W9-BRM-201

Praise for

Town in a Wild Moose Chase

"[A] terrific tale . . . With a great stunning final twist to complete a strong regional whodunit, fans will enjoy *Town in a Wild Moose Chase*." —*The Mystery Gazette*

"The third book in a well-written series, the appearance of a white moose and the big hints about a conspiracy will keep the reader enthralled. While *Town in a Wild Moose Chase* was complete, the ending leaves the reader waiting for the next in the series." —*Fresh Fiction*

"Candy is a sensible, interesting young woman who takes her time and thinks things through before she jumps in feetfirst." —*The Mystery Reader*

Town in a Lobster Stew

"[A] fun and likeable amateur sleuth . . . With a little bit of romance thrown in, this one has a recipe for success." —*The Romance Readers Connection*

"A fun, atmospheric mystery, perfect for lounging bayside waiting for the boats to bring in their latest catch." —*The Mystery Reader*

"This is a charming cozy . . . With seafood and recipes adding to the flavor of a *Town in a Lobster Stew*, subgenre fans will enjoy spending early summer in Maine." —*The Mystery Gazette*

"A savory read, which brings the people of coastal Maine to life. It leaves Candy Holliday fans with a taste for more of her misadventures." —*Bangor (ME) Daily News*

continued . . .

Town in a Blueberry Jam

"In this debut mystery, Haywood has picked a winning combination of good food and endearing characters."
　—Sheila Connolly, national bestselling author of *Sour Apples*

"This is a charming and amusing Pine Tree State cozy in which Cape Willington is vividly described so that the reader feels they are attending the Blueberry Festival. The cast is solid as the residents bring out the ambience of the seaside village . . . A fresh spin to B. B. Haywood's first Candy Holliday whodunit." 　　　　　*—The Best Reviews*

"A delicious mix of yummy food and a good, small-town mystery." 　　　　　*—The Romance Readers Connection*

"A winning combination of great characters, warm setting, and mischievous locals will appeal to cozy lovers everywhere." 　　　　　*—RT Book Reviews*

"An interesting cast of characters in a quaint Maine town. It's not Cabot Cove, and thank God for that. Candy Holliday is an intriguing new sleuth in the lighthearted mystery genre." 　　　　　*—Bangor (ME) Daily News*

Berkley Prime Crime titles by B. B. Haywood

TOWN IN A BLUEBERRY JAM
TOWN IN A LOBSTER STEW
TOWN IN A WILD MOOSE CHASE
TOWN IN A PUMPKIN BASH
TOWN IN A STRAWBERRY SWIRL
TOWN IN A SWEET PICKLE

TOWN IN A
Pumpkin Bash

B. B. Haywood

BERKLEY PRIME CRIME, NEW YORK

THE BERKLEY PUBLISHING GROUP
Published by the Penguin Group
Penguin Group (USA) Inc.
375 Hudson Street, New York, New York 10014, USA

Penguin Group (Canada), 90 Eglinton Avenue East, Suite 700, Toronto, Ontario M4P 2Y3, Canada
(a division of Pearson Penguin Canada Inc.) • Penguin Books Ltd., 80 Strand, London WC2R 0RL,
England • Penguin Ireland, 25 St. Stephen's Green, Dublin 2, Ireland (a division of Penguin
Books Ltd.) • Penguin Group (Australia), 707 Collins Street, Melbourne, Victoria 3008, Australia
(a division of Pearson Australia Group Pty. Ltd.) • Penguin Books India Pvt. Ltd., 11 Community
Centre, Panchsheel Park, New Delhi—110 017, India • Penguin Group (NZ), 67 Apollo Drive,
Rosedale, Auckland 0632, New Zealand (a division of Pearson New Zealand Ltd.) • Penguin Books
(South Africa), Rosebank Office Park, 181 Jan Smuts Avenue, Parktown North 2193,
South Africa • Penguin China, B7 Jiaming Center, 27 East Third Ring Road North,
Chaoyang District, Beijing 100020, China

Penguin Books Ltd., Registered Offices: 80 Strand, London WC2R 0RL, England

This is a work of fiction. Names, characters, places, and incidents either are the product of the author's
imagination or are used fictitiously, and any resemblance to actual persons, living or dead, business
establishments, events, or locales is entirely coincidental. The publisher does not have any control over
and does not assume any responsibility for author or third-party websites or their content.

PUBLISHER'S NOTE: The recipes contained in this book are to be followed exactly as written.
The publisher is not responsible for your specific health or allergy needs that may require
medical supervision. The publisher is not responsible for any adverse
reactions to the recipes contained in this book.

TOWN IN A PUMPKIN BASH

A Berkley Prime Crime Book / published by arrangement with the author

PUBLISHING HISTORY
Berkley Prime Crime mass-market edition / February 2013

Copyright © 2013 by Robert R. Feeman and Beth Ann Feeman.
Cover illustration by Teresa Fasolino.
Cover design by Diana Kolsky.
Interior text design by Kristin del Rosario.

All rights reserved.
No part of this book may be reproduced, scanned, or distributed in any printed or
electronic form without permission. Please do not participate in or encourage piracy of
copyrighted materials in violation of the author's rights. Purchase only authorized editions.
For information, address: The Berkley Publishing Group,
a division of Penguin Group (USA) Inc.,
375 Hudson Street, New York, New York 10014.

ISBN: 978-0-425-25188-1

BERKLEY® PRIME CRIME
Berkley Prime Crime Books are published by The Berkley Publishing Group,
a division of Penguin Group (USA) Inc.,
375 Hudson Street, New York, New York 10014.
BERKLEY® PRIME CRIME and the PRIME CRIME logo are trademarks of
Penguin Group (USA) Inc.

PRINTED IN THE UNITED STATES OF AMERICA

10 9 8 7 6 5 4 3 2 1

If you purchased this book without a cover, you should be aware that this book is
stolen property. It was reported as "unsold and destroyed" to the publisher, and neither the
author nor the publisher has received any payment for this "stripped book."

For Sarah James and Drift,
and for Matthew

PROLOGUE

At first he thought he had wandered into a graveyard.

He'd been looking down, careful of his footing in the darkness, and only when he glanced up and around, spooked by a sound in the woods nearby, had he noticed the tall, arched headstones on either side of him. Sprouting from a flat, open space, they stood like black sentinels against the shadowy landscape, lit only by the angled beam of his flashlight and the muted glow of a half-hidden gibbous moon, a few days from full, its face smeared by a swath of thin, strung-out cloud.

Instinctively he took several steps back, horrified that he might just have walked over someone's dead body.

On somewhat safer ground, he stilled himself and listened. There had been a sound, a whistle or low whisper from a stand of trees in front of him and to his left. He was sure of it. He lifted the flashlight and shined it in the general direction of the trees, flicking it around. "Hello?" he called into the darkness. "Is that you?"

He shifted the light from tree to tree, searching the shadows, but saw and heard no one.

Not for the first time, he wondered if this was a good idea. The message had been vague at best. Meet here, in this isolated pumpkin patch in Down East Maine, an hour before midnight. It was an urgent matter, the message had said, though no more details were provided. But the implications were too worrisome for him to ignore.

Had something changed? Had something gone wrong?

Did he need to alter his plan—again? He had hoped the end of his financial troubles was within reach. Now he had his doubts.

To find the key, search that which binds.
The key . . .

That's what he needed. But had it already been discovered?

That thought alone had drawn him out from his room at a hotel up on Route 1, where he'd been encamped for the night, longing for a nightcap and an early bedtime, since he had an appointment in the morning, in this very field.

He'd wondered about that. *Why this field? This place?* It could be coincidental—but, no, he'd decided after he thought it through. There had to be a reason he'd been asked to come here.

And why the late hour for the meeting? Why not meet at some cozy pub with a warm fireplace, instead of this cold patch of land?

He had a nagging feeling that he'd missed something, been lax in his research, but he pushed it down. He'd come too far to back out now.

He'd left the university earlier that day, letting a grad student take his late class so he could make the seven-hour trip from western Massachusetts, first heading east toward Boston, then northward along the coast, past Portsmouth and Portland, Freeport and Waterville, and eastward again to Bangor. He'd stopped only a few times to gas up and grab something to eat at a fast-food joint. But he was quickly back on the road.

Once east of Bangor, he'd checked into the hotel and watched the clock until the appointed hour, then let the GPS guide him as close as possible to his destination, though no address had been provided. Just a road marker and a cross street. He'd never been on this backcountry lane, and it had taken him a while to find the dirt track he sought, but finally he'd spotted the small vertical white sign, and the turnoff just beyond. After that he'd crept along at five or ten miles an hour, thinking all the time he was probably on private land, or had gotten himself turned around somewhere, or worse, had fallen victim to some sort of cruel prank. But his desperate need to know egged him on.

He eventually parked where he'd been instructed—or as close as he could determine—locked the car, dropped the keys into his pocket, and traveled the rest of the way on foot, over a low ridge and through a stand of trees and dense shrubbery, approaching the pumpkin patch from the rear.

That's when he'd stumbled into the graveyard.

He turned the flashlight back toward the tall, thin head-stones, playing the beam of light across their shadowed surfaces. *What's a graveyard doing out here in the middle of nowhere?* he wondered, confused. The message he'd received hadn't mentioned anything about it. He knew there was a cemetery just out of town along the main road, Route 192, known to the locals as the Coastal Loop. What was that place called? Something with rock or stone in the name? Stone Hill Cemetery? Yes, that sounded about right.

That's where they'd buried Sapphire Vine.

Just the thought of her made him queasy. He hadn't attended her funeral. Instead, he'd smartly skipped out of town a few days before, which had seemed like the best decision at the time, given all that had happened back then. It must be . . . what? A little more than two years ago now? He took a moment to dig into his memories to confirm the time frame and decided that, yes, she had died two summers past. It seemed like forever—and just yesterday.

He could still remember the last time he'd seen her, though he quickly shook away the unpleasant memory. Sapphire's death had caused a massive disruption in his life, both good and bad. She'd been blackmailing him, so her murder had eliminated that financial burden for him, as well as the humiliation of her never-ending demands. But his career also had taken a hit. Though he'd managed to keep most of the details of the events of those days from his employer and coworkers, the rumors had been damaging enough. Since then, he'd worked hard to rededicate himself to his craft, reestablish his reputation, and put some major distance between then and now. But admittedly it had been a struggle, and over the past year, he had experienced a number of setbacks. Someone had started spreading rumors about him again, though he couldn't determine who or why. But word had gotten around. His career had stalled. His creativity had faltered. His books weren't selling. His classes were poorly attended. His future looked bleak.

He knew he needed to find a way to break through the barriers that were holding him back.

So here he was, just outside Cape Willington, Maine, standing in a dark pumpkin patch a few minutes before eleven o'clock on a Friday night, exhausted after the long drive from western Massachusetts and the tense wait in his hotel room, feeling wired and on edge, and wishing he were anywhere else but here.

And now he had just trespassed on someone's private burial plot, a particularly distasteful development.

The tall stones were abnormally thin, which caused him to suspect their true nature. On an impulse, he took a few tentative steps forward, shining his light across their granite gray surfaces. But he knew almost at once they were not made of any sort of rock or stone. Instead, the surfaces looked as if they'd been painted on, and they had writing on them. Not engravings, but bold lettering applied in an almost comical hand. He focused in on the epitaphs:

HERE LIES OLD MAN WINTER, THE COOLEST CAT EVER, one headstone read.

MARY, MARY, QUITE CONTRARY, ARGUED IN THE CEMETERY, said another.

And on a third: RIP, REGINALD I. PERIWINKLE, A MAN OF INITIAL WORTH.

And another: C. A. GHOST, A SPIRITED FELLOW.

His brow furrowed. They were complete nonsense. *Joke lines,* he thought.

He reached out and pushed at one of the headstones. It teetered back loosely.

They weren't real.

It must be some sort of Halloween gag, he realized. *Decorations of some sort.*

He heard the sound again, more distinct this time—a low whistle from the trees off to his left.

Nervously he shifted the beam of the flashlight around, surveying the landscape. "Who's there?" he called into the darkness. "Is that you? I'm here, just like you asked."

Again, no response. He swallowed hard. Was this some sort of game?

"I'm coming over there," he called out, as if in warning, and started off toward the trees. "Give me a signal or something so I know where you are."

He moved at a cautious pace, stepping carefully over the uneven landscape, keeping a watchful eye for any sort of movement or signal. When none came, he veered toward a particularly large oak, which stood out among all the other gray trunks.

He had just stepped into a low area when the heel of his boot struck hard earth. He shined the light down toward his feet and saw that he stood on some sort of dirt road, which ran along the edge of the trees. He shined the light along the road to his left. It curved around the tree line a little farther on, where he saw a pile of pumpkins and more evidence of Halloween decorations—probably for some sort of activity, he thought, like a hayride.

Something moved in the shadows to his left.

He swung around, crouching warily as he turned, the light moving with him.

A figure had emerged from among the trees.

It was luminescent in the moonlight, a thin, gangly thing of awkwardly moving appendages, coming toward him at a steady pace. As it got closer, he could see the thin ribs and even the finger bones of one hand, curled around an old pitchfork. The face was especially troubling—a skull with a wide grin and black eyes.

It was a skeleton.

Or, rather, someone wearing a skeleton costume.

It's some sort of a prank, he realized as his hopes crashed and his stomach heaved in on itself in despair. *I've been lured out here for nothing. I'll probably get robbed—or worse.*

He heard several things at once—a shift of fabric, the deep echo of a heavy truck passing along a distant road, the faint sound of a dog barking somewhere, the closer rustle as a breath of wind kicked up a few fallen leaves that rattled past his feet.

A click, as if someone had flicked off the safety on a pistol.

There was a spark of light, a crack of sound, a slap at his chest as if a big bug had flown into him. He shuddered, his fingers tingled, his neck bulged strangely. Everything in his brain turned hot and red as he felt his knees buckle and his body collapse.

And then the ground came rushing up to meet him at a speed he'd never thought possible.

From *The Cape Crier*
Cape Willington, Maine
October 26th Edition

BLUEBERRY BITS

by Candy Holliday
Community Correspondent

THE PUMPKINS ARE COMING!
Don't get out your shovels yet! (Well, yes, get them out, but
hope we won't have to use them before Halloween this year.)
There's plenty to do in Cape Willington this October before
the cold weather sets in and the snow flies.

The town's annual Halloween festival, called the Pumpkin Bash, will be held on Wednesday, Oct. 31, in Town Park
and along Main Street and Ocean Ave. This spooktacular
event, now in its third year, kicks off promptly at noon with
the Great Pumpkin Weigh-in, as we search for Cape Willington's biggest pumpkin. I'm sure there are some *humungo*
pumpkins out there (I know because I've seen them!), so
bring them down to Town Park and enter the contest.

The pumpkin-carving tables will open at noon as well,
and we'll be carving as many pumpkins as possible. Create
the spookiest, craziest, cutest, happiest jack-o'-lanterns you
can possibly carve. They'll be displayed all over downtown
and lit at sunset. We hope to have thousands of them on
display, so we need as many carvers as possible.

Throughout the afternoon and evening, all of the shops
in town will be running special Halloween sales, and there
will be food and craft tables galore. And right after the
Vacuum Cleaner Run, the shops will start handing out
candy to trick-or-treaters. So come on down to the Pumpkin
Bash and scare up some fun!

LADIES AND GENTLEMEN, START YOUR VACUUMS!
Speaking of fun, a new event, the Vacuum Cleaner Run,
will power up at 5 P.M. on Main Street. Dress up your vacuum cleaner in a funny costume and bring it out to the

starting line in front of Duffy's Main Street Diner at 4:45 P.M. No entrance fee necessary, but there will be great prizes awarded to whoever rolls across the finish line first, as well as for best costume, oldest vacuum cleaner, and more. So come on out and see if you can make a clean sweep of the event, or just cheer on your favorite.

PUMPKINS FLY AT FINCH'S
Have you ever seen a pumpkin fly? You can if you head over to Finch's Garden Center and Farm Stand in Fowler's Corner, where the Halloween Pumpkin Toss takes place on Wednesday from 10 A.M. to 3 P.M. The students in the wood shop class at Cape Willington High School have designed and built a trebuchet, which they'll use to catapult pumpkins into the sky. They even built the trebuchet on wheels, so it's easy to move around. Those kids are amazing. They plan to send off several pumpkins on the hour, every hour, so head on over and watch the pumpkins fly.

While you're there, see if you can escape from the lobster's claws! The folks at Finch's have created a spooky Lobster Hay Maze that's sure to be fun for the whole family.

ANY WAY YOU SLICE IT, IT'S PIETOBER!
Melody Barnes, proprietor of Melody's Café on River Road, has been drawing attention to local pie bakers with a culinary celebration she calls "Pietober." All month long, she and a few local pie bakers, including yours truly, have been making just about every type of pie you can imagine. In fact, if you can eat it, you can be sure someone has made a pie out of it. Melody and her kitchen staff will have a selection of their most popular pies available by the slice at their booth during the Pumpkin Bash. So stop by and sample her wares before Pietober sadly comes to an end!

BOOKS AND DESSERT MAKE HAPPY READING
The Pruitt Public Library will hold its annual Book and Bake Sale on Friday and Saturday, Nov. 2 and 3, starting at 9 A.M., with a preview event for library members on Thursday, Nov. 1, at 7 P.M. The library is accepting book

donations prior to the sale. Also, if you'd like to contribute baked goods for the event, ask at the front desk for the sign-up sheet. See you there!

QUOTH THE RAVEN
Local thespian Elliot Whitby will bring his acclaimed portrayal of Edgar Allan Poe to Town Park on All Hallows' Eve. He tells me that he's planning to recite from a number of Poe's works, including "The Raven," which should be a real treat. He will perform two half-hour shows at 5:30 and 7 P.M., and will be present in costume in Town Park before and after each show for photos and additional impromptu readings. You don't want to miss his uncanny portrayal of the legendary writer. Nevermore!

TASTY TIDBITS
"The Importance of Tea in the History of Maine" will be the theme of a new exhibit debuting at the Cape Willington Historical Society on November 3. This unique display will include one-of-a-kind teacups, as well as collections from sea captains, merchants, and historical figures who lived in the area over the past two centuries. For instance, teacups used by William King, the first governor of Maine, and Benning Wentworth, the Colonial governor of New Hampshire, will be on display, as well as a cup used by New England writer Celia Thaxter. The society will also hold a number of tea events over the next several weeks, so keep checking back with us for further information. The exhibit runs through January 31.

Official Judicious F. P. Bosworth sightings for the first half of October:

Visible: 3 days
Invisible: 12 days

Judicious, you're scaring us!

ONE

"There's a curse on that house, I'm sure of it," Maggie Tremont said, the exasperation evident in her voice. "There's no other explanation. And I'm not the only one who thinks so. Just the other day I was talking to Sally Ann Longfellow, who lives three doors down, at the end of Gleason Street—she drives by there all the time, and she says the place is haunted."

Candy Holliday checked her watch and looked askance at her friend. "I wouldn't trust everything Sally Ann says. She keeps goats in her house, you know."

"Only in the winter," Maggie responded blithely, as if it were a perfectly normal thing, "and not in the entire house—just the kitchen. She makes a little pen for them. I've heard they're relatively well behaved . . . for goats." She paused, regrouping. "Besides, Sally Ann's not the only one I've heard it from. There're others who agree with me."

"Who?"

Maggie made a face. *"Others."* Playfully she jabbed her friend in the side with an elbow. "You must have heard people talking about that house. It's all over town. That place has a bad history. But I don't have to tell *you* that, do I?"

She glanced back over her shoulder, giving the comment a moment to sink in. A hay wagon and tractor sat behind them in the middle of the pumpkin patch, across a tumbling field of orange and greenery. A small crowd had formed behind the wagon—parents and kids, mostly, waiting to get on board for the first ride of the day. So far no one seemed to mind the delay, but that wouldn't last much longer.

"I have to be honest with you," Maggie said, turning back to Candy, "I'm starting to think there's a reason behind it all. Something else must have happened there before, well, that thing with *you-know-who*." She said the last words in an exaggerated whisper and wiggled her hand in the air, as if that explained everything.

And indeed it did. Candy knew exactly who she meant.

Maggie was referring to the woman known around town as Sapphire Vine—a beauty queen, gossip columnist, and blackmailer who had been murdered here in Cape Willington, Maine, two summers ago.

"At first, in the months after she died, it was just all those little things around the house," Maggie continued, leaning in closer to Candy and lowering her voice as a family passed by. The parents cradled smaller pumpkins in their arms, the two kids hauled a red wagon filled with several larger pumpkins, and the grandparents trailed along behind with a few smaller pumpkins as well. They all nodded politely and exchanged a few words as they passed. After they were out of earshot, Maggie picked up where she'd left off.

"I'd notice that something had been moved around, or something else wasn't where it was supposed to be. Lights turned on and off randomly at all hours of the day and night. I saw it happen myself. Faulty wiring, they said. It's an old house. Things like that just happen, they tell me. *Humph!* I wish it were that simple. Someone once said they heard music in there—and whispers. We searched but couldn't find anything. We had the Coopers living there back then. Remember them? They lasted five whole weeks. That's the longest . . . well . . ."

She didn't have to finish. Candy knew the rest of it.

After Sapphire Vine's unfortunate passing in a particularly violent manner, and the discovery of her true identity, her old house on Gleason Street had passed into the hands of her only living family member, Cameron Zimmerman, who just happened to be dating Maggie's daughter, Amanda. In the months that followed, there had been endless discussions about what to do with Sapphire's old place. For a while they'd had it up for sale but received no offers. They tried renting it out but couldn't get anyone to stay for long. It sat dark and unlived in for more than a year, dust filming the windows and spiderwebs gathering in the corners.

So, after examining various options, Maggie had offered to personally take over the management of the house as a seasonal rental. It was a good fit for all concerned. Maggie had expertise in insurance, finance, and small-business affairs, and an agreed-upon commission would help her budget and funnel some pocket money to the house's current owner until the local real estate market improved.

She took easily to the challenges of property management. She'd even signed up for an online course, which gave her a certification of sorts that looked good on a business card, and had subsequently taken on two additional properties over the summer—coastal rentals that remained fully booked through Labor Day and into the fall, thanks to Maggie's efforts.

But while most of the other seasonal rentals around town were sought-after properties with no open rental spots and lengthy waiting lists, Sapphire Vine's old place on Gleason Street, a few blocks northwest of downtown Cape Willington, sat largely empty, which only fueled its growing reputation as a haunted house, to Maggie's dismay.

"Word gets around, I guess, what with the Internet, travel sites, social networks, and all that texting stuff these days," she said with a resigned shrug. "It's too easy to find out information about anything. Just a few taps on the computer keyboard. I've seen the comments about the place. It's even been posted on a website dedicated to New England ghost stories."

"Well, at least it's not a total loss," Candy said, doing her best to sound positive. "You had those ghost hunters who rented the place a few months ago."

"Yes, but that's the problem."

Candy saw what she was getting at. "You think the house's reputation is scaring normal people away?"

Maggie raised her hands in an exaggerated gesture. "Whatever the reason, we just haven't had enough renters, even after drastically reducing the price. I don't know what to do with the place. We can barely cover the property taxes and utilities, and it's starting to show its age. The past couple of years have taken their toll. It needs some work, but Cameron and Amanda don't have the time to do it, and they don't want that house anyway—not with what's happened there. The Zimmermans are happy in their own place, so they're not interested in moving. And *I* certainly don't want to live there—since it's, you know, cursed."

"In your opinion."

"In my opinion," Maggie agreed, "but it's more than that. There've been those sightings."

"There's been only *one* sighting," Candy corrected her, "and we investigated. We didn't find anything, remember?"

"We didn't look very hard."

"We checked every room, plus that secret hidey space in the attic."

"Not the basement."

"No, not the basement. I'm sure there's nothing down there."

Candy didn't like basements much, since she'd found a body in one once.

Maggie frowned up at the gusty sky, blowing in dark rain clouds. "I don't like the looks of that," she said. Her gaze dropped to follow a scattering of brown leaves that blew across the parking lot. She let out a deep sigh. "I guess he's not coming then."

Reluctantly, Candy had to agree.

They were expecting a visitor, but he was fifteen minutes overdue, and they couldn't wait for him any longer.

The call from Sebastian J. Quinn had come out of the blue a couple of weeks earlier. The award-winning poet, who had been involved with the Sapphire Vine murder case, had contacted Candy at her office at the paper one afternoon, apologizing for calling her first, since he'd only just learned of the house's availability and didn't have Maggie's number. "Can you put me in touch with her? Is the place still for rent?" he'd asked. "If so, I'll take it for two weeks, and perhaps through the Thanksgiving holiday."

That had been good news all around. Sebastian needed a place to "get away from the rat race" for a while to work on a new book of poetry, and the "inspirational beauty" around Cape Willington in the fall and early winter was just the thing he needed, he'd told Maggie when they'd talked, and she had promptly passed on the details to Candy. Both of them questioned Sebastian's explanation for renting the place—"It just sounds a little contrived to me," Candy noted at the time. But neither of them could see a legitimate reason to turn down the offer, as generous as it was.

A deal had been quickly finalized, with occupancy to take place the weekend before Halloween and continuing into early November, with a week-by-week option after that. Sebastian had agreed to pay three hundred per week for the place, a particularly good rate for the off-season, though it included all utilities and heating oil, which could become costly if the weather turned cold, so it seemed a fair-enough arrangement to Sebastian. To Maggie's astonishment, he'd offered to pay in advance. A check for six hundred dollars, plus an additional one hundred fifty for a safety deposit, promptly arrived two days later by special delivery. A few other papers were exchanged by two-day mail, and they were in business.

Even though Maggie had offered to meet him at Sapphire's place to hand over the keys and conduct a walkthrough, Sebastian told her he'd prefer to stop by the pumpkin patch that morning to conduct their business. "I don't want to put you out," he'd said to her over the phone, and she'd relayed the message to Candy, "but I just want to get my hands on the keys and get settled in. That place has a lot of memories for me. I prefer to make the first visit alone, if you know what I mean. I'm just not quite sure what my reaction will be, after all that happened there. I'll see you at ten on Saturday morning."

And here they were. Ten fifteen on the agreed-upon morning, and no Sebastian J. Quinn.

"What do you think this means?" Maggie asked, trying not to sound despondent. "Do you think he got scared off by all the stories about the house and backed out of the deal? And what if he wants his money back? I've deposited the check, gave the kids most of the money, and already spent some of my share."

"Let's not jump to conclusions," Candy said calmly. "Maybe he's just been delayed."

Maggie shook her head and pulled out her phone, one last time, to check for new messages. There were none. She sighed. "We can't wait any longer," she said, slipping the phone back into her pocket. "The natives are getting restless. We have to get this show on the road."

To prove her point, she turned and waved toward the folks gathered around the hay wagon. "Sorry for the holdup!" she called out to them. "We'll be right there!"

Looking back at Candy, she added, "You ready?"

"Let's do it."

"Good," Maggie said as she started off, and to the crowd she called, "It's time for the Pumpkin Hollow Haunted Hayride's first trip of the day!"

TWO

They'd pulled the hayride operation together in record time, though they'd been working in the pumpkin patch since late August. That's when Maggie had approached elderly Mr. Gumm, who ran the local hardware store, about managing the field for him that fall.

It had been a fairly simple idea, the result of a conversation over salads and glasses of iced tea at Melody's Café one warm afternoon, when Maggie was feeling down in the dumps. She was still working at the dry cleaner's in town, but her hours were limited and the pay was low. She'd been looking around for a scheme to make a little money on the side, but she hadn't had much luck.

"I'm not a baker or a writer like you, so I can't make pies to sell or write stories for the local newspaper," she told Candy without a hint of jealousy, "and I've tried creating little thingamabobs to sell at the craft fairs but, to be honest, I'm not much of a quilter or a knitter. I'm too old to try landscaping or lumberjacking. I suppose I could waitress, but I don't think anyone is hiring around town this time of year."

She was right about that. Though the tourist season had been relatively strong this year, few businesses hired in the late summer, when they were usually starting to let people go. There might be a few end-of-season jobs around, vacated by college and high school students heading back to their classes, but most local businesses ran lean into the fall, and were looking to wind down in the weeks after Labor Day, rather than staff up. They'd all stay open through October, of course, in anticipation of the annual busloads of leaf peepers who swarmed over New England during the month, following peak foliage from north to south. As soon as Halloween passed, though, and the trees turned dull, the leaf peepers would head home, taking their tourist dollars with them, and businesses up and down Main Street and Ocean Avenue would begin to cut hours drastically or shutter for the season. After that, it was just a matter of finishing up the remnants of the harvest, bringing in the lawn furniture and garden tools, preparing the flower beds and fields for cold weather, winterizing the cars and boats, and getting the snow shovels and bags of rock salt out of the back corner of the garage.

"There just isn't much to do around here for a woman of my skills," Maggie had lamented that day in August, when the arrival of winter was still months away. "What am I going to do?" She had tried to keep the conversation light, but her typical good humor was failing her as the prospect of a long, lean season loomed.

"Well, we'll just have to figure something out," Candy had told her with all the optimism she could muster. She'd been reading a book about the power of positive thinking and she was determined to give it a try. "You know what? If we can't find another job for you, we'll just have to create one."

That made Maggie perk right up. "Hey, that's not a bad idea. What do you have in mind?"

Candy thought about it a moment. "We'll just have to figure out what your strengths are and then build around that."

"What an intriguing concept." Maggie straightened in her chair, liking this idea more all the time. "Which strengths do you think we should start with?"

"Let's see." Candy assessed her friend with a scrutinizing eye. "You're good with numbers, right? And you're an excellent manager."

"I like working outside," Maggie put in, "and I'm pretty good with plants."

"Plus you're bright, personable, hardworking. . . ."

"Well groomed . . ."

"You're good with customers. . . ."

"Self-motivated and organized . . ."

"You have a wonderful sense of humor. . . ."

"And I can throw together a pretty mean lasagna in a jiffy!"

They made a list of all of Maggie's attributes and another one of prospective jobs, both existing and new ones, that might fit her skill set. They tried to think broadly, even adding *lobsterman* to the initial list before scratching it off. "I tend to get seasick," Maggie admitted, "even in light chop."

Over the next few days, they fanned out, looking into options around town. They checked all the nurseries and farm suppliers in the area, for instance—all three of them—but none were hiring. They caught wind of an opening with the town maintenance crew, but it turned out to be a job for a Bobcat operator to help clear snow off the sidewalks and streets over the winter. Maggie demurred. Ditto for a job as a bus driver for the local school district. "Me on the roads this winter with a bus full of rambunctious kids? I don't think so."

Creating a new job for her proved to be trickier than they thought. Which way to go? Start her own organizing business? Or cleaning service? Collect empty soda cans by the side of the road?

She considered becoming a private tutor, opening a senior-care business, and even becoming a business coach or interior designer, but in the end it was Candy's father, Henry "Doc" Holliday, who made the suggestion that stuck, mostly because it was the easiest idea to get started on, and matched her skill set perfectly.

"Why don't you talk to Mr. Gumm about taking over that pumpkin patch of his?" Doc said absently one afternoon while he was standing on the porch cradling an armful of vegetables, including peppers, tomatoes, and onions, which he'd just picked in the garden. He planned to make his famous spicy tomato sauce that evening.

Doc went on to say he'd overheard at the diner that Mr. Gumm was thinking about selling a pumpkin patch he owned because he could no longer keep up with it, and it was starting to fall into neglect. When Candy expressed an interest, Doc elaborated, though first he ducked inside so he could set down the vegetables on the kitchen counter.

"Well, let's see. From what I've heard, that piece of land has been in the Gumm family for generations. They've grown other crops there, of course, like corns and beans, but mostly they've utilized it as a pumpkin patch, because the soil's rich and moist, and it's got good exposure to sun. They have two fields—Low Field and High Field—where they plant different varieties. Connecticut Field pumpkins—those are the traditional jack-o'-lanterns, you know—in Low Field, and more of those plus some heirlooms in High Field. From what Mr. Gumm said, they just ran a simple u-pick operation, and apparently made quite a bit of money at it over the years, when it was well managed—which it hasn't been for a long time. He talked about selling it, but I don't think he'd really ever part with it, since it's family property.

But he's clearly frustrated and doesn't know what to do with it. Maybe there's an opportunity there, especially with this Pumpkin Bash thing coming up."

That got their imaginations going. The "Pumpkin Bash thing," as Doc referred to it, was a relatively new event in town, supported and managed by a small yet energetic group of local residents and business owners. The idea was to draw trick-or-treaters and their families to the downtown area on Halloween night by keeping the stores open late, handing out candy, and creating several large displays of lit jack-o'-lanterns up and down the streets and in Town Park. Entrants for a giant pumpkin weigh-off contest would also be on display, and there'd be a few food booths, kids' games, and entertainment.

For someone with a pumpkin patch, it was, as Doc said, a golden opportunity—or more accurately, Candy decided later, an *orange* one.

She talked it over with Maggie, who quickly latched onto the idea, deciding it was a perfect fit. And she persuaded Candy to help her with it. "If we can make a few thousand dollars each, that would go a long way over the winter, and give me time to figure out my next long-term career move," Maggie said at the time.

After agreeing to work the patch together, they approached Mr. Gumm, though Maggie, who had worked at the hardware store and knew the elderly proprietor well, did most of the talking, explaining how she and Candy would take over the patch, spruce up the operations, use their business savvy to make it a profitable business again, and share some of the proceeds with him.

He readily agreed, and after a round of handshakes to seal the deal, offered them anything they needed, including the use of an old tractor he kept at an adjoining property he owned, and any tools or materials from the hardware store—within reason, of course.

And they'd delivered. Thanks to their efforts over the

past few months, the once-neglected pumpkin patch now thrived, thickly populated with mature vines, their faded green leaves nearly the size of elephant ears, helping to feed the still-burgeoning orange fruit that abundantly peppered the fields.

Mr. Gumm had been pleased with what he'd seen when he stopped by one day in mid-September to walk the two fields with them. "My two grandsons and a few of their friends helped get the fields ready for planting this year and got the seeds in the ground," he told them, wiping a handkerchief across his forehead, more from habit than the warmth of the day. "Said they'd stick around to run it through harvesttime, but then one of them headed off to Texas with his girlfriend, and the other got into a pretty good school in New York, so here I was with this field I couldn't manage. Good thing you ladies came along with your idea. I'd've hated to see all this bounty go to waste."

He turned, surveying the fields around them, finally pointing nowhere in particular. "You might want to fertilize those vines with a little fish emulsion—got plenty of that around here along the coast. I'll see some gets out to you. And when you notice pumpkins tipped over on their sides, set 'em up straight. That way they'll flesh out rounder and oranger and you'll have better-looking fruit. Helps if you put a shingle under each one too—keeps 'em up off the ground, so they look prettier, and the prettier they are, the more you'll sell. If I remember correctly, there's a stack of them behind the farm stand. Course, you'll want to start clearing out some spots for your pumpkin piles. Makes it easier for the customers if they can just pick up a few off the piles. We used to keep them arranged by size. Easier to price that way."

He'd given them a few more tips, and left the rest to them.

For the business end of the operation, they renovated the property's small, dilapidated farm stand at one corner of the pumpkin patch, modifying and expanding it to suit their needs. Ray Hutchins, the local handyman, added a wider, reinforced countertop and put angled storage bins up front, so they had plenty of places to display pumpkins of various sizes, plus squash, baskets of Indian corn, and assorted jars of homemade blueberry jam, all with the decorative Blueberry Acres label attached, as well as elegant jars of Coffin Farms honey, delivered by Marjorie Coffin herself. And on a series of narrow tables off to one side, arrayed in bins and baskets, they'd set out just-picked vegetables from their gardens, which were now deep into harvest. Today they had late carrots and beets, potatoes, squashes, garlic, and onions. There were also the last of the Macintosh apples from one of the local orchards, plus a few containers of chrysanthemums.

Then, of course, there was the Pumpkin Hollow Haunted Hayride.

They'd had good crowds throughout the fall but wanted to end the season with a big splash—and pocket a few extra dollars to help get them through the winter ahead. Earlier in the month, Maggie had spotted an old hay wagon at the farm where they'd found the tractor, which gave her the idea.

"You know, we should do a haunted hayride the last couple of weekends we're open," she'd told Candy one morning while they were out at the patch. "We could set up a few spooky displays, like tombstones and that sort of thing, then take people around the pumpkin patch in the hay wagon, tell a few ghost stories, and send them merrily on their way. Of course, we'd charge for the ride and remind them to pick up a few pumpkins on their way home, as well as a couple of jars of jam and honey and such. It could be a lot of fun, and it'd help us sweeten the profits before we close things down. What do you think?"

"I think," Candy had told her, "that you'd better brush up on your ghost stories, because *I'm* going to drive the tractor, and *you're* going to be the haunted hayride's hostess with the mostest!"

THREE

It took them ten minutes to get the waiting crowd, which included several families and a few seniors, settled on board the hay wagon.

As they climbed up a wooden step and onto the bed, the passengers all talked, laughed, and smiled in anticipation, but the children were the most excited, chattering nonstop with parents or with one another as they staked out the best places to sit for the upcoming ride. In anticipation of Halloween, some had dressed in costume, so this morning the hayride's passengers included a short-statured nurse, a princess in pink, a blue-caped superhero, and two zombies with ashen faces and dark eyes.

A few of the adults also wore some type of costume accessory, such as bunny ears or alien antennae, and one portly gentleman chuckled as he climbed aboard dressed in a bee costume. But most of the adults simply wore brightly colored hooded sweatshirts or fleece vests, ball caps, rain jackets, and even a few scarves against the blustery day, though some braved the unsettled weather with nothing more than shirts and jeans, and one shaggy-haired male teen had opted for cargo shorts and sandals, proving that the weather in Maine rarely imposed itself upon the fashion trends of the younger generation.

Maggie herself had been one of the first to climb up onto the bed of the wagon, so she could help the passengers who needed assistance in getting seated. She and Candy had placed bales of hay around the exterior sides of the wagon and spread an inches-thick layer of hay across the bed as well to provide relatively comfortable seating.

Candy stationed herself on the ground at the back of the wagon and did a quick head count. Twenty-two passengers in all—close to the wagon's limit. They preferred to keep occupancy under twenty-five, though on one run the previous weekend, they'd managed to squeeze in nearly thirty. But they both felt that was pushing the limits of safety and comfort.

As the passengers passed by her to climb up onto the wagon, Candy took their tickets and exchanged pleasantries with many of them. They'd sold the hayride tickets earlier at the farm stand, rather than here at the ride itself, so they could keep all their cash in a centralized location—though it was hardly as secure as locking it in a bank vault. They stuffed their ones, fives, tens, and twenties into a metal cash box, which they locked and tucked away behind the farm stand's front counter when they were off on the hayrides. It was an admittedly unsecure hiding spot, but folks around here were honest and hardworking, and even if someone should happen to discover the box, Candy and Maggie had no concerns that it'd be stolen.

They'd also placed a hand-lettered sign on the counter that read HAYRIDE IN PROGRESS, since inevitably customers would come along wanting to purchase pumpkins and other farm-stand items, or tickets for an upcoming ride, while they were in the back field. But the hayride lasted only ten or twelve minutes, and so far no one seemed to mind the wait.

And there was probably a good reason why—the pumpkin patch was a beautiful place to hang out, especially on a seasonally brisk autumn morning. The vines, grasses, and wildflowers that had grown up across the low, hammocklike field during the summer were fading toward winter, though they'd glimmered with a touch of frost that morning. Beyond the field, the colors were not quite as spectacular as they'd been a week ago, since the trees here along the Maine coast were just past peak. Spots of vibrant golds, reds, and oranges lingered, but the foliage was inexorably darkening into rusts and ambers and mustard yellows, eventually to wither away in the annual fall ritual.

"Don't you just love this time of year?" quipped an elderly woman as she handed her ticket to Candy. "The air is so crisp and clear, and the fall colors this year have been absolutely stunning."

"They certainly have," Candy replied. "Are you from around here?"

"We drove up from Virginia," the woman said, indicating her traveling companion, a quiet, gray-haired gentleman who had already climbed up into the wagon, "though we have lovely color there as well, especially along Skyline Drive and the Blue Ridge Parkway. But we've never been to Maine before, so we thought we'd come up for a visit this year, and it's been just lovely."

"Well, we're glad you're here," Candy said amiably as she helped the woman up.

The last few passengers were climbing aboard when Candy heard the sound of a car pulling into the parking lot. Thinking Sebastian J. Quinn had finally arrived, she looked to her left.

A silver sedan was just coming to a stop beside a bushy fringe of deep red chokeberry. Candy could see only a single passenger inside. *This could be him,* she thought. *This could be Sebastian.* And she turned and signaled to Maggie, who nodded. She also had spotted the vehicle from her perch up in the wagon.

The car's engine shut off and a few moments later the driver's side door swung open. The man who emerged was lean and tall, with thick sandy-colored hair and the rugged, athletic, educated look of someone who had played multiple sports at some Ivy League college, though he was well past college age—in his early to mid-forties, Candy guessed. His brown jacket and slacks looked comfortable yet stylish, and expensive, though in an understated way.

He slid his hands into his pockets and studied his surroundings in a casual yet seasoned way, his stance shifting fluidly as his gaze swept across the flora and fields before settling on Candy. He tilted his head, smiled, and nodded in greeting.

Candy nodded back, uncertain of who he was. Obviously not the bearded, bearlike Sebastian J. Quinn.

As the newcomer started across the parking lot toward them, Candy looked back at Maggie and shook her head. *It's not Sebastian,* her gesture said.

Maggie had seen what she'd seen, and her right eyebrow rose questioningly. *Who is he?* she mouthed. But Candy just shrugged and shook her head.

Maggie glanced a final time toward the approaching stranger, and then, as if she'd been given a signal, turned back to her passengers. "Now that everyone's on board," she began in a rousing tone, "we'd like to welcome you all to the Pumpkin Hollow Haunted Hayride!"

The passengers broke into an enthusiastic applause as Candy kicked aside the wooden step behind the wagon and reached for the back slat, which she hefted up off the ground and dropped into place as Maggie launched into her rehearsed presentation.

"In just a few moments," she told the passengers, "we're going to take a spooky sojourn back through Pumpkin Hollow's haunted history. I don't know if you've heard, but strange events have occurred on this isolated plot of land for centuries. Some folks say there's an old Indian burial ground somewhere nearby, dating back to before the Pilgrims landed at Plymouth Rock, and that the souls buried there become restless after dark. Others believe a British force from Augusta massacred a settlement of French squatters somewhere around here in the late seventeen hundreds, and that their ghosts still appear on dark nights when the mists roll in from the sea. What makes these fields so fertile yet so deadly? No one knows for sure, but whatever happened here, both good and malevolent spirits linger, and they seem to become particularly active as we get closer to Halloween. So keep your eyes open, because we just might see a few of them today!"

Several of the children simultaneously giggled and shivered in anticipation, and the adults chuckled.

As Maggie continued addressing the passengers, Candy made her way around the wagon toward the tractor, but stopped halfway there as the newcomer approached her.

"Hello!" he called out as he made his way along a path between the chaotic pumpkin vines.

The day had brightened briefly as the sun broke through an opening in the overcast sky, and she held up a hand to shade her eyes. "Hi," she said as he drew closer, "can I help you?"

He flashed an easy smile as a strong gust of wind tussled his hair, which curled around the back of his neck. "You wouldn't happen to know someone named Candy Holliday, would you?" he asked.

"I would," she said after hesitating only a moment, uncertain of why this handsome stranger would have driven out here to the pumpkin patch on a Saturday morning looking for her. "And who'd be looking for me?"

He laughed, easily as well. "Hi, Candy, I'm T.J., and I wonder if I could ask you a few questions about the haunted house. You know, the one where the woman was murdered? I've heard you know something about that place."

FOUR

If anyone else had approached her with such an odd opening line, she might have reacted differently. But this inquisitive newcomer who called himself T.J. had such a casual attitude and a disarming way about him that she could only laugh as she let her guard down. "Well, T.J., I just might be able to help you out," she said, instantly feeling at ease in his presence, "but what makes you think Sapphire's old place is haunted?"

"Sapphire? You mean the woman who was murdered there?" He gave her a quick shrug and stared off into the distant field. "I've heard the stories around town, just like everybody else," he responded vaguely.

But before he could continue, they heard a shrill whistle and turned to see Maggie wagging an arm at them. "Hey, come on you two, let's get on board!" she said, and she tapped her watch. "We're behind schedule. It's time to get rolling!"

Candy looked back at T.J., an apologetic smile crossing

her face. "You heard the woman," she said, and pointed to the wagon. "She can be quite a taskmaster. I wouldn't cross her. Why don't you climb aboard? I'm sure she can find you a spot to sit."

His eyes flicked uncertainly toward the wagon. "It looks full." He thought about it a moment or two, and finally took a few steps back. "Maybe I'll just wait here 'til you get back."

"Oh, don't be silly. You might as well ride along." And taking him by the arm, Candy led him around to the back of the wagon and pointed up at the rear slat, which she'd put in place to make sure none of the passengers tumbled out over the rougher terrain. "Up you go."

He nodded and took a few steps toward the wagon, as if to climb aboard, but then he looked over at her. "You're not coming with me?"

She pointed toward the tractor. "I'm driving."

"Oh." He glanced in the direction she'd pointed before looking back at her, an eyebrow rising.

She wasn't quite sure how to take his reaction. "I'm a blueberry farmer," she said reassuringly. "I know how to handle that thing. I'll get you there and back safely."

The look in his gray eyes told her she'd misread him. "No, it's not that," he said with a mild shake of his head. "I'm aware you're a farmer—I've read your columns. All of them. It's just that I was hoping we could ride together, so we could talk along the way."

"Together? In the wagon?"

"If that wouldn't be too much trouble." He pointed up at Maggie. "Maybe your friend could drive this time, so you and I could talk? It'll help speed things along, you know." He flashed his grin at her again, and in the brightening light she saw a swirl of lavender specks in his eyes.

Candy was caught in those eyes for a few moments. To break the spell she cleared her throat, several times. "Umm, give me a minute."

In a quick, easy motion, she climbed over the wagon's

back rail and made her way past the seated passengers, apologizing as she went. "Sorry. Short delay. This'll just take a minute. Sorry." She picked her way along quickly but cautiously, careful not to step on anyone's toes or fingers.

When she reached Maggie, her friend hissed, "What's the matter? We've got to get going."

"Switch with me," Candy said.

Maggie gave her a quizzical look. "What?"

"Switch with me. You drive the tractor this time. I'll do the narration."

"But I thought you didn't like doing the narration."

"I changed my mind."

"Do you remember how it goes?"

"I'll fake it."

Maggie's eyes widened, and she glanced around Candy toward T.J., who had climbed aboard and was coming toward them. "Who's your friend?"

"His name is T.J."

Maggie instantly grasped what was going on. She smiled craftily, patted Candy's wrist, and winked. "I've got you covered, honey." With that, she walked around Candy and waved. "Hi, T.J., I'm Maggie. Why don't you sit up there at the front of the wagon, beside Candy, and I'll go fire up that tractor."

Turning to the passengers, she added, "Folks, we've made a slight adjustment to the program this morning. I'll have the honor of shepherding you around with the iron beast, and the famed Candy Holliday herself is going to provide the narration for you. And boy, are you in for a treat, because no one knows the inside story of Cape Willington's mysterious, murderous past better than Candy Holliday herself!"

FIVE

A few minutes later, Maggie started up the tractor, and with a jerk and a lurch, the hay wagon rattled forward, to scattered cheers and applause from the passengers.

Their route would take them along a narrow dirt track through the center of the pumpkin patch to the south side, where they'd follow a spiral pattern to the left, looping around the front of the patch along the parking lot, then angling off to the left again, along the northern edge of the field, before journeying into High Field, where they'd set up several Halloween displays.

Candy perched on a bale of hay at the front of the wagon and cleared her throat one more time, suddenly aware of all the pairs of eyes gazing expectantly at her.

"Well, as my friend Maggie said, we welcome all of you to our haunted hayride," she began, doing her best to recall the narrative script for the tour, which she'd helped Maggie research and write a few weeks ago. "My name's Candy, and usually I'm the one who's driving the tractor, and Maggie serves as your host. But due to a last-minute request, we've switched places for this trip, so I hope you'll excuse me if my delivery's a little rusty." She glanced at T.J., who was sitting nearby, watching her with a bemused expression on his face.

"So, let's see." She paused, collecting her thoughts, and then decided to just say whatever came to her mind, and launched right into it, sweeping her arm out toward the pumpkin patch. "Maggie mentioned some of the strange happenings that have taken place in and around these fields we're traveling through, and we'll talk about those in a few minutes. But Cape Willington isn't the only town in Maine with a mysterious past. The entire Down East coastline has a spooky history all its own, dating back hundreds of years. This was one of the first areas of the continent explored by the Europeans, who brought all their old superstitions with them. Of course, the Native Americans had already been here for thousands of years, and they had their own myths and legends, which helped fuel the imaginations of the early settlers. It wasn't hard for them to see ghosts and phantoms and strange creatures in these dark, unexplored woods. A little later on, pirates roamed the islands and coves of Maine, and supposedly left some treasure behind, probably not too far from here, along with a few haunted caves and curses. And just like Salem, Massachusetts, Maine has its own witch stories. . . ."

She started with the tale of the cursed monument of Colonel Jonathan Buck, who founded the town of Bucksport, Maine, in the mid–seventeen hundreds. "There are a number of variations to this story," Candy told the passengers, "but they all say the same basic thing. At some point during his time in the area, Colonel Buck became secretly and romantically involved with a young woman—some stories say she was his maid, others that she was a local native woman. In any case, the woman became pregnant, which caused Colonel Buck to lose his cool. Apparently he was afraid his reputation would be damaged should the secret affair become public knowledge, since he also happened to be the local justice of the peace. So he ended the relationship and, to cover up his indiscretion, started spreading rumors that the woman was a witch. And his plan worked. In time, a few years after the birth of her child, the woman was brought before Colonel Buck with allegations that she was indeed a witch, and he pronounced her death sentence—she was to be burned, as all witches are."

There were a few gasps and nervous giggles around the wagon as Candy continued, her tone becoming more dramatic. "As the flames were taking this innocent young woman, she cursed the colonel, telling him that she would stomp on his grave until the end of time. And then a strange thing happened. While the rest of her body was being consumed, one of her legs fell out of the fire, and a child—her young son, it is believed—rushed forward and made off with it. That's all he had left of her to bury, some say. And her curse worked. Several years after Colonel Buck passed away, a tall monument was erected at the center of town in his honor, and a short time later the distinct outline of the witch's leg and foot appeared on the stone, as if she was stomping on his grave, and it's been there ever since. Some call it a stain, and there have been numerous efforts to remove it from the stone. They've even replaced the stone itself twice, but whatever they do to it, the image of the witch's leg and foot returns—and you can see it to this day if you visit Colonel Buck's cursed monument!"

As they rolled along, she told the tales of a redheaded ghost who haunted a nearby lighthouse, and a headless woman who regularly appeared to motorists on a dark road in rural Maine, asking for a lift. "Refuse her," Candy said ominously, "and you just might feel the full force of her wrath."

Next she told the tale of the mooncussers—land-based pirates who, a couple of hundred years earlier, used large lanterns as decoy beacons to lure unsuspecting ships onto the rocks of Maine's craggy coast, where they would then murder the crew and steal the ship's cargo. And she recounted the story of a pirate's moaning ghost, who still rattled his chains when anyone approached the haunted coastal cave where he had hidden a treasure centuries earlier.

"Pirates frequently sailed the treacherous waters along Maine's coast," Candy said to her passengers, "and there have been hundreds, perhaps thousands of shipwrecks on the rocky headlands and islands, leaving behind the restless souls of those who perished in the cold waters and continue to haunt our foggy shores."

At one point, as Candy paused between stories, T.J. leaned forward with a curious look in his eyes. "And what about this haunted house in town?" he asked. "I've heard you have a firsthand experience with that place."

"There's a haunted house in town? I'd love to hear that story," the elderly woman from Virginia said excitedly, "especially if you have an inside scoop."

Candy raised her eyebrows and let out a breath. How to approach this one? She indeed knew the inside scoop, but much of it was still unknown to the public.

"Yes, it's true," she finally said, "there is a ghost who haunts this town, though not in the traditional way of a haunting. It's more like her spirit looms over everything that's happened over the past few years."

"You're referring to Sapphire Vine, the Blueberry Queen who was murdered a few years back?" T.J. clarified.

"Yes, that's correct."

"And you think she has something to do with the other murders that have taken place locally?" T.J. asked, his voice low.

"I don't know," Candy said, shaking her head. Hesitant to go into the details with children and out-of-towners in the crowd, she leaned in closer to T.J. and said softly, "Why don't we talk about this later, okay? It's . . . somewhat complicated to explain."

T.J. took the hint and indicated with a tilt of his head and a slight grin that he'd drop his line of questioning—at least for the moment.

They had made the loop around the northern end of the pumpkin patch and were just heading through the line of trees into High Field. Candy took advantage of the change in geography to talk about the pumpkin patch itself.

"As you can see, we're leaving Low Field now, as this front patch is called," Candy told the passengers as the wagon bumped over the rough, rocky boundary between the two plots of land, "and heading into an adjoining patch, called High Field. You'll notice a number of different types of pumpkins in this upper area, including heirloom and ornamental varieties. Off on the right, you'll see some Long Island Cheese, which are those squat pumpkins with pale orange skin, and over there are my favorites—the Cotton Candy, which are the white ones in the traditional pumpkin shape. Most people use them for decorating, but they make great pies as well."

While Candy was talking about pumpkins, several of the children had begun pointing out the various displays along their route. In quick succession they passed a couple of mannequins dressed as a ghostly married couple, a stuffed scarecrow sporting a wicked grin, a crude wooden door over a cleft between two large rocks labeled HAUNTED CAVE—DO NOT ENTER, a series of black tombstones with funny epitaphs written on them, and several large-winged bats entwined in the limbs of a crooked tree. The kids particularly loved the sight of a hideous troll with a long white beard—also a mannequin, that of a small child they'd found at a yard sale, which they'd dressed appropriately—peeking out from behind a nearby stump, a stuffed bag of booty resting close by and gold-painted coins scattered around its feet. They'd also carved scary faces into numerous large pumpkins that lined their route.

"If you look closely," Candy told the passengers as they trundled along, "you also might see the ghostly image of the woman who died in this field decades ago and still haunts it. She's over there, hidden among the tree trunks, silently watching us."

Several passengers pointed out the sheet-draped mannequin hidden in the midst of a copse of trees, while others started laughing as they passed by one of the many piles of pumpkins that dotted the field. "And who's that?" someone asked good-naturedly. "I don't think he made it."

"Who do you mean?" Candy turned and looked.

"Over there," said the man in the bee costume, pointing and chuckling. "There's a leg right there, sticking out from under that pile of pumpkins—sort of like that leg in the witch's story you told us."

Candy wasn't sure what he meant. "What leg? Where?"

She saw it then. They were right. Not too far away, what looked like a man's leg stuck out from beneath a pile of pumpkins, showing the part of the body from the thigh down. It was cantered at an odd angle, and wore brown pants and a relatively new hiking boot on the large foot.

For a few moments it confused her, and she tilted her head, studying it. "I don't remember putting that there," she said.

In fact, she thought, *I don't remember that pile of pumpkins being there at all. Maybe Maggie or one of the helpers did it.*

But then the tractor came to an abrupt stop. Maggie twisted around and pointed urgently. She'd seen it, too, and it had confused her as well at first, but now she'd realized what it was.

"It looks like some sort of dummy or mannequin," Candy heard one of the passengers say.

But she knew that wasn't the case.

The wind left her suddenly, knocked out of her by some invisible force as she realized the truth.

"That's not a dummy!" she heard herself say, though the words sounded strangely disconnected, like she was talking underwater. "That's a real person under there!"

SIX

T.J. was the first one out of the wagon, leaping over the side and starting across the field at a sprint, but Candy was too shocked to move. Her body had frozen in place.

She wasn't sure what was happening. Perhaps it was the suddenness of this horrific discovery—and the possibility that something sinister had occurred right here, in the pumpkin patch she'd been working in with Maggie for all these months.

She watched as, after a dozen or so long strides, T.J. reached the pile of pumpkins, where he dropped to one knee and, with desperate abandon, started rolling and tossing the heavy orange globes off the body buried beneath, sometimes using his arms to sweep aside several at a time.

Could someone survive under that pile? Candy wondered as she watched, still frozen. *Could the person buried underneath still be alive?*

Candy saw Maggie jump off the tractor and dash toward

T.J., shouting toward the wagon for help, waving her arms frantically. In a few more moments she, too, was digging into the pile of pumpkins.

Candy heard movement behind her and felt the floorboard shift. One of the male passengers had jumped off the wagon and was running to help.

That snapped Candy out of whatever state she'd been in. She looked at the other passengers in the wagon, most of whom were turned toward T.J. and Maggie and the activity taking place in the field before them. But a few of them were watching her to see what she was going to do.

Candy pointed to one of the younger women with dark curly hair. "Do you have a cell phone?" she asked.

The woman nodded.

"Call nine-one-one," Candy instructed her. "Tell them there's been an accident out at Gumm's pumpkin patch on Willowbrook Road. Tell them they need to send an ambulance right away."

"What are you going to do?" asked a little girl sitting next to the curly-haired woman.

Candy did her best to smile reassuringly. "I'm going to see if I can help. You wait here. I'll be right back, okay?"

And with that, Candy rose, sidestepped her way through the sitting passengers, jumped down off the back of the wagon, and dashed across the field, trying to fight down the feeling of dread washing over her.

Not again, she thought as she ran. *It can't be happening again.*

But it *was* happening again. She knew it. She could feel it. Somehow she had known it would happen—not when or how, but someday, somewhere.

But never, she thought, here in this pumpkin patch.

By the time she reached the pile, they'd moved aside a good portion of the pumpkins, which were stacked heaviest around the body's head and shoulders. Maggie and a middle-aged man were rolling pumpkins off the legs and lower torso, while T.J. had cleared most of them away from the upper portion of the body. He was huffing, his hair was tossed about, and a line of perspiration had broken out along his forehead. His expensive-looking clothes were caked with dirt and grime. He looked up as she bent to help him.

"It looks like it's a he—and he could still be alive," T.J. said between breaths, giving her a faint ray of hope, "though how in the hell he got himself stuck under here I'll never guess."

"Maybe it was an accident," Candy said, "or a joke."

T.J. shook his head grimly but said nothing.

He didn't have to. They both sensed the truth. However this body had wound up in this place, buried beneath this pile, it must have been a deliberate act.

Together they cleared away a few more pumpkins, and Candy began to see portions of a face—a dirt-stained cheek, part of the forehead, matted dark hair. She had a pumpkin in her hand, about to toss it away, but something about the face looked familiar. She came to a standstill, trying to figure out what had caught her eye.

"Here, let me help you with that." The man in the bee costume appeared by her side. He took the pumpkin from her hands and tossed it away, then leaned forward to move more of them.

T.J. and the man in the bee costume were working side by side now, and they were making progress. Only a final layer of pumpkins remained. The body's arms, legs, and part of his chest were visible.

Candy stepped back, an expression of deep thought clouding her face.

"You okay, honey?" Maggie asked, coming over to stand beside her, brushing dust and dirt off her clothes. "You look like you've seen a ghost."

"I think I have," Candy said, and pointed.

Maggie saw it then—the face, and the beard.

She gasped, and her hand went to her mouth. "You don't mean . . . ?"

Candy nodded. "I'm afraid so. It looks like Sebastian J. Quinn made it out here to the pumpkin patch after all."

SEVEN

T.J. and the others moved aside the last few pumpkins, and they all got a good look at the person lying beneath.

Candy hadn't been mistaken—it was him all right.

Sebastian J. Quinn.

"Is he alive?" she asked, again strangely unable to move.

But T.J. was a step ahead of her. He'd already knelt close to the body and reached out a hand. He held a couple of fingers to the man's neck and felt at the wrist for a pulse. After a few moments, his jaw tightened. Raising his gaze to her, he shook his head.

Candy's first thought was for the passengers and the children. She looked back over her shoulder at the wagon, and then turned to Maggie. "We can't let the kids see this," she said, the concern evident in her voice. "I think I should take them back to Low Field."

Maggie nodded, her mouth tight. "That's probably a good idea, honey." She sidled a little closer to Candy and lowered her voice, so no one else could hear what she said. "You don't think this has anything to do with the house, do you? I mean, he was supposed to meet us here this morning to pick up the keys, right? So how does he wind up under one of our piles of pumpkins, smack dab in the middle of High Field?"

Candy shook her head. She didn't have an answer.

She was still recovering from the shock of seeing Sebastian's body. For some reason, she couldn't seem to take her eyes off him. She'd seen a dead body before, a year or two ago in the basement of an old house in town, but somehow this was different.

This death had taken place right under her nose.

"I don't know," she said finally, and with a shake of her head she started toward the hay wagon.

But halfway there she stopped, falling into deep thought. Something was itching at her—something didn't feel right. After absently studying the ground for several moments, she shook her head. She was missing something—she just had to figure out what it was. She lifted her gaze and looked out ahead of her, toward the hay wagon and then left to the line of trees. Through the thin screen of trunks and branches, she could see slivers of Low Field and the cars in the parking lot beyond.

She shifted, now scanning the trees to the north, and following them around to the west and the south, turning in an almost complete circle. She gazed up at the sky and again down to the fields around her.

Finally she turned and walked back to Maggie, who was still standing where she'd left her. "You know, that's a great question," Candy said as she approached her friend.

Maggie gave her a confused look. "Which one?"

She pointed toward the body of Sebastian J. Quinn. "How did he wind up here, under a piles of pumpkins, smack dab in the middle of *this* field?"

"Oh, *that* question." Maggie scrunched up her face and shrugged. "I have no idea. That's why I asked you. Why, have you noticed something?"

In response, Candy turned and looked back toward the line of trees and Low Field. "I don't remember seeing a car in the parking lot when we came in this morning. Do you?"

"A car?" Maggie had to think about that for a moment. "Now that you mention it, no. The lot was empty when we came in, just like it is every morning."

"Right," Candy said, her mind starting to work. "So if Sebastian didn't come here in his own car, how did he get out here? Did he walk from town? Did he take a taxi cab all the way out here? Did he fall out of a plane?"

"Maybe the murderer brought him here," Maggie mused.

"Murderer?" Candy looked thoughtfully at her friend. "So you think he was murdered?"

Maggie gave her a noncommittal look. "Wasn't he?"

A determined look came into Candy's blue eyes, and her jaw tightened. "I don't know. Let's go find out."

EIGHT

T.J. had edged back from the body but still crouched nearby, while the others who had helped uncover the corpse hovered in a loose circle among the scattered, tossed-aside pumpkins.

Candy walked up to T.J. and touched him on the shoulder. He looked up at her, a solemn expression on his face.

"We should get everyone back away from the crime scene," she told him, "so we don't disturb it any further—though granted it's a mess as far as evidence is concerned."

He nodded and rose, gazing back toward the wagon. "Right. And someone should probably get those passengers out of here."

"I'll do it," Maggie volunteered. She looked at Candy and added, "I think your job is here."

As she started off, T.J. looked at Candy quizzically. "What did she mean by that?"

"She means," Candy said grimly, "that I've had a bit of experience with this sort of thing . . . much as I hate to admit it. Unfortunately, trouble seems to keep following me around."

She waved her arm at the others who stood near the uncovered body. "Will you all please step back? In fact, it might be better if everyone climbed back into the wagon. Maggie's going to take you back to your cars. We really appreciate your help, but the police will take over from here."

Her first concern was footprints, but if Sebastian—or anyone connected with his death—left some in the immediate area around the body, most of them had probably already been disturbed or destroyed, given all those who had helped move the pumpkins and uncover the body. Still, there was no point making it worse. She took several steps back herself, pulling T.J. with her. He came away uneasily, as if reluctant to leave the body behind.

Candy knew exactly how he felt, but for the moment, she did her best to detach herself from her emotions and focused her gaze on the corpse of Sebastian J. Quinn. She noticed several things right away. He was wearing brown slacks, a white shirt, and a dark jacket, all soiled and spotted with clumps of dirt and vegetation. Seeping through his shirt, just at the edge of the jacket's right lapel, she could see a dark spot, maybe two—possibly bullet wounds, she thought.

That seemed to confirm Maggie's suspicion that Sebastian had been murdered.

But how had he wound up buried under a pile of pumpkins? And what had he been doing out here in the first place?

Candy also noticed that he still clenched a flashlight tightly in his left fist. The flashlight was either turned off or the batteries had died out.

That might be a clue to his time of death, she thought. She guessed that he must have been killed sometime during the night—otherwise why would he have a flashlight with him? *If he'd been shot out here and buried under the pile of pumpkins, how long would it have taken for the flashlight batteries to die out?* she wondered. *That could help establish a more precise time of death, couldn't it?*

Her gaze swept the body again. She noticed the outline of a cell phone in Sebastian's front pocket, so whatever had happened, he didn't have time to call for help.

And then there were the car keys clutched in his right fist, held so that several of the keys protruded from between his fingers, looking like shorter versions of Wolverine's claws. Why the heck had he held them like that?

She looked up, scanning the area. She noticed nothing more out of sorts than a stray pitchfork stuck into a pumpkin not too far away.

Hadn't that been part of one of the displays? The one with the ghostly couple? How that got there, she had no idea.

Perhaps Sebastian had moved it.

Or someone else.

"What are you thinking?" T.J. asked, breaking into her thoughts.

She looked over at him. He was watching her closely.

With a gentle shake of her head, she turned back to the body and pointed. "Something's not right about this."

"What do you mean?"

But Candy wasn't quite sure. She couldn't put her finger on it, but she sensed something odd about the body, as if it were trying to tell her something—as if it had been arranged that way.

She turned, her gaze shifting out toward the surrounding fields and woods. "I'm going to have a look around," she said to T.J., and on an impulse started off toward the far end of High Field.

"Need some company?" he called after her, a trace of concern in his tone.

Turning, she walked backward as she spoke. "It'd probably be best if you stayed by the body—to keep people away and make sure no one else disturbs the scene." When she saw his skeptical look, she managed a weak smile and added, "I'll be okay. I just want to check something out. I'll be right back."

With that, she turned forward again and walked toward the distant trees.

As much as she hated to admit it, she did have experience with these sorts of things—probably more than anyone else in town, except for a few folks in the police department—and maybe Finn Woodbury, a local friend who had once been a big-city cop. Over the course of the past few years, Candy had somehow tracked down and exposed several murderers in town, mostly by simply following clues and asking the right questions of the right people. And she'd come to realize that she had an odd knack for this sort of thing. She wasn't quite sure why. She'd never set out to be an amateur detective. But somehow these mysteries kept showing up on her doorstep, and in solving them, she'd come to trust her instincts and allowed her curiosity to take her in the right directions.

It was her curiosity that had her walking across High Field now, toward the woods on the far side. The question on her mind at the moment was a simple one. It was the same one Maggie had asked: How had Sebastian J. Quinn wound up in this field? More specifically, how did he get out here?

Candy could think of only a couple of ways. He'd either been brought here and dumped, or he'd arrived in his own car and had been murdered here. The first scenario was certainly possible, but Candy had a hunch he'd come here under his own power.

The keys in his hand—that was the clue that had caught her eye.

If his body had been dumped here by someone else, why would he have his car keys clutched in his hand?

He wouldn't, she realized—which meant he must have arrived here in his own car.

So where was it?

When she and Maggie had first taken over the pumpkin patch at the end of the summer, she'd taken a few minutes one morning to study the property on Google maps, just to get a lay of the land. She recalled that, at the far end of High Field, a dirt access road headed off in the opposite direction, back to a paved rural road that eventually wound its way out to Route 192, which led up to Route 1.

Could that have been how Sebastian got here? Had he come in the back way?

If so, that would present a new set of questions, but for the moment she tabled those and concentrated on the issue at hand.

It didn't take her long to find the car. In fact, she practically walked right to it as she followed a narrow footpath through a screen of thick shrubbery and trees, and turned to her right.

An older-model white Audi sat by the side of a narrow dirt road. It looked as if it had been abandoned. The car hadn't been washed in a while, and bore Massachusetts license plates. That would make sense. The last she'd heard, Sebastian still taught at the University of Massachusetts at Amherst, halfway across the Bay State.

But if the car was his, why had he parked it back here?

As she approached the car, Candy could see there were no passengers inside. Still, she moved toward it cautiously, just in case someone might be sleeping in the backseat—or lying in wait. But once she looked in the windows, she saw that it was indeed empty.

She walked the entire way around the car, just to make sure, and then tried the door handle on the passenger side. Locked.

She tried the other door handles as well. All locked.

In a fleeting moment, she was tempted to walk back to Sebastian's body and retrieve the keys in his hand to see if they fit this car. But that would be highly inappropriate, she knew, and more than likely unnecessary. Somehow, she was certain the keys in Sebastian's hand would fit this car. It had to belong to the man who now lay dead in the pumpkin patch.

Just to make sure she hadn't missed anything, she walked back around the car again, but nothing jumped out at her, and she knew there wasn't much else she could do at the moment, other than alert the police to the car's location.

She heard the sound of a distant siren then, signaling that the ambulance and police were on their way. Unfortunately, they'd arrive far too late to save Sebastian's life.

Before she walked away from the car, she took a final look inside. There was nothing in the backseat except a folded jacket, an umbrella, and a few old magazines. And nothing in the driver's seat.

But in the passenger's seat she spotted what looked like a manila folder. She edged in closer to the window for a better look.

The folder appeared to have a few documents inside, though she couldn't tell what they were, since she could see only their edges poking out of the folder. However, she could just make out a single word someone had written on the folder's tab with a heavy black marker.

It read, in all capital letters, *EMMA*.

NINE

"Well, Ms. Holliday, here we are again," said Daryl Durr, Cape Willington's chief of police, in a particularly calm, controlled, almost disinterested manner that told Candy he was anything but.

She nodded, arms folded across her chest. She didn't quite trust herself to talk just yet. She'd noticed on the walk back across the field that her hands were shaking, which was why she now stood with her arms crossed, her hands tucked away at her sides. The full force of what had happened—that there had been another murder in Cape Willington—had shaken her. Once again, the victim had been someone she had known. And once again, she somehow found herself smack dab in the middle of a murder mystery.

She stood perhaps a dozen paces from where Sebastian J. Quinn's body still lay in the pumpkin patch. A couple of police officers were cordoning off the area around the crime scene with stakes they'd found and yellow police tape, while another stood nearby in a conversation with two EMTs. And a dark-haired female officer was talking to T.J. and the man in the bee costume. Off to the right, the flaring lights of three patrol cars and an ambulance, parked along the same dirt farm road the tractor and hay wagon had followed into High Field, cut across the darkening day.

The whole scene had taken on a surreal aspect, causing Candy's thoughts to scatter, despite her efforts to focus them.

Chief Durr must have recognized her discomfort, for his expression softened just a bit. "I know this is difficult for you, Ms. Holliday," he told her, his eyes allowing a trace of sympathy, "but you and I have been through this drill before, haven't we?" His forced smile looked almost genuine.

Candy returned it as best she could. "Yes, Chief, we have."

The chief had arrived at the pumpkin patch ten minutes earlier, wearing aviator sunglasses and a chocolate brown bomber jacket over his standard police-issue uniform. He'd first walked around the crime scene, studying it from all angles with a practiced eye and talking briefly with a deputy, several of the officers, and a few hayride passengers before spotting Candy and heading over to her. He'd greeted her with a tip of the hat, his expression grim.

"So, you want to tell me what happened?"

She nodded, took a deep breath as she collected her thoughts, and then told the whole story, from the beginning, as carefully and factually as possible. Her voice was hesitant and strained at first but grew steadier and more assured as she talked. She told him that Sebastian had contacted Maggie a few weeks earlier about renting Sapphire Vine's old place, and how he'd failed to show for a scheduled meeting that morning, and how they'd loaded up the hay wagon, making their regular rounds of the two fields, and found and uncovered the body. She mentioned the flashlight she'd spotted in Sebastian's grip, and her guess about the time of his death the night before, and the car she'd found parked along a dirt road beyond the edge of High Field.

She left out the part about the folder labeled *Emma*. She was sure he'd find that himself when he searched the car. Whether or not it had anything to do with Sebastian's death, she couldn't say—though deep down she felt it could be important.

The chief listened to her carefully before grunting and turning back toward the activity surrounding the body, his eyes peering out from beneath his hat's bill. "And do you think it's a coincidence," he said after a few moments, "that the body was discovered here, in a field you happened to be working in?"

Candy let out a long breath at the question and shook her head. "To be honest, Chief, I just don't know. I agree it looks suspicious. . . ."

"It looks a lot more than suspicious, Ms. Holliday." His tone wasn't accusatory, just matter-of-fact.

She felt a chill. "You think there's a reason he was murdered here . . . and that it has something to do with *me?*"

The chief shrugged as he looked back toward her, his gaze sharpening. "We already know there was a connection between the deceased and Ms. Tremont, and between him and you as well. You'd met the deceased before, right? You had a relationship with him?"

Candy couldn't help grousing at that. "I wouldn't call it a relationship."

"But you knew each other?"

"Yes, we knew each other. But I haven't seen him in over two years."

"And you knew he was coming here this morning?"

"To meet with Maggie, yes, to get the keys to Sapphire's house." She involuntarily tightened her arms across her chest, a protective gesture.

"Did he tell you or Ms. Tremont why he was interested in renting the place?"

Candy shook her head. "He was . . . well, kind of secretive about the whole thing. But he might have mentioned something about it to Maggie. Maybe you should talk to her."

"I intend to do just that," the chief said as he rubbed his chin, pondering what she'd told him. "But we have to assume it's more than coincidental that the deceased was murdered here in your field, don't we? There's a definite connection between you, Ms. Tremont, and Mr. Quinn. How exactly that connection resulted in Quinn's death remains to be seen. So here's what I need you to do, Ms. Holliday . . . Candy."

He pointed toward the dark-haired female officer who was just finishing up her conversation with T.J. and the man in the bee costume. The woman was short and curvy yet solid, with big shoulders and a round face. "Have you met Officer Prospect?" the chief asked.

"No, I don't think so."

The chief waved the officer over, introducing her while she was still several steps away. "This is Officer Molly Prospect. Molly, this is Candy Holliday. I'd like you to take her statement."

Officer Prospect gave her a professional yet friendly nod. She seemed like the type of person who had a hard time keeping a smile off her face, and there was a twinkle in her dark eyes that told everyone she met that she loved her job. "Hello, Ms. Holliday," she said pleasantly.

"Hello," Candy said softly, with a nod.

"I want you to tell Officer Prospect everything you just told me," the chief instructed, looking Candy carefully in the eyes. "She'll take notes and create an initial report. I'd like you to come down to the station Monday morning to review it and make sure everything's accurate, and we'll get your signature on it. Can you do that?"

"Of course."

The chief patted her on the shoulder. "That's the spirit. Now if you think of anything else we should know about, I want you to immediately call Officer Prospect here. She'll give you her business card so you can get in touch with her.

And if you can't reach her, I want you to call the station and ask for me personally." He forced a grim smile. "And try not to worry too much, Ms. Holliday," he told her. "We'll figure out what's going on around here."

With that, he turned and made his way back toward the crime scene, while Officer Prospect began asking Candy a series of directed questions, making careful notes of the answers. Her manner was efficient and professional as she guided Candy through the series of events that had occurred that morning. Candy noticed that her black hair, which she'd tucked up under her hat, was straight and shiny, and Candy imagined that when she let it out, it must fall to her shoulders, and perhaps even farther. If Candy were to venture a guess, it would be that Office Prospect had Native American blood in her—possibly from the local Penobscot tribe.

They were going back through the sequence of events a second time when T.J. approached them. "How are you doing?" he asked Candy during a break in the questioning.

She gave him a halfhearted shrug. "I'm hanging in there."

"Well, listen, I'm headed back to the parking lot, but if you'd like, we can walk together. I think the police have the situation pretty much under control here. In fact, I think they'd prefer that we get out of their hair."

He looked over at Officer Prospect. "You have everything you need from her at the moment, right?"

The dark-haired officer jotted down a few more quick notes before she folded shut her notepad and reached into a shirt pocket for a business card, which she handed to Candy. She gave T.J. an agreeable nod. "I think so, Mr. Pruitt. We're all done."

Candy took the card, glanced at it, and slid it into her back pocket. It took her a few moments to register what she'd just heard. Her eyes widened. "Wait a minute. Did you just call him *Pruitt*?"

Her gaze shot to T.J., the surprise evident in her expression. "You're a Pruitt?"

She noticed it then—the eyes, the nose, the shape of his face. It struck her like a cold shower, sending brisk pinpricks of recognition through her as she realized who he really was. "You're Tristan Pruitt, aren't you? You're one of Helen's sons?"

Helen Ross Pruitt was the richest woman in town, from one of the richest families in New England. She regularly summered at Pruitt Manor, on the rocky point out by Kimball Light, an old lighthouse that dated back to the early years of the previous century. Candy had met Mrs. Pruitt—as the family matriarch was known around town—several times, though she'd never met any of Helen's siblings or children. But she'd seen a few photos of them, and now noticed the family resemblance.

In response, T.J. held out his hand. "Actually, I'm her nephew," he said smoothly, "and the full name is Tristan James Hawthorne Pruitt. It's a pleasure to finally—and formally—meet you, Candy Holliday."

TEN

"So you're Helen's nephew?"

Tristan Pruitt nodded as the wind caught his fair hair, flicking a few strands across his forehead. "The family history's a little muddled, but, yes, I'm the son of her younger brother, Judson. He's the middle child. Aunt Helen has four siblings in all. She's the oldest, and she has two sisters and two brothers, including my father."

"And you decided to keep that fairly significant piece of information to yourself? Why the secretive use of initials?"

The two of them were walking along the dirt road that led back to Low Field and the parking lot. They'd left behind the hushed, solemn atmosphere that centered on Sebastian J. Quinn's body. The corpse had been covered with a sheet, and several of the officers were fanning out across the field, searching for evidence while they awaited the arrival of the crime scene van from Augusta.

Candy had to admit she was glad that T.J.—or, rather, the man now known to her as Tristan Pruitt—had pulled

her out of there. The suddenness of all that had happened
in the past hour had left her feeling emotionally on edge.
But now that they were headed away from the scene of the
crime, she found herself breathing a little easier, and the
tightness in her chest and tingling in her arms and fingers
were beginning to abate.

As they walked, she found herself stealing glances
at Tristan Pruitt. Despite the subterfuge of disguising his
name, she found herself intrigued by him. She decided she
liked the way he held himself, the square of his shoulders
and the leanness of his body. Her eyes were drawn to the
line of his jaw and the shape of his hands. She liked the way
he'd reacted when they'd first spotted Sebastian's leg pro-
truding from beneath the pile of pumpkins. While she'd
stood there frozen in indecision and dread, he'd leapt out
of the wagon with urgency and decisiveness. He'd worked
harder than anyone to remove the pumpkins that covered
the body, and his hands and clothes now displayed the results
of his efforts, spotted with dirt and grime, though he barely
seemed to notice—or care. She imagined he wasn't the type
of person who pursued fashions or fads or the latest hot
spots, and probably would be equally comfortable throwing back a couple of beers with the local lobstermen or
climbing out of a limo in a tux for a night at the opera. There
was an earthiness and yet an elegance about him, an unmis-
takable confidence that appealed to something deep
inside her.

"It wasn't my intention to be deceptive," he said sincerely,
responding to her question. "I suppose you could say I just
wanted to keep a low profile initially. The family name car-
ries quite a bit of cachet around here, as I'm sure you know.
Sometimes that's beneficial, but other times it can be a
burden."

Candy couldn't conceive how being a member of the
wealthiest family in Cape Willington would ever be considered a burden, but she let that go for the moment. Instead,

she gave him a mischievous grin. "So . . . Tristan, huh? What's the whole thing again? Tristan Hawthorne something?"

He caught her look and laughed easily. "Tristan James Hawthorne Pruitt, if you must know the truth. And, yes, it is a bit of a mouthful."

"Why Tristan? That's a British name, isn't it?"

"Welsh, actually." He squinted up at the sky, which momentarily brightened. "The Pruitts are originally from Wales, you know. There's a medieval story about a hero named Tristan, who was one of King Arthur's knights of the Round Table."

"Tristan and Isolde," Candy said, recalling the story.

He lowered his gaze toward her, his head tilting slightly to the side. "That's right. The Wagner opera. Isolde was an Irish princess, said to be very beautiful. She was betrothed to King Mark of Cornwall, who sent his trusted nephew, Tristan, to Ireland to fetch his future bride and escort her back to Mark's kingdom for the wedding. But along the way Tristan and Isolde took a potion and fell helplessly in love, creating a very sticky romantic triangle. Anyway, my family was obviously fond of the name, since quite a few of my ancestors were named Tristan, including one of my great-grandfathers—one of the old Welsh Pruitts. I'm his direct namesake."

Candy was intrigued. "And the Hawthorne part?"

He suddenly looked sheepish. "It's after Nathaniel Hawthorne. That was my mother's idea. She was a socialite from Boston who had a classical education. She insisted on naming all her children after New England literary figures in some way or other, either with first or middle names, or in some cases both. I have a brother named Henry Longfellow Pruitt, and a sister Charlotte, after Brontë."

"My, my, that's pretty fancy." Candy's eyes twinkled in amusement at his apparent discomfort over the current line of questioning. "And James?"

"That was my mother's father. He was a Hutchinson. Very old Boston family."

Candy whistled. "Wow, that's quite a genealogy. You're practically a walking New England history book, aren't you?"

He chuckled. "That's probably true. I guess I never quite thought of it that way. When I was younger I thought the whole name was too long and pretentious, and since I'm not the pretentious type, I started calling myself T.J., and my family and friends followed my lead. But once I grew up I decided I needed something more mature, so I've reverted to Tristan."

"Well," Candy said sincerely, "I think it's a very nice name."

He grinned. "I'm glad you approve. But you have a fairly unique name yourself. Where did Candy come from?"

It was a question she'd heard many times before, especially when she was growing up, and she'd even been teased about it a number of times. But she didn't mind answering the question again, considering who was asking. "My mother came up with it. She was born on Christmas Day, so her parents named her Holly. And she lived up to her festive name. She was a wonderful, warm, caring person."

"She's gone now?" Tristan asked, catching the past tense of the verb.

Candy nodded. "A few years back."

"I'm sorry to hear that. But, again, why Candy?"

"Like my mother, I was born on a holiday—in my case, Halloween. So my mother decided to continue the tradition."

"Halloween?" Tristan pondered that for a moment. "So you have a birthday coming up in, what, four or five days?"

Candy gave him a dark look. "Don't remind me."

Her reaction surprised him. "Why not? Birthdays are a time for celebration, aren't they?"

"Usually, yes," Candy agreed, "but this is a big one."

"I see."

She waited for him to say more, but like a gentleman, he kept any further questions about her age to himself, unwilling to pry too far into her personal history. So she filled in the blanks for him. "It's the big four-oh," she said reluctantly, as if the very thought of it was too much to bear. "I'm getting old!"

He laughed again, charmingly. "I'd hardly consider you old, but I do understand." He studied her face, the same way she'd studied his earlier. "Well, Candy Holliday, I guess we'll just have to figure out a creative way to ease this obviously stressful transition for you," he said seriously. "But as someone who's several years on the north side of that rather significant age milestone, I can tell you it's not nearly as bad as you think it might be."

Candy shot him a skeptical look. "Hmm, I'll take that under advisement."

Impulsively, he reached out to give her hand a squeeze. "Trust me, you'll be just fine."

As the sky lowered and the wind picked up, they angled to their left, following the dirt track, and had just reached the lower pumpkin patch when they heard someone huffing and puffing behind them. They turned to see the man in the bee costume running to catch up. He had lingered around the scene of the crime but apparently had finally been shooed away.

After he'd introduced himself as Eric and they'd exchanged pleasantries, the three of them made their way through the pumpkin patch toward the hay wagon, which had come to a stop next to the parking lot. By this time all the passengers had disembarked, and some had already driven off in their cars, though quite a few customers still wandered around the field, picking out pumpkins and perusing the wares at the farm stand, where Maggie was busy adding up prices for customers, taking money, and making change.

Everything looked more or less perfectly normal, Candy

thought. It was as if nothing strange had happened that morning, and all the customers were just enjoying the day, completely unaware of the dead body lying in the next field.

As Eric the Bee said his good-byes and made his way to his car, Candy and Tristan headed over to the farm stand to help out Maggie. By the time they'd finished with the last few customers, the crime van had arrived, bouncing carelessly along the dirt track through the pumpkin patch to the field beyond.

A short time later, Chief Durr drove down to have a talk with them.

"We're going to have to close the entire pumpkin patch— both fields—for the rest of the day," he told them, as a few heavy raindrops fell from the sky. "Looks like it's turning stormy anyway. It's probably a good time to close up shop."

"What about tomorrow?" Maggie asked, the concern evident in her voice. "There are only a few days left until Halloween, and Sunday tends to be one of our biggest days of the week."

"We have a lot of pumpkins we have to clear out of here by midweek," Candy added, aware that Halloween—and her birthday—fell on a Wednesday this year. After that, the demand for pumpkins would disappear—and she would have to face the fact that she was on the north side of forty, as Tristan had called it. "We'd sure like to open up tomorrow. Is that possible?"

The chief tugged off his hat and ran a hand through his graying hair. "It all depends on the forensics team," he replied, replacing the hat firmly on his head. "It's their call. Best I can tell you is it'll be a day-to-day decision. We'll see what the morning brings. But for now, I'd like the cooperation of you three, since you're the primary ones who found and uncovered the body."

He turned his gaze on Maggie. "Ms. Tremont, as I told you back in the other field, I'd like to see the printouts of all your e-mail exchanges with Sebastian Quinn, and details about your phone conversations with him as well. I need you to gather all that information together and drop it off at the station this afternoon."

Maggie clicked her heels together and saluted. "Aye, aye, Captain. I'm glad to help out."

His gaze lingered on her for only a moment, as he quickly decided to let her theatrics pass without comment. "And, Ms. Holliday and Mr. Pruitt, I'll need you both at the station Monday morning to review and sign your statements, and answer any additional questions we might have. We hope to get this investigation wrapped up as quickly as possible, so if any of you think of anything else that might help us out, get in touch with us pronto. Got it?"

They said they did, and once he had their assurances, he gave them all a brusque nod, climbed back into his car, and drove off.

"Well, I guess that does it for today," Maggie said. "We'd better close this place up and do as the chief says." She stuffed the final few bills into the money box, shut the lid, and looked up at the sky. "Besides, he's right—the weather's not cooperating. Looks like we would've gotten rained out anyway."

Working quickly, they covered some of the items in the stand, tucked others behind the counter, and packed the most valuable ones into the back of Candy's teal-colored Jeep, which she'd pulled up next to the farm stand. The Jeep was showing its age, and bubbles of rust were beginning to attack the rear wheel wells and lower running boards, but it still managed to get her where she was going.

As Maggie finished stowing away items at the farm stand, Tristan helped Candy carry the last few boxes and bags to the Jeep. They worked in silence, Candy deep in her thoughts, until Tristan, gauging her somber mood, said softly, "Rough morning, huh?"

Something in the way he'd said it made her mood lighten just a bit. "Well, to be honest, it's not what I expected when

I got out of bed this morning." She paused, noticing the concerned look in his eyes. "It's just that—well, we'd been expecting him . . . Sebastian, I mean. He was scheduled to meet us this morning here in the pumpkin patch to pick up the keys to Sapphire Vine's old house. He wanted to rent it for a couple of weeks and . . ."

Her voice trailed off as another thought came to her. She narrowed her gaze on Tristan. "But you're here, too, aren't you?" she said, not in an accusatory way, but more as if she'd only just recalled the real purpose for his sudden appearance in the pumpkin patch that morning.

He responded with a lopsided grin. "My timing is impeccable, it seems."

She stuck to her point. "But you came out here for a reason, didn't you? Something about a haunted house?"

The grin disappeared, and his eyes took on a guarded look. "Yes, that's right. Sapphire Vine's old place. Apparently Sebastian Quinn was interested in it too. I didn't realize it was so popular."

"You said you wanted to talk to me about it. You had some questions?"

He nodded curtly. "I still have them," he said, all flippancy gone now. "In fact, I was hoping to invite you out to the house today for lunch, so we could have a longer talk about it."

"The house?" It took her a moment to understand the reference. "You mean Pruitt Manor?"

"Yes, Pruitt Manor. I'd hoped you might join Aunt Helen and myself for lunch. The offer still stands. Of course, with all that's happened . . ."

Candy understood what he was getting at, and she instantly appreciated the fact that he gave her a way out. "Thank you so much for the invitation, but today's probably not the best day for it."

If he was disappointed, he didn't show it. "Of course. I completely understand."

They carried a last load to the Jeep, and once they'd stuffed all the items inside, Tristan reached into a coat pocket. He, too, withdrew a business card, which he handed to Candy. "For your collection," he said, "and in case you change your mind today, or would like to reschedule for another day. Just give me a call."

A few minutes later, he was gone, driving off in the silver sedan.

"Well," Maggie said, sidling up beside her friend, eyeing the swirl of dead leaves kicked up by Tristan's disappearing car, "you and Mr. Pruitt seemed to be getting along fairly well, considering the two of you just met." She'd already heard the story of how T.J. was actually Tristan James, scion of the wealthy Pruitt family.

Candy shut the Jeep's back hatch. "He seems like a nice guy," she said noncommittally.

"Hmm, yes, very nice—and very rich."

Candy frowned. "That has nothing to do with it."

"Of course not."

"Besides, the last thing I need right now is a boyfriend."

"True . . . since you already have one. So how is Ben doing out on the West Coast, by the way?" She was referring to Ben Clayton, Candy's sort-of boyfriend and the editor of the *Cape Crier*, Cape Willington's local newspaper.

"We talked yesterday. He's calling again tonight," Candy told her friend as she walked to the driver's side door, while Maggie headed around the other side and climbed into the passenger seat.

"Are you going to tell him about Tristan?" Maggie asked when they were both seated inside.

Candy shrugged and snapped on her seat belt. "I hadn't really thought about it."

But Maggie wasn't quite ready to let the whole episode go. In fact, she decided to double down. "So," she said breezily, "it sounds like our soon-to-be birthday girl has not one but *two* admirers."

"Now cut that out," Candy replied with mock sharpness as she fished the car keys out of her pocket. "You know there's nothing between Tristan and me. It's like you said— we just met. And I don't need any more complications in my life right now. We have enough trouble on our hands."

"You got that right." As they backed up, Maggie glanced out over at the pumpkin patch, toward High Field. "Can you imagine Sebastian J. Quinn showing up dead like that under a pile of pumpkins? Isn't it unbelievable? Now we not only have a dead body in our field, but I still have that damned vacant haunted house on my hands." She let out a deep sigh as Candy headed out the dirt lane back toward the main road. "If you ask me, I still blame that house."

"What do you mean?" Candy asked, looking over at her friend.

"Sapphire's house. I'm telling you it's cursed, just like I said. And the evidence is clear. First Sapphire dies, and now Sebastian. It seems like anyone who's connected to that place winds up murdered."

"That's crazy talk."

"No, it's not!" Maggie said, her voice rising to emphasize her point. "I'm totally serious about this! That house is cursed, I'm telling you . . . and I just hope the curse doesn't transfer to us!"

ELEVEN

Normally, Candy didn't believe in curses, or haunted houses, or ghosts, for that matter—other than the Halloween variety, of course. But she'd seen some strange things going on around Cape Willington over the past few years—like a man who thought he could turn himself invisible, and a trio of sisters who were said to have uncanny premonitions, and a white moose that had an affinity for discovering dead bodies and old hermits in the woods. So she wasn't quite ready to rule anything out—at least not yet, not until she determined for herself what was true, and what wasn't.

So even though Maggie was probably exaggerating about the curse—*probably*, Candy admitted—her friend was right about one thing: Whatever was happening around town, whatever had happened to Sebastian J. Quinn, it seemed to revolve around Sapphire Vine and her old house.

Sapphire Vine.

It was a name that continued to plague the residents of Cape Willington. Even though she'd been dead for more than two years now, struck down in the prime of her life in her own home by a vicious murderer, the former gossip columnist and blackmailer somehow managed to continue to reach out from the grave, casting a dark shadow over their quiet coastal village.

How was that possible? Candy wondered. She knew the hold Sapphire had had on a number of individuals, including Sebastian, but had there been something else—something none of them knew about?

Why had Sebastian been interested in renting Sapphire's old house? Candy asked herself. Was there something still there, in the house, that Sebastian wanted?

And if so, what could it be?

Candy thought back to the file she'd seen laying on the front seat of Sebastian's car. *Emma*, it had been labeled.

Emma.

Who was Emma? Why had Sebastian left that file sitting on the seat? And did it have anything to do with Sebastian's death?

Candy thought she knew a way to find out.

It had come to her after she'd dropped off Maggie at her house in Fowler's Corner, so she could locate, print out, and assemble the e-mails Sebastian had sent to her over the past few weeks, at the police chief's request. Earlier in the day, Candy had vaguely recalled seeing the name Emma somewhere before, and it had nagged at the back of her mind for the past couple of hours. But as she backed out of Maggie's driveway and turned toward town, she suddenly knew where she must have seen it.

She found a parking spot along Ocean Avenue, one of the town's two primary commercial streets, and headed up to her second-floor office at the *Cape Crier*, where she worked part-time as a community columnist and occasional reporter.

She'd inherited the position of columnist from Sapphire Vine herself, who spent years with the paper before her death, covering local events while secretly amassing a collection of documents, photos, and files on many of the town's citizens. Sapphire had then used some of the more damaging information she'd collected to blackmail several individuals.

She'd kept some of the files in her office at the newspaper, but had hidden away the more damaging ones in a secret hideaway in the attic of her house, where only she could access them. After Sapphire's death, Candy had inherited many of the files, and her first instinct had been to burn them, destroying the secrets they contained. But after careful consideration, she'd had second thoughts, and had decided to hold on to them, in case they were ever needed in an emergency.

Out of respect for the privacy of others, Candy had largely avoided going through the files, and had dug into them only once before, when she thought the information they contained might help her solve a mystery.

Now she was about to search through them again, since she was almost certain that somewhere in those files, she'd once seen a reference to someone named Emma.

Upstairs, she found the maze of second-floor offices deserted; it was late Saturday morning, almost noon, and none of the staff members were working today, since the paper had recently reverted to its twice-a-month publishing schedule, after putting out an issue twice weekly during the summer months, which often meant weekend hours.

Like the other offices, the one belonging to Ben Clayton was dark and deserted. Ben had flown out to San Francisco earlier in the week to attend a journalism and social media conference, at which he'd been booked as a panelist for a Sunday-morning session. Taking advantage of the trip, he'd also managed to snag an interview with an Internet billionaire who had local roots. The interview was scheduled to take place early the following week, but Ben had promised Candy he'd make it back to Cape Willington in time for her fortieth birthday.

Once in her office, Candy pushed the door closed behind her and stepped right to the filing cabinet in the corner, where she dropped into a cross-legged sitting position. Directly in front of her, the cabinet's bottom drawer was labeled with only two letters: sv.

Sapphire Vine.

Candy took a deep breath, moved her hand to the dull metal handle, slid aside the button with her thumb, and pulled open the drawer.

She leaned in for a closer look as the files fanned out before her, extending deep into the cabinet. All the tabbed labels were neatly printed in Sapphire's own handwriting, usually in purple, green, or red ink, often embellished with various curlicues, hearts, and even little drawings of flowers, kitties, and stars. Many bore the names of individuals Candy knew well: *Alby Alcott, Melody Barnes, Judicious F. P. Bosworth, WB* (for Wanda Boyle, a file Candy had already peered into at an earlier time), *Delilah Daggerstone, Charlotte Depew* . . .

And there it was, directly in front of a file labeled *The Foxwell Sisters*—an old, well-worn one simply labeled *Emma.*

Gently Candy removed the file, laid it flat across the top of the other files in the drawer, and flipped it open.

Inside, she found only two items.

One was an old black-and-white, eight-by-ten-inch, somewhat crinkled photograph of a gravestone. The other was a photocopy of an aged index card, like those from an old library card catalog.

She examined the photo of the gravestone first. It looked as if it had been blown up from a smaller photo, for it was too blurry to see anything in any sort of detail. She could make out the word *EMMA* in large, indistinct capital letters near the top of the stone, but there was no last name, or at least one that was readable. She saw several smaller inscriptions engraved into the bottom of the gravestone, but those, too, were impossible to read due to the poor quality of the photo.

Candy studied it for several moments, her gaze focused in on the singular inscription.

Emma.

So, she thought, *here's the proof that I was right.*

There *was* a connection between Sebastian, Emma, and Sapphire Vine.

And it appeared Emma was dead—that she had, in fact, died quite a while ago, judging by the age of the photo.

She noticed, then, that the gravestone showed no dates. No birth date. No date of Emma's death.

Candy frowned. That was strange. What gravestone failed to show the life span of the deceased? Wasn't that the whole point of one—to commemorate and help others remember a person's life?

She also now noticed that the gravestone appeared to be in a small, grassy cemetery, somewhat overgrown and unattended, surrounded by vegetation and what looked like some sort of stone wall. There were only a few other dark gravestones surrounding Emma's, their inscriptions blurred as well. They appeared to be quite old.

A family plot? Candy wondered.

Leaving those questions for later, she set aside the photo of the gravestone and turned to the other document she'd found in the file—the photocopy of the index card.

But before she could study it in any detail, she was interrupted when her cell phone buzzed. Momentarily distracted, she fished it out of her pocket and checked the name on the display screen.

It was Wanda Boyle calling her. Wanda was the town busybody, who about a year ago had started a popular local blog called the *Cape Crusader.* She and Candy routinely butted heads over just about everything that went on in town.

Candy pursed her lips and shook her head. She had no interest in talking to Wanda at the moment, so she slipped the phone back into her pocket without answering it and returned her gaze to the document she held in her hand.

She noticed now that the index card depicted in the photocopy was from the Pruitt Public Library, since the library's name was faintly visible in the upper-left corner of the card. The library was still housed in a historic building named for its primary benefactor, Horace Roberts Pruitt, the grandfather of Helen Ross Pruitt—and Tristan's great-grandfather.

Sapphire must have photocopied the card at some point in the past few years, though Candy knew that card catalogs had almost totally disappeared from libraries in this digital age. However, she imagined that the library might still maintain the old card catalog in some back corner of the building.

In the photocopy, the index card appeared to be a few decades old. Across the top, typed in bold letters, were the words, *A History of the Pruitt Family in Maine, 1789–1975; in 26 Volumes.* Below that were the appropriate reference numbers, supporting publishing data, and author information.

Stamped across the bottom in faded block letters was the declaration WITHDRAWN, and off to the side, written in a neat librarian's pen, was an additional note: *Volume XXIII missing. Returned to the family's private archives at Pruitt Manor, as per Mrs. A.P.—*

Another stamp, also faded with age, established the date of the transfer as 17 AUG 72, presumably for the entire collection of Pruitt histories.

Again, another mystery. Why would Sapphire have photocopied this old index card? What value could it have had to her? What was her interest in it? And why had it been hidden away in a file labeled *Emma*?

There must be a link, Candy realized, between the missing volume of Pruitt history and the woman named Emma, now dead.

Candy focused in on the librarian's handwritten inscription on the card: *Returned to the family's private archives at Pruitt Manor, as per Mrs. A.P.—*

Who was Mrs. A.P.? she wondered.

And what had Sapphire—and Sebastian—been after?

Her phone buzzed again, making her jump.

She fished it out of her pocket and checked the screen.

Wanda Boyle. The woman was relentless.

Again, Candy let Wanda's call go to voice mail, but as she was replacing the phone, she felt something else she'd slipped into her back pocket.

She pulled it out. A business card. Two of them, actually—one given to her by Officer Prospect, and the other by Tristan Pruitt.

She stared at the two cards for several moments, and then on an impulse took out her mobile phone again and dialed the number of one of them.

The person at the other end answered right away. "Hello?"

"Tristan, it's Candy Holliday."

"Candy!" He sounded genuinely pleased to hear from her. "This *is* a surprise. I'm glad you called. What can I do for you?"

"Well, remember that invite for lunch today? I wonder if the offer still stands?"

TWELVE

Pruitt Manor occupied a prime piece of property along the Coastal Loop, sitting for more than a hundred years on a rocky, pine tree–covered promontory that jutted out into the sea, with unhindered views of the ocean to the south and east. Its only neighbor on that stretch of coastline was the historic Kimball Light which sat at some distance from the main building on a ledge of land donated by the Pruitts in the early years of the previous century. It was now in private hands.

Hobbins, the butler, must have heard her coming as she rolled to a stop in the cobblestoned courtyard that fronted the English Tudor–style manor, for he opened the stately front door as she came up the flagstone walkway. The stocky, pug-faced butler, smartly dressed in a starched white shirt, black tie, and dark suit, his salt-and-pepper hair trimmed down into a tight crew cut, gave her a gracious nod.

"Ms. Holliday, good afternoon," he said in greeting, with not even a trace of a smile on his fleshy lips.

"Hello, Hobbins," Candy said politely. "It's good to see you again. How's the Bentley?"

"Finely tuned and running like a charm," he assured her, allowing the hint of an eye twinkle to break through his emotionless expression.

It was a small moment that passed between the two of them, a remembrance of an episode that had occurred a couple of years earlier, when Candy had been snooping around the garage at Pruitt Manor, searching for a murder weapon. When Hobbins had chanced upon her, practically catching her red-handed, she'd quickly invented a story about her interest in the Bentley. Apparently buying the ruse, Hobbins had told her more than she'd ever needed or wanted to know about the car.

She'd been out here to Pruitt Manor only once since then, for tea with Mrs. Pruitt a few months later. Maggie had come along for that visit, and they'd had a wonderful time.

Now here she was again, on the trail of another mystery that somehow seemed to lead to the front door of Pruitt Manor.

The manor's foyer, into which she stepped, looked just as Candy remembered it. The Queen Anne–style chairs were in their proper places, and the ornate wood paneling had been freshly polished until it gleamed. The men and women depicted in the austere portraits hanging on the walls— obviously Pruitts of generations past—still stared down their patrician noses at her, but now she noticed some family resemblances to Tristan, which made them a little less intimidating.

"Tristan and Madame await you in the conservatory," Hobbins said, returning to his formal demeanor. "If you'll follow me." The butler turned on his heel and started off, leading the way through the house.

Tristan and Helen Ross Pruitt were waiting for her in a magnificent, glassed-in room at the back of the manor, over-looking the rear lawn and the sea beyond.

As she entered the conservatory, Tristan rose and came to greet her, holding out his hand. He had changed his clothes, and now was wearing gray slacks and a dark shirt. They shook hands warmly.

"Candy, thanks again for accepting my invitation," he said, unable to hold back a grin. "You've met my aunt, right?"

Candy smiled at the thin, elderly woman who sat straight-backed in a wicker armchair. Mrs. Pruitt looked much the same as Candy remembered her. She was dressed in shades of gray and lavender today, her long skirt and jacket well tailored to fit her bony frame, and accented by a single strand of pearls and small silver earrings. Her carefully coiffed bluish gray hair was pulled back from her high forehead and pinned elegantly behind her head, which caused the eye to focus on her pale, creamy skin, thin rose-painted lips, and long, Romanesque Pruitt nose. Her wide-set eyes were intelligent and ever watchful.

Typically around town, Mrs. Pruitt put on a stern demeanor, but today she seemed distracted, even a little flustered, though she appeared to gather herself as Candy stepped forward to shake her hand, tucking away any concerns she had.

"Hello again, Candy," the elderly woman said softly but pleasantly, managing a subdued smile. "How nice to see you."

"It's wonderful to see you again too. I hope I'm not causing you any inconvenience by showing up on such short notice."

"Of course not," Mrs. Pruitt told her. "You're Tristan's guest, so of course you're welcome. And Cook has held lunch for us. I believe everything's ready." She pointed to a small white garden table set up near the conservatory's rear windows, and draped with a cream-colored linen tablecloth.

Lunch was promptly served once they were seated, and started with fresh-baked rolls and a crisp garden salad with small grapes, sunflower seeds, thin slices of cucumber, and green onions, topped with feta cheese and balsamic vinegar. That was followed by broiled lamb chops with a delectable rosemary-mint sauce, diminutive roasted potatoes, and asparagus tips in a light cheese sauce.

Their conversation was occupied by small talk as they ate, with Tristan asking about the farm and Candy's job at the newspaper, while Mrs. Pruitt was curious about Maggie's activities. "Your friend has such a delightful sense of humor," Mrs. Pruitt observed, and she cast a sharp glance at Tristan. "We should have thought to invite her to join us today as well."

Tristan returned his aunt's rebuke with a casual smile, unprovoked by her comment, but Candy came to his rescue nevertheless. "Maggie has a little homework to do for Chief Durr," she said simply.

"Oh, yes." Mrs. Pruitt's lips drew into a tight line. "Tristan told me about the unfortunate incident that occurred today out in the field where you've been working." There was a hint of disdain in her words, as if she had no use for the type of manual labor required for farmwork. But she let any further comments go unspoken.

Candy, however, used the shift in conversation to pursue her true reason for agreeing to lunch at Pruitt Manor. She turned to Tristan. "This morning, when we were out at the pumpkin patch, you mentioned something about Sapphire Vine's house—the *haunted house*, you called it. You said you wanted to ask me some questions about it."

Her comments resulted in a sudden silence around the table. Candy peered at him, raising an eyebrow.

He responded by taking up his cloth napkin, which he used to dab at the corners of his mouth. His gaze shifted toward his aunt before flicking back to Candy. "Well, yes," he said finally. "I suppose we should talk about that."

But before he could proceed, Mrs. Pruitt leaned forward and placed her thin hand on her nephew's wrist. "Tristan, where are your manners? It's not polite to talk about business at the dining table," she told him in a gently admonishing tone. "I agree this is a conversation we need to have. But please, we must be civilized. Let's finish the delicious dessert Cook has made for us before we reveal our most intimate family secrets."

THIRTEEN

So they had dessert—fresh-baked pumpkin pie topped with a dollop of homemade whipped cream—before they adjoined to the library with their coffee and tea to hold their conversation about "intimate family secrets," as Mrs. Pruitt had called them.

The library was cozy and comfortable, a middle room tucked between two larger ones on the north side of the house. A tall, narrow window overlooked the shedding trees in the side yard and let in some light. The library, Candy saw as she scanned it, was well stocked with newer books as well as a number of volumes that looked like they dated back a hundred years or more. And Candy imagined some of them did. Here, too, were a few smaller portraits hanging in nooks and alcoves, presumably of more Pruitt ancestors. But she also recognized some familiar faces in smaller black-and-white photographs that hung around the room or sat on shelves and side tables.

Tristan helped her identify some of them. They'd settled

into wingback chairs, and he pointed around the room casually, as if he'd identified these images for hundreds of people before her. "That's Eleanor Roosevelt with my grandfather," he told Candy, "and over there is Henry Ford with a great-great uncle."

"And that one?" Candy asked, pointing at a framed photo that sat in a prominent spot on a nearby shelf.

Mrs. Pruitt answered. "That's my father, Cornelius Roberts Pruitt, with Andrew Carnegie. It was taken in the early nineteen hundreds in New York. My father was still a teenager then, and Carnegie was in his late seventies."

Candy was impressed. "Your family has quite a fascinating history," she said, her gaze still wandering around the room, studying the old books, photographs, and furniture.

"We do," Tristan admitted, "and that's one of the reasons I invited you out here today. You see, part of our family history is missing."

"Oh, really?" As she spoke, Candy noticed out of the corner of her eye that Mrs. Pruitt shifted uncomfortably at the change in conversation.

Tristan appeared to notice also, but he cleared his throat and pressed on, his voice lowering. "We—Aunt Helen and I, as well as the rest of the family—believe there's been a theft, you see, and we thought you might be able to help us figure out what's happened."

"A theft?" Candy's gaze swept the room again, her curiosity piqued. "What was stolen?"

In response, Tristan rose and walked to a shelf lined with older books that had worn leather covers. Some of the old books were greatly aged and spotted, as if they'd been left outside for weeks, while others were more elegant and gently used, with faded gold leaf on the edges. They were of various shapes, sizes, and thicknesses, and took up the better part of two shelves.

Candy's gaze focused in on several of the leather-bound books, looking for the titles on their spines, but she could see none. As her gaze swept along the shelves, she noticed an open spot, as if one of the books had been removed but never returned.

Tristan indicated the spot. "It's a journal. A diary, actually, written by my grandmother, Abigail."

"Abigail?" Candy's gaze was locked on the spot.

"My mother," Mrs. Pruitt clarified, "married to Cornelius."

"Oh!" Candy finally made the connection. She'd heard stories about Cornelius Roberts Pruitt, and knew some of his history, but she'd been only vaguely aware of his wife's name.

It was all starting to make sense.

Abigail Pruitt.

Mrs. A.P., she thought, remembering the handwritten inscription on the library index card she'd found in Sapphire's files.

Helen Ross Pruitt continued, her gaze fixed firmly on Candy. "As Tristan said, we believe someone has stolen one of my mother's diaries."

Candy scrunched up her face. "Why would someone do that?"

"That's exactly what we'd like to find out," Tristan emphasized, returning to his seat and dropping into it.

"My mother had her secrets, that is certain," said Mrs. Pruitt, folding her hands into her lap and straightening herself in her chair. "We've speculated that her diary was stolen because of something she might have written in it, but we haven't been able to determine what that could be. You see, Mother was a prolific diarist. She felt someone needed to chronicle the family's history here in New England, and she took that task upon herself. She was actually Father's second wife. The first died giving birth. She was quite a frail creature, from accounts I've read. The child died a few days later. My father was obviously distraught at the loss of both his wife and first child, and remained unmarried for many years until he met my mother. He was nearly twenty years older than her, so he would have been in his late thirties then, though Mother was barely out of her teens when they met. He'd spent the war years—this was World War I— mostly in Boston, managing the family's shipping and timber businesses, and that's where he met my mother in the years after the war."

Mrs. Pruitt paused to take a sip of tea. Candy and Tristan waited in silence until she carefully returned the teacup to its saucer and continued. "Mother was from a fairly well-off family, and she liked to have things a certain way around the house, as she'd been taught. When Father first brought her here to Pruitt Manor, she was horrified, for the place had fallen into disrepair. It had been practically abandoned by the family for nearly a decade at that point, during the war years. It was built in the 1880s—around the same time my grandfather, Horace Roberts Pruitt, built the Pruitt Opera House and the Pruitt Public Library. The estate's yards and gardens were a disgrace when my mother arrived, the furniture was dusty and out of date, and the staff was without direction. With Horace's blessing and Father's money, Abigail immediately set out to make things right. She began a complete renovation and restoration project."

Mrs. Pruitt pointed toward the back of the house, where they'd had lunch earlier. "The conservatory was one of her additions, and the Garden Room at the opposite end of the building, as well as the Lavender Wing, which was named and decorated by Mother herself. That became the family wing, with a nursery and our bedrooms when we were young. As you may have noticed, lavender remains one of my favorite colors to this day."

Mrs. Pruitt glanced down at the gray and lavender outfit she was wearing before she continued. "Mother spent several years remodeling and expanding the mansion. She specified the manor's exterior design, which remains unchanged to this day, and extensively redecorated the interior. She grew to love this old place, and in her later years, spent more and more time here. She often said that being so close to the sea rejuvenated her."

Mrs. Pruitt paused again, as if swept away by a memory, her gaze wandering out a window into the distance, but after a few moments, it shifted back to Candy. Abruptly Mrs. Pruitt rose. "Come, I'll show you."

Taking Candy by the hand, she led the way out of the room, along a hall, and to the front foyer. Tristan followed, his hands entwined behind his back. Once in the foyer, he leaned nonchalantly against a doorjamb as his aunt indicated one of the portraits hanging on the walls.

"This is my mother, Abigail," she told Candy, who looked up at the image she'd indicated.

It was one of the larger portraits—nearly a yard wide and perhaps four feet tall, with an elaborate gilded frame. It hung above them, centered on the wall, obviously in a place of honor. Candy had noticed the portrait earlier but had been unaware of the woman's identity. Now that she knew who it was, she studied the portrait with a more scrutinizing eye.

Abigail Pruitt had obviously sought to look her best during the portrait sitting, for she was elegantly dressed and decked out with a stunning jeweled necklace and matching bracelet. Her hair was drawn back from her face, much as Mrs. Pruitt's was today, and she had the same firm set of the mouth, the same long nose, the same sharp yet inquisitive eyes above high cheekbones and a pointed chin. Her stern expression made her look a little scary, Candy had to admit, and she sensed from the portrait that Abigail would have been a formidable woman to deal with, and a tenacious enemy to anyone who crossed her.

"She's very . . . handsome," Candy said diplomatically.

"She was a tough, no-nonsense type of person," Mrs. Pruitt agreed, "but she had to be, given her status and the day and age in which she lived. Father ran an empire, and she ran it along with him. But underneath that gruff exterior, she had a warm heart, I can assure you. Her loyalty to the family and love for her husband and children knew no bounds. She would go to the ends of the earth to protect her family, and the Pruitt name, if she had to—and more than once, she did exactly that. I never saw her fight a battle she didn't win."

At this, Mrs. Pruitt turned to Candy and gave her a slight smile. "My father knew that about her as well, and did his best to avoid any confrontations with her, for her wrath was something to behold. Yet, despite his efforts to avoid it, he felt the full force of it on more than one occasion, I can assure you. We all did. But we still loved her."

Mrs. Pruitt moved on then, indicating a smaller portrait of a well-groomed, well-dressed man on Abigail's left. "That's my father, Cornelius, painted in the forties. And over here," Mrs. Pruitt said, taking a few more steps and pointing up at another portrait, "is my grandfather, Horace Roberts Pruitt, who in many ways is the father of what we consider to be modern-day Cape Willington. He loved this sleepy little coastal village more than anyplace else in the world. And he did much to ensure the village survived long after he was gone—the building of the opera house being one example."

Mrs. Pruitt turned to face Candy. "I have now taken on the burdens borne by my ancestors. I cherish my family, and I love this town and the people in it, and I will do anything within my power to protect all that is dear to me. But I must admit to you that I am concerned, for I feel, in the past few years, that we have come under siege."

This odd comment took Candy by surprise. "What do you mean?"

"I mean," Mrs. Pruitt said dramatically, "that there are forces aligning against us—against my family and against the people of this town. This recent rash of murders we've experienced—well, murder is not all that common here in Maine, is it? Not like in the larger cities to the south. That's why we all treasure this village so much, and why we all seek to protect the special way of life here in Maine. Don't you agree that murder seems to have become commonplace in Cape Willington, and that it is completely out of sorts with what's happening in the rest of the state?"

Candy nodded, for she'd been feeling the same thing for quite some time. "I do."

"And now this most recent murder—this Sebastian Quinn fellow . . ." Mrs. Pruitt's voice trailed off, and she shook her head sadly. "Something is not right, Candy. Something terrible is happening here, and it's threatening not only my own family, but all Capers. And I cannot, I *will not* let it stand."

She took a calming breath, and Candy realized that the elderly woman was shivering.

Tristan noticed it also, and he stepped forward, coming to his aunt's aid, but she waved him back, straightening and steeling herself. "I may be old," she told Candy with a firmness in her voice, "but I have plenty of fight left in me, and like my mother, this is a battle I will not lose."

Candy took a moment to think about that, and decided to bring the conversation back to where it had started. "So what does the stolen diary that belonged to your mother have to do with all of this?"

"We don't know for certain," Tristan said, "but we do feel there's some connection between it and the death of Sebastian J. Quinn—and perhaps with some of the other deaths that have occurred around town over the past few years."

Candy shook her head. "But I don't understand. How could it have anything to do with Sebastian's death?"

"Because of the person who was involved in the theft of Mother's diary," Mrs. Pruitt said simply. "You see, I believe I know who stole it. That's why Tristan went out to see you this morning in that pumpkin patch you've been running with Ms. Tremont. That's why he invited you here to lunch with us today—so we could ask for your help in getting to the bottom of this mystery that seems to be consuming our town."

Now Candy found herself shivering as another question came to her, though she hesitated to ask it, for she wasn't sure she wanted to know the answer. Softly, as if approaching the most delicate of topics, she asked, "And who do you think stole your mother's diary, Mrs. Pruitt?"

"I believe," the Pruitt family matriarch said, stiffening, "that the diary was taken by Sapphire Vine before she died."

FOURTEEN

Sapphire Vine.

There she was again . . . continuing to haunt them, rising from the grave like a ghostly presence, her dark influence lingering in everything she touched when she was alive.

But what could she possibly have wanted with a beat-up old diary written by Abigail Pruitt? Candy wondered. *What was she after?*

Mrs. Pruitt's words echoed in Candy's mind. *Mother had her secrets,* she'd said.

That was it then. Sapphire had found out something about the Pruitts—a family secret of some sort—and perhaps hoped to use it to blackmail them, as she'd done to others in town.

But what secrets could Abigail have written down in her diary?

This mystery, Candy realized with a chill, *goes deeper than I thought.*

She looked back at the portraits. As her mind worked,

her gaze lingered on Abigail Pruitt's eyes. *What were you up to?*

After a few moments, Candy turned abruptly and walked out of the foyer, past Tristan, and back along the hallway they'd just come through, to the library. Once inside the door, she turned right and headed straight to the shelves that held Abigail Pruitt's old diaries. "How many of them are there in all—the diaries, I mean?" Candy asked, running her gaze along the rows of leather-bound journals.

Mrs. Pruitt had followed her, and now came up behind her. "There are a total of thirty-seven. She started the first one shortly after she arrived at Pruitt Manor, in the 1920s. The last one—well, it's only partially finished, as that's the volume she was working on when she passed away. Each volume is numbered, by the way, on the first page."

"Thirty-seven in all," Candy said, repeating what Mrs. Pruitt had just told her. She noticed that the missing volume was close to the end of the row on the second shelf. "What was the number of the one that was taken?"

"It was number thirty out of thirty-seven," Mrs. Pruitt said.

On an impulse, Candy reached up and withdrew diary number twenty-nine from the shelf. Almost as an afterthought, she turned around and faced Mrs. Pruitt, indicating the volume, which she held up. "May I?"

Mrs. Pruitt nodded, ever so slightly. While it appeared she was not used to having outsiders examine her mother's private diaries, she knew it was part of the investigative process.

Candy returned a nod before shifting her gaze to the diary she held in her hands. It had a well-worn chocolate brown leather cover, while most of the others were gray or black. The pages were not gilt edged. As delicately as possible, she flipped open the cover and scanned the first page.

The Thoughts and Reminiscences of Abigail Pruitt, read

the line at the top, written in a controlled yet delicate script, with numerous flourishes. It appeared that, despite her stern demeanor, Abigail had a fondness for expressive penmanship.

In the top corner of the page, Abigail had noted: *Volume N° 29.*

The first entry started a few lines down:

Friday Morning, 4:48 A.M., June 21, 1963—Sunrise on the Summer Solstice . . .

The fog broke just at dawn, giving way to the Glorious Sun in its Orange and Lavender morning veils, which flowed as a flock of multicolored Seagulls, winging away to the North and South, a wondrous display of God's own beauty, Who made the Creation beyond my window, a sight I shall never forget. And so begins another journey through these plain, unwritten pages. . . .

It was certainly flowery enough. Abigail seemed to imagine that she had a poetic soul. But Candy's attention was drawn to the more specific parts of the entry. Her mouth tightened and her brow furrowed in thought as she pondered the possible significance of the date and time of the first entry. But, she quickly realized, that was of no importance. So she read no further, but instead flipped back to the diary's last page, and the final entry, which read:

Wednesday Evening, 6:01 P.M., September 22, 1965, Sunset on the Autumnal Equinox . . .

I have, at the close of this day, reached the conclusion of another Journal, having laid out the contents of my Life, and of those around me here at Pruitt Manor, in an effort to truthfully inform the inquisitive minds that might follow me in Time. . . .

Thoughtfully Candy closed diary number twenty-nine, replaced it on the shelf, skipped her finger across the open space once occupied by the missing book, and withdrew the next one in line, diary number thirty-one, from the shelf. It was a little larger than the one she'd just perused, with heavier paper. Again, she turned to its first page.

Abigail had started this new journal at dawn on Monday, March 20, 1967—the spring equinox.

Obviously Abigail liked to begin and end her diaries on important astronomical dates. But for the moment, that was beside the point. What were important, she thought, were the dates of the missing journal.

"She must have started diary number thirty—the missing one—sometime around mid-September 1965 and finished it around mid-March 1967," Candy mused out loud. "So most of the year 1966 . . ."

She turned back to Mrs. Pruitt. "Did anything significant happen in your mother's life during the mid-1960s?" Candy asked. "A special event or milestone in Abigail's life during those years?"

Tristan had wandered back into the room, and he settled into his chair again, running a hand wearily through his thick, sandy-colored hair. "We've asked ourselves that same question a hundred times and keep coming up blank."

Mrs. Pruitt gave a more thorough answer. "I was living in New York City at the time," she told Candy, "raising two children of my own, who were still young. My husband was in the financial business, but when he passed away unexpectedly in the early 1970s, I reassumed my maiden name and took up the family business. I didn't return to Boston—or to Pruitt Manor—until the early eighties, when my mother grew ill. Cornelius had passed away in 1959, and for most of the years after that, Mother lived alone—either at one of the family's homes in Boston or, increasingly, here at Pruitt Manor. What she might have been up to in those days, none of us really know."

But something happened, Candy thought, *something she wrote down that caused Sapphire to sneak into Pruitt Manor and steal diary number thirty off the shelf.*

"How did it happen?" Candy asked. "How did Sapphire manage to get her hands on that journal and steal it from . . . ?"

But she stopped in midsentence when she heard music drifting to them from somewhere else in the house. It was a classical piano piece, and after a few moments, Candy realized it was being played live—not a recording—with great skill, at least to her ears. She turned to Mrs. Pruitt, a questioning look on her face.

" 'Raindrop,' Chopin," the elderly woman replied by way of explanation.

Candy's brow fell and she shook her head. "I'm sorry?"

Tristan filled in the blanks. "Hobbins is in a melancholy mood." After a moment, he added, "Could be the weather, could be something else."

Mrs. Pruitt cast her nephew a silencing look before turning back to Candy. "It's Hobbins. He's playing Chopin's 'Prelude No. 15' in D-flat major, also called 'Raindrop.' It's one of his favorites."

"He always did have a thing for Chopin," Tristan put in.

Candy finally grasped what they were saying. "Oh!" She turned toward the doorway and the music coming from beyond it. The piece had turned darker, falling into lower notes that drummed menacingly. She was entranced. "I didn't know he could play the piano like that."

"There're a lot of things you don't know about Hobbins," Mrs. Pruitt said cryptically.

"There're a lot of things we don't *want* to know about Hobbins," Tristan added with a touch of sarcasm.

But Candy only half heard their comments, for she was captivated by the sad, haunting melody echoing through the halls of Pruitt Manor. The notes had begun to literally beat like musical raindrops—until, abruptly, they stopped in midpiece, hanging in the air, leaving remnant echoes to fade through the hallways and empty rooms.

It was Mrs. Pruitt who brought her back to the moment.

"To answer your question," the elderly woman said into the silence as she crossed to a chair and seated herself, "it was during one of Ms. Vine's rare visits out here to Pruitt Manor, a few weeks before she . . . well, before her death." Mrs. Pruitt reached for her teacup and lifted it daintily. "I didn't even notice the diary was missing until more than a week later, when it was brought to my attention by one of the cleaning staff. Of course, I didn't immediately make the connection to Ms. Vine—Sapphire, as you call her. That only came later, after her death, and several weeks after I saw you at her funeral. I was checking back through my appointment book one day and was reminded of Ms. Vine's visit by an entry that caught my eye. That's when I began to put the timeline together, and to suspect her of the theft."

"What was her appointment about?" Candy asked curiously, knowing she was prying.

Mrs. Pruitt answered the question without hesitation. "She told me she was conducting research about the Pruitt family's history for a story she was planning to write on Cape Willington's founding families. She contacted me and she asked if she could interview me for the article. I agreed, and it was scheduled in."

"How long was she here?"

Mrs. Pruitt raised her bony shoulders in a subtle gesture. She shook her head, uncertain. "Perhaps an hour, maybe a little longer."

"Was she alone during that time?"

"Yes," Mrs. Pruitt said. "I later recalled that she was. It was for only a short period of time—a few minutes at most—when I was called away by Cook to review plans for that evening's dinner. We were expecting guests, you see. Only later, much later, did I begin to realize that Sapphire had been in the house alone for that period of time, and could easily have sneaked into the library and stolen the diary. She had a number of folders and documents with her in a large red purse, and could have simply slipped the diary inside with her other papers. No one would have ever noticed. I came to the conclusion that she was the only person who could have taken that book from the shelf."

"Are you sure it's not just lost somewhere in the house," Candy asked, "or that it wasn't taken by one of your family members—perhaps one of your brothers or sisters, or a grandchild?"

Mrs. Pruitt pointed out the door toward the hallway and the rooms beyond. "I had Hobbins question everyone who had been in and out of the house during a fairly long period of time surrounding the disappearance of the diary. He personally conducted a thorough search of the house with the rest of the staff. If it was hidden somewhere here at Pruitt Manor, he would have found it. And no family member has it."

"So there's only one real suspect," Candy concluded.

"That's correct." Mrs. Pruitt nodded her head firmly.

"But"—Candy crinkled her brow again—"I'm not quite sure how I can help. I mean, you're asking me—at least I think you are—to help solve a mystery that's more than two years old. It's a cold case with little or no evidence. Why me? And why now?"

Mrs. Pruitt gave her a look that told her she'd anticipated these questions. "To answer your second question first, we received a . . . communiqué recently."

"About the diaries?"

"About the entire collection," Tristan said, twirling his finger around the room.

"Does that happen often?"

"It never happens," Mrs. Pruitt said emphatically, "which is why it made us immediately suspicious. I've asked Tristan to help me get to the bottom of this issue with the missing diary once and for all."

"So that's why you came out to see me at the pumpkin

patch this morning," Candy finished, "and it's why you asked about Sapphire's house?"

"Yes, that's why I came out to see you, and because of the sensitive subject matter, why I thought it best to travel incognito," Tristan confirmed with a slight grin. "I even drove Cook's car, since I didn't want to take my own. And it turned out to be a rather interesting morning."

Candy had to agree with that. "But again," she asked, "why me?"

"Because," Tristan replied patiently, "if Sapphire Vine *did* steal Abigail's diary, as Aunt Helen believes—as both of us believe—then we suspect she might have hidden it somewhere inside her house."

Candy's head went up in a nod of realization. "Ahh, I see. You want me to search that old haunted house of hers and see if I can find this missing diary."

Tristan cast a glance at his aunt. "See, I told you she was quick."

The elderly woman simply shook her head at her nephew's flippant comment and sipped at her tea, which had started to grow cold. She made a face and set the cup back down on the saucer. "Of course," she said, "we'd be willing to pay you for your detective services—perhaps a per diem, depending on how long your investigation takes, plus a reward for the safe return of the diary. If that sounds acceptable?"

Candy didn't have to think long about it. "Of course," she said. In truth, it sounded like a fairly easy assignment.

"There is one other thing," Mrs. Pruitt said, her face tightening as if she'd just sucked on a lemon.

"And what's that?" Candy asked.

Mrs. Pruitt cleared her throat. "This is a private affair, of course, so we would require your complete discretion."

Candy smiled. "I can be discreet."

The matriarch of the Pruitt clan settled back into her chair, a satisfied expression on her thin face. "Good. Then it seems we have an arrangement."

FIFTEEN

Tristan walked with her back out to the Jeep, hands thrust deep in his pockets, huddled against the raw afternoon.

"I do apologize again for all the secrecy this morning," he told her sincerely, squinting as a gust of wind whipped past them. "As Aunt Helen indicated, we're not really sure what's in that diary of Abigail's, or why Sapphire Vine would have had any interest in it, or why some lawyer representing an anonymous buyer would suddenly contact us with an offer to buy our entire collection—and offering a lot of money for it, I might add. So until we know what's going on, and who's behind it, we'd like to keep a very low profile on this."

"I understand." Candy held a finger up to her lips, her eyes twinkling just a bit at all the furtiveness. "I promise I won't tell a soul."

Tristan was looking up at the weather, but now angled his gaze toward her, a corner of his mouth pulling up in a lopsided grin. "I knew we could count on you."

A few minutes later, back out on the Coastal Loop, Candy called Maggie. "Wait until you hear what I have to tell you!"

She knew she'd promised to be discreet, but there was no help for it, she'd decided. After all, Maggie had the key to Sapphire Vine's old house. Candy had to get inside to search it, and Maggie was the only way in, so she had to know at least part of the story—didn't she?

They coordinated their efforts, and met at Sapphire's house just after two thirty P.M., as a light rain began to grow heavier, and a stiffening breeze blew up the carpet of fallen leaves, which rattled noisily across the streets, sidewalks, and driveways.

"Good thing we abandoned the pumpkin patch when we did," Maggie said as she dashed from her old Subaru, which she'd parked in front of Sapphire Vine's house, to the front porch, where Candy waited for her, just as the rain came on. "Whew! Made it just in time."

She raised a hand to brush back a few strands of her curly brown hair, which had been blown over her eyes, and bent to unlock the front door.

Candy noticed that her fingertips were black. "What's up with that?" she asked, pointing.

"What?" Maggie pushed open the door and twisted around to look behind her.

"That," Candy said, still pointing. "Your fingers. Trying out a new shade of nail polish?"

Maggie looked at her fingers as if she'd never seen then before, then held up all ten digits, splayed out, palms toward Candy. She'd been inked.

"They fingerprinted me," she said.

"Who?"

"The police."

"When?"

"Just a little while ago, when I dropped off those e-mails at the police station." Maggie lowered her hands and rubbed at her fingertips. "I tried soap and water, but it doesn't come off. I might have to resort to something more powerful, like industrial bleach." She leaned in closer to Candy and whispered loudly, "You don't think they suspect *I* killed Sebastian, do you? Are they going to arrest me?"

Candy shook her head as she entered the house behind Maggie. "It probably just has something to do with the crime scene. Our fingerprints are all over those pumpkins—though I don't know if they can lift prints from a fruit. I'll have to check that. But my guess is that they can get fingerprints from just about anything these days. They'll probably fingerprint all of us—all who were out there this morning helping to uncover Sebastian's body—so they'll know which prints are ours and which are someone else's."

Maggie gulped. "Like the killer's?" she asked, casting a wary glance back over her shoulder as Candy shut the door behind them and locked it.

"Like the killer's," Candy confirmed. Together they started along the dark central hallway toward the kitchen at the rear of the house. "They'll probably also ask us about our shoes."

"Our shoes?"

"Lots of footprints around that body," Candy explained. "They'll probably try to sort out whose prints belong to who."

"They can do that sort of thing?"

"They can do just about anything these days, with all that forensic investigative stuff they have going on. Don't you watch TV?"

They'd reached the kitchen, where they dropped some of their things on the table. "Only the cooking and travel channels," Maggie admitted.

"So, did you hear anything interesting about the murder case while you were at the station?"

Maggie shook her head and clicked her tongue. "Not a thing—and I really made an effort, because I knew you'd ask. I tried grilling Carol, the receptionist, and even turned on the charm with the nice young police officer who finger-printed me—but they're not saying a thing. They're all but-toned up tighter than a lobster claw."

"I bet they are," Candy said. "Another murder in town. It's becoming an epidemic. They have to be going crazy over there."

Just then her cell phone buzzed. She scooped it out of her back pocket and checked the readout. It was Wanda Boyle again—the fourth time she'd called, Candy noticed from the display. And four voice mail messages were wait-ing for her as well.

Candy slid the phone back into her pocket. She had no intention of talking to Wanda right now—not ever, if she could help it. Instead, she looked up and around her, and rubbed her hands together. "Okay, you ready?"

"Sure."

"So where do you think we should start?"

"Ummm . . ." Maggie dragged out the word, looking back and forth around the kitchen, a serious expression on her face, as if she was in deep thought. "What are we look-ing for again?"

So Candy explained it all from the beginning, how she'd seen the file labeled *Emma* on the front seat of Sebastian's car, and how she'd remembered a similarly labeled folder in Sapphire Vine's old files, and how she'd found the old black-and-white photo of Emma's gravestone and the pho-tocopy of the index card from the Pruitt Library, with the notation about the missing volume of Pruitt history. And how Sapphire Vine had allegedly stolen a diary written by Abigail Pruitt from Pruitt Manor.

When she finished, Maggie looked at her, impressed. "You found all that out all by yourself in just a few hours?"

"I've been busy," Candy admitted, "and I even had time for lunch at Pruitt Manor."

"Oh, really? I'm so jealous."

"We had salad with sunflower seeds and grapes, and after that, broiled lamb chops with this wonderful rosemary-mint sauce."

"I love lamb chops," Maggie said.

"And we had those little roasted potatoes, and some lovely sprigs of asparagus."

"You're starting to make me hungry. Don't rub it in."

Candy was silent for a moment, then added quietly, "Pumpkin pie for dessert."

"With whipped cream on top?"

"Homemade," Candy confirmed.

"Hmm." Maggie sighed. "Maybe someday I'll get a chance to go out there again with you. So . . . why don't we start at the top of the house and work our way down? And remind me again how this works . . . we're looking for *two* missing books?"

Sapphire's secret lair at the top of the house turned up nothing interesting, since they'd already gone through everything up there years ago, when they'd first discovered it. The closets on the second floor held a few dusty boxes of knickknacks and books, but none were the missing volumes they sought—neither the Pruitt history nor Abigail's missing leather-bound diary.

As they worked, Candy thought back over everything she'd learned today, searching in her mind for clues and connections. She realized, once she'd thought about it, that she'd forgotten to ask Mrs. Pruitt about the missing volume of history, which supposedly had disappeared from the public library, prompting the return of the rest of the collection to Pruitt Manor's private library at the request of *Mrs. A.P.*—obviously Abigail Pruitt.

Also, Candy realized, she had neglected to ask Mrs. Pruitt if she'd ever heard of someone named Emma.

I'll have to go back and follow-up, she thought, running a series of additional questions through her head.

But she realized a few moments later that most of those questions might be moot if one or both of the books she sought turned up right here at Sapphire's house.

Did she get a per diem for an hour's worth of work?

However, after searching for a couple of hours, they found nothing resembling either the history volume or the diary.

Only when they were back down in the kitchen, taking a break, did Candy dash out to the Jeep and grab her tote bag from the front passenger seat, where she'd left it. Once she was back in the kitchen, brushing raindrops from her honey-colored hair, she plopped the tote on the table and pulled out the photocopy of the index card. Maggie had switched on the overhead light but it wasn't very bright, and Candy squinted as she studied the black-and-white image.

After a few moments, she threw up her hands. "Well, darn," she said.

"What?" Maggie had put a kettle of hot water on the old gas stove and scrounged up a few mugs in the cupboard, as well as a couple of tea bags. The tea would help warm them against the chilling house.

"I got this completely mixed up," Candy said, sounding frustrated. "There's no way Sapphire could have stolen the volume of Pruitt history from the library."

"Why not?"

Candy held up the photocopy. "It went missing in the early seventies. Sapphire didn't show up in town until the late nineties. So she couldn't have taken it."

"What's that mean? Are we back to square one?"

Candy turned toward the rear window to think, let out a breath—and nearly jumped out of her skin, yelping at the top of her lungs.

Maggie screamed as well, and dropped the tea kettle she was just lifting off the stove. It clanked noisily back down onto the burner. "What! What!"

"Did you see that?"

"See what?" Maggie spun around frantically.

"That! I just saw a face in the window!"

"A what?"

Candy was out of her chair, scooting back so she'd be closer to Maggie. "A face! I just saw someone's face in the window!"

"Whose face was it?" Maggie asked, turning toward the back window.

"I don't know," Candy said, shivering with sudden fright, "but it looked like . . . a skeleton!"

At that moment a heavy gust of wind tossed itself at Sapphire Vine's old house, rattling the shutters and knocking tree limbs against its south side, and the few lights they'd turned on flickered once, twice, and went out. In fright, both of them screaming in terror, they threw themselves into each other's arms.

SIXTEEN

Henry "Doc" Holliday had a good laugh at that—the first in some time, as it happened.

Doc had been out in the fields behind the farmhouse at Blueberry Acres all day, mowing. It was an annual fall ritual, initiated by the region's Native Americans long before the first European settlers arrived, and followed by wild blueberry farmers ever since. Wild blueberries were low-bush plants, and left unpruned, their yield would decrease each year, until they reached an unproductive low point. But cutting the plants down to near ground level every other year caused them to send out new, stronger stems, which produced more blueberries per stem, increasing overall yield.

There were two ways to prune the wild blueberries—to simply mow the fields, which reddened in the autumn, looking like seas of fire, or to mow and burn them—literally putting them to fire. Using a tractor attachment called a flail mower, and working over the past couple of weeks, Doc and

Candy had pruned down some of the berry bushes to about one-half inch from ground level, which was adequate. Those areas of the fields would now lay dormant for a year as the plants responded to the pruning by generating new underground rootstocks, called rhizomes, which in turn produced new shoots and stems. Because it took a full year and more for the plants to regenerate, wild blueberry farmers pruned only half their crop each year.

The flail mower method was quick and efficient, but they could use it only in areas that were relatively flat and rock-free. In rocky areas or through rougher terrain, they used another attachment called a bushhog, a large rotary mower pulled behind the tractor. But because it was higher off the ground, it couldn't prune the bushes down to the required height. So the areas they'd mowed with the bushhog would have to be burned in the coming weeks. They'd start as soon as all the mowing was finished and burn through November and into December, until either they were finished or the first snow came.

Doc had been far out in the back field with the bushhog since midmorning, mowing until the oncoming rain drove him indoors. He'd spent another hour fiddling around in the barn and talking to the chickens until, dusty and hungry, he'd finally wandered into the house and checked the messages on his cell phone after he'd grabbed a cold one from the fridge.

He frowned right away. There were seven messages waiting for him, all from his "posse"—his close-knit group of buddies, including William "Bumpy" Brigham, Artie Groves, and Finn Woodbury. Finn had a secret source inside the Cape Willington Police Department, and usually had the inside scoop when something dirty went down in town.

There were four messages from Finn alone. *They've fingerprinted Maggie,* the most recent one read.

Doc hightailed it out of there without even looking at the rest. He headed straight for the diner, calling Candy on the way over. "Where are you?" he asked gruffly. "What's going on?"

"You mean you haven't heard?"

"No. What the hell's happened this time?"

At that point, he heard someone talking in the background and recognized the voice. "Is Maggie there?" he asked, sounding increasingly concerned. "Where are you?"

More background talking. Finally Candy said into the phone, "We're at Sapphire Vine's old place, and we've just had the scare of our lives."

"You need help? Want me to come over there?" Doc tried not to sound too worried, but in truth he *was* worried. He had all the regular worries for a man approaching his late sixties—health, money, health, his daughter, health, the farm—and, of course, his health.

But other than health issues, his daughter had been in his thoughts a lot lately. Candy had been living with him out at Blueberry Acres for more than four years now, and he loved every minute of having her there. She was more help, and better company, than he'd ever hoped for when he'd bought the place. He had planned on running the farm himself postretirement, but he had to admit, it had proved to be more work than he'd expected, and the place had gotten out of his control fairly quickly. If Candy hadn't come along . . .

But she did, and they'd lived and worked well together over the past few years. However, in time, her presence at the farm had given rise to new concerns for Doc—most prominently, what the future held for the both of them.

He knew he wasn't getting any younger, and he didn't know how much longer he could continue to work the farm, even with Candy's help. But he worried more about Candy herself—that she wasn't moving on with her life, that she'd become too dependent on him as a friend and companion, that her love life seemed stagnant. . . .

Today, however, he'd been focused on something more

immediate. Candy's fortieth birthday was just a few days away, and as always, Doc wasn't as prepared as he'd hoped to be. He'd wanted to throw her a big party, but Doc wasn't the party-planning type. That had always been the forte of his wife, Holly. She'd been a master at it. So despite his best intentions, he hadn't taken the time or effort required to pull it together, and now it was almost too late.

So out in the barn that afternoon, after pondering it all day, he'd decided to contact his buddy Finn and see if he could help pull something together. Finn was pretty good at organizing that sort of thing, and the other boys would pitch in and help, Doc knew. Working together, maybe the four of them could put something memorable together in a short amount of time.

So he'd headed inside the house with this plan on his mind, intent on giving Finn a call, only to find the seven messages waiting for him.

And he'd immediately started worrying that it was all happening again—that his daughter was once again being drawn into some dark mystery in town, one that would put her life in danger.

"No, Dad, we're okay," Candy said over the phone. "We've just lost the electricity. We're getting out of here fast."

"Meet me at the diner in ten minutes," he instructed her, anxious to find out what was happening around town.

But once they'd entered the warm, familiar buzz of Duffy's Main Street Diner, settling into the cozy corner booth that had been the posse's home on weekday mornings for years, sandwiched in between folks they knew and loved, all their concerns had eased somewhat.

Still, Doc listened, grim-faced, as his daughter, accompanied by input from Maggie, with additional commentary courtesy of Finn, Artie, and Bumpy, told him the news of the day. He shook his head in disbelief when he heard the story of the unearthing of Sebastian's body, right there in the middle of the pumpkin patch, and what had followed.

When they'd finished, he looked over at Maggie. "And your fingerprints?"

She explained that as well.

He was about to ask Candy another question when his cell phone rang. He didn't recognize the number on the readout screen, but it was a local call. When he found out who it was, he stepped away from the table so he could talk in private in a quieter location, back along the hallway leading to the bathrooms in the rear.

It was Tristan Pruitt calling him.

A few minutes later, his spirits lifted measurably, Doc returned to the table, which was when Candy told him about the skeleton face in the window—which had prompted him to throw back his head and laugh, caught up in the moment.

But when he looked around the table, they were all staring at him like he was an idiot.

SEVENTEEN

"Dad!" Candy said the word sharply, in admonishment, surprised at his odd reaction.

Doc crinkled his nose, his good humor fading when he saw her expression. "What?"

Candy looked at her father with a confused shake of her head. "It wasn't really funny. We were scared out of our wits."

"It was a skeleton! In the *window*!" Maggie emphasized, before adding in a less emphatic tone, "Well, at least, that's what I think it was. I didn't actually see it myself. But Candy said she saw it, and I believe her!" She stamped her foot for emphasis.

"Thanks for the support," Candy said across the table.

"Anytime." Maggie crossed her arms and nodded her head.

"It was probably just some neighborhood kid," Doc said in an attempt to defend himself.

"You're probably right," Finn said seriously. "Still, it

appears there's another murderer around town, so everyone should be keeping an eye out for anything strange. And the body was found smack dab in the middle of that pumpkin patch where they've been working. How were they supposed to know this skeleton wasn't someone with nefarious purposes?"

"Yes . . . but . . . but . . ." Doc sputtered, and tried to put on an accommodating smile. "Look, I know this is serious business but . . . it was just an early trick-or-treater. He was just goofing with you—looking around for a little mischief before the big day."

"I don't know, Dad." Candy was still shaking her head, still surprised by her father's odd reaction to the appearance of a skeleton in a window at Sapphire Vine's place. "It didn't really look like a kid to me. I'm sure I would have noticed something like that. It was . . . weirder. Like someone was watching us, checking us out, seeing what we were doing."

"Spying on us," Maggie put in helpfully.

Candy wiggled a finger at her. "That's it exactly! It was like someone was spying on us."

"But that doesn't make any sense," Doc said. "Why would someone be spying on you? How would anyone even know you were there, or what you were doing?" He paused, considering that statement, before he asked, "What *were* you doing there?"

Candy waved a hand. "That's beside the point."

"Which is . . . ?"

"Like Maggie said. Someone in a skeleton costume was spying on us!"

"But . . ."

"Dad," Candy said, her voice tensing, "I didn't just dream this up. Whatever it was, someone—or some*thing*—was staring at us through that window."

"I know, I know," Doc said, kowtowing to her from a seated position and motioning with his hands for all of them to calm down. "Look, I know what you think you saw, and

I didn't mean anything by my reaction. I just . . . well, I just . . ."

"Who was that on the phone?" asked Artie Groves, breaking into the conversation as he adjusted his glasses on his thin nose, his gaze focusing with curiosity. He'd combed his thin, steel gray hair straight back from his high forehead, and had grown out a thin goatee, which gave him a slightly more distinguished appearance.

Doc cleared his throat. "Oh, it was no one . . . just an old friend."

But Artie caught the little white lie in Doc's statement. A trace of a wicked smile crossed his face. "You're hiding something from us, aren't you?"

"Am not," Doc replied.

"Maybe it was a call from his girlfriend," Bumpy said, bemused by the turn of the conversation.

"He has a girlfriend?" Candy asked, surprised.

"Of course not!" Doc sputtered, his face turning red.

"I agree with Artie," Finn said firmly. "You're hiding something, Doc. So spill the beans. What is it? Is everything going okay?"

Feeling himself boxed into a corner, Doc considered his response carefully. "I'm taking the fifth," he replied, his jaw firming up.

But Candy was studying her father. "Dad, are you all right? You seem a little . . . strange."

Doc blew out a breath as he settled back in his seat. "No, it's just . . . I'm worried about you, pumpkin, that's all, with everything that's happened today. It's just been one thing after another, and this most recent news took me by surprise, that's all. And I've been out in the back field all day and I'm feeling a little . . . stressed. That's all."

"That's a lot," Finn said. "All this murder stuff can cause all sorts of emotional and physical problems in people—and not just the victims. Stress is bad for the ticker, too, you know."

Doc glowered at him. His buddy wasn't helping matters.

And as he feared, Finn's comment prompted the wrong reaction.

"Dad, are you sure you're feeling all right?" Candy asked, genuinely worried, and she gestured toward her friend. "Maggie, feel his forehead. Tell me if he feels hot to you." Candy and Doc were seated at opposite sides of the booth, but Maggie was wedged in next to Doc.

"Well, okay," said Maggie, shifting as she raised an eyebrow. "Let me just feel how hot you are, Doc."

That set them off.

"Yes, Doc, how hot are you?" Artie asked, suppressing a grin.

Bumpy fueled the flames. "He looks pretty hot to me," he said, a dribble of salad dressing gleaming at the corner of his mouth.

"Naw, he needs a shave and a haircut, but he might clean up okay," Finn put in, and they all laughed.

Doc flashed a look of mock anger at them and brushed away the palm that was approaching his forehead. "Now cut that out! I'm feeling just fine, I tell ya. And I don't need any babying. Besides, here comes our dinner. . . ."

While they ate, they chatted about the day's events, chewing over the latest developments as they dug into an olive-and feta-laden Mediterranean pizza, grilled pita sandwiches, and a Greek sampler plate, complete with calamari, fried eggplant, and mini-kabobs, which Artie had ordered but insisted on sharing with everyone.

Finally, after they'd loaded up, Finn settled back and filled them in on what he'd heard out of the police department. "Word is Sebastian was shot all right, smack dab in the middle of his chest, at maybe ten to fifteen feet, sometime before midnight last night. Right now they're trying to piece together his whereabouts before he died, and they're searching his cell phone records, hoping that'll give them some clue about the killer. . . ."

Finn continued, but Candy was only half listening. She'd seen the outline of the cell phone in Sebastian's pocket and had wondered if it might shed some light on how he'd wound up buried under that pile on pumpkins in High Field. She also wondered about the file labeled *Emma* she'd seen on the front seat of his car.

The police had that now, but had they opened it? she wondered. And if so, what had they found inside?

"Have you heard anything about a file I saw sitting on the front seat of Sebastian's car?" she asked Finn straight out of the blue. "I'm sure the police must have found it."

But Finn only shook his head. "Haven't heard anything about that. Don't even know if it's part of the investigation. Why, do you think it's important?"

She was about to respond when a generous slice of pumpkin pie miraculously showed up in front of her.

Surprised, Candy turned and looked up.

Juanita Perez, one of the diner's longtime waitresses, was standing beside the booth, a broad smile on her oval face and her long, straight black hair pulled back into a thick braid, which hung down her back almost to her waist. "On the house, Candy. Enjoy!" Juanita said, patting Candy on the shoulder.

"Juanita, you don't have to keep giving me free stuff," Candy told her in an almost beseeching tone.

But Juanita would have none of it. "It's a lifetime thing," the waitress said earnestly.

This had been going on for some time, ever since Candy had been a judge at a lobster stew contest, which Juanita won. And as a way to show her appreciation, the waitress had been plying Candy with free coffee and desserts ever since.

"Besides, you gave us the recipe for that lobster stew, which is one of our bestsellers, especially in the fall and winter," Juanita added, "so enjoy!"

But Candy continued to protest. "Juanita, I've already

had a piece of pumpkin pie today. I can't eat another. I'll gain ten pounds."

"Then I'll bring you something else," the waitress said, undaunted.

"No. Juanita . . ."

Candy knew the waitress meant well, and the last thing she wanted to do was hurt Juanita's feelings or, worse, seem like an ingrate.

Looking for a way out, she scanned the faces at the table, then turned to search the rest of the diner. She quickly spotted a female police officer sitting at the counter, reading the newspaper and just finishing a burger and fries. Candy remembered the officer from earlier in the day, and her name—Molly Prospect.

Candy discreetly pointed in her direction. "Do me a favor, Juanita, and give the pie to the police officer, would you? With my compliments? She's probably had a rough day, and deserves a treat."

The waitress turned, spotted the police officer, and said happily, "Sure thing, Candy!" before she headed off to deliver the pie to Officer Molly Prospect.

A few moments later, when the pie was placed in front of her, Officer Prospect turned toward Candy with a questioning look. Candy could see her hesitation to accept the free offering, but after Juanita explained, Molly shrugged and dug in, after a wave of thanks to Candy.

Candy waved back.

Doc, who had surreptitiously watched the whole thing, winked at his daughter. "Making new friends?"

"I'm trying, Dad," Candy said with a weak smile. "I'm trying."

EIGHTEEN

Ben called her a few minutes after ten P.M.—just like he said he would.

She was upstairs in her bedroom, already in her pajamas—partly because she was tired and had decided to turn in a little earlier than usual, and partly because she wanted to review a file out of sight of Doc's ever-watchful eyes. She'd taken a cup of chamomile tea with her and had settled on her bed. She'd just opened the file and started scanning the first few pages when Ben called.

After they'd left the diner, Candy had dropped Maggie off a home and then returned to her office downtown, intent on pulling another file from the cabinet's bottom drawer, the one labeled SV.

She'd found what she was looking for after digging deep into the drawer. And again, she had known it existed, because she'd spotted it at an earlier time, though she'd never opened it up and looked inside.

It was a fairly thick folder, with a faded green rubber

band wrapped around it to hold all the documents together. On the label, printed in Sapphire Vine's hand, was a single word: *PRUITT.*

Maybe, she'd realized at dinner, Sapphire had left behind a few clues about Abigail Pruitt in the file. And, Candy had realized, maybe she'd even find the diary in there, wedged in between all the papers, since she and Maggie had seen no sign of it during their cursory search of Sapphire's house.

But Ben called before she could look beyond the first few documents.

Still, as he talked, she thumbed through the rest of the papers in the folder.

At first glance, it appeared there was no diary stuck inside.

"I just heard what happened," Ben was saying from the other end of the line—and the other side of the continent. He sounded weary. "Hard to believe there's been another one in town, isn't it?"

She agreed that it was.

"Do you think there's any significance that the body was found in the pumpkin patch?" he asked.

She said she believed there was, though what the connection might be, she had no idea.

"Well, I have a feeling you'll figure it out," Ben said. "Look, I've been thinking of cutting my trip short and heading back to Cape Willington early, with all that's happened there today. Maybe I can be of help. Maybe I'm needed there."

But Candy would have none of it. "What about your panel tomorrow morning? And your interview? You tried for months to get that guy to sit down with you. You can't back out now. If you do, he'll never talk to you again."

After trying for months, Ben had managed to land an interview with a reclusive Internet mogul originally from Down East Maine, who now managed a multibillion-dollar business in Silicon Valley. Ben was thinking of working it into a larger piece, perhaps even a book-length project. The time for the interview had been firmed up. It was scheduled to take place after the weekend conference, on Tuesday morning.

Ben sighed. "I don't know. You're more important right now. I don't want you facing all this by yourself."

"But I'm not by myself," Candy protested. "I have Maggie and Dad and the boys here to help me out if I need it. And, of course, the Cape Willington Police Department is on the case. I even made a new friend in the department—Officer Molly Prospect. If I get into trouble, I'll give her a call. She looks like she can handle just about anything, and I have her card right in my pocket. We'll be fine, trust me."

"But . . ."

"Trust me," Candy said emphatically. "Look, if you come back home now, you'll always regret missing that interview—and you'll probably blame me for making you miss it."

"I wouldn't do that," he said, sounding slightly wounded.

She softened her tone, and even found herself smiling a little. "Look, don't worry about me, okay? I'll be fine. I've been through this before, remember? I know how to handle myself. Besides, you're going to hop on a plane the second that interview is over, right? You'll be back here in time for my birthday?"

She could almost see his expression lightening over the phone. "Absolutely. The moment I shut off the recorder, I'm jumping in the rental car and speeding to the airport."

"Well," she said, smiling into the phone, "don't drive too fast. We wouldn't want you getting a ticket and delayed even more."

He was silent for a moment, as if still evaluating his decision. But finally he said, "I'll see you in a few days."

"Okay," she said. "Miss you."

"Miss you too."

Her smile disappeared as she keyed off the phone.

She knew he had a job to do—and she knew it was the right thing for him to stay on the West Coast until he'd finished the interview. But still, it *would* be nice to have him here, just in case. After all, there *was* a murderer loose around town.

She thought back to the skeleton's face in the window. Despite Doc's skepticism, mimicking what she knew his buddies were thinking privately, she was certain it had not been an accident—a stray trick-or-treater randomly peering in that window.

Whatever it was—whoever it was—it had been watching them, watching what they were doing.

She thought back to the stories they'd heard from the people who had stayed in the house when they'd rented it out.

Was that the answer? Had someone actually, physically been "haunting" the place?

She shivered uncontrollably.

If so, who? And why?

Suddenly tired, she closed the Pruitt file, pulled the green rubber band back around it, dropped it to the floor, and snuggled down under the covers after turning out the light.

Whatever was going on, she'd figure it out in the morning.

NINETEEN

But the morning brought no more answers than the night before.

She was up early, making coffee and a toasted English muffin spread thickly with her own homemade blueberry jam, then heading outside to check on her chickens, all the while thumbing through her smart phone, catching up on the weather and the latest farm news as well as e-mails and text messages. There were half a dozen from Wanda Boyle alone, most left the day before—but she'd already sent one this morning, Candy noticed.

It was labeled *URGENT—PLEASE RESPOND!*

That caught Candy's eye, and she considered giving Wanda a call, just to get it over with. But she hesitated, and ultimately decided to ignore the messages for now, just as she'd done the day before. She knew she'd probably hear about it later—Wanda was not the type of person who easily tolerated any sort of perceived slight—but Candy wasn't ready to deal with her just yet. She had other, more pressing tasks on her plate this morning.

Doc helped her load up the Jeep with boxes of items they planned to sell at the farm stand, and after a few quick words together, he jumped into his truck, headed to the diner for breakfast with the boys to catch up on the latest news, and Candy started up the Jeep. She swung by Fowler's Corner to pick up Maggie, and together they drove out to the pumpkin patch, uncertain of what they'd find, or if they'd even be able to open for the day.

The place was busier than they'd expected this early, but they weren't completely surprised. They'd anticipated a good crowd on this last weekend day before Halloween and the town's annual Pumpkin Bash celebration. These would also be the last few days they'd sell pumpkins before closing down the patch for the season, and the townspeople knew it, so they'd turned out in full force to get the final pickings.

And, Candy thought, some of them were probably curiosity seekers who wanted to see if they could catch a glimpse of the latest crime scene in town.

The police were already in place, however, and apparently had no intention of letting anyone get beyond them into High Field.

Candy spotted Chief Durr standing by his squad car near the farm stand, surrounded by a small crowd of people, some with recorders and notebooks, others just hanging around curiously. She pulled the Jeep to a stop nearby, at the edge of the patch, since the parking lot was nearly full. As she shut off the engine and climbed out, she could hear the chief speaking to the crowd.

"Now I've got nothing more to say at this time," he said in an abrupt tone. "We released a statement last night, and the investigation is continuing. I have nothing new to report."

There was a jumble of voices as several of the reporters fired questions at the chief, with one voice overwhelming the others. "Can you confirm that the victim was in the process of renting a local house that's reported to be haunted?" inquired a tallish, smartly dressed woman with shoulder-length blonde hair, attractively arranged.

"I'm not getting into that," Chief Durr said tersely.

"What about the murder weapon?" asked a dark-haired man, who Candy believed was a reporter for a Bangor newspaper.

"Now, I'm not going to answer any more questions at the moment," the chief reiterated. He was beginning to sound annoyed.

"Is Cape Willington turning into the murder capital of Maine?" asked the blonde woman pointedly, shoving a small digital tape recorder closer to the chief's face.

"Course not." The chief threw her a sharp look. "Where'd you hear a thing like that? It's completely untrue."

Nevertheless, Candy noticed, several people were jotting down notes on their pads.

"Is there any evidence this most recent murder is tied to the others that have occurred in Cape Willington over the past two years?" the blonde woman pressed.

The chief gave her a tight smile. "Now, Ms. March, you know there's no way I can answer that at this time."

"Are you going to hold a press conference?" she continued.

"Yes, this afternoon at four," the chief confirmed. "It'll be at the station. I'll see you all there, and provide any updates at that point." He glanced around the group. "That's it for now, ladies and gentlemen."

He turned away from the group, and seemingly appeased for the moment, the reporters began to fan out across the field to other areas of the pumpkin patch, getting the lay of the land and hunting down locals to interview.

Unfortunately, Chief Durr next headed directly to Candy and Maggie, a sour look on his face.

Candy and Maggie both stopped in their tracks, hovering together as the chief approached them.

When he was still several steps away, he touched the bill

of his hat. "Ladies." He forced a smile and squinted against the brightening day, though a chill lingered, and some of his words formed faint plumes in the clear air. His clothes were wrinkled, his nose was red, and his eyes were watery. He looked like he'd been up for a while. "We're just about finished with the forensic part of the investigation—and the rain has washed away most of what was left anyway—but we're going to keep that upper field cordoned off for the rest of the day, and perhaps for the next few days, so no more hayriding up there. And I'd like to see if we can clear some of this crowd out of here as quickly and as quietly as possible. I need your help with that."

"Of course, Chief," Candy said solemnly. "What do you want us to do?"

"Just what you usually do. Help them make their choices and take their money, so we can send them merrily on their way." He glanced back over his shoulder. "They caught us a little by surprise this morning. I thought about sending someone out to the junction to turn cars away, but that might be counterproductive, so I'm gonna allow you to do business this morning as usual. You can keep the farm stand open. . . ."

"Thank you, Chief!" Maggie said, clasping her hands together and shaking them. "We really do need to get some of these pumpkins out of here today, and we really do need the money!"

"I understand that." Chief Durr gave them both an appraising look. "But we need to keep everything civil, right? Don't want the situation to get out of hand, so let's keep the crowd numbers manageable. Move them through here quickly, like I said. And if anyone asks about what's going on, just tell them the police are investigating a possible homicide, got it?" He nodded toward High Field. "I'm keeping my men in place for now, so they'll secure the area and turn away anyone who gets too close." He turned back to Candy. "I want all civilians to stay away from that field—including you, Ms. Holliday. Right?"

"Right," Candy said obediently.

"All right then." After nodding to both of them, he stomped up through the field toward his officers.

The moment he left, before Candy had a chance to breathe, the blonde-haired reporter stepped into his place. She jabbed a well-manicured hand first toward Candy, then at Maggie. They both shook with her hesitantly.

"Olivia March, *Boston Herald*," she said, looking at both of them in turn. "You're the ones who discovered the body, right? Uncovered it from under that pile of pumpkins. That must have been pretty horrific for you." She said this lightly, as if she were commenting on the morning traffic, or the weather, or what she'd had for breakfast. "So, which one of you is Candy Holliday?"

After a few awkward moments, Candy spoke up. "That would be me."

Olivia's gaze turned to her, looking her up and down. "You're the blueberry farmer, right? And you write for the newspaper? You're something of a local celebrity, aren't you?" She smiled as she spoke, and looked pleasant enough, but she also seemed hungry for a story. "You've solved a few recent murders around town?"

"Just doing my civic duty," Candy replied vaguely. "And I had lots of help."

"So why do you think the body was buried here?" Olivia continued, asking the question easily. "Seems strange, doesn't it? Given your history with some of the other murders in town?"

Candy felt uncomfortable with that. "I wouldn't say I have a *history* with the other murders."

"That's not what I've heard," Olivia said, still smiling warmly. She had dark brown eyes, Candy noticed, and a mole—a beauty mark, some might call it—on her right cheek, near the corner of her mouth. Her makeup gave her skin a creamy color. She pointed down to her digital tape recorder. "Would you mind if I recorded our conversation?" she asked.

Candy thought about it a moment, and finally shook her head. "I don't think either of us is ready to make a public statement right now. We've both talked to the police about what happened, and we'll let them handle everything from here on out."

"The chief just told us to keep our noses out of it," Maggie confirmed.

"Can I quote you on that?"

Maggie paused a moment, caught off guard. When, tight-lipped, she looked to her friend for help in formulating a response, Candy said diplomatically, "The police are handling the matter. It'd probably be best if you talked to them."

Olivia pressed on, undeterred. "Well, then, can you tell me the condition of the body when you found it? Was it—"

But she was interrupted by the sound of a deep beeping horn, which came from the direction of the parking lot.

They all turned and watched as a multicolored minibus, filled with passengers, jounced across the grassy parking lot, wending its way through all the other parked cars, before it came to an abrupt stop at the edge of the pumpkin patch, not far from where Candy had parked her Jeep.

After a few moments, the door flew open, and they heard a voice coming over the bus's intercom system.

"This is stop number four on this morning's tour, the site of two deaths, including one currently being investigated. We'll be here for fifteen minutes, so you'll have enough time to look around before we continue our Halloween Mystery Tour. I'll be answering questions and conducting a brief tour, for those of you who are interested. And I have several booklets for sale. Now, if you'll all follow me out the door . . ."

A few moments later, Wanda Boyle, regaled in a retro-tourist-guide outfit in shades of turquoise and orange, stepped off the bus, followed by nearly a dozen passengers.

TWENTY

Their mouths agape, Candy and Maggie both watched
Wanda, first in surprise, then in growing exasperation, their
expressions darkening as the reality of what they were seeing sunk in.

"What the heck is *she* doing here?" Maggie asked, her
voice dropping to a low growl. "And what is she *wearing*?"

"I don't know, but I don't like the looks of it."

"Me neither. Those colors do *not* flatter her. Who does
she think she is, anyway?"

"I think," Candy said, "that she thinks she's a tour guide,
and she's trying to hone in on our territory."

"She can't do that, can she? What is she up to?" Maggie
was starting to fume.

"I don't know," Candy said adamantly, "but I'm going to
find out right now."

Before she headed off, though, she turned to her friend.
"Listen, while I'm on diplomatic duty trying to deal with

Wanda, maybe you should open the farm stand, so we can get things moving along? You know, like the chief said?"

Maggie nodded, and cast one last glare toward Wanda, for good measure. "Good idea. We don't want to gang up on her, do we? Maybe you should handle this one alone." She patted Candy on the shoulder, for moral support. "Good luck!" And off she went, her mood brightening noticeably as she waved and called out to a few customers who were already lining up at the farm stand, pumpkins in hand.

"Thanks," Candy said under her breath, "I think."

She turned to Olivia, who had been listening with great interest to their exchange. "You'll have to excuse me a minute," Candy told the reporter, "but I have some pressing business to attend to."

"Friend of yours?" Olivia asked, nodding toward Wanda.

"Not exactly."

And doing her best to keep her emotions under control, Candy headed across the field toward the minibus to finally face her rival.

Wanda stood at the center of a small group of passengers who had gathered around her, chattering like a flock of hungry birds in their excitement. But despite her practiced smiles and twitters of delight, Wanda seemed distracted. Candy noticed that her gaze kept shifting away from her admirers, out through the field, past the tractor and the hay wagon, to the line of police officers stationed along the boundary between Low and High Fields. And then to Chief Durr, who was talking to someone who looked like he was from the forensics team, before finally shifting right, toward the farm stand, and catching sight of Candy herself.

In that moment Wanda's demeanor abruptly changed, and her expression turned inscrutable. The smile was gone from the expansive face, and she watched Candy approach with dark, unblinking eyes.

Candy stopped several paces from the small crowd of

admirers and crossed her arms. "Wanda, I wonder if I might have a word?"

At first Wanda gave no reply. She simply studied Candy imperiously, her mouth a tight line. Finally, however, she said a few words to the folks around her, and then took a few steps toward Candy, so they could talk in relative privacy.

"Well, well, look who stopped by to say hello," Wanda said evenly. "I thought you were ignoring me."

Candy gave her a tight smile of acknowledgement. "I've been busy, Wanda. So, what did you want to talk to me about? Why all the messages?"

"I'm glad you asked, because I wanted to tell you all about my latest entrepreneurial venture." She motioned toward the minibus and the cadre of passengers. "I call it the Halloween Mystery Tour. I think it's my cleverest enterprise yet." She handed Candy a flyer from a stack she was holding in her hand. "Your little haunted hayride through the pumpkin patch here was a cute idea, but it was just small potatoes. This town deserves something better, so I decided to step in with something more upscale." She indicated the minibus. "I offer all the comforts of home, including soft drinks and snacks. I even have climate control in that thing. The customers love it."

"And when did all this happen?" Candy asked, trying hard to hide the fact that she was impressed by Wanda's latest endeavor.

"Funny you should ask. This is my inaugural tour this morning, but I'm planning on continuing it right through Halloween night, and maybe even for the next couple of weekends, depending on the feedback I get from customers."

"And just where are you taking your customers on this 'mystery tour' of yours?" Candy wondered.

Wanda indicated the flyer with a be-ringed pinky. "It's all right there. Plus there's a press release on my website.

You might want to check it out, just to make sure you get all the facts straight when you write about my new operation in your next column."

Candy closed her eyes, shook her head, and let out a breath. "Okay, Wanda, I'll write something up about it. Anything else?"

Wanda gave her a smug look. "No, that's about it. I've already talked to the chief this morning, so I'm up to date with all the official stuff. And I don't suppose I'd get much out of you if I interviewed you about the most recent murder in town, would I?"

"Probably not," Candy admitted honestly. "Maggie and I have made our statements to the police, and we're letting them handle everything from here on."

"There! You see! I could have predicted that response in my sleep." Wanda's gaze narrowed. "Though I must admit, I am surprised to find you at the center of *another* mystery in town. How do you do it? How do you always manage to turn the spotlight of fame on yourself when these terrible little deeds happen in our town?"

"It's not something I ask for," Candy said a little heatedly, as she tried to tamp down her anger. Then another thought came to her. "Is that why you're here this morning?" Candy asked, looking around at the bus and the passengers. "Are we part of your tour now?"

Wanda gave her a curious look. "You mean you don't know?"

Something in Wanda's voice made Candy stiffen, and she felt a chill. "Don't know what?"

Wanda chuckled genuinely and pointed again at the flyer. "I suggest you read that. And if I were you, I'd take my tour. You just might learn a thing or two, Candy Holliday. I might even give you a discount."

She flashed a wicked grin at Candy, turned smartly, her red hair flying, and sauntered back to her customers.

Candy's brow fell together.

What the heck was Wanda talking about?

She looked down at the flyer she held in her hand.

WANDA BOYLE'S HALLOWEEN MYSTERY TOUR, it read across the top. *Presented by your host and narrator, Wanda Boyle.*

Underneath that was some bio information about Wanda and details about her website and blog, and following that, a paragraph about some of the mysteries, past and current, that plagued the little coastal town of Cape Willington, Maine. It talked about departed sea captains, and pirates, and ghosts in lighthouses, and apparitions of young Victorian-age women. And it mentioned some of the local murders, including one that had occurred at the Pruitt Opera House in 1911, and another down near the docks in the late 1940s, as well as a series of strange murders in the 1980s and early nineties.

Following that information was the tour route, which hit eight "hot" spots around town, including the Pruitt Opera House, the lighthouse and historical society, Town Cemetery, the houses once owned by James Sedley and Wilma Mae Wendell, out to the pumpkin patch, and finally a stop at Sapphire Vine's house—*a true haunted house!* the flyer declared, *and the scene of one of Cape Willington's most brutal murders!*

But it was the paragraph describing the mysteries at the pumpkin patch that caught Candy's eye:

Gumm's Pumpkin Patch, it read. *Site of two deaths, twenty years apart. This week, the body of renowned poet Sebastian J. Quinn was found buried beneath a pile of pumpkins in the area known as High Field. Police are currently investigating that death, which has been unofficially ruled a homicide. And two decades earlier, the body of a mysterious young woman was discovered in nearly the exact same spot. The death was ruled suspicious, and the woman was never identified. Records list her only as Jane Doe. At the time of this writing, neither mystery has been solved.*

TWENTY-ONE

Two deaths. Right here in this pumpkin patch.

So Sebastian wasn't the first to die here.

Candy sucked in a breath of surprise. *Could that have any significance?* she wondered. *That there was another death here, in this same spot, twenty years ago?*

Again, she read over the flyer's description of the mysterious death, but details were scant: *The woman was never identified,* it said. *Records list her only as Jane Doe.*

Candy had never heard anything about this second death—obviously a cold case of some sort.

But where, she wondered, *had* Wanda gotten her information?

Was it even true?

By the time she looked up, Wanda had moved on. Candy caught sight of her wandering up through the pumpkin patch, greeting the early-morning customers and handing out flyers as she went.

She's drumming up business, Candy thought, *right here in our pumpkin patch, right under our noses.*

Her anger swelled again, and she was tempted to follow Wanda, to give her a piece of her mind—and to ask more about the woman who had allegedly died here twenty years earlier. But Maggie called out to her then, needing help with customers and unloading the boxes from the Jeep, so Candy dashed over to the farm stand, where she dealt with a burgeoning group of people, and then finished unloading the Jeep, so they could finish setting up the farm stand.

When she looked up again twenty minutes later, Wanda and her minibus were gone. So were Chief Durr and Olivia March, though a few policemen remained behind to turn curious onlookers away from High Field.

The next few hours flew by, and Wanda's minibus came and went several times, bringing along new waves of customers. And since those were the busiest times at the farm stand, Candy never had a chance to break away to talk to Wanda again.

In midmorning the sun finally broke through the thin haze of clouds, drying out the pumpkin patch and warming all those who had come out to enjoy one of the last beautiful fall days before winter set in. The cash box on the shelf behind the farm stand's counter filled with bills as Candy and Maggie sold dozens and dozens of pumpkins, as well as most of the other items they'd brought. And the crowds left happy.

Doc and the boys arrived around eleven, bringing with them a large thermos of coffee and a box of doughnuts, courtesy of Juanita, and stayed to help out with the customers. A little later on, around twelve thirty, Bumpy and Artie called in a lunch order to the diner for all of them, and ran out to pick it up.

Candy and Maggie both were glad to see the crowds dwindle in the early afternoon, although smaller waves continued to arrive every hour or so with Wanda's bus tour. *The woman certainly knows how to hustle for a buck,* Candy thought as she watched Wanda shepherding around her brightly colored flocks. *And as much as I hate to admit it, she's also helping our business.*

That at least made Wanda's actions a little easier to take, and Candy did her best to put her personal feelings aside for the moment—especially since she still had questions that needed answers.

Right after lunch she finally managed to snag Wanda, who was walking past the farm stand, handing out flyers. But when Candy pulled her aside to ask about the unidentified woman found dead in the pumpkin patch twenty years earlier, Wanda just waved the inquiry away. "It's in the book," she said, pointing back to the van. "I've been selling them, by the way. I got a deal with the author."

"And who is that?"

"That Seabury guy."

Candy knew exactly who she was talking about—Julius Seabury, a retired businessman who had written several volumes of local history, which he self-published and sold through area bookstores and the town's historical society.

Candy had to swallow her pride to get out the next question. "Can I get a copy from you?"

Wanda shrugged her wide shoulders. "Sold the last one an hour ago."

Candy let it go. It didn't matter. Doc had several copies of Seabury's books back at the house, many of them signed by the author, and there might even be a few copies sitting on the dusty shelves in Ben's office at the newspaper. As soon as she had a chance this afternoon, she'd locate a copy and start digging through it.

But a little while later, she had a better idea. She'd go right to the source.

Her opportunity came just before two o'clock in the afternoon. Doc approached her as she was looking out over the field, noticing how much the piles of pumpkins had dwin-dled. She felt suddenly melancholy at the sight, knowing that after all the work they'd put into this place over the past few months, it was finally coming to an end, in a matter of days. Still, they'd done what they'd set out to do, and they'd made a success of it.

Doc told her as much. "You and Maggie did a great job with this place," he said, pulling off his ball cap and wiping his brow with the sleeve of his flannel shirt. "You both should be proud of yourselves."

Candy gave him a smile and put a hand on his shoulder. "We had lots of help. Thanks for coming out today and bringing the boys."

"Ahh, we figured you'd need some backup, after every-thing that's happened. Speaking of which—I've talked it over with the guys, and we all agree that we should give you and Maggie the rest of the day off. You two deserve it. We'll keep an eye on the place for you. So, you know, plop your-selves down somewhere, have a glass of wine, and take a breather."

She leaned forward suddenly and gave him a hug. "Thanks, Dad. That would be wonderful."

He nodded happily and pointed out to the field. "You've sure sold a lot of pumpkins today. It should be a great Pump-kin Bash this year."

"It certainly should," Candy said. "I imagine it's going to be memorable in more ways than one."

TWENTY-TWO

She managed to catch Julius Seabury at the Cape Willington Historical Society, which was located in the Keeper's Quarters out at English Point Lighthouse. She'd remembered that he often gave impromptu tours of the historical society's museum on Sunday afternoons, and used the opportunity to sell some of his books, which he signed with a flourish and a wink of the eye.

Candy caught him between tours as he was explaining a diorama of the lighthouse property to a young boy, who watched and listened, mesmerized, as Julius explained how the property had changed over the years from a small wooden outpost with a whale oil light to the present-day complex, which included several buildings and a prized Fresnel lens atop the nearly ninety-foot tower.

When he'd finished, sending the excited young boy off with his parents, Candy approached Julius with a wave and a smile.

"Mr. Seabury," she said, holding out her hand. "It's

Candy Holliday, from the *Cape Crier*. Good to see you again."

"Why, Candy, hello, this is a pleasure!" Julius said, taking her hand in both of his and giving it a warm shake. He was in his late seventies, with thinning white hair and a grandfatherly face. He wore a pressed shirt under a gray cardigan with forest green corduroys. "Nice to see you again too. How's Doc doing?"

"Great, thanks. I just left him."

"Well, give him my best when you see him. Is he still working on his book?"

"Still working on it. I think he enjoys the research more than the writing though."

Julius laughed. "Ahh, I can certainly understand that!" he said, eyes twinkling.

"And to be honest," Candy continued, "he hasn't had much time to devote to his writing projects lately, with all the work we've had out at the farm and at the pumpkin patch. He's out there this afternoon, at the patch, helping out and giving me a breather."

Julius's expression turned solemn. "Yes, I heard what happened out there yesterday. It's truly a dreadful occurrence. Truly dreadful. I'm sorry it happened, and that you had to find the body that way. I hope it wasn't too traumatic for you."

"No, we've . . . we've been able to manage it okay. But that's the main reason I came out here to see you today. I'd like to ask you a few questions, if that's okay? And maybe show you an old photograph and see if you recognize it?"

"Why, certainly. I'd be glad to help any way I can." Julius looked around. "Why don't we sit over here," he said, indicating two padded chairs angled together off to one side of the main exhibit room, "so I can take a load off my feet and give you my undivided attention."

Once they were seated, she showed him the black-and-white photograph of Emma's gravestone first, placing it carefully into his hands. "I wonder if you would take a look at this and tell me if you've seen it before, as you've conducted the research for your books." She indicated the engraving on the tombstone. "As you can see, there's no last name for the deceased—and no dates of her birth or death, which I think is rather peculiar, isn't it?"

"Hmm. Yes, I would think it is. Is that what it says?" He squinted at the photograph for a few moments before fishing a pair of reading glasses out of his shirt pocket. He perched them carefully on his nose, tilted his head a little, and studied the photograph again. After a few moments, he indicated the lower areas of the tombstone with a swirl of his finger. "There's more writing down here but I can't make it out," he observed.

"That's right. It's too blurred."

"Hmm," Julius said again. He tapped a finger on his chin, then rose and crossed the room to the long wooden counter that served as the museum's information hub. He sidestepped around it and opened a drawer on the back side. Briefly he searched through it before pulling out a magnifying glass, which he used to study the photograph again. But finally he shook his head. "I can't make out the smaller engravings, I'm afraid," he said apologetically.

"Does the tombstone look familiar?" Candy asked. "Have you seen it anywhere around town, in one of the cemeteries, maybe a private cemetery somewhere?"

Julius gave her questions some thought, but in the end he had to admit he didn't recognize it. "It does look as if it's located in a private cemetery, but none of the ones I've visited in the area has that specific type of stone wall surrounding it."

"Would you be able to tell me where some of the private cemeteries around town are located, so I can check them?"

"Of course," Julius said. "I'll draw you a map. In fact, there's a good one in one of my books. I can mark the spots on that for you."

He sidled to the far side of the counter and pulled a narrow,

trade-sized paperback book from a display stand. He licked
his index finger before flipping open the book to the page he
sought, then placed it on the counter, leaned over it, and
started marking down several sites on a map with a red pen.
When he was done, he closed the book, crossed back over to
her, and placed it in her hand. "If I may ask, why the interest
in these cemeteries and this old photograph of a tombstone?
Does it have anything to do with the murder?"

"Honestly, I don't know," Candy said, and as he eased
back down into the chair opposite her, she leaned in a little
closer to him, her voice dropping to a low tone, so only he
could hear her. "But I am following up on a number of clues,
which brings me to the other reason I came to see you. I
wanted to ask you about a story you wrote for one of your
books, concerning a young woman who died in Gumm's
Pumpkin Patch about twenty years ago or so. It was a mysterious death—apparently they were never able to identify
the body. You've written about that death in one of your
books, right? Do you remember it?"

"I remember it well," Julius said. "It's in that book you're
holding in your hands."

Candy glanced down at the book's title. *Cape Willington
Ghost Stories and Mysteries*, it read.

"Tourists love it," Julius said. "Can't get enough of those
Maine ghost stories, can they? I've gone back to press with
it a dozen times."

Candy smiled warmly. "That's wonderful to hear. I can't
wait to read it. So, the story about the dead body in the
pumpkin patch . . ."

Julius nodded and continued. "I was living here in town
when it happened. I was in insurance in those days, and a
member of the Rotary and the chamber, so I used to pay
attention to the local news, especially when it affected the
town's reputation. But that story pretty much baffled us all—
this young woman who just showed up dead in that pumpkin
patch one morning."

"Do they know how she died?"

Julius shook his head. "Not specifically. Exposure, possibly. Or natural causes. Something like that."

"I've heard they labeled the death 'suspicious.'"

"They did initially, but to the best of my knowledge there was no indication of foul play."

"Do you remember what time of year it was—when she was found?" Candy asked.

"Well, it was right around this time, I seem to recall, in the fall, though it might have been a little earlier in the season. I remember that, in the photographs I saw, the trees still had their leaves on them. So maybe late September or early October."

For some reason that gave Candy a chill. "And they were never able to figure out who she was?"

"Never figured it out, at least that I heard."

"During your research, did you learn anything special about her—the color of her hair, or what she was wearing, or where she was from?"

"Well, they didn't release much information, I can tell you that," Julius said. "I know, because I looked. I went back and read over all the old newspaper clippings I could find about that incident, but there wasn't much to tell. The authorities put out the word that they'd found the body and were looking for her next of kin, but as far as I know, no one ever stepped forward to claim her."

"So what happened to the body?"

Julius shrugged. "I was never able to find out. It just seemed to . . . disappear."

"Disappear?"

"A few weeks after it happened, we'd all pretty much forgotten about it. I think there are probably some police records about the incident, but I haven't been able to get my hands on them—but this was a good while ago when I checked. I wrote that book more than ten years ago. Those records might not even exist now. I've never gone back to look for them again. So everything I know about the incident is written down in that book."

Candy offered to pay him for it but he refused. "Doc's bought more than his fair share, so consider that one on the house. Sort of a buy-one, get-one-free sale."

"Thank you for all the information, Mr. Seabury," Candy said, but as she started to rise from her chair, he put a hand on her arm. Under its gentle weight, she settled back down, perching on the edge of the seat. "Yes? Is there something else?"

His brow had pulled together and he looked puzzled, as if he'd just remembered something troubling from long ago. "There *was* one peculiar tidbit I heard about that incident with the poor dead woman," he said. "Due to the nature of the . . . information, I decided not to publish it. But I might as well tell you now, given what happened out in that field yesterday. I got this story from a farmer who lives out that way—Tom Wharton. You might remember him, he . . . but, no, he passed away a while ago, didn't he? Not many people around here probably remember him anymore. I don't even think it's called the Wharton place anymore. Not sure who owns it now."

"So what did he tell you?" Candy asked, prompting the elderly gentleman.

"Well, he told me he was up late the night before they found that woman's body. Couldn't sleep, he said. Indigestion. His wife's meat loaf, he told me. Too many onions. Anyway, he was gazing out the bedroom window at the moon, which was almost full. And he said he thought he saw, by the light of that almost-full moon, a Bentley driving down the road past his house, with its lights out. Don't know if he told that to the police, but that's what I heard."

TWENTY-THREE

Her conversation with Julius Seabury buzzed in her brain as she set off to search the town's cemeteries.

A Bentley. With its headlights out.

Could it have been the same Bentley that belonged to the Pruitts? she wondered. *Had Hobbins been behind the wheel?* Could he have had something to do with the dead woman found in the pumpkin patch twenty years ago?

Or what about Mrs. Pruitt?

And if so, what was the link? What tied everything together?

Had Hobbins even been working for the Pruitts two decades ago?

She had plenty of questions, but for the time being there were no answers. Still, she thought, trying to stay positive, maybe she'd find some today.

She started at Town Cemetery, which was adjacent to Town Park, just a few hundred yards up the Coastal Loop from the lighthouse's parking lot.

It was a small cemetery, the town's first, dating back to the mid–seventeen hundreds. Surrounded by a tall black wrought-iron fence, it was officially part of the Unitarian Church next door, and was relatively well maintained. Candy estimated there were a few dozen slate and granite tombstones within the fenced area. A historical plaque near the entrance gate, weathered from years of exposure to harsh elements, provided a two-paragraph description of the old graveyard.

Candy could tell without even entering that the tombstone she sought was not here. The look of the place was all wrong—not at all like the cemetery depicted in the old black-and-white photograph. Nevertheless, just to make sure, she walked inside and wandered among the tombstones, reading the inscriptions and the family names—Littlefields and Thayers, a few Wilsons and Pollards, all surnames she still saw sometimes around town, borne by current generations. But there was no gravestone for someone named Emma.

Her next stop was Stone Hill Cemetery, the largest on the cape, and where the relatively fresh graves of Sapphire Vine and James Sedley were located, among many others.

Here, the tombstones—mostly marble and granite, though there were a few tall, black slate stones in the older sections of the tree-spotted cemetery—were spread across a gentle slope and ridge overlooking the English River. And today, the quiet, picturesque landscape epitomized autumn in New England—still-colorful trees beginning to bare their dark, artfully twisted limbs and branches; the swirling waves of dry, curled, parchmentlike leaves, scattering among the gravestones and monuments, nearly knee-deep where they gathered in the low spots; the weak, slanting light filtering through the late-afternoon sky, illuminating open patches of gray, dying grass so that they almost shone, like pools of pale water.

Candy had been out here on a number of occasions, but had never taken much time to walk around the property. It was a large graveyard, perhaps five or six acres in all, stretching across a long, narrow strip of land marked by rocky outcroppings in some spots—a lot of ground to cover.

She toured as much of it as she could from behind the wheel of the Jeep, cruising along the narrow two-wheel dirt lanes that wound among the various sections and wove between the oaks, maples, and chestnuts. Several times Candy stopped the vehicle and climbed out to check a certain tombstone or to look down on sections of the cemetery from certain vistas. She didn't have time to check every stone, but she inherently knew that what she was looking for was not here.

She glanced at her watch. Just past three. She had a little while before she headed over to the police station for the press conference at four P.M., so she reached for Julius Seabury's book, which she'd laid on the Jeep's front passenger seat, and thumbed back through it until she found the map with the private cemeteries marked on it.

Most of them looked like they were associated with private families—Blackwoods, Clarks, Merritts, Hollands, and McCays—and were located on private land. There were a few that might be located on town or conservation land, though, so Candy headed for those first, thinking that might be the most logical place to bury an unidentified body.

She spent twenty minutes searching for a cemetery supposedly located off a dirt road that ran along the river, past the site of an old settlement, now in ruins, but when she finally located it, she was disappointed to find only a dozen or so tombstones, most commemorating the resting places of Yorks, with a few Tripps and other names mixed in.

She had better luck with a cemetery up toward Route 1, at the northwestern corner of the cape near the western coastline, where she found a walled cemetery next to a white clapboard building called the Blair House, home to a small private historical society. It was closed for the day. In the graveyard she found tombstones for the family members who had once lived there, but not surprisingly, most were from a single family—the Blairs—all of whom had passed away during the eighteen hundreds.

No Emma.

So she scratched the Old Blair House Cemetery off her list and drove back to Cape Willington, arriving at the police station just as Chief Durr began his remarks at a temporary podium that had been set up in front of the building.

Parking was at a premium, so Candy pulled the Jeep into a tight spot out by the main road, grabbed her tote bag from the backseat, and joined the crowd gathered around the chief, with her digital recorder in hand.

After all, she had a story to write, too, though her deadline was not until the end of the week for the following week's edition.

But ten minutes later she'd heard nothing new, as the chief was just rehashing old information: the identity of the victim, the manner in which he'd been found, the apparent fatal wounds on the body, his academic career in Massachusetts, his ties to the town—but Candy knew all that already. The chief officially declared this a homicide investigation, and named a state detective who was assisting on the case. Then, with a barely disguised grimace in anticipation of what might come, he said tightly, "Now I'll take a few questions."

Olivia March, the reporter for the *Herald*, had stationed herself in the front row. "What can you tell us about the victim's whereabouts in the forty-eight hours leading up to his death?" she asked in what Candy thought was a very professional manner.

"Well, we've contacted the authorities at the University of Massachusetts at Amherst, where the victim—Mr. Quinn—taught, and they're cooperating with us. We're also working with the Amherst PD to follow up on a few local leads there. There's not much else I'm prepared to say about that at this time."

"What about the victim's cell phone and e-mail records?" asked another reporter, who Candy didn't recognize.

"We're looking into that," the chief said in a clipped fashion.

"Why do you think Sebastian J. Quinn was murdered in that pumpkin patch?" Olivia March asked.

"That's part of the ongoing investigation. I can't discuss it at this time."

"Was he murdered in the pumpkin patch or was his body moved there from another location?" Olivia pressed.

The chief frowned and shook his head. He looked like he had a bad case of indigestion. "Again, no comment."

Wanda Boyle piped up from the back of the crowd. "Do you have any suspects?"

"I can't discuss that," the chief said, and rapped the top of the podium with a knuckle. "Now, if there's nothing else, ladies and gentlemen . . ."

Candy's hand shot up, almost before she was aware of it. "On a different subject, Chief, where might a Jane Doe—an unidentified, unclaimed body—be buried in town? Is there a certain local cemetery where they'd inter the body?"

Chief Durr's neck craned toward her and he squinted in her direction. He looked immensely displeased. "I'm not sure I know what you're referring to, Ms. Holliday."

"You know, if an unidentified body—a Jane Doe . . ."

But she never got a chance to finish.

"I know what a Jane Doe is, Ms. Holliday. What does that have to do with this investigation?" he asked pointedly.

"It's . . . for another story I'm working on," she said, spouting the first thing that came to her mind.

His expression grew even tighter as he studied her. Candy realized that most of those in the crowd were looking in her direction as well.

Finally the chief responded, and it was clear to see he was unhappy with the question. Nevertheless, his expression told her, he'd do his best to answer it, especially since he was standing out here in public, talking to all these fine people who were also asking him questions he didn't want to answer.

"Well, since you asked—for this *other* story you're working on, of course—I'd have to say that I don't recall burying any Jane Does in this town for quite a while, so I don't know for sure how to answer your question. But you might want to visit Town Hall and check the burial records. That'd be the best place to start."

He held her gaze for another moment but finally looked away, back to the crowd. "All right, folks. That's about it for now. I have to get back to work."

Candy watched him go, turning and heading into the police station, followed by a small cadre of support staff. She was tempted to follow him, since she had another question for him:

What was in the file labeled Emma, *which had been sitting on the front seat of Sebastian's car?*

Candy suspected at least a few of the answers she sought might be found within, but surely by now the file was in a cardboard box somewhere, locked in an evidence room, out of her reach.

Or was it?

Her eyes followed the chief as he disappeared into the one-story brick building that served as the village's police headquarters. She considered heading into the station, perhaps to talk to Carol at the front desk, maybe ask about her husband Phil's lumbago. But then what? *Can I please have a look around your evidence room, Carol? I'm sure the chief won't mind. I'll just take a quick little peek. I promise it won't take more than a few minutes. I just want to get a look at a certain file. . . .*

"I think he's starting to like you."

Candy jumped at the low voice that spoke from behind her left shoulder. She whipped around . . . and her startled expression relaxed into a smile.

It was Tristan Pruitt, looking windblown and bemused.

"Who . . . the chief?" Candy laughed at the thought of it. "Unfortunately our relationship goes back a ways, and it hasn't always been pleasant."

"I can't imagine any encounter with you being unpleasant," Tristan said with a grin.

"Well, I guess you had to be there. Most of the time me and the chief are like an old married couple—we bicker a lot but we're stuck with each other."

Now it was Tristan's turn to laugh. But when he noticed the tape recorder in her hand, his tone turned serious. "I came in late and missed part of it. Anything new in the investigation?"

Candy noticed her recorder was still on and flicked it off, then dropped it into her tote bag. "No—at least nothing official. They're not releasing much."

"Maybe they don't know much," Tristan surmised.

Candy's tone turned serious as well. "To be honest, I think they're worried."

"About what?"

She took a moment to collect her thoughts, and finally said, "This is the sixth murder in town in less than three years. That's not normal. I heard someone ask this morning if Cape Willington is becoming the murder capital of Maine. I can even see that in a headline somewhere, on a blog or something."

"So you think they're worried it's becoming an epidemic?"

"Exactly."

"And here you are, stuck at the middle of it."

Candy nodded. "I think on one level that irks him," she said, referring to the chief, "but on another level, he's worried for me. I think he's truly interested in protecting me, but he also realizes that in some weird way I may be part of what's happening."

"Why do you say that?" Tristan asked with a touch of concern in his tone.

"Well, this makes two mysteries in a row that have involved me directly—they've literally walked into my life," Candy said.

"What happened the first time?"

Candy paused, recalling the incident. "Solomon Hatch, the town hermit, walked into the back field at Blueberry Acres and collapsed in front of me. He told me there was a dead body in the woods, and then he disappeared."

"Yes, I heard something about that." Tristan's jaw tightened. "That happened when? Earlier this year?"

"January," Candy said, remembering darkly how that mystery had ended—with another mystery.

"And now this—a body found in the pumpkin patch you've been working in."

"Now this."

They were both distracted by the beep of a horn and turned to see Wanda Boyle, heading off in her minibus, apparently done for the day.

"Listen," Tristan said, and Candy turned her attention back to him, "you've had a few difficult days, and obviously you have a lot on your mind. But I'd like to see if I can help take your thoughts off these pressing matters for a few hours. Why don't you let me buy you dinner?"

Candy gave him a curious look. "At Pruitt Manor again?"

"No, at an actual real restaurant this time. My treat."

"Where?" she asked in mock suspicion.

"The Lightkeeper's Inn. I have a reservation for eight fifteen."

"How can you have a reservation?" Candy asked. "They've been booked up for weeks." She knew. She'd written a story last month about the inn's rising popularity, thanks to its young French Canadian chef, Colin Trevor Jones.

"You forget," Tristan explained. "I'm a Pruitt."

"Ahh." Candy's eyebrows flicked upward. "Rank has its privileges, right?"

"Plus I have a standing reservation there on weekends when I'm in town."

"Cook doesn't know how to make your favorite dishes?" Candy guessed.

He chuckled. "No, it's not that. Let's just say there are times when I feel like I need a little space. Aunt Helen can be . . . stifling at times."

Candy nodded. She could certainly understand that. She'd been intimidated by Mrs. Pruitt from the start. "Do you stay out at Pruitt Manor regularly?" Candy asked.

He grinned. "Why don't we discuss it over dinner?"

She glanced at her watch, then out to the crowd.

She felt she had so much to do, so much research and writing waiting for her.

And then there was Ben.

They'd never talked about their relationship being exclusive. It had always been more casual than that. On the other hand, she hadn't gone out with anyone else since they'd met.

She looked back at Tristan. "On one condition," she said.

"And what's that?"

"It's not a date. It's a business dinner."

"A what?" he asked in mock horror.

Candy smiled at his reaction. "Well, maybe not quite as serious as that. But you and your aunt asked me to find Abigail's missing diary, so I thought we could talk about your family a little more. And Hobbins."

"Hobbins?" Tristan made a face. "Why would you want to talk about him? It'll spoil our appetites for sure."

Candy laughed. "I promise that won't happen. Do we have a deal?"

Tristan sighed and rolled his eyes in a completely charming way, before a warm smile crept across his face. "You drive a hard bargain, Candy Holliday. What time should I pick you up?"

TWENTY-FOUR

He arrived at Blueberry Acres promptly at eight, driving a classic forest green Jaguar with well-worn leather seats and burl walnut trim on the dash, doors, and center console.

Doc walked out to greet him, admiring the car and shaking hands with Tristan, while Candy threw on a cocoa-colored wool shawl she'd bought the previous spring at a clearance sale at Macy's up in Bangor. She wore it over tan slacks and a draping cream-colored, midsleeve blouse with a silver belt. Turquoise earrings and a silver-and-turquoise necklace added some color. She'd fixed up her hair as best she could, and put on some lipstick and makeup.

It had taken her a while to decide on the toned-down outfit, and she still wasn't sure she'd made the right choice. She'd spent the better part of an hour on the phone with Maggie trying to figure out what to wear. She'd tried on four or five dresses, including a low-cut red number and a less revealing black dress, but none looked right for the occasion. She wanted to make sure she emphasized the point that this was a *business* dinner, and not a *date*. So she'd finally opted for the slacks and shawl, which she thought were more casual yet appropriate for dinner at the inn.

Doc was telling Tristan about his latest writing project when Candy came down off the porch and climbed into the Jaguar's passenger seat. The leather felt warm underneath her. "Heated seats?" she asked of Tristan.

He nodded. He was wearing a starched white shirt, open-collared, and a dark gray jacket. With gold cuff links. Which had diamond studs. And he was wearing aftershave. Something that smelled earthy and expensive.

She eased down into the warm seat. "Perfect for a cool autumn evening."

Doc was just finishing up, and Candy waved to him out the driver's side window, leaning across Tristan. "Would you check the chickens for me? I didn't get a chance to look in on them this evening."

"Sure thing, pumpkin." Doc slapped the roof of the car and backed away, thrusting his hands into his pockets. "Okay, you two have a good time . . . doing whatever you're doing," he said.

"It's a business dinner, Dad!"

"That's right, I keep forgetting," he said with a grin, and waved as they drove off.

The Lightkeeper's Inn was crowded and the parking lot was full, but Tristan dropped off the car with a valet, and they were promptly seated at one of the best tables in the dining room, in a softly lit alcove with a bay window over-looking the front of the inn toward the sea.

It was a beautiful night, cool and crisp. The sky had cleared and the stars were bright. The moon was just rising above the horizon out over the ocean.

As they'd come down Ocean Avenue, they'd seen some volunteers who were just finishing up their work in Town Park, setting up display stands for the Pumpkin Bash festival taking place on Wednesday. And tonight, the inn was completely decorated for Halloween, with carved and lighted pumpkins on display outside and in, autumnal wall and floor arrangements with cornstalks and sheaves of multicolored leaves, and a general spiderweb and bat motif weaving through the banisters, chandeliers, and lounge area.

A waitress came by, took their drink orders, and chatted briefly with Tristan, smiling widely the entire time, before heading off toward the bar. Tristan waved a friendly greeting to the bartender as well, and both Oliver LaForce, the head innkeeper, and Alben "Alby" Alcott, the assistant innkeeper, stopped by to say a quick hello. Mason Flint, the chairman of the town council, also paid his respects.

"My," Candy said as she sipped from a chilled glass of white wine, "you're certainly a popular person tonight. When I agreed to have dinner with you, I didn't know I'd be sitting at a table with a celebrity."

"It is a bit embarrassing, isn't it?" Tristan said sheepishly, as a half smile slipped out of the corner of his mouth. "It's just that I've known some of these folks for the better part of my life. I spent most of my summers here when I was a kid. We used to eat here at the inn way back when the place was owned by the Whitby family. They eventually sold out to Oliver, whom I've known for almost twenty years. And I've known Alby since he started here eight years ago or so." He pointed toward the bar. "I've known Hank since I was in high school—I dated his daughter one summer when we were both teenagers—and I played pool with Ted Frank, whose dad owned Zeke's back in those days. We had insurance through Stone and Milbury, until they closed down. I've been to Town Hall and met with the town council a number of times over the years on the family's behalf. I've worked with some of the local charities, we support local arts through the opera house, and of course I know most of the business leaders in town."

"Of course," Candy said, lazily twirling her finger around the rim of the wineglass.

"Well, you probably do too," Tristan said, motioning toward her, "with your job as the community columnist."

"True. And at the bakery as well," Candy added. "And, yes, I've gotten to know many of the people around town. If I haven't interviewed someone for the newspaper, then I've seen them at Herr Georg's place." Herr Georg Wolfsburger ran the Black Forest Bakery, where Candy worked during the spring and summer. But the place had closed for the season a few weeks earlier, and as far as Candy knew, Herr Georg had already left town, heading south to warmer climes.

Their drinks arrived, with an appetizer—courtesy of Oliver LaForce. It was one of Chef Colin's seasonal creations—lobster dumplings with goat cheese, accompanied by a spicy apple dipping sauce, and on another warmed plate, roasted butternut-squash bruschetta sprinkled with olive oil and aromatic herb seasoning. They were also treated to glasses of authentic Colonial cider, prepared especially for Chef Colin's kitchen.

As they dipped, munched, and drank, Candy felt herself loosening up, and finally decided to segue into the questions that were burning in her mind, using a tactful approach.

"So . . . tell me a bit more about Pruitt Manor," she said, starting broadly.

Tristan tilted his head. "What do you want to know?"

She played coy, at least for the moment. "Well, what was it like visiting there in the summers—you know, hanging out with your family, and the help, like Cook and Hobbins, and all those folks?"

He made a face. "Why would you want to know about them?"

Candy's gave him an enigmatic smile. "Humor me."

He studied her for a few moments, until the waitress came and took their dinner orders. He watched Candy the entire time as she chose blackened tilapia with rice pilaf and a fall vegetable medley, and then she watched with interest as he scanned the menu, flipped it closed, and crisply handed it back to the waitress. "I'll have the usual."

"And what's that?" Candy asked curiously.

He shrugged. "Their prime rib here is excellent. Chef Colin uses this amazing bourbon glaze."

"What, you're not ordering a cigar too?" she asked, amused.

"That comes later."

After the waitress left, he dropped his eyes into a half squint as his gaze narrowed in on Candy. "You're up to something, aren't you?" he asked.

She batted her eyes, feigning puzzlement. "Whatever do you mean?"

"There's something going on, isn't there?"

"What makes you say that?"

"Oh, the way you're fishing for information. The way you're dressed . . ."

She leaned back. "What's wrong with the way I'm dressed?" she asked, looking down at her carefully selected wardrobe.

"The ensemble looks quite beautiful on you, I'll admit, but it does seem like you're attending a business meeting," he said simply, gesturing with his hand. "I thought you were joking about that, but apparently you weren't. Honestly, it's not what a woman wears to a dinner engagement unless she's trying to deliver a message. And I'm reading yours loud and clear." He drummed his fingers on the tabletop. "So, Miss Detective, what can I help you with?"

Candy's heart sped up just a bit at the way he'd seen through her charade so easily. *This one is not easily fooled,* she thought, and vowed to be wary of that during future encounters with him.

At the same time, she found herself liking this right-to-the-point Tristan Pruitt, and she gave him a quick smile, before it faded. "Okay, here goes: How long has Hobbins been employed out at Pruitt Manor?"

Tristan frowned, looked down at the table, and played with his fork. "Hobbins again." He sighed and considered his answer carefully before speaking. "The Hobbins family has served the Pruitts for decades—I believe since the time of Cornelius, my grandfather. Possibly back even further. I'd have to check on it, really. It's all detailed in our family history, but I confess I haven't read all those dusty volumes, so I suppose I don't really know the answer to your question—not precisely, at least." He paused. "Aunt Helen would though." He paused again as his gaze rose to her. "Why?"

Now it was Candy's turn to take several moments to formulate an answer. *What should I tell him?* she wondered. *Do I want him to know what I know?*

She looked back over one shoulder, then the other, and leaning across the table, she finally said in a low voice, "I think Hobbins—or someone from Pruitt Manor—might have been involved in a death that took place out at the pumpkin patch twenty years ago."

TWENTY-FIVE

A little more than an hour and a half later, they walked out to the Jaguar and drove to Pruitt Manor.

It was just past ten in the evening, and the bar and lounge at the inn were still fairly active—for a Sunday night. But outside, the streets of Cape Willington were deserted, strafed only by the fallen leaves that tumbled down the dark pavement toward the sea. A light fog had rolled in, and might have been a problem if they were traveling far, but Pruitt Manor stood nearby, on the rocky point just a short drive down the Coastal Loop. Tristan barely had time to warm up the Jaguar's cabin before they were pulling into the manor's cobblestoned courtyard.

"I think Hobbins is off tonight," he said, motioning to one of the empty stalls in the garage. "His Explorer's missing."

"Does he ever drive the Bentley when he's out alone—on errands or that sort of thing?" Candy asked.

"Not that I'm aware of. He usually takes his own vehicle.

The only time he drives the Bentley is when he's chauffeuring Aunt Helen around. Come on, let's go inside. Most likely she's gone to bed, but we can still dig around in the library a little, if we do it quietly."

Over dinner, Candy had explained what she'd heard earlier in the day—that a Bentley had allegedly been seen in the vicinity of the pumpkin patch twenty years ago, around the time the body of an unidentified female was found there. Of course, the Bentley could have belonged to someone other than the Pruitts. But how many Bentleys were there in Down East Maine? She knew of only one. And if it *had* belonged to the Pruitts, then its appearance on that particular road on that long-ago night could simply have been a coincidence—and most likely that's exactly what it was, she and Tristan had concluded together after talking it through. But as they'd considered other alternatives, the implications became trickier. For instance, could someone in the Bentley have *dropped off* the body in the pumpkin patch—dumped it there and then driven away with the headlights out, so as not to be seen?

If so, why? And who?

Over dessert—creamy pumpkin sherbet spiced with cinnamon and accompanied by a thin wedge of dark chocolate, along with hot tea for Candy and a bourbon on the rocks for Tristan (he'd decided to eschew the cigar for now, despite mischievous prompting from Candy)—they'd come up with several scenarios, none of which shined a positive light on Pruitt Manor, or whomever had been in occupancy at the time.

It had been Tristan's idea to search the library, and specifically the volumes of Pruitt history, for clues. "At least we can find out who might have been living in the house at that time, and who was on staff. Neither Aunt Helen nor Hobbins would probably remember details from that long ago anyway, so the histories are the best place to start."

But then the realization had struck Candy—the missing

volume of Pruitt history that had been noted by the library, prompting the removal of the collection and its return to Pruitt Manor. *What had the dates been?* she'd wondered. She wished she'd brought the photocopy of the index card with her.

But one way or another, she thought, she was about to get some answers.

Tristan braked to a stop, shut off the engine, and told Candy, "Wait a minute." Then he dashed smartly around the front of the car to open her door for her. As Candy climbed out, she looked up. The place rose above them in the moonlit night, its angled rooftops and elaborate nautical weather vane silhouetted against the rising moon. Several exterior lights illuminated their way, but the large oak door sat in a shadowed recess, and Tristan had to search for the right key. "Someone should put a light out here," he muttered.

Candy pointed up. "Maybe they did. Maybe it just burned out."

He looked up, a flash of annoyance crossing his face. "I'll have to talk to the maintenance people about that," he said, and finally found the right key. He inserted it in the lock, twisted it, and swung the door open for her. "After you."

It was like walking into a museum after hours. Low lights were lit through the foyer, but the side rooms were dark. And the grand staircase leading to the second floor was in shadows.

Candy instinctively inched closer to Tristan. "Are you sure we should be in here?" she asked, barely above a whisper.

"It's my family's home," he said, his casual attitude returning.

"Are you sure *I* should be here?"

He laughed gently. "You're my guest. Come on, the library's over here."

Inside the dark, book-lined room, he walked to a side table and flicked on a lamp. "I could start a fire if you'd like."

Candy crossed her arms and rubbed her shoulders against the chill. Like most old houses in New England, Pruitt Manor had a few drafts. "That would be lovely."

"Would you like some tea? I can warm some up for us."

"I don't want to put anybody to trouble," she said.

"Right." Tristan held up a finger. "Tea first. Then the fire. Then the histories. I'll be right back."

And off he went into the house.

Candy was all alone at Pruitt Manor.

She stood in the center of the room, her gaze rising to the shadowy ceiling, then to the shelves of books surrounding her. Slowly she twirled, until she'd made a complete circle, her eyes raking the volumes upon volumes of books.

Where to start?

She raised her shoulders and gave her head a shake. The best place to start was always straight forward. So she stepped up to the wall of shelves directly in front of her.

But she paused, and as if drawn by a string, her head swiveled to the right. Over there, in another section of the library, Abigail Pruitt's diaries were arranged chronologically on two shelves.

Candy had studied them the day before but had been so focused on those specific journals that she hadn't noticed what other books were shelved around them.

Maybe all the Pruitt materials are shelved together, she thought.

Changing her mind, she turned and walked to the shelves along the right wall, stopped a few feet in front of the dusty leather bindings, and began to scan the titles of the volumes stacked around Abigail's diaries.

It took her only a few moments to realize there was a common theme to all the books shelved in this section of the library. She saw an extensive collection of biographies, including multivolume sets devoted to the founding fathers, captains of industry, political figures, and the great names of the ages.

She moved sideways a few paces. A bay or two to the right were volumes of poetry, language, and literature, and several shelves near the corner and around to the next wall were devoted to popular fiction.

Candy stepped back toward the center of the room and scanned it again. Like any typical library, it was organized by subject matter, she realized. She just had to find the section devoted to history.

She walked back toward the shelves where she'd left off and began circling the room, pausing every few steps to identify each section.

Beyond the fiction section, toward the door through which they'd entered, were several bays devoted to scientific volumes on botany, anatomy, astronomy, geology, and archaeology, as well as books on engineering, math, transportation, and economics.

She pursed her lips thoughtfully and moved on, past the door. Volumes on business and management lined the shelves here, followed by travel books, arranged by continent, with Africa, Asia, and Australia first, then Europe and the Americas, which stretched to the corner. She stepped around, spotting several shelves devoted to the great philosophic works and volumes on mythology, folklore, and the world's religions. And beyond that, numerous works on the arts, music, photography, and architecture. They filled the wall into the back corner. She noticed the bottom shelves were lined with oversized books chronicling the works of the world's grand masters.

Finally, around the corner again, was a wall filled with volumes of history. Here she stopped and focused her gaze on the titles.

Again, she noticed a simple pattern, essentially chronological, from the Egyptian, Greek, and Roman eras to a surprisingly large section on ancient Chinese history, with a respectable collection on Charlemagne and the Dark Ages, as well as the medieval centuries. Those were followed by volumes on the Renaissance, Reformation, industrial era, and modern era, and then localized volumes on New England and Maine history—and finally, a series of shelves devoted to the Pruitt histories.

She stood looking at them for several moments, then dropped into a crouch. The family histories all had similar tan-colored covers, and started about midway down the bay of shelves. She dropped a little lower, checking to see if one of the later volumes was missing.

Maybe, she thought, after the library returned the collection to Pruitt Manor, the missing volume—number twenty-three, if she remembered correctly—had been found. If so, that at least would clear up one mystery. But she noticed right away that one of the volumes was unaccounted for, as an index card had been inserted between two volumes on the lowest shelf. She moved in for a closer look.

"What on earth are you doing down there?" a voice croaked somewhere behind her.

Surprised, Candy jumped to her feet and spun around, her heart thumping in her chest.

And spotted a shadowy specter in a floor-length black cape, lurking in a seam of darkness just beyond the open door.

TWENTY-SIX

Caught off guard, Candy didn't know what to say. She tried to speak, but her tongue seemed stuck to the roof of her mouth with fright. She backed up a step and finally managed to stammer, "What? I'm sorry. . . . I . . . I . . ." She stopped, searching her brain for more words, but none came out.

Tristan walked in at that moment, rescuing her. He carried a silver tray with a pot of steeping tea and several porcelain cups. "Ah, Aunt Helen, there you are," he said casually to the specter confronting Candy. "What are you doing lurking by the door like that? You're scaring poor Candy. She probably thinks you're some cadaver risen from the dead. Come over here and have a seat, and I'll pour you a cup of tea. Candy has some questions for us."

The specter moved forward, through the door into better light, and Candy saw now that it was indeed Mrs. Pruitt. She wore a floor-length dark purple robe, and her hair was wrapped in a green and gold scarf. "I thought I heard voices," she said, her voice low and coarse, as if she'd just been awakened from sleep. "What are you two doing in here, causing a disturbance at this hour of the night?"

Ignoring the sharpness in his aunt's tone, Tristan set the tea service on a small mahogany side table, lifted the pot, and expertly poured three cups. "Candy's turned up some interesting information," he said in response. "We came back to the house to research the histories."

"The histories?" Mrs. Pruitt stopped halfway across the room and turned her sharp gaze on Candy. "Why would you have any interest in those dusty old books?"

Tristan flopped down into a wingback chair, his long legs sprawled out in front of him. "It seems we have not one but two missing volumes. And Candy thinks she's made a connection to at least one of them."

Mrs. Pruitt's mouth tightened, and her gaze narrowed on Candy. "Explain."

"Well," Candy said, thinking quickly and feeling the pressure, "I'm still putting the pieces together, but it all seems to lead back to the body of an unidentified female, who was found in the pumpkin patch twenty years ago. She allegedly died of exposure, and after the investigation into her death, her body seems to have mysteriously disappeared. But I think she might be the same woman as this person named Emma, who has some connection to Sebastian J. Quinn" She explained about the folder she'd spotted on the front seat of Sebastian's car, all the while gauging Mrs. Pruitt's reaction to this news. She knew she was fishing, but she also suspected there was some link between the Bentley and the dead woman's body. "Does that name ring a bell? Someone named Emma?"

The matriarch had listened attentively, and now shook her head almost imperceptibly as she crossed the rest of the way to a chair near Tristan. "No."

Candy continued, undeterred. "It's a little confusing, I know. Like I said, I'm still trying to fit it all together. But Sapphire Vine was looking for her tombstone—for Emma's tombstone," she clarified. "It all seems just a little too coincidental, doesn't it?"

Mrs. Pruitt frowned and she leaned forward, plucking a cup of tea from the silver tray with bony fingers. "Sapphire Vine was involved in this?" She sounded dismayed, but there was an undertone of interest in her words.

Candy nodded. "I found a black-and-white photo of Emma's tombstone in a folder Sapphire left behind. She must have been searching for it for some reason, but I don't know why, and I don't know if she ever found it. And she was also interested in the missing volume of Pruitt history, which struck me as odd."

Mrs. Pruitt shook her head. "That nasty woman was involved in all sorts of wicked schemes. Who knows what she was after." Her scrutinizing gaze turned to Candy again. "You say she was looking for a missing volume?"

Nodding, Candy turned back to the section of the shelves that held the histories and dropped to one knee. "She was looking for this right here." She pointed to the index card, which she delicately pulled out from between the books. There was a brief note written on it, which she read at a glance, and then held up for Mrs. Pruitt to see. "Volume twenty-three of the Pruitt family history. It's still missing, according to this card." She pointed to the old books lined up on the shelf. "I just checked myself. It still hasn't been returned."

"I'd forgotten about that," Mrs. Pruitt admitted. "But now that you mention it, I seem to recall that that book has been missing for decades. We thought it was lost forever. Sapphire Vine took that as well?"

Candy shook her head. "This volume went missing from the Pruitt Public Library sometime before August 1972, according to a notation made by a librarian at the time. That was more than twenty-five years before Sapphire showed up in town. So she couldn't have taken it, since she wasn't in the area back then. But for *some* reason she was interested in it, and she must have been looking for it."

"But why?" Mrs. Pruitt asked. "What interest could she have had in an old history book?"

"That's exactly what I said," Tristan pointed out.

"And it's what we're trying to figure out," Candy added. "It's why we came back here tonight."

She paused. There was more she wanted to say but she wasn't quite sure how to broach the subject. So Tristan did it for her.

"There's something else, Aunt Helen. Candy's heard through a source that a Bentley was seen driving near the pumpkin patch twenty years ago, right around the time the body of that unidentified woman was found."

"A Bentley?" Mrs. Pruitt stiffened her back noticeably. "*Our* Bentley?"

"Who else owns a Bentley around here?" Tristan asked pointedly.

Several moments passed in which no one spoke. Mrs. Pruitt suddenly looked very frail. She carefully considered the ramifications of this latest, possibly incriminating piece of evidence before she finally responded in a barely perceptible voice. "You don't suspect *me*? Or"—she gasped as her eyes widened—"*Hobbins*?"

"We don't suspect anyone," Tristan said easily. He'd risen and crossed to the fireplace, where he began to lay out a bed of kindling with practiced hands, snapping twigs and branches to the proper size, then arranging them on the grate as he went. "Candy has simply unearthed some intriguing information that seems to indicate our family's implication— perhaps in some small way, perhaps in a larger manner—in a twenty-year-old mystery, which is in a roundabout way linked to some of the more recent murders in town."

"So why are you here," Mrs. Pruitt demanded of her nephew, "searching through these histories?"

He shrugged. "We're simply trying to discover who might have been in residence here at Pruitt Manor during that time period."

"When was this again?" Mrs. Pruitt asked, her head swiveling back toward Candy.

"Twenty years ago, at around this time of year," Candy said, then added, "That would have been in the fall of 1992."

Mrs. Pruitt nodded and pursed her thin, pale lips as she thought. "Mother had passed away by then," she confirmed. "Of course, if it was around Halloween, other members of the family might have been in residence. But I can't imagine anyone would . . . certainly Hobbins wouldn't . . ." She broke off, her expression falling into confusion.

"Let's not get dramatic just yet," Tristan said evenly. "We're just trying to figure it out."

Gently, Candy asked, "How long has Hobbins worked here at Pruitt Manor?"

Mrs. Pruitt frowned and looked affronted. "How would I know such a thing?"

"Well, you'd have to think back," Tristan said helpfully, coaxing his aunt along. "Was Hobbins working here when Abigail was still alive? Or did he start after she'd passed on?"

Mrs. Pruitt thought about that for quite a while. Finally she spoke softly and hesitantly, as if under interrogation. "His father—Hobbins Senior, we came to call him—was hired by my father, Cornelius. He devoted his life to our family and worked for us for decades, although his health worsened considerably toward the end of his life. I can't recall exactly when Hobbins the son took over his father's responsibilities—possibly around the same time Mother fell ill. At the end of her life, she would have relied increasingly on the son . . . Gerald," she confirmed. "Of course, we never called him by his first name when he was professionally engaged at the manor. He was always just Hobbins, like his father."

"And that was long after you'd left the house, of course, to attend college, marry, and start your own family," Tristan said.

"Of course."

"So Abigail died in, what, 1987? So we can accurately guess that the younger Hobbins has been working here for, what, twenty-five or thirty years, something like that?"

"Something like that," Mrs. Pruitt agreed. "I don't keep track of those types of things." She turned back toward Candy. "Do you really think he could have had something to do with this . . . other death?" the elderly woman asked directly.

"It's possible," Candy replied. "That's why I'm here." She hesitated, considering her next words carefully. "There is one other thing: Tristan told me about a locked drawer in Abigail's writing desk." He had mentioned it to her at dinner, when he'd been describing some of Abigail's eccentricities.

Mrs. Pruitt stiffened perceptibly at the remark but, true to her breeding, responded in a controlled manner, although she shot a questioning look at her nephew. "So you've learned of that as well?"

"It all could be connected," Tristan interjected. "I've said so for years. You have your suspicions as well. You might as well come clean and tell Candy the whole story."

"There's nothing to tell," Mrs. Pruitt said firmly, folding her hands in her lap. "It has nothing to do with whatever else is going on in town, I'm sure of it. My mother's writing desk is an antique. It's been in the family for generations, and it's quite valuable. And yes, a small document drawer containing, we believe, some of Mother's most personal items has remained locked since her death. We haven't been able to open it for fear of damaging it."

"Because we've never found the key," Tristan pointed out.

"It wasn't among Mother's belongings or keepsakes," Mrs. Pruitt confirmed with a nod of her head, "or in any of the safe-deposit boxes, or any other secure place we can think of to look."

"So there's a locked drawer, and a missing key as well," Candy said thoughtfully, biting her lip. "This just keeps getting more and more confusing. But there has to be some link between all of these items—the drawer, the key, the diary, the missing volume of history, and the tombstone. Find one," she said, her gaze drifting to the shelf that held Abigail Pruitt's diaries, "and the rest might just fall right into our laps."

TWENTY-SEVEN

Tristan lit a fire and, as it caught and began to warm the room, they freshened their tea and talked about the mysteries swirling around them. Candy settled briefly into a stiff-backed chair near Mrs. Pruitt but felt too restless to sit for long, so she finally rose and walked back to the shelves, where she closely examined several volumes of Pruitt history. They had finely tooled leather covers, thick linen paper, and lines upon lines of small black text that would take days, if not weeks, to read through. She delicately flipped through several volumes but her mind wasn't focusing on the words before her.

Instead, she was thinking about the missing history volume—the one Sapphire had been looking for. What had happened to it? Had it simply been lost—misplaced by some innocent library patron? Or, like Abigail Pruitt's missing diary, had it been purposely taken by someone? If so, for what purpose? And could the dates encompassed by the volume—the 1940s—have any significance?

The index card she'd pulled out from the lower shelf was simply a placeholder, containing no information, other than an alert that the volume was missing from the series. So she replaced it and stepped back, studying the collection as an entirety.

What's the link, she wondered, *between all these seemingly unconnected pieces of information?* What was the thread that wove through them?

But even as she asked herself the question, one name stood out from the others in her mind.

Emma . . .

Could she have taken the volume from the library all those years ago? How old would she have been then? How old had she been when she died? Candy had no way of knowing, since the dates of Emma's birth and death weren't displayed on her tombstone.

But why not?

Who *was* this ghost person, buried somewhere in an unidentified graveyard?

Emma was at the center of this mystery, Candy felt. *Find Emma's grave,* she thought, *and you find the answers to everything else.*

But where was Emma buried?

Candy resolved to continue her search the following day. She might even have to enlist Wanda Boyle's help.

As their conversation wound down, Tristan rose and told Candy he'd drive her back home. But before she left Pruitt Manor, Mrs. Pruitt insisted on showing her Abigail Pruitt's bedroom. "It just might help you in your investigation," the elderly woman told her.

So with Mrs. Pruitt leading the way, and Tristan bringing up the rear, Candy climbed the main staircase to the manor's second floor.

"Mother chose a small bedroom for herself in the Lavender Wing," Mrs. Pruitt said, pointing left as they reached the top of the stairs. "She slept there most nights as we children were growing up. But her primary bedroom was next to Father's in the South Wing." She pointed to her right and gathered her robe about her. "This way."

The upper hallway was carpeted and dark, lit only by a single table lamp set into an alcove halfway along. They passed by several closed doors before Mrs. Pruitt opened the last one on the left. She pointed to a final door at the end of the hall. "Father's room is there, overlooking the sea. Mother usually slept in here."

Mrs. Pruitt entered the dark room and flicked on a light. "We've preserved it almost exactly as it was when my mother was alive," she told Candy. "We've moved a few of her belongings into the attic for safekeeping, since there are times we do use this room when my granddaughters are visiting—we allow them to stay in here on special occasions—and of course I have a few of Mother's most personal items in my own bedroom, but many of her other belongings are still here."

The place was tastefully decorated in muted shades of rose and gray, which had faded over the years. A large window, framed by heavy burgundy brocade curtains, looked out over a dark landscape. Candy imagined that in the daytime, one could look out that window and see part of the rear lawn and the sea off to the right. Around the room she saw touches of Victorian decoration here and there, and even a bit of whimsy in the arrangement of keepsakes and items Abigail obviously cherished. Her canopied bed stood against the right wall, opposite a small marble fireplace. Next to the bed, a cleverly disguised door led to an adjoining room, presumably that of Cornelius Pruitt, Abigail's husband.

The writing desk was positioned against the outside wall to the right of the window. It, too, was of Victorian design, made of a dark wood—mahogany, Candy guessed—with numerous drawers and distinctive brass hardware. Two raised rear structures, also with various drawers and shelves, were connected on top by a galleried centerpiece.

Walking around the bed to the desk, Mrs. Pruitt pointed to a narrow drawer on the desk's right side, under the writing surface. Candy followed her, focusing on the drawer. She'd seen something like this before. A document drawer, Mrs. Pruitt had called it. It was small, and would hold only folded documents and letters, not larger files or books. A small brass lock with a flat vertical keyhole held it tightly shut.

Candy studied the lock for a few moments, trying to imagine what its key might look like and how large it might be. She was tempted to reach out and tug on the drawer's single brass handle, just to verify that it indeed was locked. But she held herself back. She could see, though, that the desk itself was well built. She could see no way to break into the drawer without damaging the desk.

She noticed that the desk's worn leather writing surface had faded to a pale green, and that sheets of cream-colored writing paper, embossed in black with the initials AWP, still filled a small tray that sat off to one side, as if awaiting Abigail's hand. A silver oval frame, containing a black-and-white photo of Abigail as a young woman, sat on one ledge.

Mrs. Pruitt allowed Candy a few more moments to look around, but she saw nothing else that might help her solve the mysteries at hand. So a short time later, they headed downstairs, and after bidding farewell to Mrs. Pruitt, she climbed back into the Jaguar, and Tristan drove her home.

"I don't know if we actually learned much tonight," he told her as they angled around the shoreline, following the dark, damp Coastal Loop, the Jaguar's headlamps cutting through sea mist and trails of fog. They were the only car on the road.

Candy had her shawl pulled tightly around her, though the heated seat beneath her kept her warm. She thought a few moments before she responded. "Well, we learned that the volume of Pruitt history is still missing, and I found out about a missing key to a drawer in Abigail's room. And we learned that Hobbins was probably working at Pruitt Manor when a dead woman showed up in that pumpkin patch twenty years ago, and so he *could* have been driving that Bentley when it was spotted with its lights out."

"Hmm, that's troubling," Tristan admitted, and he fell silent, lost in his thoughts.

Doc had left the porch light on at Blueberry Acres. Tristan pulled up in front of the house, pulled on the emergency brake, and let the motor run as again he dashed out around the front of the car to open her door.

"Listen, thank you for having dinner with me tonight," he said when she'd climbed out, and he leaned over and kissed her on the cheek before she could react. "I had a wonderful time."

"Me too," she admitted with a smile.

He had one more question for her as he walked her to the front porch. "What are you doing Wednesday night?"

"Wednesday?" The question caught her off-guard, and she had to think about it for a moment. "Well, that's Halloween, isn't it?"

"And it's your birthday," Tristan said. "Listen, I've been thinking. As you've probably heard, my family throws a party—a masquerade ball, really—at the house on Halloween night. It's sort of a tradition around here. All the movers and shakers in town usually show up, as well as quite a few of Aunt Helen's more famous friends—artists, writers, politicians, that sort of thing. I'd like you to come as my guest, and we can celebrate your birthday in style."

Candy hesitated. "Well, I . . .'"

"I've already checked with your father," he said, "and it's fine with him."

This surprised Candy. "You called Doc?"

Tristan gave her his half smile. "Just to check to see if he had anything planned for you that evening. I didn't want to cause any sort of conflict within the Holliday family."

"And what did he say?" Candy asked, curious to hear the answer.

"Well, I'm asking you now, aren't I?" He squeezed her hand and then started away. "I'll tell you what. Talk to him about it and I'll give you a call tomorrow to confirm, okay? And remember, it's a masquerade ball."

"A masquerade ball? But . . ." Candy started to say, but she was speaking to a rapidly disappearing back. A few moments later, he'd jumped into the Jaguar and driven off.

Doc was in his room, reading, so she didn't disturb him. She locked up the house, turned out all the lights downstairs, and went up to her bedroom, where she got undressed, put on her pajamas, and climbed into bed. Once she was settled in, she opened the Pruitt file she'd started going through the night before, picking up where she'd left off.

She was only a quarter of the way through when she fell asleep with papers scattered around her and across the bed.

TWENTY-EIGHT

Candy was up and out the door early, as she had a quick errand to run before she picked up Maggie and headed out to the pumpkin patch.

On Monday mornings during the spring, summer, and into the fall, Candy usually worked at the Black Forest Bakery up on Main Street. But Herr Georg had closed down his shop for the season right after Columbus Day, and Candy was still getting used to the idea of having her Mondays free.

Of course, she had plenty to do out at the farm helping to get the fields ready for winter, and she and Maggie still had a few days left at the pumpkin patch. And she still worked part-time at the *Cape Crier*.

That's where she was headed this morning.

Just after eight, she drove down Ocean Avenue and found a parking spot near the wood-and-glass door, identified as number 21B, that led to a set of well-worn wooden stairs and the second-floor offices of the *Cape Crier*.

The place officially opened at eight thirty, but she expected to be well out of there by then. She'd arranged to take these few days off, now that they were on a biweekly schedule, and she didn't want to have to explain why she was in the office this morning. Especially with everything that had happened out at the pumpkin patch. She knew there'd be too many questions she didn't want to answer right now, so she wanted to avoid any conversational entanglements.

But there was something she wanted to check— something she'd thought of the night before as she was going through the Pruitt file left behind by Sapphire Vine.

So she planned to sneak in early, get what she needed, and leave quickly.

As she'd expected, the place was deserted. She hurried through the rabbit warren of hallways to her office, where she flicked on the light and closed the door behind her with the side of her hip.

Knowing exactly what she was looking for, she dropped to one knee in front of the filing cabinet in the corner and pulled open the bottom drawer labeled sv. This was the third time she'd been in this drawer in as many days, so she made quick work of it. She dug back through the files with nimble fingers, scanning the handwritten names on the labels, looking for a specific one.

And there it was—a quarter of the way back, a file labeled *Hobbins*, with a smaller annotation in parentheses, *(Gerald)*.

She snatched it out of the drawer and dropped it into her tote bag without looking at it further. She wanted to review it when she had time to focus on it, which she'd have later in the day. And she didn't want to get caught in her office right now. Besides, she had a schedule to keep. It was time to skedaddle.

She made her next stop at the police station, where she read and signed the written version of the statement she'd

given to Officer Molly Prospect on Saturday morning. She
felt an odd vibe in the station as an assistant took her into a
side room to be fingerprinted. After they were done with
her, she drove to Fowler's Corner, wiping at the ink on her
fingers with a paper towel.

Maggie was anxiously waiting for her in the driveway of
her house at Fowler's Corner, bundled up against the chilly
morning. She held a commuter cup of coffee in one hand
and brandished a color printed-out sheet of paper in the
other. "Have you seen the headlines this morning?" she
asked, waving the sheet in front of Candy's eyes. "I just
printed this off of Wanda's blog. She linked to the *Herald*'s
site. Can you *believe* it? We're *famous*!"

Candy squinted and tried to focus. "What is it?"

"The front page. Look at that headline!"

"I would if you'd quit waving it around." Candy finally
snatched it out of the air and held it steady for a few moments
so she could read it.

It was a printout of the front page of the *Boston Herald*'s
website. Since the entire web page was squashed to fit onto
an eight-by-eleven sheet of paper, some of the print was too
small to read easily. But the headlines stood out. The large
main one in the middle column read, *PUMPKIN PATCH
KILLER STRIKES IN MAINE VILLAGE*.

And in smaller type underneath that, *BY OLIVIA
MARCH*.

Candy read the first couple of sentences—*Local farmers
in the quiet coastal Maine village of Cape Willington were
in for a pre-Halloween surprise on Saturday morning when
they unearthed a dead body from beneath a pile of pumpkins in a popular local patch. The deceased was identified
as . . .*—before her gaze broke off and shifted to Maggie.
"Oh, no, this isn't good. Everyone in New England will be
talking about the Pumpkin Patch Killer. We won't be
famous—we'll be *infamous*!"

"I know! I don't know whether to be thrilled or horrified!"

Maggie said, and she looked both. "I'm quoted in the third paragraph." She pointed at the sheet of paper, then jabbed at it farther down. "Wanda's in there too. What a terrible way to get your name in the *Herald*."

"I'm sure it makes good copy though," Candy said, and she passed the paper back to her friend. "They'll probably sell out on the newsstand, especially with a story like this right before Halloween. It's custom-made for papers and the Web. The story might even go viral, given Sebastian's quasi-celebrity status." She put the gearshift into reverse and looked back over her shoulder. "Read it to me while I drive."

The quotes were fairly accurate, and Olivia provided some decent background about Sebastian. She also mentioned the fact that the murder was the latest in a string of deaths that had occurred in town over the past few years, and questioned whether they could be connected. She then quoted Chief Durr's response when asked if Cape Willington was becoming "the murder capital of Maine," and provided a few more details about the investigation, although there was nothing Candy hadn't heard already.

More importantly, no mention of Emma. No mention of a body found in that same field twenty years earlier.

Maybe those points aren't relevant, Candy thought. *Maybe they have nothing to do with the murder of Sebastian J. Quinn. Maybe it's something else entirely.*

Or maybe, she told herself, Olivia simply hadn't discovered all the details yet. Maybe, like Candy, she was still digging around.

The story ended with a few quotes from Wanda Boyle about all the recent murders, and how the latest crime wave in town had to be stopped. She concluded by suggesting that a wider investigation might be in order—though she stopped short of officially criticizing the work of the local police department.

Given the prominence of the story in the Boston paper, Candy and Maggie weren't quite sure what to expect out at the pumpkin patch. But despite their newfound fame, and a mention of the patch's location in the paper's story, traffic at the pumpkin patch was fairly light that morning, giving them time to set up shop before they had a small rush of customers around nine, many of them asking about the story.

Wanda Boyle showed up in her minibus a little after nine thirty, hosting the first Halloween Mystery Tour of the day, but Candy noticed the bus was less than half full. A little later on, the reporter from Bangor, who introduced himself as Denny Brite, drove up with a photographer in tow. Denny asked a bunch of questions, but Candy could barely remember how she answered them, since the photographer kept snapping shots of her, Maggie, the farm stand, and the fields, distracting her.

They left just about the time Wanda showed up with her second load around ten forty, and this time Candy was surprised to see the bus was nearly full. As the passengers spread out across the field, more vehicles started showing up—including a TV truck from Bangor and, a little later on, one from Portland.

The word is spreading, Candy thought as she watched the activity and answered more questions than she wanted to.

"If I'd known there were going to be cameras around," Maggie told her at one point, "I would've had my hair done yesterday."

"You and me both," Candy said, looking down at her farmer's clothes. "I would've worn clean jeans."

During a lull in the action, after the bus and TV trucks had departed, Candy spotted a battered old white van coming along the unpaved road, its springs creaking. Blue letters on the side of the van announced GUMM'S HARDWARE.

The van drove up the field's access road close to the farm stand and the engine shut off. The driver waved. Candy waved back.

"Mr. Gumm's here," she said, and went out to greet him.

Maggie, who was helping a customer, just nodded in acknowledgement.

Augustus Gumm, the eighty-something owner of the pumpkin patch, and the proprietor of the hardware store in town that bore his family's name, was shaking his head and gazing out at the patch as he climbed out of the van's front seat. "It's a real shame," Candy heard him say as she approached. "Just a real shame."

"What's that, Mr. Gumm?"

"Ohh"—he pointed out toward High Field—"just all that trouble you had out here a few days ago. With that body and all. And now that story about the Pumpkin Patch Killer in that Boston paper. Terrible thing."

"It'll give the town a bad reputation, that's for sure," Candy said, "and that's something we don't need right now."

"Nosiree bob, nosiree," Mr. Gumm said, still shaking his head. He looked over at Candy. "I would've been here sooner but I was out of town—visiting my sister down in Kittery. She isn't feeling too well these days. Legs are bothering her. But I came back as soon as I could. Can't believe it's happening again."

"Again?" Candy said, emphasizing the word. She knew the story but wanted to hear Mr. Gumm's take on it.

"Yup, happened twenty years ago or so, I guess, sort of just like this latest death . . . mysterious and everything, and even right around this same time of year, if I remember correctly, sometime in the fall. We had the police out here to the field back then, too, and a reporter or two, if I remember correctly. She had no ID on her, and they said they could never match her fingerprints to anyone. They called her The Woman Without a Name—no one knew who she was."

"How did she die?" Candy asked, to clarify the information she'd already heard.

Mr. Gumm had to think about that for a moment. "Don't know if I ever heard the whole story," he said, "but word was she just died of exposure. It was mighty cold around that time, I seem to recall. Early hard frost. Think we had an early snow that year too."

"And they never found out who she was?"

"Nope, never did, far as I heard. The stories about her continued for a few months, and then, like everything else, they eventually died away."

"Do you know what happened to her body?"

Mr. Gumm rubbed at his chin. "Well, that's the curious thing. Never heard about that either."

"So you wouldn't know if she was buried around here somewhere?"

The elderly gentleman turned to look at her then, a curious expression on his face. "You're the second person who's asked me that recently."

Candy felt a chill. "Why? Who else asked you?"

Mr. Gumm shrugged. "Some reporter woman called me about it yesterday. I don't know how she tracked me down—I was still over at my sister's place—but she found me. Though I told her the same thing I'll tell you—I just don't know. Never heard what happened. That young dead woman just seemed to . . . disappear. . . ."

He turned his gaze back out toward High Field. "There was one thing I heard about her, though, back in those days. Can't quite remember where I heard it. Must have been from someone around town."

"And what did you hear about her, Mr. Gumm?" Candy asked quietly.

"Well, it's funny . . . but someone told me she was one of the island people."

TWENTY-NINE

Doc and the boys showed up at half past noon, just as a third TV truck—this one from a station in Manchester, New Hampshire—was heading out of the parking lot on its way home. They'd shot a live feed for the noontime newscast right from the pumpkin patch, and somehow Candy and Maggie had allowed themselves to be lassoed into it, talking live on the air for a minute or two. Artie got a call from a friend in Concord, who just happened to be watching the broadcast, and Doc and the boys hurried right over to the pumpkin patch.

"It all happened so fast," Candy told him, still sounding a little bewildered by the whole thing. "There we were, live on the air, before we knew what was happening."

"Candy did most of the talking," Maggie added, pointing at her friend. "All I told them was what I saw from the tractor's seat."

"The place has been crawling with reporters all morning," Candy said, "ever since word got out."

"We heard about it too," Doc said grimly. "I was out in the fields all morning and decided to run into town for lunch. Didn't know what was going on until Finn and the boys filled me in. All this talk about a pumpkin patch killer. Sure got the business folks around here—including me—worried about the town's reputation."

"They're plenty concerned over at the police station as well," Finn informed them.

"Have they said anything else about the investigation?" Candy asked. "Any suspects?"

Finn just shook his head. "Not that I've heard, no, though I'm sure they're looking into Sebastian's past and current acquaintances. My guess is it was someone he knew— someone who lured him here. But I haven't been able to confirm that. I've been trying, but whatever's going on, the police aren't saying."

"They're feeling the pressure," Artie surmised, "especially if this latest murder puts them in the national spotlight."

"And like Doc said, we don't need that kind of publicity," Bumpy added.

Candy tilted her head. "No, we sure don't." Her brow fell in thought. "So the quickest way to end this mystery is to solve it. Find the Pumpkin Patch Killer."

"That's right," Artie said, "and the sooner the better."

"Then maybe we can all get back to our regular lives," Bumpy added.

"I'm sure that's exactly what the police are trying to do—solve this thing," Doc said hopefully, watching his daughter, "so maybe we should leave it to them."

"Maybe we should, Dad," Candy said, still thinking, "but what if there's something they're missing? Something that no one else knows about?"

"And what would that be?"

"I don't know yet."

Finn gave her a stern look. "You investigating again?"

Candy turned to him. "Let's just say I'm following up on a hunch. It could lead nowhere."

"But it could lead *somewhere*," Doc said, "and that's what worries me."

"Look," Candy said, trying to keep the conversation light, "I just have to check something out—do a little research. And it might help us get to the bottom of all this. I promise I won't get into any trouble."

"But to quote someone who's near and dear to me, trouble seems to have a way of always finding *you*," Doc pointed out, with a wry smile.

"I know, Dad, but I can't help that. I can only do what I have to do." And leaving it at that for the time being, she turned toward Maggie. "I hate to ask, but can you cover for me for an hour or two?"

"Sure, boss!" Maggie saluted her. "No worries. Consider yourself covered."

"Thanks. You're a saint."

"Hmm, Saint Maggie," she mused. "It *does* have a ring to it, doesn't it?"

"Well, as long as you're handing out sainthoods, I guess we can help out around here for a few hours as well," Doc said. "Especially since you seem set on doing whatever it is you're doing. But remember, you promised—don't go getting yourself into trouble."

Now it was Candy's turn to give him a half smile. "Dad, you know I'd never do that."

She glanced at her watch. Twelve thirty-five. She walked to the farm stand, grabbed her tote bag from its hiding spot behind the front counter, and flung it over her shoulder. By the time she turned back around, Wanda Boyle's minibus was trundling up the unpaved road toward the parking lot.

She turned lastly to Finn. "You'll let me know if you hear anything else from the police department, right?"

Finn nodded gruffly. "The moment I catch wind of something new, I'll let you know."

She nodded gratefully. "Thanks. Now if you'll excuse me," she said to her friends as she started off across the field, "I have a bus to catch."

THIRTY

She headed to her Jeep first and grabbed the printout of the *Herald*'s front page that Maggie had left laying on the passenger seat. She glanced back over it as she crossed the parking lot.

By the time she reached the bus, all the passengers had disembarked and were headed off across the field or meandering over toward the farm stand. Wanda was the last one down the step and out through the folding door.

She'd passed on the retro-tourist-guide outfit today and instead looked like a zookeeper, in khakis, a wide black belt, and an Aussie slouch hat with a leather chin strap, one side turned up against the crown. She saw Candy coming, crossed her arms, and waited.

"Morning, Wanda," Candy said as she approached.

"Morning, Candy." There was more than a touch of suspicion in her tone.

Candy stopped a few feet away, cleared her throat, and

continued. "I wonder if you'd mind if I asked you a few questions?"

"Depends on what you're asking."

Candy held up the printout. "I read the quote you gave to that reporter from Boston. The one where you said you thought there should be a wider investigation. I'm just wondering what you meant by that?"

"You know *exactly* what it meant."

Candy scrunched up her face. "And what would that be?"

Wanda frowned and waved a hand out toward High Field. "All these murders that have been going on. Something's not right."

"In what way?"

Wanda gave her an annoyed look, glanced around quickly to make sure they were alone, and lowered her voice. "You know what I mean. That article was right. We're becoming the murder capital of Maine. There's something going on—and I'm keeping my eye out for anything strange."

"Is that why you're running these tours of yours? Keeping an eye out?"

"Something like that," Wanda said, nodding her head a little.

"You've done a lot of research for your tour, haven't you?"

Again, a look of suspicion flicked across Wanda's gaze. "I did some reading and some day trips around the area, sure. Why do you ask?"

Candy slid the printout of the *Herald*'s front page into her tote and pulled out the black-and-white photo of Emma's grave. "Have you visited the cemeteries in the area?"

"Of course. I've researched them all."

Candy held up the photo so Wanda would see it. "Have any idea where this particular tombstone might be?"

Wanda glanced suspiciously at Candy before looking down at the photo. She leaned forward a little and focused in on it, finally reaching out for it, taking it in fingers with red-painted nails. She studied it for several moments before pointing at a spot on the photo with a pinky. "What's it say down here?"

She was pointing to the lower area of the tombstone. "I don't know. It's too blurred to read."

She looked up at Candy, handing the photo back to her. "Emma?"

"That's right." Candy slid the photo into the tote bag.

"Who's she?"

Candy wasn't quite ready to answer. Instead, returning to the original subject, she asked, "So, have you seen the tombstone?"

Wanda was silent for several long moments. "What if I have?"

"You mean you have?" Candy's voice rose in excitement.

But her enthusiasm disappeared the next moment as Wanda gave her a smirk. "No, I didn't say 'I have.' I said, 'What *if* I have?'"

"So you haven't found it?"

"I'm not saying I have and I'm not saying I haven't."

Candy sighed. "Then what *are* you saying?"

"I'm saying I might have seen it. I'm not sure. I'd have to check it out."

Again, Candy's hope grew. "Where do you *think* you saw it?"

"There's only one place it could be." Wanda tilted her head toward the bus. "Buy a ticket and I'll show you."

Candy nodded. She'd planned on taking Wanda's tour anyway. "Okay, so how much is it?"

"For you, ten bucks."

"Ten bucks! But what about the discount you promised?"

Wanda gave her a vengeful smile. "Lady, that *is* with the discount."

THIRTY-ONE

The passengers were soon back on the bus, and Wanda drove off to the next stop, talking as she went. "As you may have noticed, we're a little ahead of schedule," she told her riders over the bus's PA system, using a surprisingly pleasant and professional-sounding tone. "So as an added bonus, before we head to our final stop on the tour, I thought it might be fun to take a brief detour to one of Cape Willington's hidden cemeteries. Who's up for that?"

There was some scattered applause and a few ragged cheers around the bus, prompting Wanda to continue. "Now this particular cemetery we're headed to is located a few miles outside of town, off a little-known back road, among the ruins of an old settlement that existed there back in the eighteen hundreds."

As she talked, Wanda spun the steering wheel, and they turned left from the dirt farm lane onto the paved road, heading northwest, away from town.

"Not many people know about it, but it was called Notch

Town, because as you'll see, it sits near a notch between two low hills separated by a stream. On an interesting side note, the fall color won't be quite as wonderful in that area as it was a week or two ago, the last time I was up there, but it should still be a beautiful spot."

As they drove farther out of town, turning onto one of the narrow back roads that wound up through the cape, she continued, "This place we're about to visit is mentioned in only one or two old histories of the town, which I found on a back shelf at the Cape Willington Historical Society while I was conducting research for an educational project with my son. We love doing historical research together. He's such a smart kid, and it's such a wonderful way for a mother and son to bond."

She went on to explain how she had found the old histories wedged behind several books on a back shelf, misplaced and forgotten years earlier. "I'm afraid I have to report that this sort of thing has happened several times up in the archives at the Keeper's Quarters," she told her passengers. "We're still in the process of getting everything organized. But because I've been digging around so much, I've made a number of interesting discoveries, which you can always read about by visiting my community blog, the *Cape Crusader*," she added, giving herself a plug. "It's your best source for local news and events."

Sitting near the back of the bus, Candy knew some parts of Wanda's speech were intended as digs at her, but she let them pass. The idea of finally tracking down Emma's grave made her temporarily immune to minor slings and arrows.

But in the end, the whole side trip turned out to be just another wild-goose chase, as the cemetery in question—a small plot of land surrounded by a rusted vine-covered iron fence, containing no more than a dozen gravestones in the midst of a few worn-down foundations—was not the one she sought.

Wanda parked nearby and gave the passengers a few

pointers before turning them loose to look around. She and Candy found a gate into the cemetery, and Wanda pointed to a tombstone in the corner. "If it's any one of them, it'll be that one."

It was certainly the right size and shape, with an arched top, and it looked to be even the right color—a dark smoky gray (though it was difficult to be certain of the tombstone's color in the black-and-white photo). "I remembered seeing it on an exploratory trip out here a few weeks ago," Wanda told her, "but I don't recall the name on it."

The engraved name, as it turned out, read, ALBERT TILSBURY, B. 1857, D. 1925. BELOVED BY FAMILY AND FRIENDS.

Candy turned away, disappointed. "It's not the one."

"Then there's nowhere else it can be," Wanda told her, "at least not that I've seen. And I've been to every known cemetery on the cape. If it's not that tombstone in the corner there, then I haven't seen it, because no place else looks like that graveyard in the photo you showed me. Which leads me to think it's not around here. You're looking in the wrong place."

You're looking in the wrong place.

Those words echoed in Candy's mind as they drove back toward town. Along the way, she stared out the window, lost in her thoughts, watching the late October scenery slide past her in all its fading glory.

If Emma's not buried in Cape Willington, then where is she?

The answer, Candy thought dismally as the minibus pulled up in front of Sapphire Vine's house on Gleason Street, was a simple yet discouraging one:

The tombstone could be anywhere. Anywhere else in the state.

Or anywhere else in the country.

She was following a dead end.

Wanda parked along the curb and, out of respect for the neighbors, didn't let the passengers roam around at this stop.

But she told the story of how Sapphire Vine, a former community columnist for the local newspaper and a onetime reigning Blueberry Queen, had been murdered in the front living room of her home, struck down in fury by an assailant wielding a red-handled hammer.

Something about the story struck a nerve in Candy, and she rose suddenly from her seat, grabbed her tote bag, and made her way up the aisle, excusing herself to the passengers she bumped along the way. At the front, Wanda scowled and waved her back. "No passengers off at this stop. You'll have to return to your seat."

"Wanda, I'm getting off. Open the door."

"The tour's not over."

"It is for me."

They locked gazes for a few moments, but Wanda finally relented, after she realized that all the passengers were staring at them. "Oh, all right," she said reluctantly, flipping the handle that opened the folding door. "But no reentry! Once you're off, you're off."

"Fair enough," Candy said, and with a good-bye nod of her head, she walked down the step and around the back of the bus. Wanda closed the door with a quick slap behind her.

A few moments later, as Candy walked up onto the porch of Sapphire Vine's old house, the minibus drove off with a snort of sound.

Candy waited until it was around the corner and out of sight before she made her way down off the porch and around to the back of the house. When Sapphire was alive and living here, she always left a key outside, hidden on top of one of the rear window frames. A few years ago, Candy and Maggie had used that key to "break in" to Sapphire's house to help solve the mystery of her death. They'd put it back when they'd locked the place up, and as far as Candy knew, no one had disturbed it since.

So she wasn't surprised to find it still there.

Maggie had a key to the place, of course, but she was out

at the pumpkin patch, and Candy had decided on an impulse, while listening to Wanda tell Sapphire's story, that the clues she sought *had* to be here, hidden somewhere within the house that had once belonged to the former Blueberry Queen.

She resolved to search it from top to bottom until she found what she sought.

After unlocking the back door and replacing the key, she dropped her tote bag on the kitchen table and glanced at her watch. It was a little past one in the afternoon. She figured she'd take a couple of hours and dig around, and then give Maggie a call, asking her to swing by in the Jeep to pick her up.

She started back at the very top of the house, in the secret hideaway Sapphire had established for herself beneath the home's peaked roof, and retraced the steps she and Maggie had made two days earlier, searching back through all the boxes, shelves, drawers, cubbies, files, and anywhere else she could think to look for the missing diary. She double-checked each book, flipping through its pages to make sure Sapphire hadn't cut out a hiding spot inside one of them.

She also paid attention to the book titles, looking for any clues there. She found a lot of romances and mysteries, in both hardback and paperback, as well as a decent collection of historical novels by popular authors.

Most of the nonfiction consisted of biographies of celebrities and royalty. But, Candy noticed, Sapphire also had a number of books on local travel and history, including several guides to hiking and biking trails.

A bookmark was sticking out of one of them, a guide to Maine's islands. Candy flipped it open to the bookmarked page. It was a section on the Cranberry Isles, a group of small islands, including Grand Cranberry, Little Cranberry, and several others off the coast of Mount Desert Island. A black-and-white photo on the bookmarked page showed one of the ferry boats that regularly shuttled passengers between the islands and the mainland.

Mr. Gumm's statement earlier in the day floated through her mind: *Someone told me she was one of the island people.*

Island people.

Could these be the islands he'd been talking about?

She closed the book, set it aside, and continued her search.

Working her way down to the second floor, she dug through closets and searched in drawers, all the way to the back ends. She even took a few drawers completely out and flipped them over, checking to see if Sapphire might have taped the diary to the bottom of one. But she found nothing.

She searched under mattresses and in coat pockets and even tapped the floorboards in several places, checking for a possible hiding spot. She emptied out boxes and went through the contents item by item. An hour passed. Another. But she didn't find what she was looking for. So she went down one more level, to the first floor, where she stood in the living room, surveying it.

This was where Sapphire had reached the end of her life, in the center of this room. Candy and Maggie still tended to avoid it as much as possible. At one time there'd been a masked-tape X on the floor where Sapphire's body had fallen, but it had been removed, and the floor scrubbed, years ago. Sapphire's rust-colored mission-style furniture set remained, but the bookshelf had been cleaned out, now holding only bric-a-brac.

They'd sold the old upright piano, and many other items, and given even more away, though they'd held on to many of Sapphire's more personal belongings, just in case—those were the items they'd boxed away.

Candy made a cursory search, but they'd been through this room fairly extensively in the past months and years. If there had been anything that resembled a diary here, Candy or Maggie would have remembered it.

It was close to three thirty by the time she put on a kettle of water to heat and pulled a mug out of the cupboard for tea. She turned to her tote bag then and removed the files on the Pruitts and Hobbins, which she'd brought with her. She decided to finish going through them first before she gave up for the day.

Fifteen minutes later, she gave Maggie a call. "You have to come right over. I think I've found something."

THIRTY-TWO

She laid out the black-and-white photographs on the kitchen table before them. "Two photos," Candy said, "taken at different times. Both showing the same tombstone. And found in two different files."

Maggie was munching on a bag of trail mix she'd brought with her. "Which files?"

"This one," Candy said, pointing to the first photo she'd found, "was in a file labeled *Emma*, which I found in the cabinet in my office at the newspaper."

"Right, the bottom drawer labeled sv," Maggie said, and raised an eyebrow. "The one you swore you'd never go into again."

"I changed my mind after I saw a similarly labeled file on the front seat of Sebastian's car the morning after he was murdered. I figured this was an emergency, and made an exception. Anyway, *this* one," she continued, pointing to the second photo, "I found in a file labeled *Hobbins*."

"And did that file come from the same place as the other one?"

"Same place."

"So Sapphire put those two photos in those two files."

"Correcto-mundo."

"Why'd she do that?"

"That's exactly what I asked myself," Candy said. "Obviously Sapphire wanted to remind herself of something she'd discovered—a link between Emma and Hobbins."

Maggie looked uncertain. "Um, obviously."

"But what about the Pruitts?" Candy continued, thinking out loud. "If Hobbins had something to do with Emma's death—and I'm assuming it was her body that was found in the pumpkin patch twenty years ago—were the Pruitts also involved? And if so, how?"

"I don't know," Maggie said, thoughtfully chewing a few nuts and raisins. "You're the detective. You tell me."

"I don't know either," Candy admitted, "but I think Abigail's diary is linked to all this, and the missing volume of Pruitt history as well. Exactly how all those pieces fit together, I haven't figured out yet. But I'm working on it."

As if demonstrating that very fact, she leaned across the table so she could get a better look at the two photos.

They were remarkably similar, though the second photo—the one she'd found at the very back of the file labeled *Hobbins*—was taken from a little farther away. Unfortunately, that meant the writing on the tombstone itself was still indecipherable, except for the name *Emma* engraved at the top. But it also meant a wider shot, so Candy could see a building in it now—at least a small part of one, a stone structure, perhaps a house, with a slate roof and white window frames.

And a small piece of ocean in the distance.

"It's near the coast," Candy said, leaning even closer to the photo, wishing she had a magnifying glass, "so at least that narrows down our search a little."

"Maine has about two hundred fifty miles of coastline, as the crow flies," Maggie said, squinting at the ceiling as if recalling the statistics from memory, "but around thirty-five hundred miles of actual shoreline, if you count all the bays and inlets and capes and such."

When Candy gave her a questioning look, Maggie shrugged. "I just read it in a magazine article a few days ago."

"Thanks for sharing," Candy said, looking back down at the photo.

"Well, we don't have to search all thirty-five hundred miles," Maggie said. "I mean, we don't have to search the heavily settled areas, like Kennebunkport or Old Orchard Beach or Portland. So that rules out a few dozen miles."

"You're not helping," Candy said, and she lifted the photo, holding it up and angling it toward the light, so she could get a better look at it. "It's definitely a rocky coastline—but that doesn't help narrow it down much either, does it? I suppose I could jump on the Internet and do a quick search for coastal cemeteries. It might give me a few ideas."

"What's that?" Maggie asked, pointing with her pinkie to the back of the photo.

"What's what?" Candy flipped it around.

"That smudge up there in the corner—looks like some sort of scribbling."

"Where?" Candy realized that, in her haste upon discovering the photo in the file, she had neglected to turn it over and look at the back of it.

"There." Maggie pointed again, jabbing her finger.

Candy squinted. She saw the spot on the back of the photo now, and studied it for a few moments. "It *is* writing. It's just faint."

"What's it say?" Maggie asked, leaning in closer.

"I don't know, I think"—her mouth opened slightly as she continued to try to decipher the writing—"I think it says, *sked in pru file*."

"What in where?"

"Sked in pru file," Candy repeated, her brow furrowing. "That doesn't make any sense, does it?"

"What's a sked?" Maggie asked.

"What's a pru?" Candy countered.

But a moment later it dawned on her. "Schedule," she said. "Sapphire must have written that message to herself! And she's talking about a schedule!"

The rest of it came to her the next instant. "In the Pruitt folder." She looked over at her friend, amazed. "*Schedule in Pruitt file*. You know what this means?"

"No," Maggie asked. "What?"

"It means you've found another clue!"

"I did!" Maggie said excitedly, but her jubilant expression changed a moment later. "But what does it mean?"

"Exactly what it says. I think I remember seeing something that matches that description." She grabbed the Pruitt folder, flipped open the cover, and starting digging through it. "I saw it a little while ago when I was going through it, but I mistook it."

She found what she was looking for, a torn-out page from a magazine. "It's an article about the Pruitt Opera House— one of their plays a few years ago," Candy said, pulling the page out from the file. "But look."

She turned the page over. "I glanced at it but it never registered with me." Candy pointed to a half-page ad on the other side.

"What is it?" Maggie asked, focusing her gaze on it.

"An ad for the Cranberry Isles ferry.

"The Cranberry Isles?"

"Don't you see? That's it! That's the answer!"

"The answer to what?" Maggie asked.

In response, Candy flipped the black-and-white photo around again and jabbed at it with her finger. "The location of Emma's tombstone."

THIRTY-THREE

It all made sense now, though Maggie looked at her quizzically as Candy dashed out of the kitchen and up the stairs to the attic hideaway. A few minutes later, huffing a little, she returned with a book in her hand.

"I found this earlier when I was going through some of Sapphire's things upstairs," Candy said as she walked back into the kitchen. "It's a guide to Maine's islands. Sapphire had a page bookmarked—a description of the Cranberry Isles. She actually had this all figured out. She knew that Emma was one of the island people, just like Mr. Gumm told me this morning. That's where Emma's from. One of the Cranberry Isles. She was one of the island people. And that's where she must be buried. On an island."

"Yes, but which one?" Maggie asked as she looked back at the photos, her gaze zeroing in on them. "How many of them are there in that group? Five or six?"

"I don't know, something like that." Candy studied the photos along with her friend for several moments, her gaze shifting back and forth, searching both for any clue. But the first photo showed only the tombstone and a small section of the cemetery—nothing of the building or the surrounding landscape—and the other showed only a small portion of the stone building and a glimpse of the ocean through the trees.

"Can't tell from those." She laid the book out on the table beside the photos, open to the spread Sapphire had bookmarked. Then she started paging forward and backward through the book, searching for anything that caught her eye.

And she found it fairly quickly. "Here it is," Candy said, her finger skimming halfway down one of the pages. Sapphire had bracketed a paragraph in pencil. Candy read it quickly. "It talks about Wren Island. Is that one of the Cranberries?"

Maggie picked up the ferry ad, which included a small map of the isles. "Yup, here it is." She pointed at the smallest of the islands, angling the map toward Candy so she could see it.

The two largest islands—Grand Cranberry and Islesford, also known as Little Cranberry—were on the southern side of the small group of islands, while several others, including Bear and Wren, were to the north, closer to the southern tip of Mount Desert Island.

Candy took the ad from Maggie and studied it. The Cranberry Isles were served by both a mail boat, which set out several times a day from Northeast Harbor, and by the Cranberry Cove Ferry, which set out daily from Southwest Harbor. The mail boat from Northwest Harbor was probably closer to them, Candy figured. Since it was off-season, there were fewer trips per day. Other than an early-morning trip, the mail boat set out for the isles at eleven A.M. and at two and four thirty in the afternoon.

"How far are we from Northeast Harbor on Mount Desert Island?" Candy wondered out loud.

Maggie shrugged. "You have to go up to Ellsworth first, and then south. Maybe an hour or so?"

Candy checked her watch. It was nearly four o'clock. There was no way she'd make the last ferry today. "It'll have to be the eleven A.M. trip tomorrow then." She looked over at her friend. "Want to go on a boat ride?"

In response, Maggie held up her hand and waved it. "Thanks, but no. Like I said a while ago, me and the ocean don't get along well. Gives me the heaves. But you go—and have a good time. I'll keep an eye on the pumpkin patch for you."

Candy nodded and returned her attention to the photos. "It shouldn't be too hard to find a cemetery on an island that small. How many can there be?"

"Maybe the captain would know," Maggie said, waving toward the photographs, "if you show him those."

Candy nodded and sighed. "I just hope this isn't another wild-goose chase, because I'd sure like to figure out what's going on. But whatever happens, tomorrow will certainly be an interesting day."

THIRTY-FOUR

Finn called the following morning at eight, waking her. "Got some news," he said without introduction.

Groggy-eyed and dry-mouthed, Candy inelegantly swiped a hand across her face. She and Maggie had downed a bottle of wine with their dinner of spaghetti, salad, and fresh-baked garlic bread the night before as they'd discussed the events of the day, and Ben had called her, and then Tristan had called, and she'd fallen into bed later than she'd planned.

She pressed the phone to her ear, still under the covers. "Finn? What is it?"

He hesitated, uncertain. "Are you sure you're awake? I thought farmers got up early."

"I'm up, I'm up," she said, throwing aside the covers and swinging her legs over the side of the bed. The floor was cold. Her toes searched for her slippers. "I have to get moving anyway. What's up?"

Reassured, he plunged ahead. "Well, remember that file

you asked me about a couple of days ago? The one you said you saw on the front seat of Sebastian's car?"

"Yeah, I remember." If she hadn't been fully awake before, she was instantly alert now. "What have you heard about it?"

"Well, according to my source, the police investigators have taken a look at it, but all they found inside was a bunch of documents—paperwork for some woman named Emma Smith. Most of it dated back in the early nineties. It listed her home address as some place in Lewiston—an orphanage run by the Sisters of Charity—nuns. I wrote down the name of it somewhere if you want it. Anyway, most of the paperwork consisted of files from a mental institution in Portland. It appears this Emma person was a resident there. The local authorities are checking into it. Just thought I'd let you know."

"A resident in a mental institution? Why would Sebastian be interested in that?"

"Good question."

And then, in an instant, something clicked in Candy's brain, as a piece of the puzzle dropped into place.

Sapphire Vine.

Hadn't Sapphire been in a mental institution in Portland? When had that been?

"Finn, can you give me the exact dates on that paperwork. I want to check something."

"You think there's a connection to the murder?"

"I don't know," Candy said. "It's just a hunch."

"You get those too?"

"All the time," Candy admitted.

He told her he'd call her back as soon as he had the information, and she dashed off to grab her computer.

She logged on remotely to the newspaper's server, which gave access to back issues, as well as her own password-protected personal folders and files, stored on the server's hard drive. After conducting a global search, she found what she was looking for.

Sapphire Vine's obituary.

Candy had written it herself for the newspaper, a week after Sapphire's passing, but she couldn't remember exactly what she'd written, so she scanned the final version of the obituary first. Almost at once she knew that the specific information she sought was not there, since she'd avoided writing about certain aspects of Sapphire's life—certain aspects that even now were unknown by the general public, due to Sapphire's dark past. But she'd kept her notes for the obituary in a separate document in the same folder, and searched that next.

She finally found what she wanted.

About two-thirds of the way down through her notes were the dates that Sapphire Vine, as a young woman, had spent in an institution in Portland.

This information had first come to her from Cameron Zimmerman, in the days after Sapphire's murder. During a tense encounter at a cabin by the sea, he had filled them in on this particular part of Sapphire's background—unknown to any of them except Cameron until that moment. Days later, after they'd unmasked Sapphire's killer, Candy had taken it upon herself to follow up on Sapphire's past, contacting the institution in Portland and gathering the information, which she had dutifully recorded—and then filed away.

And it was still there: Sapphire had been in the institution in Portland from the summer to the late fall of 1991.

A few minutes later, when Finn texted her, she had a match: *Dates of Emma's stay at the mental institution: April '91–Jan '92*, read his message.

Bingo.

Sapphire Vine and the woman previously known only as Jane Doe, and now almost certain to be Emma Smith, had been in the same place at the same time in the early nineties.

Candy pondered what she'd learned as she jumped into the shower, got dressed, checked the chickens, and made herself a toasted bagel for breakfast.

Then she packed for her journey. She'd switched out her tote bag for a dark green daypack, and checked it carefully to make sure she had everything she needed, including a small digital camera, her recorder, notebooks, phone, and other gear. She threw in a banana, a sleeve of wheat crackers, and some hard cheese, in case she couldn't find a place to eat. She also dropped in a map she'd found in Doc's office, hidden among the clutter; it gave her a fairly detailed look at the Maine coastline. And finally, she slid in a color print-out of Wren Island, which she'd studied from the air on Google maps. The resolution wasn't great, and the quality of her printer made it look even worse, but she could make out eight or ten houses on the island, and several docks. One or two of the buildings could have a cemetery attached—she'd have to check when she got there to make certain. It looked like there were no roads on the island because there were no cars—only footpaths for people and bicycles. She'd be walking, so she wore her sneakers, and took along a Windbreaker, hat, and gloves, since she knew it would be cooler out on the open water.

She left the house at nine thirty, first heading northward up the Coastal Loop to Route 1, then turning west to Ellsworth, and finally swinging south toward Mount Desert Island and Northeast Harbor, a thousand things on her mind.

THIRTY-FIVE

After loading up with passengers and freight, the mail boat left the Northeast Harbor dock at precisely eleven A.M., pushing off with a chug of engines, scattered calls and waves from those onshore and on the boat, and a few toots of the horn. Candy had to steady herself as the deck vibrated violently for a few moments, and she caught a whiff of gas fumes hanging in the air. Seagulls whirled hungrily overhead, and the swish and slaps of the waves grew more frenetic as the captain turned the boat about and pushed the throttle forward.

Candy plopped down on a bench seat that ran along the middle of the rear deck and watched the dock slide away behind them. The sky was overcast, and the brisk, damp air carried the smell of the sea. She put her face into it, enjoying the way it slipped around her cheeks and across her skin, tugging her hair out behind her.

It was a small mail boat, capable of carrying no more than a dozen passengers, not like the larger car-hauling ferries that crossed Lake Champlain in Vermont or toured the islands of Casco Bay off Portland. Before they'd left the dock, the captain had come around to collect the twenty-five-dollar round-trip fare, and Candy had asked him about stopping at Wren Island.

"That's privately owned," he'd told her, "although there are a few unrelated families living there. You know someone on the island?"

"I'm going to do research," Candy answered, "at the cemeteries." And she explained that she was a reporter from Cape Willington.

He gave her an appraising look and finally nodded. "It'll be our first stop then," he said. "I'll let you know when to jump off." And he started off toward the other passengers

"Will you be able to pick me up?" Candy called after him.

He stopped and turned back toward her. "Ayuh, but it'll be about three hours. That's how long it takes me to make the circuit, with stops."

"That's fine."

"No restaurants on the island," he added, "and no public bathrooms. Just so you know."

"How long 'til we get there?"

"Twenty minutes."

Once away from the harbor they headed almost due south, slipping through the short, narrow channel between forested banks that were golden brown in color before chugging into the cold blue waters of the Atlantic. The overcast day unleashed a few heavy droplets on them, and the wind whipped the sea into a mild chop, tossing up light spray that occasionally fanned at them. But the mail boat cut through it gleefully as the passengers settled in for the trip.

Candy eventually found a spot out of the weather, inside the small passenger cabin, at the end of a bench. She set her daypack beside her and stared out the opposite window. She loved being out on the ocean. The air smelled sharp and full, as if it had been infused by the sea, and she took several deep breaths as she studied the vistas around her. There was a fair amount of marine activity going on around the islands today—she saw lobster boats, personal motor craft, and several sailboats, plus a good-sized yacht headed north toward the sound. Cruise ships often came past here on their way from Portland to Bar Harbor, which was just up around the coastline to the northeast, before heading to points farther east—though she saw none of the larger ships today. And a catamaran made daily trips up along the coast to Nova Scotia, also with a stop at Bar Harbor.

As she took in the landscape, her mind drifted, and she found herself thinking about her conversations last night, as well as the one this morning with Finn, which provided a solid link between Sapphire Vine and the woman now known as Emma Smith.

On the drive down, she'd decided that *something* must have happened at the mental institution in Portland during the early nineties, when the two women had both been residents. More than likely Emma had told Sapphire a choice bit of news—possibly something about the Pruitts, which Sapphire tucked away in her devious brain.

But what had Emma told her? Why had Emma gone to Cape Willington in the first place? What had she been doing in that pumpkin patch when she died?

And what had Sapphire been after? Why steal Abigail's diary? And where had she hidden it?

It was possible, Candy thought, that it could be secreted away at the newspaper office, where Sapphire had worked before she died. Maybe it was stuck in some forgotten cubbyhole or ditched on a shelf in the back of a closet. Ben had cleaned out some of Sapphire's papers after her death, Candy recalled, and the police had taken some of her files as well, though they'd eventually been returned. Candy had been through much of it years ago. But could she have missed something—a lost file, a forgotten shoe box filled with Sapphire's mementoes, or a book passed on to a colleague but never returned?

She'd asked Ben about it, in a roundabout way, when he called the night before, but he seemed to barely register the question. "Possibly," he'd allowed only as a passing statement before he moved quickly to the topic that had been the point of his call. His interview on the West Coast had been delayed again—until late today, Tuesday, or possibly even until tomorrow morning. "I'm still not sure when I'm going to get out of here," he'd told her, sounding frustrated. "If we finish by ten P.M. I still might make it to the airport to catch the red-eye. If not, I won't be back until late Wednesday. But I promise I'll be there in time to wish you a happy birthday in person. . . ."

Her birthday. She hadn't quite forgotten about it—though in truth she'd kind of tried. *This is my last day in my thirties,* she realized ruefully as she looked around the cabin at the other passengers, *and here I am on a mail boat, headed out to a mysterious island with a bunch of strangers, chasing a murderer.*

Her gaze scanned the passengers. Most of them wore rain slickers or hooded sweatshirts against the uncertain day. Many of the men wore ball caps, and some of the women did as well. A few might be tourists, Candy thought, but most simply looked like working folk and islanders.

She had to admit that the sudden shift in the investigation was almost surreal in nature. Just yesterday afternoon she'd been searching for a tombstone in a forgotten cemetery with Wanda Boyle, and now here she was, headed out to a private island in an attempt to uncover the secrets of a woman she'd never known. In fact, so much had happened over the past few days, starting with the discovery of Sebastian's body, that she'd barely had time to think about it, to process it all.

Another dead body, she thought, and that made her feel

even more melancholy. She shook her head and let out a sigh.

Who shot Sebastian J. Quinn? And why?

And what was he *doing in that pumpkin patch?*

Something else bothered her, something Wanda had confirmed—a general feeling going on around town that *something* else was going on below the surface—something none of them had yet guessed. Was Wanda right? Were all these murders, or at least some of them, connected?

And if so, what was the connection?

After Candy thought about it a few moments, she knew at least one connection—everything, in one way or another, led back to the Pruitts.

The wealthy family seemed to have a link to just about every murder in town over the past few years. Twice now Candy had talked to Mrs. Pruitt on two different murder investigations. But there was still something she was missing—still an important piece of the puzzle she had yet to discover.

But what?

Tristan had called her around ten last night, just to check on her, he'd said, to make sure she was okay—and to make sure she was still going to the masquerade ball on Halloween night.

She'd almost backed out when he'd asked her about it, almost given her regrets and begged off. Better to sit at home alone on the night of her fortieth birthday, she thought, than to entangle herself in another possible relationship she wasn't sure she wanted.

But she hadn't been able to speak the words she'd been thinking, and she'd realized that, in truth, she found herself feeling a little hurt. No one had said much about her upcoming birthday, and the milestone that it was for her. Sure, Maggie and Doc had mentioned it in passing, but no one seemed to be paying it much mind.

Maybe, she thought, that's the way they thought she wanted it. Maybe that's what she was projecting.

But not to Tristan, who had waited patiently on the phone for her answer.

She knew inherently that if she tried to beg off, he'd somehow convince her to change her mind. He seemed to care about her, and sensed that she didn't *really* want to be alone. And why should she? Once she'd thought about it from a different angle, she realized that maybe a masquerade ball was the *perfect* way to spend her fortieth birthday.

At the very least, it would be memorable.

So she'd told him yes, she'd be there—though again, she found herself being asked out to a formal event with no idea in the world of what she was going to wear.

The last time this had happened, at the Moose Fest Ball back in January, she'd worn a little black dress Maggie had found for her. It had indeed looked beautiful on Candy, but due to an intentional mix-up, she'd wound up being mortified. Fortunately, everything had eventually worked out in the end. A week or two after the ball, Maggie had come clean and explained to the dress's owner what had happened. She'd also offered to make amends, but an alternative arrangement had been struck, and one day Maggie had presented the sleeveless Givenchy number to her best friend as a gift for all Candy had been through. "We both thought it looked better on you anyway," Maggie had told her friend, referring to the dress's previous owner. "She thought you should have it. It's yours to keep."

"But how did you arrange *that*?" Candy asked, truly surprised and grateful as she admired the dress again.

"I used my charm, of course." But that was all Maggie would say about it. The dress was still hanging in Candy's closet.

She couldn't wear it tomorrow night to the masquerade ball though. She'd have to come up with something else. A costume.

Maybe she'd ask Maggie for help again . . . if she dared.

They'd angled west out of the harbor, and after fifteen

minutes of traveling at a good clip over the open water, Candy could see the first island approaching up ahead, off the port side. The captain brought them around the headland and toward a small, protected cove on the west side, where a single pier stretched out from the rocky shore. The captain guided them toward it, spun the wheel, and laid the boat in neatly alongside the dock. A young deckhand hopped over to tie them off.

Grabbing her daypack, Candy walked out of the cabin and across the rear deck, where she waited. Once the boat had settled, the captain leaned out of the wheelhouse door and called to her, loud enough to be heard over the low chug of the engines. "Be out here on the dock at two fifteen this afternoon. If I don't see you I won't stop, but I'll look for you again on the last run of the day. That'd be around quarter to five. After that, you're on your own."

Candy nodded her understanding. She hesitated for a moment as she was about to step over the side onto the pier, but someone else beat her to it.

A craggy-faced woman, perhaps in her early seventies, wearing a long raincoat and carrying a green canvas bag filled with groceries and a few magazines and books, unapologetically angled in front of her, stepped expertly over the side, and started up the pier without saying a word. Candy had barely noticed she was aboard. The elderly woman walked briskly toward the rocky shore with a determined gait.

The young deckhand, a dark-haired boy of high school age, nodded after her. "Have a good afternoon, Mrs. Trotter."

He received no response.

Candy watched the woman curiously before adjusting the daypack on her shoulder. Then she, too, stepped over the side onto the dock.

With a touch to the brim of his ball cap, the deckhand loosened the lines, tossed them back aboard, and hopped over. The captain powered up the boat's engines again, and expertly guided the craft away, water churning up behind it.

A few moments later the boat was gone, and Candy was left standing on the dock, alone.

THIRTY-SIX

As she started toward the shore, she surveyed her surroundings. Ahead of her, a few old sheds with weathered gray-shingled sides cluttered on the hard-packed earth just beyond the end of the pier, but they all looked deserted and locked up. Lobster buoys had been tacked up on the sides of some of the buildings, though Candy sensed they were more for decoration than for an actual fishing operation. A dirt lane that started where the pier ended twisted off into the dense woods at the center of the island, and footpaths meandered away from the sheds to the left and right, along the coastline in both directions. The elderly woman who had disembarked with Candy had disappeared along the footpath to the left, following the rocky curve of the island until it cut through a thick stand of trees and shrubbery that crept down to a rocky point. Anything beyond that was lost in a hazy mist that hugged the north side of the island.

Candy turned back the other direction, scanning the tree- and rock-strewn shore that angled southeastward. She could see a few shingled cottages, aged by the elements, dotted around the edge of the island in that direction, but other than the gulls, she saw no signs of life—no one else out walking, no bikers, no one tending to boats, no one else like her visiting the island for the day, hiking its narrow paths and exploring its nooks and crannies.

It was as if she were entirely alone here, and she felt strangely out of place, even a little ill at ease. To make matters worse, the sky was lowering, the day growing more gray as visibility lessened with the encroaching mists.

Better check what you came here to check and get back on the mainland, she encouraged herself as she reached the end of the pier. She stopped for a few moments, surveying the path to her left, wondering what had become of the elderly woman she'd seen headed off in that direction. Next she turned to the right, running her gaze along the southward path again, until she let out a breath and continued straight ahead, following the dirt lane toward the center of the island.

She recalled the layout of the island in her head, and knew the first place she wanted to look for a cemetery was at the opposite end of the island, where a fairly large house stood—or, at least, that's the way it had looked to her on Google maps the night before.

After a few hundred feet, the foliage began to close in around her, and as she continued on, toward the island's center, the wind died out and the day grew eerily hushed. She was walking through woods made up of both deciduous and pine trees, and they seemed to insulate her from outside sounds. She could hear birds calling high in the branches above her, and occasionally a distant slosh as a strong wave pushed against a rocky shore somewhere nearby. But other than that, she could hear very little of the world beyond this forested patch on this small island—no human voices, no music, not even the sounds of motorboats out on the water.

The forest floor, she saw, was rich and dark, peppered

with swaths of decaying pine and spruce needles under a covering of fallen leaves, creating a carpet of dark browns and rusts, grays and yellows. Leaves lay scattered across the path as well, so thick in some places they reached her calves as she waded through them.

Farther in, the quietness intensified and became its own sound, a soft, underlying murmur, disturbed only by the crunch of her sneakers on the pebble- and leaf-strewn lane. And then another sound—gentle plops falling from the tops of the trees, down through the remaining leaves and denuded branches. One or two struck her face as she looked up.

Raindrops.

Up ahead, a rocky formation rose up from the ground, monolith-like, blocking her way, but the lane simply curved around it, and she followed. Once on the other side, she could see patches of blue through the trees, and the sound of the ocean became more constant.

The woods opened up again, and after another few dozen steps, she emerged from the forest to find herself at the edge of a grassy meadow, which sloped down to a rocky shoreline, providing her with a panoramic view across a wide expanse of the water, from the mainland on the left, with its whale-humped hills arcing away to the northeast, out to open water straight ahead, and off to the south, where she saw another island a short distance away.

She had reached the end of the lane and the far side of the island—in a less than ten-minute walk.

Unfortunately, it looked as if she couldn't go much farther in this direction, since between her and the shoreline, neatly bisecting the meadow, stood a seven-foot-tall wrought-iron fence, with an arched double gate directly in front of her, closed and blocking her path. The fence extended all the way to the left and right, deep into the trees and shrubbery, until it disappeared from view. Candy assumed it went all the way to the shoreline in either direction, cordoning off the island's eastern tip.

Beyond the fence, framed by a sparse grove of tall-trunked pines that dotted a flat piece of ground stretching right to land's end, stood a majestic house, a stone and chocolate-shingled affair with a steep, weathered roof, multiple stories, two gables, overhangs, and at one end, a three-story tower with windows all around at the very top—a sort of widow's walk, Candy imagined. *The views must be spectacular from up there,* she thought as she gazed at it. She also saw two stone chimneys, one at either end of the house, and part of a porch on the building's seaward side. And beyond the porch, a pier that led out to a platform twenty feet from the shore.

The house was fancifully designed, in a summer-cottage style that resembled something built in the late eighteen hundreds by a wealthy businessman as a retreat from the city. Or perhaps it was only a dozen years old. These days, it was hard to tell.

As she approached the iron gate, she looked to the left and saw several outbuildings inside the fence, tucked among the trees—one that looked like a garage or a large storage shed, and another possibly a guest cottage.

But there was another building farther back in the trees. After focusing in on it for a few moments, Candy decided it looked like a steep-roofed stone chapel.

And behind it, shadowed by the dense branches of the surrounding pines, she could see what looked like a stone wall.

Just like in the black-and-white photo.

Her heart quickened as she studied it, wondering. She'd reached the gate now, but she saw no lock, only an iron latch, which she tested with a finger. It seemed to move easily in its bracket. She lifted it all the way up, and much to her surprise, the gate swung open.

She hesitated. No doubt this was private property. She wondered if she should first announce herself at the house, just in case someone was in residence.

But like the rest of the island, the building looked deserted, its windows dark, with no lights on inside. No sign of even the slightest whiff of smoke from either of the two chimneys. No sounds or movements to indicate someone might be about.

Making up her mind quickly, she passed through the gate, deciding it would take her only a few moments to determine if this was the cemetery she sought. She'd be gone before anyone knew she was here.

Walking back along the property inside the fence, she started toward the chapel. It was small—probably with no more than a few benches inside, able to hold maybe a dozen or so parishioners. As she got closer, she saw that it had no steeple—only a simple cross above the white wooden door frame. The chapel's tall, narrow windows were dark as well, just like the main house's. The door was closed and presumably locked.

Candy didn't stop to check it. She walked around the side of the building, toward the stone wall she'd seen behind it, as if drawn by a magnet.

The wall stood about four feet high and enclosed a plot of land perhaps twenty-five feet square. Thick vegetation hugged the wall in places, while low branches of nearby pines shielded other parts of it from view.

When Candy reached the wall, she walked around one side, then another, until she found an opening with another iron gate. This one, too, was unlocked, and she went through.

It was indeed a cemetery—probably a family plot, she thought. She walked to the nearest gravestone, which was black and nearly waist high, and read the name. It was a Wren—Chester P., born 1815, died 1881. She checked another, and found another Wren buried there, this one a Martha, born in 1819 and died in 1849. She checked the others. They were mostly Wrens, with a few Butlers, Steeles, Sturlings, and Gilfords mixed in.

But there was one gravestone in particular that drew her

attention. It sat in a grassy area in a rear corner of the cemetery, nearly hidden behind larger, darker gravestones.

Candy recognized it the moment she saw it. She walked toward it almost in reverence, and stopped a few feet away.

"Hello, Emma," she said softly into the silence.

THIRTY-SEVEN

It looked exactly as it had in the photo she'd found in the files Sapphire Vine had kept. The name *EMMA* in capital letters across the top. No last name. No dates.

Candy's gaze dropped to the lower portion of the tombstone, where she'd seen other inscriptions that were too blurred to read in the photos. And now she knew why. Dirt had been throw up against the stone, and tendrils of ground-cover ivy clung to the lower area, obscuring some of the inscriptions and making them hazy in the images. Candy approached the tombstone, knelt before it, and brushed away some of the dirt while pushing aside the ivy. Finally she could make out what was written here.

There were actually three inscriptions—well, two inscriptions and an image.

In the lower-center portion of the tombstone, made up of several simple flowing lines, was the stylized outline of a bird—a wren, Candy imagined. She'd seen a similar image on some of the other tombstones in the cemetery. It must be a family symbol or icon.

Below that and off to the side, in the lower-right portion of the stone, a phrase in Latin was engraved, in capital letters using an archaic font: *SAPIENS QUI ASSIDUOS.*

Candy stared at it for several moments, wondering what it meant. Then her gaze shifted to the opposite side of the stone, where in the lower-left portion, another phrase in Latin was engraved, its letters dark and shadowed on this overcast day: *DEUS PASCIT CORVOS.*

There was nothing else carved into the stone—still no dates to tell her when the tombstone had been erected, when Emma had lived, died, or been buried.

But she could guess at least one of the dates.

More than likely, she thought, the woman who was buried here was the same one who had died in a pumpkin patch in Cape Willington twenty years ago, and been interred here shortly after.

The Jane Doe had been an island person, Mr. Gumm had told her, so that piece fit. Here was Emma buried on an island. It also meant the woman she'd previously thought of as Emma Smith, according to legal documents from the nineties, was more likely Emma Wren—or at least had some connection to the family after whom the island had been named. That much at least seemed apparent. Again, Emma was buried here, on Wren Island, in a private cemetery occupied primarily by deceased members of the Wren family, with a stylized bird engraved on the stone.

Candy mulled over what she'd just discovered, and linked it to other clues she'd found over the past few days—and the one she'd learned just this morning from Finn.

The institution in Portland. She surmised that Emma had met Sapphire Vine there sometime in the early nineties. At some point after that, perhaps only months later, Emma must have left the institution and shown up in Cape Willington, and had later died in the pumpkin patch. And then, Candy thought, turning and gazing out toward the sea, her death had been hushed up for some reason, and she'd been buried here, in a back corner of this largely forgotten family cemetery on a deserted island off the coast of Maine.

That much, at least, seemed to fit together.

That was part of the puzzle, but what was the rest?

Candy reached into her daypack, took out her phone, swiped her finger across the screen to unlock it, and checked the readout at the top of the display. As she'd suspected, there was no signal out here on the island.

She couldn't jump online to check the meanings of the Latin phrases, so instead she used her phone to take a few quick photos of the tombstone and the grave before she slipped it into her back pocket, switching it out for her regular camera. She snapped a dozen more images, including some close-ups of the inscriptions at the bottom of the stone. She also took out a notebook and pen and carefully wrote down the inscriptions, making sure she had the exact spellings, just in case. As soon as she was back on the mainland and could get a signal on her phone, she'd search for the phrases on the Internet and see if she could find out what they meant.

Once she'd finished, she replaced everything in her daypack, zipped it up, and swung the strap up on her shoulder. Then she walked around the back of Emma's tombstone and checked the stones nearby as well, but after a few minutes, she realized there was nothing else she could learn here.

She left the cemetery and walked to the main house.

If someone was around, she wanted to talk to them.

She knocked politely on the back door, waited, knocked again. When no one answered she walked around to the seaward side of the building, climbed up onto the porch, and knocked again at the front door.

Again, no answer.

It appeared she'd been right. The place was deserted. No one was home.

She thought for a few moments, and quickly decided on her next course of action.

Since she'd been on the island she'd seen only one other person.

It was time to find Mrs. Trotter.

Candy made her way back along the dirt lane, through the small woods and out the other side to the foot of the pier, where she turned right, following the footpath she'd seen the elderly woman take. The path hugged the shore for a short while before angling northeast and turning inland. It skirted a patch where the sea had carved its way into the land, creating a rock-strewn inlet, then swerved back to the shoreline again.

After four or five minutes of walking, Candy could see around the north side of the island. She spotted what looked like a small, steep-roofed cottage out near a point, half hidden among the mists and foliage. It was not nearly as large as the gated estate she'd found on the island's eastern end, but it had similar architecture on a smaller scale.

She could see no other buildings around, so this must be where Mrs. Trotter had been headed.

Candy approached casually, as if she were simply a tourist out for a walk. She didn't want to appear threatening or spook anyone. She started humming a pop song as she approached the house, just to make a little noise and perhaps alert the person inside that a visitor was nearby.

She walked up the path that led to the front door, knocked, and waited.

It took a few moments, but finally the door creaked open. A wizened old eye set in a thin face peered out. "Yes," said an uncertain voice.

"Hello, Mrs. Trotter? I . . . um . . . I heard the deckhand

on the mail boat call you that. I hope I'm not being too much of a bother." And in a genial manner, Candy introduced herself and explained who she was.

"I'm afraid we don't have any public bathrooms here," Mrs. Trotter said in an apologetic tone, apparently misunderstanding Candy's reason for knocking.

"No, I'm . . . I'm not really looking for a bathroom. I'm a reporter. From the *Cape Crier*. In Cape Willington. I'm . . . I'm researching a story about some of the local families and I have a question about the cemetery at the eastern end of the island. The one by the big gated estate? I wonder if you know anything about it, and if you'd be willing to answer a few questions for a story I'm writing?"

"A story?" The woman gave Candy a look up and down, her eyes showing sudden wariness. "Where did you say you were from?"

"Cape Willington. I'm wondering about that cemetery over by the little chapel. Inside the gated estate. Do you know which one I mean?"

"Yes."

Candy waited for her to say more, but when that didn't happen she plunged ahead. "There's a gravestone in the cemetery for a woman named Emma. There's no last name, and no dates for her birth and death. Would you happen to know anything about her?"

The elderly woman blinked rapidly several times, and her mouth seemed to physically twist, as if she were actually chewing on her words. She looked at Candy with no small amount of caution. "I'm not sure I can say much about that. It happened a while ago. I'm afraid I can't help you."

She started to close the door but Candy persisted. "Mrs. Trotter, please, this is important!" she blurted, realizing she had only seconds to explain what she was after before the door shut in her face, and deciding in an instant that blunt honesty was the best approach at this point. "I'm here because of a murder that took place in Cape Willington a few days ago. It's possible Emma was somehow linked to the victim. Maybe you've heard about him—he was a poet named Sebastian J. Quinn."

The door stopped moving, and for the longest time, the elderly woman studied Candy from the house's shadows, her face frozen, saying nothing. But finally she coughed very deep in her throat, backed away, and pulled the door open wider.

"So, you've traced her here, have you?"

"I have," Candy said simply.

The elderly woman's narrow shoulders sagged. "I was beginning to think—to hope—she'd been forgotten by now. We've had a few visitors over the years asking about her, you know, but they always went out to the big house, where no one has lived for years. No one's ever stopped here before—I'm too far off the main path, I guess. But I thought sooner or later someone might come knocking at my door. And here you are." She turned and started off into the house. "You might as well come in," she said over her shoulder. "I'll put on some tea."

They sat in the kitchen, near a window that overlooked the sea to the north. "This is the caretaker's cottage," Mrs. Trotter told Candy, after she'd put on a kettle to boil. "My husband was the caretaker, of course—not me. His name was Ellis. Ellis J. Trotter. He was a wonderful man. He passed away a few years back."

"I'm sorry to hear that," Candy said. "What was he the caretaker of?"

"Why, Wren Estate, of course—the big place." The elderly woman waved off toward the far end of the island. "Where you saw the cemetery. By the way, that house was designed by John Patrick Mulroy. You've heard his name, haven't you?"

"I have, Mrs. Trotter," Candy said, with a faint smile. "I've been inside a few of the houses he designed in Cape Willington. A friend of mine lived in one of them for many years. She had an extensive collection of ketchup bottles. She showed me a hidden document drawer in a built-in cabinet Mulroy had designed. He was a contemporary of John Calvin Stevens."

"That's correct. You've done your homework." Mrs. Trotter gave her guest an appraising look. "And please, call me Nettie. I was born Annette, but everyone's just called me Nettie. No use for airs around here anymore. Anyway, Stevens designed a number of summer cottages on some of the nearby islands, and over on the mainland, of course. But the Wrens chose Mulroy to design that estate house you saw, and the outbuildings, including this cottage. The chapel dates back decades earlier though. It was the first building on the island, you know. Anyway, the family was up here quite a bit around the turn of the century and up through the thirties and forties, or so I've heard. But during the fifties, many of the older Wrens passed on, and they hadn't produced enough male heirs. It was quite a concern at the time. The line here on the island almost died out, but a few held on. One of the daughters, Cornelia, lived out at the estate for years. But she eventually passed on as well, and the place sat empty for many years, so Ellis—that's my husband, the caretaker—mostly looked after it himself, and I helped him take care of it. In time the Wrens lost some of the property around the west side of the island, but another daughter managed to keep control of the estate. No one's lived there much since Cornelia though. She rarely left the place, until she fell ill in her later years. She kept a ward out here with her for a while, you know—a young girl, during the late sixties and early seventies."

"A ward?" Candy repeated, curious at the woman's use of that specific word. "Was it Emma?"

Nettie nodded and rose as the kettle began to whistle. Candy waited as she pinched two tea bags from a glass jar on the counter, set out two mugs on the table, dropped a tea bag into each one, and began to fill the mugs with hot water.

"Was Emma a Wren?" Candy asked, breaking the silence, hoping to finally attach a real last name to the mysterious woman who had died in the pumpkin patch two decades earlier.

But Nettie shook her head. "No—not a Wren. Though I can see where you'd get that idea, considering where she's buried. But she was something else."

"Who was she then? Why is she buried in that cemetery? And why no last name on the tombstone?"

Again, there was silence for several moments as Nettie returned the kettle to the stove and settled again in her seat at the table. She appeared to be thinking carefully about what to say. Finally she pressed out a breath of air, as if she'd made up her mind—or perhaps it was a deep sigh of resignation, an indication of the realization that she could no longer keep the secrets she knew to herself.

"They tried to keep it hushed up," she said in a voice barely above a whisper, "and mostly it worked. That's why they brought her out here when they found her, and it's why she's buried here. They didn't want anybody else to know about her. But Ellis finally figured out what was going on, and he told me—though of course we never told anyone else. We kept it to ourselves all those years. The Wrens were good to us. They paid us well, and left us this piece of property, free and clear, so we couldn't say anything against them, could we?"

Candy leaned in closer to the elderly woman. "What did you find out? Who was Emma?"

In response, Nettie rose and walked to a cabinet that stood along one wall. She opened a lower drawer and pulled out an old photo album.

"Here, let me show you." She crossed the room, set down the photo album on the table in front of Candy, and opened it. "There are some photos taken at the estate in here, from back when the family was still around."

With short, sturdy fingers roughened by decades of manual labor, Nettie turned to a page near the back of the album. "Yes, here they are." She pointed to a small, square black-and-white photo, probably forty or fifty years old. "Here she is. That's Emma."

Candy looked first to Nettie, and then down at the photo album. She focused in on the image the elderly woman had indicated.

It showed a skinny girl of medium height, with pretty curled blonde hair, wearing a crisply pressed white linen dress with a flowered belt, white socks, and shiny black patent leather shoes, standing near the stone house on the point with the sea in the background. Flanking her were three people—a handsome, rugged-looking man in work clothes, probably in his early to mid-thirties, and two middle-aged women, of similar build and features. One wore a dark skirt and shawl while the other—the taller of the two—was in high-waisted khaki slacks, a navy blue jacket, and rubber-soled boat shoes. She also wore sunglasses and a patterned scarf over her dark hair, though her distinctive face was still recognizable.

"This is Ellis, a year or so after we came out here to the island," said Nettie, pointing to the man in the picture. "He was quite handsome, wasn't he? And so good with his hands."

She then tapped at the image of the taller woman who stood next to the skinny young girl. "I don't suppose you know who this is?"

Candy did. It came to her in a rush.

It was the same woman whose portrait she'd seen hanging in the front hall at Pruitt Manor.

"That's Abigail Pruitt."

THIRTY-EIGHT

There was no mistaking it. In the photograph, Abigail's clothes were unadorned yet well made, and her accessories looked expensive. She had the same firm set of the mouth, the same long nose, the same high cheekbones and pointed chin.

The same stern, scary demeanor.

"But what was Abigail Pruitt doing out here on the island?" Candy asked, looking up at Nettie. "And what did she have to do with Emma?"

In response, the caretaker's wife sat back down in her chair, clasping her hands on her lap, remembering. In a soft, even tone, she said, "I remember it was late spring—May, I think. We cleaned the house for a week before she arrived. We didn't know who she was at first. We heard an important visitor was coming out to the estate for a visit. There was to be some sort of celebration. We heard it had something to do with Emma, but again, we didn't know exactly what. So we worked our fingers to the bone to make the place shine.

Ellis toiled on the yards until well after dark for several nights in a row to make sure the place looked nice. And on a Tuesday morning, our important visitor arrived in a private boat, spent most of her time in private talks with Cornelia, attended a brief party—a dreary, low-key affair, from what I've heard—and left on the boat that same afternoon, well before dinnertime. She was on the island for less than four hours, and seemed to barely notice all the work we'd done. In fact, she said practically nothing to us at all, and we were told not to speak to her unless she addressed us first. So we didn't. Mostly they kept us in the dark."

Nettie paused, her gaze flicking to her guest and then out the window. "We didn't know much about the island in those days. We'd only recently arrived ourselves. Ellis had been working as an electrician and maintenance man in Brunswick when he saw the ad in the local newspaper. We drove up to visit the place and fell in love with it. How could we not? We were just youngsters then, looking for a better life. I was still in my mid-twenties, and Ellis eight years older. Cornelia was the one who interviewed and hired us, and she's the one who paid us. She was a widow who lived out here much of the year, even during the winter months. Back in those days, when we first arrived, she had several servants with her over there at the estate, including two maids, but she told us she needed a maintenance man to help with the upkeep of the place and extra help inside as well, so she hired us both after carefully checking our references. It changed our lives. We had a place to live and a future. Ellis took care of the house and worked on the yards and gardens, and I helped clean the place and did the laundry. Cornelia also had a cook back then, so we didn't have to worry much about that. But everything changed when *she* came to live here."

A stab of Nettie's eyes, which then returned to the sea, indicated the photo of Emma.

"When was that?" Candy asked, looking back down at the faces in the image.

"Well, let's see. Ellis and I came here to the island in the spring of 1965—April, to be exact. I remember it was still very cold and raw out here on the island when we moved into the caretaker's cottage. And Emma arrived that fall."

At that point, Nettie paused as she considered her previous statements. But finally she nodded. "Yes, I'm sure that's right," she said, reassuring herself. "Emma was living at the estate for our first Christmas here, so she arrived later that same year."

"And you said everything changed after her arrival. How did it change?"

Nettie took a deep breath as she collected her thoughts. "Well, the atmosphere at the house changed. It became very secretive. There were lots of whispers in the hallways and behind closed doors. Within weeks of Emma's arrival, both maids were let go. Then they found a new cook who lived on the mainland, and only came out to the house during the day. Ellis and I were the only ones Cornelia kept on the permanent staff, probably because we didn't live at the big house like the other servants—we had a place of our own, here on the north side of the island, hidden out of sight. Cornelia took advantage of that to ensure her privacy. She changed our work schedules as well. She allowed us to work at the big house only at appointed hours. Ellis mostly worked out there in the mornings, for instance, and then in the afternoons he helped out at some of the other properties on the island, and for a while he even took some work on the mainland. And I worked at the estate only two days a week, usually in the mornings as well, helping with the laundry. Both of us dealt directly with Cornelia but we rarely saw the girl—Emma. She was kept hidden away in her room. She almost never came out. In the entire time she was here, over a period of several years, I probably saw her no more than a dozen times. I rarely spoke to her. Even when I did, it was only to exchange brief pleasantries. I never had a conversation with her."

Nettie pointed to the photo again. "That picture was taken about a year after we arrived, on the day Abigail came out on the boat. As I mentioned, it was a special occasion of some sort. Later, Ellis told me it had been a birthday party."

"For Emma?" Candy looked down at the photo again, studying the skinny girl in her crisply pressed white linen dress and shiny black shoes, with her hair neatly curled.

Emma's wearing a birthday dress, she realized.

She looked back up at Nettie, who nodded. "After we'd cleaned up the place for Abigail's visit, I helped Cornelia put up a few decorations around the place. I wasn't allowed at the party itself—they said it was a private affair—but the cook was there, and Ellis. He said he was asked to witness the signing of a document by Emma."

Candy's brow fell. "What sort of document?"

Nettie shrugged. "Ellis never found out. He said he wasn't allowed to see the whole thing—just the last page. He wasn't sure he should have signed it without reading it, but he told me later that he felt he didn't have much choice in the matter. He said it was a legal document of some sort, brought out by the woman we later learned was Abigail Pruitt. That's when they took the photo—after they'd signed the document. As I said, it was some sort of commemoration, we thought—or a documentation."

"But commemorating what?" Candy asked, still confused. "What was Abigail's connection to the whole thing?"

Nettie arched an eyebrow. "We asked ourselves the same question, but Ellis finally figured it out," she answered. "It was something Cornelia let slip at one point during the day—she said something to Ellis about her sister."

"Her sister?"

Suddenly it dawned on Candy, and she looked back down noticing the resemblance between the two adult women. "That's it, isn't it? Cornelia and Abigail were sisters!"

And it struck her then. Abigail's initials, which she'd seen on the stationery on her writing desk, were *A.W.P.*

Abigail Wren Pruitt.

"We believe so," Nettie said with a nod. "But as I've explained, we didn't know the whole story for many years, until after Cornelia passed away. But finally we were able to patch together at least some of it, from bits and pieces of conversations we heard while working around the house. As best we could determine, Emma had been living in an orphanage in Lewiston when they found her and brought her out to the estate."

"An orphanage?"

It fit exactly with what Finn had told her that morning. The paperwork found in the folder sitting on the front seat of Sebastian J. Quinn's car had dated back to the nineties, and gave the home address for a woman named Emma Smith as an orphanage in Lewiston, run by the Sisters of Charity.

They'd found Emma in an orphanage.

Candy looked up at Nettie again. "Who found her?" she pressed. "In the orphanage? Who found her there?"

The elderly woman thought about it a moment, but finally shook her head. "I don't know. As I said, they kept it all hushed up. Cornelia never spoke about it with us—she only told us what was needed around the house—and Emma certainly never said anything to us about her background. She was a very reserved girl, very shy, and lived under the ever-watchful eye of Cornelia. As I've said, she never left the property, and rarely left her room. It was as if she was imprisoned in the place. That's why we were only allowed to come' out to the estate at specific times, we soon came to realize. They wanted to control our access to Emma. They didn't want anyone else to speak to her, or to even know she was there."

"But why? Why were the sisters so secretive?"

Nettie pressed her thin lips together and again shook her head.

Candy took a sip of tea, thinking. There were so many questions twirling around her head, she didn't know what to ask next. Finally, she said, "So what happened to her? To Emma, I mean?"

Nettie pursed her lips, and her eyes became shadowed. "Cornelia had her first stroke in 1970. She was in the hospital and then the rehabilitation clinic for several months as she recuperated. In her absence, Abigail returned to the big house on occasion, and spent a few nights there, but mostly she stayed at her sister's bedside. When Cornelia finally returned to the island, she was never the same. She spent the last few years of her life in a nursing home. During that time, Abigail continued to check in at the big house from time to time, but Emma stayed out at the estate mostly on her own. Ellis still kept up the place and I still did the laundry, and the cook still came out during the day. But Emma stayed in her room. The place became like a ghost house. Most days, when I was there cleaning, there was not a sound inside that building other than my footsteps as I did my chores around the place."

"You didn't talk to her?" Candy asked.

Nettie shook her head. "She never came out of her room. I believe she did her best to avoid us. We used to leave her meals on a tray outside her door, and she would only open it after we were gone."

Candy shivered, thinking of what a lonely life that must have been, and what could the young girl have possibly done to condemn her to it? "How long did that go on?" she asked.

"For some time," Nettie admitted. "I felt so bad for that girl, but nothing I tried could get her to talk to us. Eventually Abigail hired a governess to watch over her—a very strict Catholic woman by the name of Mrs. Murphy. I think she might have been a nun once, or perhaps she still was one, though she never wore a habit. She did tend to favor dark colors though. For some reason she didn't like me much, I can tell you that. She followed me around as I worked, pointing out any spots I'd missed or chore I'd forgotten. But Ellis got along with her fairly well." She smiled wistfully. "Ellis got along well with just about everyone. He was just that type of person. Anyway, Mrs. Murphy kept Emma on an even tighter leash than before, if that was possible. I wasn't allowed upstairs at all, and for the most part, Ellis was kept out of the house as well. She was here for a year or so, until Cornelia passed on. And then, one day, shortly after that, Emma was gone too."

"What happened to her?" Candy was almost breathless.

Nettie looked out the window one last time, then rose to clear away the tea service. "No one knows," she said as she worked. "I heard that Abigail searched everywhere for her but couldn't find her. They read Cornelia's last will and testament, and Ellis and I learned that we'd been given this cottage. After Abigail passed on, lawyers took over the estate. We always thought it might have been left to Emma, but we never saw her again . . . until . . ."

"Until she was buried here," Candy finished for her.

The elderly woman nodded. "Even that was done in secret. They must have brought her body in at night, by boat. We didn't even know about it for a week or so, until one day Ellis was tending to the cemetery, and there it was—that gravestone with just her first name on it."

Candy filed all this information away, along with everything else she'd learned over the past few days. She had an even stronger feeling now that everything was connected, and that she was close to putting all the pieces of the puzzle together.

But there were still a few pieces missing.

She closed the photo album and sat staring at its cover for several moments, until she finally pushed it back across the table, thinking as Nettie finished cleaning off the table.

She was over at the kitchen sink when Candy turned to her and asked, "Who owns it now—the estate?"

Nettie stopped what she was doing and faced Candy, wiping her hands on a towel as she spoke. "I believe it's currently being held in some sort of a trust," she said, "though I couldn't say for sure. Every once in a while, someone in a suit stops by to check on the place, and occasionally a workman comes out and makes repairs. But no one's lived there in quite a while. I've heard there's talk they might sell the place, though that rumor's been going around for some time, and there's still no for-sale sign on the gate. So it sits out there on the point, deserted."

"Hmm." It struck Candy as odd that such a prime piece of property on this busy stretch of the coast should sit empty for so long. Surely there must be an heir somewhere who would want to get his or her hands on it—and whatever fortune went along with it.

So why was the place kept in limbo like that? Candy wondered. It seemed like such a waste.

Unless, she thought, there was a reason behind it.

Maybe the reason was simply to keep people away from the place.

But why?

Again, the only obvious answer was Emma.

On an impulse, Candy reached into her daypack and pulled out her notebook. She flipped back to her most recent entries: the texts of the inscriptions she'd seen on Emma's tombstone.

"There are two Latin phrases engraved on Emma's stone," Candy said to Nettie, and she laid her notebook flat on the table, angling it so the elderly woman could see what she'd written. Candy did her best to read the phrases correctly; she'd missed Latin in high school. "One says, *Deus pascit corvos* and the other reads, *sapiens qui assiduos*." She looked over at Nettie. "Do you have any idea what those phrases might mean?"

Nettie had walked back to the table, and now she looked down at the phrases in front of her, a melancholy smile on her face. "I never took Latin myself," she said, "but Ellis did. He was classically trained, despite his vocation. He had four years of Latin, so he told me what those passages meant."

"And what do they mean?" Candy asked.

"Well, let me see. I believe *Deus pascit corvos* translates to *God feeds the ravens*, and *sapiens qui assiduos* means *he is wise who is industrious*. Or something like that. I have the exact wording written down somewhere around here."

Candy's face twisted.

God feeds the ravens?

He is wise who is industrious?

They sounded like old, random sayings. "What do they mean?" she asked.

"Well, it was Ellis's idea that they were family mottoes. We never thought about it much more than that, until one day, about a year after Emma disappeared, we received a box in the mail. It was from her. When we opened it up, we were surprised to find some of her mementoes inside, including that photo I showed you, and a book or two. She wrote us only the briefest of notes, saying she had moved far away but wanted us to hold on to the items for her. She never explained why, and she never came back for them."

Candy was intrigued. "You say you found some books in the box? What kinds of books?"

"Well, that's the interesting thing," Nettie answered, suddenly animated. "One was a volume of Pruitt history, and on an inside page there's an image of the Pruitt family crest. You'll understand once you see it. Here, I'll show you."

Again, the elderly woman crossed the room, but this time she climbed a steep set of wooden stairs to the second floor, where Candy assumed the bedrooms were located. Candy could hear her moving around up there. Nettie was gone for several minutes before she came back down and into the kitchen.

"Here it is," she said, cradling a box perhaps two feet square. "I had to look for it. It was in the back of a closet. I almost thought I'd lost it there for a few minutes."

As she set the box down on the table, Candy rose from her seat. She watched as Nettie delicately opened the box's four flaps, folding them back one at a time.

As Nettie had said, inside were a girl's mementoes—a mirror and hairbrush, a small doll, ribbons and necklaces, as well as two old hardcover books and a few faded color photographs. The photos showed a young, pale woman with a painfully solemn expression, though in one of the images, in which she held an infant, she smiled wistfully. The photos were perhaps twenty or thirty years old, Candy guessed.

"That's Emma, I presume," she said, pointing to the young woman in the photos. With her pinky she indicated the infant. "And who's this?"

Nettie shrugged and shook her head. "We don't know."

Candy hesitated. "May I?" she asked, and when Nettie nodded, she reached inside the box and took out the photos. She studied them closely for a few moments, and then flipped each one over to check the back. But she found no writing, nothing to identify the date or the people in the images.

She placed the photos back in the box and retrieved the two hardcover books.

The smaller one was a well-read copy of *Walden* by Thoreau. Candy opened it gently to peer through the pages, and as she thumbed through, she found several small wildflowers pressed and dried between thin slips of colored paper.

Candy smiled. She'd done much the same thing when she'd been younger.

The other volume was larger. She hefted it in her hand. It had some weight to it.

"Now I wonder what this could be," she said.

She checked the spine, and then the title page.

It was, indeed, Volume XXIII of a larger collection with

the overall title, *A History of the Pruitt Family in Maine, 1789–1975.*

This particular volume encompassed the years 1940 to 1949.

It was the book stolen from the Pruitt Public Library in 1972.

"The family crest is near the front," Nettie told her, indicating with a wiggle of her finger for Candy to turn a few pages.

Candy nodded and complied.

And there it was, a two-color crest with a red shield at the center, showing a prancing lion, and above it, surrounded by filigree, was a steel helmet, as if from a suit of armor.

And in an elaborate ruffled banner across the bottom, in Old English script, was the phrase *DEUS PASCIT CORVOS.*

God feeds the ravens.

It was, Candy realized, the Pruitt family motto.

THIRTY-NINE

By two fifteen, Candy was out on the pier, watching the sea to the north. Five minutes later she was back on the mail boat heading home—though they were going the long way around, since the boat first had to make stops at Grand Cranberry Island and Islesford, also known as Little Cranberry, before heading back to Northeast Harbor.

Candy settled herself on a bench inside the cabin, as she'd done before. It was more crowded now than on the last trip, and she had to wedge herself in between a teenager and a fisherman. But most of the passengers disembarked at Grand Cranberry, and on the final leg back to the mainland, there were half as many people on board, so Candy had a chance to stretch out a little, and to finally take a look at her treasure.

She'd tucked away the volume of Pruitt history in her daypack. After she'd explained to Nettie that the book had been taken—perhaps stolen—from the Pruitt Public Library in the summer of '72, and that the rest of the volumes subsequently had been returned to Pruitt Manor, the elderly woman had placed it in her hands and insisted that she return it to its rightful place.

And that's exactly what Candy intended to do.

But first she planned to have a look through it, in an attempt to answer at least two questions that were buzzing around her brain.

First, why had Emma stolen the book from the library—what was in it that she sought?

And second, why had the Pruitt family motto been engraved into Emma's tombstone?

Was Emma a Pruitt? And if so, which of them was she descended from?

There were several scenarios Candy could think of right off the bat. For instance, Emma could have been Cornelia's child—or, more likely, Abigail's.

That, at least, would explain all the secrecy.

But if that were true, who had the father been? She guessed the second Latin phrase engraved on the tombstone—the one that read, when translated, *he is wise who is industrious*—might answer that particular question.

Was it another family motto? And if so, for whom?

There were any number of possibilities.

Candy could think of several herself.

Or perhaps she was all wrong about it. Perhaps Emma had simply been a long-lost Wren heir—a cousin or a distant relation.

But then why make a mystery of her burial? And why neglect to put the dates of her birth and death on the tombstone?

That was the real clue, Candy realized—the tombstone itself, and specifically the second engraving. Whatever it meant, she'd be able to get to the bottom of it once she got back on the mainland and had a signal on her smart phone, so she could search the Internet.

Until then, she was going to have a look through the book on Pruitt history.

As she'd discovered before, when she'd paged through a volume in the library out at Pruitt manor a few days ago, it was fairly dry stuff—names and dates, places and events that meant little to her: extensive biographies, long explanations of legal affairs and financial issues. . . .

She considered the dates—the 1940s.

Why had Emma been interested in that decade?

Candy sighed and flipped toward the back—and that's when she spotted the folded piece of paper inserted between two pages. It looked as if it had been torn from the bottom of a writing tablet—perhaps as a bookmark, Candy thought.

She lifted out the slip of paper and unfolded it.

There was a single sentence written on it, in a small, neat hand with an unsharpened pencil:

To find the key, search that which binds.

That was all it said.

Candy stared at the note, wondering what it meant, when a passenger walked past—a thick, hooded figure wearing a sweatshirt and sunglasses. He nipped the end of Candy's knee with his leg as he passed by, almost sending the book flying from her lap. He reached out to grab it, evidently to keep it from falling to the floor. But Candy was able to catch the book first and folded it into her arms.

"Sorry," he said in a low voice, his face turned away from her.

She wanted to say, "Hey, buddy, watch where you're going," but held herself back. No point in getting into an argument over something that had obviously been an accident.

"Don't worry about it," she told him.

"Sorry," he said again gruffly, with a deep cough, as he straightened and moved off, looking back only once.

She watched him as he walked out of the passenger cabin onto the stern deck, and then turned her attention back to the handwritten note.

To find the key, search that which binds.

Had Emma written it and slipped it between these pages? Or had it been there longer, from before Emma had taken the book? Perhaps it had been put there by another library patron. Perhaps it was simply what it looked like—a bookmark.

And perhaps not.

She still had the book open on her lap, to the place where the note had been inserted, and was about to start reading that page, when the boat's horn tooted. Looking up, she saw they were approaching Northeast Harbor. She folded the note back into the book and closed it, then slipped the volume snugly into her daypack and prepared to disembark.

It was almost four by the time they were docked again. The clouds over the mainland were dark and blowing quickly northeast along the coastline. For the most part the rain had held off, she thought absently as she walked to the parking lot and climbed into the Jeep, dropping the daypack into the passenger seat.

When she started the engine, she noticed she was low on gas and decided to fill the tank before she left Mount Desert Island to drive back home. She remembered seeing a gas station up the island road about ten minutes, in a little settlement called Somesville, so she headed in that direction.

Fifteen minutes later, she pulled up beside an empty pump, jumped out of the cabin, and dashed into the brick-sided convenience store to pay for the gas. It was rush hour on the island, especially with the last of the tourists headed back to their hotels or out for dinner, so she found herself standing in a long line.

As she waited, she glanced out the window toward the gas pumps.

Her brow fell, and she had to focus in on what she was seeing.

A strange person was lurking around the side of the Jeep.

What's he doing there? Candy thought, tensing.

He was looking in the side windows, moving toward the front of the vehicle.

With a quickening of her heart, she realized it was the same beefy guy in the hooded sweatshirt who had bumped her on the boat, almost knocking the book from her lap.

Before she could register what she was seeing, he'd opened the passenger-side front door, snatched the daypack out of the front seat, and dashed off toward the main road.

Candy's eyes widened as her instincts took over. "Hey!" she yelled. "Hey! That guy just stole my daypack!"

She ran out the front door in disbelief, only to see the hooded thief jump into a late-model sedan and tear out onto the main road headed north.

Without hesitation, Candy dashed out to the Jeep, fishing the keys out of her pocket as she ran. She slipped into the driver's seat, started up the engine, and roared after him.

FORTY

The back end swung out, tires spinning on the damp, leaf-strewn pavement as she mashed down on the gas pedal. The Jeep leapt out onto the two-lane road, its engine whining. She heard someone beep a horn behind her as she cut into the traffic but she didn't care. She could feel the heat rising in her face and her hands were clamped tightly on the steering wheel.

How dare the thief take her bag! she thought as she searched the twisty two-lane road ahead, which wound through forested land. There were several cars in a tight line before her, but none of them looked like the sedan she sought. She thought she might have spotted it farther ahead, but she couldn't be sure.

She gunned the Jeep and started passing cars one by one when she could, making sure she had adequate room as she leapfrogged forward, though once or twice she cut things a little too close. But she was upset. She wasn't about to let some thief make off with her bag.

As she drove, her mind assessed what exactly she had put in the daypack, and what exactly he might have been after. Perhaps he'd thought there was money in it, or other valuables. And, to Candy, it did contain her valuables—the tools of her trade, including her notebooks, camera, and digital recorder. Items that were valuable to her but to no one else. It's possible the thief could have been after any one of those items.

But, no.

She was almost certain he'd been after the book. The Pruitt history. He must have seen her paging through it on the boat and for some reason decided it was of some value. He'd tried to knock it off her lap. He must have been trying to take it from her then.

But now he had it, and with it, the note.

The note.

She didn't know if it was significant or not, but she hated to lose anything at this point. At least it was easy to memorize; she'd write it down in her notebook the moment she had a chance.

But then she shook her head. He'd taken her notebooks! And her camera, and recorder, and all her research and important papers, and everything she needed for work.

In a sudden moment of panic, she reached around and felt her back pocket. She couldn't remember where she'd put her phone. Was it in her pocket—or in the daypack?

But after a few moments of frantic searching, her fingers finally found the hard plastic outline of the phone, and she touched it reassuringly through the pocket's jean fabric.

At least the thief hadn't stolen everything.

And if she had her phone, then she also had photos of the tombstone, so she still had a record of the exact wording of the two inscriptions in Latin.

But why had the thief been interested in the book? She never had a good look at his face—she vaguely remembered that he'd looked like a younger person, perhaps in his thirties—but she hadn't noticed anything else about him . . . his eyes, the color of his hair . . . anything.

Because he'd been wearing the hood and sunglasses—as if he were trying to disguise himself, as if trying to blend into the crowd.

He was stalking me! she realized with a start.

That's why he'd been wearing that sweatshirt with the hood—to hide his true identity.

For some reason, that thought angered her again, and she stepped back down on the accelerator pedal as the indicator on the speedometer jumped forward. She came around a tight curve and saw a straight stretch of road, and there, far up ahead, where the road curved again to the right, she saw the sedan she was looking for.

She stood on the pedal as the engine's whining grew more shrill and the wind raced past her windows. She was clocking near seventy on this narrow island road. She'd surely get a ticket if she came across a patrol car right about now.

The sedan disappeared around the curve in the road, hidden again behind a thick screen of dull green spruce and pine, with a few rust-colored deciduous trees mixed in. She coaxed the Jeep a little faster, knowing she was pushing it to its limits—and knowing she couldn't sustain this pace for too long on this road.

Up ahead, a car pulled out of a side road, headed away from her in her own lane, and began to accelerate, but slowly. She considered passing the vehicle but another was coming toward her in the opposite lane, forcing her to back off on the accelerator pedal. She was approaching another settlement of perhaps a dozen or so buildings, and a crossroads, and she had to back off even more. And as she slowed, she could feel her resentment and frustration rising.

She wasn't going to catch him, whoever he was.

He had disappeared. And he'd taken her daypack—and the book—with him.

FORTY-ONE

Dusk was near as she drove back into Cape Willington—and mischief was in the air.

It was the night before Halloween, and jack-o'-lanterns were lit in the windows of homes all along the Coastal Loop. In some of the yards, children in costume played or romped about excitedly. It was clear to Candy, as she passed by, that some of the kids could barely contain themselves, and she could understand why. Halloween had an energy and mystery all its own among the holidays, and next to Christmas, was probably the most fun of all.

Candy herself had mixed feelings about the holiday, due in no small part to the fact that she'd been born on Halloween. Not being an ostentatious type of person, she'd never been much for dressing up, but having been born on the thirty-first, it had been expected of her. Many of her earlier birthdays had, in fact, been Halloween costume parties, and she'd often been expected to have the most stupendous costume of all. Many times she did, with her mother's help.

Holly Holliday had been born on a holiday as well—
Christmas—so she knew something about having a birthday
on a day of celebration. She'd done everything she could to
make sure her daughter's birthdays were always special and
individual.

So as Candy grew older, the parties had become more
low-key and personal, and since her mother had passed
away, she had lowered her birthday expectations even more,
since party planning was not one of her father's top skills,
and everyone else's Halloween plans usually took them in
different directions.

And, for the most part, that was fine with her.

Still, she was looking forward to the Pumpkin Bash celebration in town tomorrow, since at least there would be *some*
celebrating going on by *some* people, and maybe she could
experience that in *some* way vicariously, since she was sure
little had been planned for her.

Besides, she didn't have time to party. She had a mystery
to solve—and she still had a number of clues that needed
following up.

And now, suddenly, there was another layer—and another
theft of an old book.

What was so important about that old volume of Pruitt
history that made it worth stealing—twice?

Most of all, she was saddened that she'd let it slip right
through her hands—an important piece of the puzzle,
snatched away from her before she'd had a chance to really
study it, and all because she'd let her guard down for a few
seconds.

Now she wasn't quite sure what to do.

After finding the book at the caretaker's cottage on the
island, she'd planned to drive straight over to Pruitt Manor
and deliver it into Mrs. Pruitt's hands. But that plan changed
the moment the thief had opened the Jeep's passenger-side
door and made off with her daypack.

Should she still drive out to Pruitt Manor and explain

what had happened? Should she tell Mrs. Pruitt and Tristan about the note she'd found slipped inside, and ask them if they knew what it meant?

To find the key, search that which binds.

Should she tell them what she'd found out about Abigail Pruitt, and her mysterious trip to Wren Island?

And what should she tell them? That she suspected Abigail, or her sister Cornelia, might have given birth to an illegitimate child? That the young girl had been placed into an orphanage in Lewiston until she was in her teens, and then practically imprisoned at an isolated old house out on the point of an island reachable only by boat?

Should she ask them why the Pruitt family motto was engraved on the girl's tombstone?

Did they even know the tombstone existed? Or the estate? Or Wren Island itself?

Surely Helen Ross Pruitt had to know *something* about that.

She had given all these questions a lot of thought as she drove back home, trying to sort out all the links, names, and relationships. She'd established that Abigail's maiden name was Wren, which was her link to the island and the estate. But why had she visited Emma on her birthday, bringing along a document for the young woman to sign? And if Emma really was Abigail's child, then that meant she was also Helen Ross Pruitt's half sister, wasn't she? Or perhaps her cousin, if Emma was Cornelia's child? Was that why they'd hidden her away on Wren Island? To keep her existence a secret, and to keep her away from the rest of the family so as not to cause a scandal?

In the end, as she drove down Ocean Avenue toward the traffic light at the foot of the broad boulevard, Candy decided it was all too much to dump on the Pruitts without having more evidence and a better idea of what was really going on.

She needed someone to talk it over with, to help her organize her thoughts, before she went any further.

So she drove to the house of the one person she thought might be able to help her figure it all out—and the one person she decided she'd like to spend a little time with on her last night as a thirty-something-year-old.

She drove to Maggie's house in Fowler's Corner.

The green Subaru wagon was in the driveway, so Candy knew her friend was home. She also knew she should have called ahead, but it had been a last-minute decision, and she knew Maggie wouldn't mind if she dropped in unexpectedly. Maybe they could even order a pizza for dinner and have a glass of wine or two to celebrate Candy's impending milestone.

She rang the bell and waited. Maggie finally opened the door, looking flustered. "What are you doing here?" she asked, as if the tax collector had knocked on her door.

Candy smiled. "I thought I'd stop in and see you."

"But it's not ready."

"What's not ready?"

"Well . . . I . . . uh," Maggie stammered, looking like she'd been caught doing something she shouldn't have been doing. "You weren't supposed to know until tomorrow."

"I wasn't supposed to know *what* until tomorrow?" Candy asked, giving her friend a puzzled look, then gazing past her, into the house. "What have you been up to all afternoon?"

Maggie abruptly swung her hands behind her back. She'd been holding a needle and thread, and a piece of cloth. "Nothing."

"What's that in your hands?"

Maggie did something behind her back, and then brought one hand forward, waving it in the air. "Empty. See? There's nothing behind my back."

"It's in your other hand." Candy leaned over, trying to

look behind her friend's back. "Blue cloth and thread? You stitching up some jeans or something?"

Maggie's eyes widened. "Yes, that's it exactly! I was just stitching up some jeans and . . . I'm not done yet, so you have to go."

She made a move to close the door, but Candy had already started inside. "Don't be silly. I'll help you," she said, unaware of the expression of surprise on her friend's face. "Maybe we can get some dinner while we work."

"Well, I . . . I . . . I . . ." Maggie said, not moving.

Candy stopped and looked back at her. "Are you okay? Something wrong?"

"No, it's just—" Maggie finally threw down her hands. "Oh, I can't keep a secret from you any longer. It's almost your birthday, right? Close enough, anyway. Besides, you can't spend your last night in your thirties alone, can you? So you might as well come in and have a look."

She stayed several paces behind as Candy walked into the living room—and saw the gown thrown over the back of the couch. It was a shimmery blue strapless number that looked like it might once have been a prom dress.

"What's that?" Candy asked.

"It's one of Amanda's old prom dresses."

"What's it doing here?"

"I'm modifying it."

"For who?"

"For you."

"Why?"

"Well, you're going to the masquerade ball tomorrow night with Tristan, right? You can't go to a masquerade ball without a costume—especially on your birthday."

"But . . . how did you know? That I needed a costume, I mean? I was actually going to ask for your help with it, but . . . I didn't expect it to be done already."

Maggie waved a hand. "Well, that's what friends are for, right? And it's not quite done. I'd actually planned to spring it on you tomorrow as a surprise, but it's probably better this way. We can finish it together. And, yes, we should order some pizza, because I'm famished. And I have some Chardonnay chilling in the fridge."

"But . . ." Candy kept looking at the dress, wondering how she might look in it. "So it's a costume?" she asked.

"That's right."

"And just what exactly will I be going as?"

Maggie gave her a look and put her hands on her hips. "Well, isn't that obvious, honey? You're going to be a Blueberry Queen!"

FORTY-TWO

She woke in the middle of the night.

For a few moments she wasn't quite sure where she was, or even if it was day or night. She lifted her head and turned to look back over her shoulder at the darkness outside the window, then checked the clock. It was just after two A.M.

She'd fallen asleep in her own bed with the light on, she realized. She still had her clothes on, the ones she'd worn to the island the previous day, and to Maggie's house. She remembered now that, when she'd finally made it back home late in the evening, she'd taken off her shoes, wrapped herself in a homemade flannel blanket she'd bought at a craft fair a few years ago, and snuggled down onto her bed, with the intent of closing her eyes for only a few minutes and taking a quick nap. But she must have been more tired than she'd realized. She'd slept for more than four hours.

She blinked several times and sat up. Her brain protested at the abrupt movement, fogging her thoughts, and for a few moments, she was tempted to turn out the light, lay her head back down on the pillow, and go right back to sleep. But she couldn't—not quite yet. There was something she needed to do.

Experimentally, she sneaked a foot out from under the blanket to test the air. The room was chilly, since this early in the season they set the thermostat at sixty-five to conserve fuel. She was tempted to pad downstairs and notch it up a couple of degrees, but she didn't want to wake up Doc.

So instead she climbed quickly out of bed, grabbed her laptop from where it sat on a dresser nearby, and jumped back into bed. She sat cross-legged and pulled the blanket tightly around her again as she set the computer down in front of her and booted it up.

She knew what had awoken her—the nagging thought, even while asleep, bubbling up from deep in her subconscious mind, that there were unanswered questions she needed to resolve.

As she waited for the computer programs to load up, she glanced at the clock again.

It's after midnight, she realized. *That means it's Wednesday, the thirty-first of October.*

"Happy birthday, girl," she said softly to herself. "You're forty years old now."

She smiled wryly. It didn't feel too bad, actually.

She let out a deep breath as she moved her index finger over the computer's touch pad and opened the browser window.

She had stopped at Maggie's house the previous evening with every intention of discussing all the information she'd learned on the island. She'd wanted to tell Maggie about the Wren Estate, and the lost tombstone she'd finally found, and about her conversation with Nettie Trotter, and how she'd found the volume of Pruitt history. She wanted to talk about the thief who had stolen her daypack—and everything in it—and describe her wild chase up the two-lane island road, on the trail of the unidentified culprit. And she'd wanted to see what she could find out about the second Latin phrase inscribed on Emma's tombstone.

But Maggie had been so excited about the Blueberry Queen costume she'd designed for Candy, and had seemed so resolved in making sure Candy enjoyed her final night in her thirties, that there'd never been a good time to start a discussion about the island, or Emma, or the inscription, or the murder of Sebastian J. Quinn, or tombstones, or books, or whatever. Candy had tried a couple of times to bring up the subject of her island adventure, first over pizza, and then later on in the evening when they were talking about their final day at the pumpkin patch. But in the end, she'd decided against ruining the increasingly jovial tone of the evening, especially after they'd both had a few glasses of wine and were giggling about something or other. She'd never found an appropriate time to disturb the evening's lighthearted mood.

And, she realized now, it was probably for the best. She wasn't sure anyone else could help her at this point. She had all the puzzle pieces she needed. Now she just had to fit them together.

So she moved the cursor to the browser's search box and keyed in the English translation of the second Latin phrase she'd found on Emma's tombstone:

He is wise who is industrious.

She hit the return key and leaned in for a closer look as the results came up on the screen.

The first few search results were for Biblical phrases that contained the words *wise* and *industrious*: one a passage from Ecclesiastes and another from Proverbs.

Candy scanned those quickly but dismissed them just as quickly. She knew that wasn't what she was looking for.

But a little farther down the page she saw a search result that was a better fit—and one that didn't totally surprise her.

It was a link to a website that specialized in family names and crests.

The underscored link was titled, *Sykes Family History and Crest.*

The Sykes family.

So that's it, Candy thought as she felt a small twist in her stomach.

The motto in question was part of the Sykes family crest.

She clicked on the link. On the resulting page, her eyes were instantly drawn to the right, where she saw an image of the crest with the Latin inscription *SAPIENS QUI ASSID-UOS* in a wavy banner above it.

Candy leaned back a little, her brow furrowed and her mouth a tight line as she considered the ramifications of what she had just learned.

The two Latin inscriptions engraved on Emma's tombstone were the mottos for two prominent New England families who had long histories in Maine and Cape Willington—the Pruitts and the Sykes.

So why were those two mottos on the tombstone?

Candy leaned in again and focused in on the web page. The Sykeses were an Old English family, she read, just as the Pruitts were Welsh. *Sykes* was an old Anglo-Saxon name, and had had a variety of spellings going back to the Middle Ages—Sikes, Syks, Sikkes, and the like. Members of the Sykes family had first settled on the North American continent during the late sixteen hundreds in places like Virginia and Maryland.

And, she knew, at least a few of them had put down roots in Down East Maine, and specifically in Cape Willington, sometime in the seventeen hundreds—around the same time the Pruitts first arrived in the area.

During a historical presentation at the annual Moose Fest celebration last January, Doc had discussed Cape Willington's famous families, and she'd sat in and listened to some of it. He had described, among other things, how the Sykes family had come to the cape, and some of the difficulties they had early on. One of them, Captain Josiah Sykes, had fallen on hard times and reportedly gone mad.

Several members of the Sykes family still lived in New England. If she remembered correctly, the main family home was in Marblehead, Massachusetts. But a nearby, abandoned mansion that had also belonged to the Sykes family had burned down back at the beginning of the year. And Candy had already had run-ins with several members of the current family, including Porter Sykes, a Boston developer, and his brother Roger, a restaurateur—both of whom also just happened to be old college friends of Candy's sort-of boyfriend, Ben Clayton.

But as Candy pondered all these apparently coincidental connections, other parts of the puzzle began to click into place.

The Pruitts. And the Sykeses.

Mottos for the two wealthy families listed side by side on Emma's tombstone.

But why?

It must have something to do with the missing volume of Pruitt history, Candy thought. Why had Emma taken that book, covering those years in the family's history? What significant events had occurred during the 1940s?

Certainly much must have happened during the war years—as well as the prosperous years that followed.

Candy felt a spark of realization, and recalled a story she'd heard once that provided a link between the Pruitts and the Sykeses.

And one specific individual from each family.

Cornelius Pruitt.

And Daisy Porter-Sykes.

Candy felt a jolt as a thought swept through her:

They'd been together at a resort in Maine during the late 1940s.

It was a story she'd heard from Wilma Mae Wendell, an elderly former resident of Cape Willington. Wilma Mae had been the keeper of a valuable lobster stew recipe, given to her by a friend and admirer, James Sedley. When Mr. Sedley was murdered and the recipe stolen from a secret document drawer in Wilma Mae's house, she'd commissioned Candy to find it for her—and along the way solve the mystery of Mr. Sedley's death.

Wilma Mae had also been an avid collector of ketchup bottles. Her collection numbered in the hundreds. She'd kept them throughout her house on Rose Hip Lane, on shelves and in cabinets, in boxes and drawers—and one day she had shown Candy the bottle that had started it all.

It was an empty bottle of ketchup that had once been used at the Lodge at Moosehead Lake sometime in the summer of 1947—and when it was still filled with ketchup, it had been used by Cornelius Pruitt, the husband of Abigail Pruitt and father of Helen Ross Pruitt, one morning when he'd been having breakfast with his mistress, Daisy Porter-Sykes.

Candy remembered Wilma Mae telling her that, during the late 1940s, Cornelius had taken to spending a week or two every summer at the lodge, ostensibly to be alone so he could "cleanse his soul and commune with nature," as Wilma Mae had put it. But that was all a smoke screen so he could arrange for some personal time to dally in illicit affairs.

On that certain summer morning at Moosehead Lodge in 1947, Cornelius had tipped a ketchup bottle—the very one in Wilma Mae's collection—over a plate of steak and eggs, and slapped the bottom so firmly that ketchup had squirted all over the tablecloth, and right onto the morning dress of his current paramour, the very married and very attractive Mrs. Porter-Sykes. Daisy had been so upset at Cornelius for ruining her dress that she'd broken up with him on the spot and stormed out of the room.

But what if, Candy wondered, she had been pregnant at the time?

And what if the child had been Cornelius Pruitt's?

What if, months after breaking up with Cornelius, Daisy Porter-Sykes had given birth to a child in secret?

And what if Emma had been that child?

Candy shivered, and it had nothing to do with the chill in the room.

What would Daisy have done with the child?

Given it up for adoption?

Sent it to an orphanage in Lewiston?

That's how unwanted pregnancies were often dealt with in those days, Candy knew. Daisy had been a relatively young woman, wife of wealthy Gideon Sykes of Marblehead. If she'd become pregnant by Cornelius Pruitt, it would have been scandalous, and she'd more than likely have lost everything, disavowed by both men. So what would have been the sensible thing for her to do? Keep the pregnancy a secret from both men? Take an extended "vacation" before she started showing? Have the child in secrecy, and afterward give it away? Or arrange for an orphanage to take the child?

That had to be it!

It would explain so much, Candy realized—including the lack of a last name on the tombstone.

Was Emma Smith, alias Emma Wren, actually Emma Pruitt?

But how, Candy wondered, did Abigail Pruitt fit into all this? If Emma had been Cornelius's illegitimate child, how had Abigail found out about it? Had Cornelius even known he'd borne a child? And why did they keep Emma out at Wren Island . . . and bury her there?

And, perhaps most importantly, how was it all connected to the death of Sebastian J. Quinn, and the theft of Abigail's diary by Sapphire Vine?

And what about the note Candy had found hidden between the pages of the book on Pruitt history, before it had been stolen from her?

To find the key, search that which binds.

The key to what?

Candy's head was spinning, and her brain was feeling foggy again. So much to think about, so much to sort out—and so much still unknown.

She felt she was making progress though. She was onto something. But as she powered down her laptop, set it on the floor beside the bed, and settled back down under the flannel blanket, too tired to change into her pajamas, she knew she still had work to do.

She also knew that, step-by-step, she was getting closer to finding the killer.

FORTY-THREE

Doc was waiting for her downstairs in the morning with coffee made and a beaming smile on his face. He gave her a hug and a kiss on the cheek. "Happy birthday, pumpkin," he said warmly, and held out her chair for her as she settled at the kitchen table, which was decorated with a bouquet of autumn flowers. In the middle of the place mat in front of her sat a small, wrapped jewelry box with a card beside it.

"Did you sleep well?" Doc asked, walking back to the counter to fill mugs of coffee for them.

Candy studied the jewelry box with interest. "Pretty good, I guess. I slept in my clothes."

Doc gave her a curious look. "Why did you do that?"

Candy shook her head. "I don't know, really. I just never put on my pajamas. Too tired, I guess."

"Well, I can see why. A lot's been going on around town lately, that's for sure," Doc said knowingly as he set a mug of coffee down in front of her, and a plate of something that looked perfectly scrumptious.

Candy's eyes widened at this unexpected treat, and she inhaled its rich, fruity aroma. "Is that what I think it is?"

"Yup, probably is," Doc said with a smile. "Sent over by special messenger this morning."

Now it was Candy's turn to give him a curious look. "Special messenger?"

"I'll explain later." He pointed at the German breakfast pastry he'd set down in front of his daughter and grinned. "So?"

She turned her attention back to the heavenly confection. "Well, it's an *apfeltasche*, isn't it? Like a sort of strudel, with a fruit filling?" She studied it more closely. "Looks like apples and blueberries, with some cinnamon, judging from the aroma."

It was delicately brown, a crisp, flaky pocket pastry stuffed with a warm fruit filling that literally burst out of it in a passion of color—mostly purplish blues and cinnamon golds—and topped with a delicate framework of icing. Candy lifted the fork Doc had also laid on the table for her and used it to test the pastry's flakiness, then cut off a corner and sampled it. For the next few moments, she savored the mixture of flavors and textures. "Mmm, that's amazing," she said when she'd finished. "There's only one person I know who makes pastry like that. Is Herr Georg in town?"

Doc smiled slyly. "Like I said, I'll explain later. Once you've finished your little snack and opened your present, I'll warm up the truck and we'll head to the diner for the next course."

Candy arched an eyebrow. "The next course?"

Half an hour later, as they slid into the corner booth at Duffy's Main Street Diner, Candy received a round of birthday wishes and even a few scattered cheers and applause, not only from Bumpy, Artie, and Finn, but also from the diner's staff, including Juanita and Dolores, the two waitresses, and even a few of the regular patrons. Juanita rushed over with a second cup of coffee and a stack of warm blueberry pancakes dripping in butter and fresh maple syrup.

"Happy birthday, Candy!" the waitress said, giving her a hug. "And what's this?" Juanita asked, admiring Candy's latest piece of jewelry.

"Doc gave it to me this morning." Candy held out her wrist. "It's a handmade blueberry bracelet. See, the blueberries are actually blue coral, but don't they look amazingly like real blueberries? And these little blueberry leaves are bronze with a hand-painted patina. Isn't it beautiful?"

"It is," Juanita said admiringly. "Which reminds me, I have a gift for you too."

She dashed away again but was back in an instant with a neatly wrapped package, topped with a red bow. Inside was an autumn-colored scarf with matching hat and gloves. "The snow will be flying before we know it!" Juanita said cheerfully as she hurried off to tend to her other customers.

There were birthday gifts from the boys as well. Bumpy presented her with a Vermont Teddy Bear dressed like a farmer, Artie gave her a first-edition Stephen King novel he'd bought on eBay, and Finn bestowed upon her an expensive-looking bottle of French wine. Then Maggie burst through the diner's front door and made for their table, a large flower-and-balloon bouquet in hand, just as Juanita and Dolores came out of the back with a freshly baked blueberry muffin topped by a single candle. Candy was genuinely touched as everyone in the diner sang "Happy Birthday"—and the muffin wasn't too bad either. Because she'd just had some of a mysterious baker's *apfeltasche*, however, she sliced the muffin in half. She took one half for herself and offered the other to Maggie, who had slid in beside her.

"I wasn't going to worry too much about what I ate today, since it *is* my fortieth birthday, you know, and I'm allowed to party a little," Candy said to her friend. "But if I'm not careful, I'll gain ten pounds today."

"Tell me about it. Luckily for you, I'm here to help out." Maggie broke off a chunk of her half and popped it into her mouth. "After all, what are friends for? And just so you know, I have a feeling this isn't the last celebration you'll be experiencing today, so better get used to it—and maybe sign up for a gym membership."

"Thanks for the warning. I'll try to moderate myself—though I have a feeling that will be difficult to do."

"Honey, look at you—you're forty and you have the body of a thirty-eight-year-old! That's a cause for celebration. Live a little!"

"You know, you're right," and Candy defiantly broke off another piece of the muffin for herself.

Later, they climbed into Maggie's Subaru station wagon and drove out to the pumpkin patch for their last few hours of operation. They planned to close the patch down for the season at noon, and then head over to Town Park to take in some of the Pumpkin Bash events.

The morning hours whirled by as Wanda's bus tour came and went a few times, and each time the crowds swelled, with many carrying away multiple pumpkins for the day's upcoming events. Over the past few days, Doc and the boys had consolidated the piles of pumpkins, moving them closer to the front of the patch, and had cut the last few remaining pumpkins from thick vines. Now even those last few piles were dwindling.

Around eleven, Doc and the boys showed up to help, but there wasn't much left to do. Candy and Maggie made their last few sales, the last few customers trickled away, and everyone helped close the place down.

"We'll take the tractor and hay wagon back to Mr. Gumm's other farm over the weekend," Candy told Doc after they'd cleared away and packed up the last few crates and stands. "And who knows, maybe we'll give all this another shot next year."

"Maybe we will," Maggie said, draping her arm around her friend's shoulder. "We worked pretty hard, that's for darn sure. And we did pretty good. Only next time, it would be great if we could do it without the dead body buried under the pile of pumpkins."

"You got that right."

As the morning had progressed, whenever they'd had a spare moment, Candy had told her friend all that had happened over the previous day or two, and Maggie had listened with interest. And like Candy, she'd hadn't been totally surprised to hear that the Sykes family was somehow involved. "I wondered if that name might turn up again," she'd told her friend. She'd come to Candy's aid during a run-in with a Sykes once.

"You don't know the half of it. If you asked me, I'd say there was some sort of conspiracy going on. Of course, other than the inscription on the tombstone, there's no real proof that they had anything to do with this, including Sebastian's murder. Or anything else that's been going on in town."

"So what's the next step?" Maggie had asked.

"Well, I've been giving that some thought. One way or another, we have to find Abigail's stolen diary. That might contain the clue we're missing."

"And which clue is that?" Maggie had asked, becoming slightly overwhelmed at the sheer amount of information she'd had to process in a short span of time.

Candy had then told her about the note she'd found in the volume of Pruitt history, adding even another layer to the mystery. But before they'd had a chance to discuss this latest discovery any further, they'd both been drawn away with customers, and it was a while before they had a chance to talk again. But as Candy hurried around the field, carrying pumpkins and taking customers' money, a certain phrase kept buzzing through her head.

To find the key, search that which binds.

Binds what?

She'd been pondering that question ever since she found the note, and the answer had finally come to her.

A bookbinding.

The binding of Abigail's diary.

It all made sense, she realized—and explained why Sapphire stole the diary in the first place.

She'd been searching for a key, too, hidden in the binding of the diary.

Had she told Sebastian about it? Was that what he'd been looking for as well?

It all seemed to make sense, and was worth checking out—if they could find the missing diary.

"It must still be in that haunted house of Sapphire's," Candy had told her friend just before Doc and the boys showed up. "We're going to have to go back there this afternoon and search the place one last time. It *has* to be there somewhere. That *has* to be what Sebastian was after when he rented the place."

But first, she had a festival to cover for the newspaper—even though she'd have to do it the old-fashioned way, with a pen and notepad, since her digital recorder and camera had been stolen with the daypack.

So once they'd loaded the last few items into the back of Maggie's wagon, and put out signs announcing that the patch was closed for the season, they all headed downtown to the Pumpkin Bash.

FORTY-FOUR

The end of October was upon them, signaling the close of the annual leaf-peeping season, yet a sizable crowd—a good mixture of locals and tourists—turned out to enjoy the day-long celebration. Cape Willington's two intersecting streets, which represented the village's business district, were aswarm with people. As the town had done for previous events like the Blueberry Festival, held every August, they'd blocked off Main Street and Ocean Avenue, allowing only pedestrian traffic to wander the thoroughfares. Crews had worked for the past few days setting up booths, tables, viewing areas, and display stands for the thousands of pumpkins they expected to light at dusk. Folding tables located throughout Town Park were laden with mature pumpkins of all shapes and sizes, some carved and ready for display, while others awaited the artist's touch. Children, parents, seniors, teens, and anyone else who could lend a hand were helping out with the carving, and finished pumpkins were being shepherded by wagon or wheelbarrow to the waiting displays up and down the street.

Cape Willington's pumpkin event wouldn't be as big as the one in Keene, New Hampshire, where they regularly displayed more than twenty-five thousand pumpkins, or a record-breaking Boston event, where a little over thirty thousand were carved and lighted on Halloween night. But the citizens of Cape Willington planned to put several thousand carved and lighted pumpkins on display—and to achieve even that number, everyone in town had to pitch in and help.

Candy and Maggie, along with Doc and the boys, were ready to do their part. So after spending a few minutes watching the pumpkin weigh-in—the results of which would be announced at two P.M.—they found places at the carving tables and set to work.

An hour and a half later, Candy blew away a few strands of hair that had fallen over her face and let out a long, deep breath. "Boy, these things sure have a lot of guts in them," she said, pulling her hand out of a particularly plump pumpkin and withdrawing a clump of pale orange plant goop consisting of damp, stringy clumps and clots of seeds. She looked over at Maggie. "How many have you carved so far?"

Maggie held up her plastic-gloved hands, coated with the same organic material, and wiped an arm across her forehead. "I think I'm working on my sixth or seventh. Something like that. I've lost count."

"I've done about the same," Candy said. "My arms are getting tired."

"Mine too. Why don't we take a break after we're done with these and see what else is going on around town?"

"Sounds like a brilliant idea."

But a little later on, as they toured the craft booths and food tables, checked out the other carving stations, and watched volunteers shuffling back and forth with their wagons and wheelbarrows, Candy felt at a sudden loss. "I don't have my camera," she said, somewhat morosely, "or my recorder. I feel empty-handed."

"You still have your phone," Maggie said helpfully as she

eyed a beautifully decorated, ruby red candy apple that was calling her name from a shelf in a nearby food booth. "That looks so delicious but I absolutely, positively know I shouldn't."

"What? Oh, here." When Candy saw what her friend was indicating, she fished a few dollars out of her pocket. "It's my birthday. I'll splurge and we'll both take a few bites."

Maggie flashed a smile. "Well, if you insist. And don't worry, honey—we'll figure out a way to get your stuff back. And if we don't, we'll just buy you all new stuff. That actually might be fun, you know. And the newspaper will spring for some of it, won't they? Or they'll have something they can loan you until you get a chance to replace it, right?"

Candy thought about that as she took a bite of the apple. "Now that you mention it, you're exactly right. I think I have some extra notebooks in my office, and maybe I can borrow a little digital camera from Jesse, if he's around." Jesse Kidder, a rail-thin twenty-five-year-old, was the newspaper's graphic designer and on-call photographer who had a second-floor office near Candy's. "Come to think of it, I'll text him right now and see if he has something he can lend me."

Taking alternate bites of the apple until they'd eaten it to the core, they swung by the pumpkin weigh-in station to find out who won, and following Maggie's suggestion, Candy took a few quick photos of the winners with her smart phone, and entered the winning names in a note-taking app. After that, they walked out of Town Park and up the gently sloping Ocean Avenue toward the newspaper's second-floor offices. By the time they reached the wood-and-glass door to 21B, Jesse had texted her back and told her where she could find a point-and-click digital camera in his office. She could borrow it for as long as she needed it.

The office door at the top of the stairs was locked, and after fishing out her keys, Candy unlocked it, stepped inside, and disarmed the security alarm before she ushered Maggie in and locked the door after them. "I thought someone might be up here today, but I guess they're all out covering the

Pumpkin Bash," Candy observed as they walked past the unoccupied offices—including Ben's, still shadowed and deserted like the rest. He'd texted her earlier that morning from the San Francisco airport and told her he was on his way home, but he wasn't expected to arrive back in Cape Willington until later in the evening.

Candy led Maggie through the rabbit warren of offices to her own. But as soon as she walked in the door, she stopped abruptly and scanned the room. "Someone's been in here," she said to her friend, who came up short behind her.

"What?"

"Someone's been riffling through my stuff."

Maggie was suddenly sharp-eyed, her gaze sweeping the room as well. "How do you know?"

"Things have been moved."

"Has anything been taken?"

"I don't know," Candy said, "but someone's been riffling through my filing cabinet."

"And someone left a note for you."

"What?"

Candy turned around. Maggie was pointing at something that had been left in the center of her desk, right in front of the computer terminal and keyboard. A white envelope, with her name on it.

She eyed it suspiciously, hesitant to approach it. "Do you think we should call the police?"

"Because of a letter?"

"Well, what if it's . . . you know, toxic or something?"

Maggie studied the envelope carefully for a few moments, then took several steps toward the desk, snatched it up, opened it, and looked inside. After a moment, she reached in and withdrew a folded letter. "There's just this old letter inside. Doesn't look toxic to me." She unfolded it, scanned it, made a face, and handed it to Candy with a frown.

"But you might want to think twice before you call the police."

FORTY-FIVE

The letter was a typical computer printout, on nondescript white paper, in an average font. She doubted it was traceable. Too generic.

The message was short and to the point:

> **Bring the key to Pruitt Manor tonight. Upstairs, 9 P.M. I have a hostage. Someone you know. Her name is Olivia March. Fail to bring the key and she dies. Tip off the police and she dies.**

That was it. Candy read it again, and then a third time, shocked.

She finally looked up at Maggie with worried eyes. "What are we going to do?"

Maggie made a gesture with her hands. "I suggest you take the key to Pruitt Manor at nine P.M."

"But I don't have it. I think it's hidden in some binding somewhere."

"What did that note say again?" Maggie asked, trying to recall what Candy had told her in the pumpkin patch that morning. "The one you found in the history book?"

"It said, *To find the key, search that which binds*."

"So we just have to search that which binds, right?"

"Right."

"Any ideas?"

"I think it could be referring to the binding of Abigail's missing diary."

"Okay, good, that makes sense. So then we just have to find this diary, right?"

"Right. But that's what we've been trying to do for the past few days. We've spent hours looking and still haven't found it."

"Yes." Maggie paused. "But we haven't searched the basement of Sapphire's house yet."

"No, but there's nothing down there. We cleaned it out, right?"

"There are a few boxes of old stuff left, I think—things we were going to take to the thrift store but never did. But maybe it's something else. Maybe there's a secret hiding spot down there, or some back cubby where Sapphire hid things away, or something like that."

"Hmm, maybe," Candy said, "but basements aren't the best places to hide books. They're dark and musty and filled with spiderwebs."

"And dead bodies."

"Right, there's that too. So if Sapphire went to all the trouble of stealing the diary, why would she hide it in a musty old basement where it could get ruined?"

For a few moments they thought in silence as Candy began reequipping herself. In her excitement that morning, she'd left her main tote bag at home, but she found her old one in a corner of the office, and it still had some old pens and small notebooks in it, as well as assorted paper clips, loose change, some old folded-up tissues, stray makeup cases, a few stamps and sticks of gum, and lots of scribbled reminders to herself on numerous small pieces of paper, mostly receipts and old grocery lists. She cleaned out some of it before she began to refill it. "Isn't it funny what we leave behind in our old bags?" she said as she worked. "It's like an archaeological dig, except it's usually from just a year or two ago, rather than a few millennium. But in some ways that makes it even more interesting. You know, I've found stuff zipped into hidden pouches or buried in pockets of bags I abandoned years ago. Something will suddenly just disappear, and years later I discover it in an old bag somewhere, zipped away, almost lost forever. Has that ever happened to you?"

She looked over at Maggie, who had a frozen expression on her face.

"Hey, what's wrong? You look ill."

When Maggie didn't immediately speak up, Candy squinted at her. "Are you okay?"

Maggie blinked several times. "Yes, it's just . . . I just . . . It's what you just said."

"What?"

"About the bags."

"What bags?"

"Old handbags and tote bags and things like that. About how you're always leaving stuff in old bags you've used."

"Yes? And?"

Maggie looked pale. "One of the boxes in the basement of Sapphire's house—the ones we were going to give to the thrift store? One of them had her old purses and bags in it."

FORTY-SIX

"We thought they were worthless," Maggie said as they hurried out of the office. They'd made a quick search of the place to determine if anything was missing—and as far as Candy could tell, nothing was—and they'd swung by Jesse's office to pick up the loaner digital camera. Candy now carried her backup tote bag, having replaced most of the items she'd lost when her daypack was stolen.

"We checked them all," Maggie continued as they headed back along the hallway, "and cleaned them all out but . . ."

"But we could have missed something," Candy said as she set the alarm and locked the office door behind them. "Like in a hidden zipped pocket."

"Or a little slip-in side pocket or something like that."

Because of the Pumpkin Bash celebration, they'd had to park in the lot behind the buildings on Main Street, and it took them several minutes to make their way up the street. The pumpkin displays were beginning to fill, and the carving stations were still churning out more jack-o'-lanterns.

Downtown Cape Willington had taken on a festive feel for the afternoon. Candy was tempted to stop and shoot a few candid photos with Jesse's camera, but she knew a life might be hanging in the balance, so they hurried along—though Candy wasn't sure what else they could do at the moment other than follow up on their hunch. The meeting with the kidnapper of Olivia March wasn't until nine. Would Olivia even still be alive by then? Should they call the police and report what was happening, and risk Olivia's life? Or should they keep their mouths shut, as the kidnapper had told them to do?

For the moment, Candy decided, all they could do was follow up on the current clue and see where it led.

Less than ten minutes later, they pulled up in front of Sapphire Vine's old place, and again they went around to the back door. Maggie hadn't brought the house keys with her, so they used the one hidden above the window frame to get inside.

The house was dark and gloomy. "No wonder people think this place is haunted when it looks like this," Candy said as she stepped into the kitchen and flicked on the light.

The stairs to the basement led down from the hallway, through a door lined with shelves so it could double as a pantry. After Sapphire's death, they'd cleaned out all the cans of peaches and sauerkraut and tomato paste, and old boxes of macaroni and potato flakes. The shelves were empty now.

"You go down first," Candy said as she pulled open the basement door and stood aside so Maggie could go through.

"Why me? You always go first."

"Because I don't like basements."

"Well, neither do I."

"But it was your idea to go down there in the first place."

"Yes, but it's your investigation."

"Hmm. Okay," Candy said after a moment. "Then we'll just have to go down together."

"Great idea," Maggie said, and she flicked on the basement light.

But it didn't go on.

"Bulb's probably burned out," Candy observed grimly as she looked down the dark wooden staircase. "Got a flashlight? I think I left mine in my other bag."

Maggie kept one under the kitchen sink, and with their arms linked and the flashlight lighting their way, they descended the stairs into the basement.

They found no dead bodies this time, but they did find several cardboard boxes sitting on a side shelf, filled with odd bric-a-brac, mostly yard sale and thrift shop material.

At the far end of the shelf, they found a box filled with Sapphire Vine's old tote bags and pocketbooks.

And once they had the box back upstairs, after an exacting search, they found Abigail Pruitt's diary, smelling a little damp and musty, hidden in a side pocket of a large red purse.

FORTY-SEVEN

Tristan Pruitt arrived in the Jaguar just after eight to whisk her off to the masquerade ball.

It had taken her more than an hour to get ready, and the entire time she'd wondered what she should tell Tristan—and what she should keep secret.

Should she tell him that they'd found Abigail's diary? Or that apparently the item sought by Sebastian J. Quinn—as well as by the person who had murdered him—was a key that Candy believed had been wedged into the diary's binding by Abigail Pruitt?

And should she tell him that she suspected the key hidden in the book's binding would open the small document drawer in Abigail's writing desk—a drawer no one had been able to open since her death?

Should she tell him that she'd found the missing volume of Pruitt history, only to lose it again within an hour? And that the thief who had taken it had apparently also taken a hostage, and was now threatening that hostage's life?

Should she tell him she was to meet that same thief and kidnapper—and possible murderer—this very night, in an upstairs room at Pruitt Manor?

And should she tell him the rest of it, the hardest part: that in her mind, at this point, everyone—including Mrs. Pruitt, Hobbins the butler, and even Tristan himself—was a suspect?

But that just confused her even more. Why would Mrs. Pruitt hire her, Candy, to find a missing diary in the first place, if Mrs. Pruitt herself was implicated in the crime? Or her butler? Or her nephew?

And what if someone else was involved—someone she hadn't counted on? Like someone from the Sykes family?

Was she in danger? Were the Pruitts in danger? Was Olivia March really in danger—or was it all just a ruse?

She didn't know the answers to any of those questions. So until she did, she decided to tell Tristan none of these things. Better to wait until she had all the facts before she started pointing fingers.

She'd figured out part of the puzzle, yes—or, at least, she thought she had. But the person behind it all, and that person's motivations, were still a mystery to her—though she could make a few educated guesses. But until she knew the whole story, she was hesitant to discuss her discoveries—and her secrets—with anyone.

Maggie knew a lot of it, but she had promised to keep quiet until after the evening's events played out—though, naturally, she was worried about her best friend.

"Just don't go getting yourself killed on your birthday," she'd said before they'd parted earlier in the day. "That would be a real bummer. And try to have a great time!"

Candy would, she decided, do exactly that—it was, after all, her birthday. And she'd also try to avoid getting herself—or anyone else—killed. But she knew she might need help in that particular area, so just in case, she'd made a last-minute phone call. Then she pushed aside her doubts and concerns, and mentally prepared herself for the evening ahead.

So at eight o'clock on the night of her fortieth birthday, dressed as a Blueberry Queen, wearing an altered prom dress, sparkly blue shoes, and a silver tiara with fake blueberries hot-glued onto it, and carrying a sequin- and feather-decorated mask attached to a ribbon-swirled stick—some *fantastique*-style fashion accessory Maggie had picked up at a flea market a few years back—Candy locked the farmhouse door behind her and walked down off the porch toward the Jaguar. She was wrapped in a white cashmere shawl against the chilly night air, and carried in one hand a nondescript silver clutch purse, one just large enough to hold a slim diary, as well as a few other things she thought she might need.

Tristan held the car door open for her. "Good evening, and happy birthday," he said as he glanced up and down at her. "You look absolutely amazing."

"You think so?" she asked, spinning for him in the driveway, showing off her costume.

He crossed his arms appraisingly across his chest. "Yes. Blue is definitely your color."

"You look pretty amazing yourself," she said, letting out a bit of a laugh as she studied his outfit. He was dressed in white breeches, knee-high boots, a blue waist-length, gold-buttoned jacket with epaulets and braids, and a tricorn hat with a feather. "Very dashing. You're a sea captain, right?" She gathered her dress around her and slid past him into the front passenger seat—again, luxuriously heated. It was, she thought, just about the best car accessory ever invented.

"Something like that," he said easily as he closed her door, quickly rounded the car, and tossed his hat into the back before dropping into the driver's seat beside her. He pulled the gear shift into drive and they started off toward town. "To tell you the truth, I was instructed by Aunt Helen to dress as a commodore, but this was the closest thing I could come up with."

Candy laughed again. "Why a commodore?"

"Excellent question. First, you'd have to understand my aunt. And second, it was sort of a nickname of mine when I was growing up around here during the summers. The family owns a couple of boats, including one we keep here in Cape Willington. When I was around fourteen or fifteen, I had this brilliant idea one summer that I was going to start my own ferry service, just like Cornelius Vanderbilt did—and that's what they used to call him, you know. The Commodore. So when I took the boats out, I insisted that everyone call me that, and it stuck for a summer or two."

Candy found all this quite amusing. "But why commodore instead of captain?"

"Well, in my way of thinking as a fifteen-year-old, it was a more accurate description of my rank."

"And how's that?"

He flicked his gaze toward her and grinned. "Commodore's a higher rank, you see, although it's not used much anymore. Essentially a captain is in charge of a ship, but a commodore is in charge of a squadron or a wing or a task force—that sort of thing."

"Or a fleet?"

He nodded. "And since the Pruitts owned a fleet of exactly two boats, technically I was a commodore. Anyway, it must have stuck in my aunt's mind, because when she heard I was coming to her party this year, she insisted I dress this way."

"Well, it seems fitting then," Candy agreed. "In fact, it suits you."

Tristan took the compliment with a shrug. "It's not like I have much of a choice. It's a required obligation for family members when we're in town. That's why most of us usually stay away."

"So why did you come up at this time of year?" Candy asked mischievously. "Certainly not because you wanted to dress as a commodore?"

"Certainly not. But I had some business I needed to attend to. And I wanted to meet you. So here we are."

"Here we are," Candy agreed.

They'd made a left onto the Coastal Loop and were already approaching Pruitt Manor. He pointed ahead, out the windshield. "We're a little early. Do you mind if we make a brief side trip?"

She shook her head. "No, of course not. What do you have in mind?"

"A quick walk through the park?"

Traffic grew heavier as they drove down the Coastal Loop past the Lobster Shack, which sat alongside the ocean on their right. By the time they reached the downtown area and the turnoff on the left for Main Street, they'd slowed to a crawl. The village's business area was blocked off to traffic for the festival, but they could see along the street, and all the jack-o'-lanterns that had been carved and lit for the evening—hundreds and hundreds of them on display.

"It looks beautiful," Candy said as they drove by.

"It sure does. Let's have a look."

A little farther on, Tristan flicked on the turn signal and swung into the parking lot behind the Lightkeeper's Inn. He pulled into a spot marked PRIVATE.

Candy indicated the sign. "Let me guess. You know the owners?"

He grinned. "Like I said, being a Pruitt has its benefits." He shut off the engine. "Hang on, I'll get your door."

Once he'd locked the car, he led her up the steps onto the inn's wraparound porch, festively decorated for the holiday. "Just a brief stop," he said, bouncing his keys in his hand, "for a quick celebration."

He had a table waiting for them in the lounge, with red roses as a centerpiece and a bottle of Dom Pérignon on ice.

"A little prelude to our evening," he told her as they were seated, "and to celebrate your birthday in proper fashion, as befitting a Blueberry Queen and her escort, the Commodore."

The sommelier poured for them, and Tristan raised his glass. "To the queen of the evening, the birthday girl—and the most beautiful woman in town. Happy birthday, Candy Holliday."

She blushed, and they drank together.

FORTY-EIGHT

Both the head innkeeper, Oliver LaForce, and the assistant innkeeper, Alby Alcott, stopped by their table to say hello and wish Candy a happy birthday. Several waiters, waitresses, and bartenders, many of whom both Candy and Tristan knew by name, stopped by as well to give Candy their best wishes and say hello to the "commodore." And Colin Trevor Jones, the inn's young French Canadian executive chef, popped out of the kitchen personally to deliver a selection of hors d'oeuvres he'd prepared especially for them.

After they'd had a glass or two of champagne and sampled the hors d'oeuvres, they headed outside to take in the sights and sounds of the Pumpkin Bash. Ghosts, vampires, and witches ruled the night, though superheroes, robots, and princesses were also well represented. Entire families were dressed up, moving from booth to booth and display to display, pointing out their favorite jack-o'-lanterns and stopping by the storefronts, where costumed employees handed out candy and prizes to the kids.

Candy and Tristan wandered up one side of Ocean Avenue and down the other, pausing to admire the various pumpkin displays, including a particularly impressive one in front of the Pruitt Opera House. At the bottom of the street, they angled into Town Park, and managed to catch an impromptu reading of "The Raven" by local thespian Elliot Whitby, dressed in period garb.

Nine months ago, at the center of this very park, an ice sculpting exhibition had taken place, and Candy had found a clue buried in the ice. Tonight, in the spot where the ice sculptures had once stood, rose the tallest of the pumpkin displays, a pyramid-shaped affair with the high point nearly twenty feet above the ground. There were hundreds of pumpkins lined up on this display alone, all lit, giving the night a spooky orange glow.

They lingered for a while in the park, enjoying the crisp autumn air and the festive atmosphere, full of laughter and excitement, until Tristan glanced at his watch and said, "It's time to go."

He put his arm around her, and she couldn't help leaning against him as they headed back to the Jaguar and drove out to Pruitt Manor.

The mansion looked particularly spooky tonight. It, too, was decorated with jack-o'-lanterns as well as Halloween displays of ghosts, tombstones, and witches, along with several large autumnal-themed arrangements. As they drove into the courtyard, they saw that guests were still arriving for the ball. Several cars were lined up near the entrance, their passengers awaiting to alight for the evening's high-society affair. They idled in line for a few minutes until the other cars cleared out, and Tristan pulled the Jaguar up in front of the manor. It had barely come to a stop when he jumped out and tossed the keys to a waiting valet, while another valet, dressed as a zombie, opened the door on Candy's side.

"Ma'am," the young valet said as he took her hand and helped her out of the car.

As she stepped out, Candy looked up at the manor's facade. Its English Tudor–style exterior was brightly lit with colored spotlights, though most of the upstairs windows were dark. She could hear voices coming from inside, and music, mixed with the sound of the ocean breaking on the rocky shore behind the house.

"You know, there should be a pretty interesting crowd here tonight," Tristan said as he came around the car and held out his arm for her, so he could escort her inside. "Aunt Helen's parties always draw a lot of movers and shakers from the area. There's usually a senator or two, a couple of mayors, a few famous writers and TV personalities. Of course," he said as they passed through the front door into the foyer, "everyone's in costume, so technically we're not supposed to know who anyone is. But I'll point them out to you when I see them."

He'd put on a black mask and his hat as well. The voices and music grew louder, and Candy raised her mask to her face, too, as they traversed the foyer and entered the room on their right.

It had been a large sitting room, Candy recalled, but now it was transformed. Colorfully dressed partygoers were everywhere, all wearing masks and costumes, some quite elaborate. The place had been festively decorated for Halloween, and a three-piece band played in one corner. As Candy and Tristan entered, several people around them applauded and welcomed them, and a waiter swept past carrying a tray with flutes of champagne. Tristan expertly plucked off two and held one toward Candy, then nodded at the crowd. "Shall we mingle?"

One of the first people they ran into was Helen Ross Pruitt herself, dressed regally in purple silk and chiffon, with a high white wig and a mole on her cheek, reminding Candy of someone who might have been right at home in the Sun King's court at Versailles.

"You look stunning, as always," Tristan said as he greeted

his aunt with a kiss on her cheek. "Marie Antoinette would be jealous."

"Let's only hope I don't meet her fate," Mrs. Pruitt said dryly.

"A good turnout, I see," Tristan pressed on, looking around the room.

Mrs. Pruitt jutted out her chin. "Of course it is. I know how to throw a party." She reached out then and took Candy's arm. "You look lovely tonight, dear. The color blue suits you."

They chitchatted for a few minutes, and Mrs. Pruitt pointed out a few prominent personalities in the crowd, before she went off to greet several of them herself, and Candy and Tristan continued to make the rounds as well.

All the while, Candy kept an eye on the discreet silver-banded wristwatch she wore, right next to the blueberry bracelet Doc had given her that morning. The nine o'clock hour was approaching, and she nervously scanned the crowd, wondering when, and if, she should head upstairs for her rendezvous with Olivia March's kidnapper.

She didn't have to wonder about it too long, for something odd caught her eye.

At the far end of the room, moving slowly through the crowd in her general direction, she saw someone wearing a skeleton costume and mask, carrying a black plastic pitchfork.

First she caught just a glimpse of it—an arm or leg, the bones imprinted on the black fabric oddly luminescent, or just the skull itself as it wove through the partiers. At times it seemed to be looking straight at her, watching her. Candy felt a chill as she realized it appeared to be exactly the same mask she'd seen looking in through the window at Sapphire Vine's house a few days ago.

Candy turned, about to say something to Tristan, but he'd disappeared. She searched the room, and spotted Mrs. Pruitt talking to an elderly couple, laughing and joking with them. But there was no sign of Tristan.

He must be mingling, Candy thought, as she surreptitiously searched for the skeleton costume again.

But it, too, had disappeared.

Candy drifted to the right, weaving her way through the crowd, half-empty champagne glass in hand, feeling strangely out of place without Tristan. Several masked and costumed guests nodded politely at her has she passed, and a few offered brief greetings, but Candy was too preoccupied to engage anyone in conversation.

What had happened to Tristan?

And the skeleton?

She saw it then, standing near the door that led out of the room. It seemed to be watching her again, grinning. And then suddenly it was gone, ducking out of the room into the front hallway and foyer, where the staircase to the second floor was located.

Candy hesitated.

Should she follow? Was the person in the skeleton costume the same one who had kidnapped Olivia March? Was it the same person who had killed Sebastian J. Quinn?

She looked back down at her watch. It was a few minutes before nine.

There was only one way to find out.

She scanned the room one last time, hoping that her backup was near, and watching.

Then she took a deep breath and started across the room, following the skeleton figure out into the foyer and up the stairs to the second floor.

FORTY-NINE

At the top of the stairs, she paused, holding tightly to the banister as she looked both directions.

The skeleton had disappeared. On either side of her stretched the two hallways, one leading to the left, to the Lavender Wing, where Mrs. Pruitt's bedroom was located, as she'd told Candy a few days earlier. To the right were the bedrooms of the late Cornelius Pruitt and his wife, the late Abigail Pruitt, maintained as they'd been when both were alive.

Candy heard a creak coming from that direction, the smallest of sounds, as if a door had swung open a fraction of an inch. "Hello?" she called in a loud whisper. "I'm here, just like you asked."

She took a few steps to the right, but heard no other sounds coming from the hallway. The door to Cornelius Pruitt's room, straight ahead at the far end of the hall, was closed. But it looked as if the last door on the left—the one that led to Abigail's bedroom—stood open a few inches.

"Hello?" Candy called again, taking a few steps closer, her back hugging the wall.

The voices from the party downstairs drifted up to her, crescendoing as the nine o'clock hour chimed somewhere in the house. In the mix of voices and sounds from below, she thought she heard someone call her name.

For a moment, she hesitated. Perhaps this wasn't a good idea, following a stranger—and supposed killer—along a shadowed, deserted hallway into a dark room. She thought briefly about heading back downstairs, but something prevented her from retreating. She wasn't the only one involved in this mystery anymore. Someone had been taken hostage. Someone's life was in danger. And at this moment, she was the only one who could help, because she carried in her purse the item the kidnapper wanted.

So she took a few more steps forward, toward the end of the hall. When she reached the last door on the left, which stood ajar an inch or two, she placed her hand on the knob and pushed.

The door swung open with the barest creak, a skittering sound that swelled in the sudden stillness.

Candy stopped at the threshold, standing perfectly still, her breath held deep within, her skin tingling as she scanned the scene before her. The room was dimly lit and deeply shadowed—and empty, as far as she could see. Only a single pool of light, cast by a small shaded lamp sitting on Abigail's writing desk, provided illumination on the far side of the room. But the area of the room immediately to Candy's right, off to the side of the canopied bed, was hidden in shadow.

The drapes were pulled shut, but Candy could hear faint sounds of the dark sea beyond. "Are you in here?" she breathed into the eerie stillness. "I've got what you want."

Hesitantly, she took a few steps forward, into the room. "Hello?"

There was a shift of shadows then, a swish of movement.

Candy jumped back, halfway out the door, her pulse quickening and her heart catching in her throat as the skeleton emerged from behind the brocade curtains that covered the far left window, near the opposite corner.

"Shut the door," a voice croaked.

The costume's bones glowed in the faint light, and the rest of the black fabric almost entirely disappeared, making it seem as if she were being addressed by a real skeleton.

Candy hesitated for a moment, finally taking a few steps back into the room. She shut the door softly behind her but remained alert and ready to run if required.

The area around her darkened even more, as the faint light that had been coming in from the hall was cut off. She was left standing in shadows.

"So you have it?" the skeleton asked in its harsh, muffled voice.

"Not the key, like you asked. But I found the diary," Candy said. "It's right here." She opened her small clutch purse and withdrew the leather-bound volume. It smelled a little musty, having sat in a dark, damp basement for more than two years. But otherwise it was in good shape.

She considered for a moment what to do with it. Finally she walked forward and placed the diary on the center of Abigail's bed.

"I thought I should return it to where it belongs. Abigail probably wrote that diary sitting in this very room—at that very desk." Candy pointed before retreating again to the interior wall, near the door, just in case she had to flee fast.

"I want the key," the skeleton said, touches of anger and impatience in its voice.

"You read the clue . . . right? You're the one who stole that volume of Pruitt history from my car, right? And my daypack? You must have seen the note inside the book."

The skeleton grunted and shifted again. It reached a bony hand inside its costume, and withdrew a small shiny object—a silver pistol, Candy realized.

The skull mask seemed to grin as the skeleton leveled the weapon at Candy. "No more games. I want the key."

"Why?" Candy asked, knowing she was pushing her luck, but also knowing this might be her only chance to get answers to her questions. "Why do you want the key so badly?" She paused a moment, her gaze shifting toward Abigail's desk. "It opens the document drawer, doesn't it? That's what you want. You want what's inside." Candy looked back at the skeleton. "What's in there that's worth murdering someone for?"

The skeleton seemed to tense, and Candy stiffened, too, not knowing what was coming next. She almost closed her eyes, fearful this might be the end. But after a few moments the skeleton waved the pistol at her, signaling for her to stay where she was. Then it walked forward to the bed, and still holding the gun on Candy with one hand, snatched up the diary with the other.

"Don't move," the skeleton said.

"Not a muscle," Candy assured it.

The skeleton retreated to its far corner, taking along the diary. A few moments later, Candy saw a small pen-sized flashlight click on. The skeleton turned the narrow beam of light into the diary's binding, searching the tight pocket along the spine. The skeleton then pulled out another tool, a thin blade, sliding it along the length of the narrow space.

It took a few moments, and Candy waited anxiously, knowing exactly what the person dressed in the skeleton costume would find in the book's binding.

The same thing she and Maggie had found.

"Nothing," the skeleton said after a few moments of careful searching. Finally, it tossed the diary back onto the bed. "The key's not there."

"No," Candy agreed, "it's not there anymore . . . but it *was*."

The skeleton took a step toward her, holding out the weapon dangerously, aiming it at her chest. "You're not listening to me. Don't play games!" it repeated in a forced, gravelly voice, brandishing the pistol. *"Where is the key?"*

"Sapphire Vine found it first—and she hid it in a different place."

"Where?" the skeleton demanded angrily, the pistol shaking in its hand.

Candy swallowed hard. "I'll tell you," she said, "but first show me Olivia March. I want to make sure she's alive and unharmed."

"What makes you think she's unharmed?" the skeleton asked. "I made no such promise."

"But you . . ."

"The key!" The skeleton thrust the pistol forward. "Now! Or I can guarantee you, both you and Olivia March will die!"

FIFTY

Candy knew she had no other choice, and had no more cards to play—except one.

Pressing her lips tightly together, she opened her clutch purse again and withdrew an old metal key ring with perhaps a dozen keys hanging from it, as well as a well-worn miniature metal lighthouse, painted white and red. Many of the keys on the ring looked old and unused, their nickel and brass surfaces worn and dull.

Candy pointed to the diary. "Like I said, Sapphire figured it out first, several years ago. She got her hands on that diary long before you or I had any idea what was going on. But that was Sapphire's skill, I guess. She always was a step or two ahead of everyone else. She always knew *exactly* what was going on around town—and how best to use that information for her own benefit. And in the end, that's what got her killed."

"Where is the key?" the skeleton demanded impatiently.

Candy sighed and held up the key ring, jangling it in the

air. "It's right here. You're looking at it. I've been looking at it, too, for quite a while, not even knowing what it was. This key ring has been sitting in a junk drawer in the kitchen of Sapphire Vine's old house on Gleason Street. We thought they were just duplicate keys—and most of them are. But there were one or two we could never identify. We never found the locks they opened. They're sort of like orphan keys, you know? Keys without a home. Anyway, as close as we can figure, after Sapphire stole Abigail's diary from the library downstairs, right from under Mrs. Pruitt's nose, she stashed it in her red purse and took it home to examine it. She must have found the key almost immediately. She probably did the same thing you just did the moment she was alone with the diary. She knew exactly what she was looking for—and there's only one way she could have known."

Candy saw the eyes behind the skeleton's grinning skull mask shift curiously. "And what's that?" By the tone of the voice, Candy could tell the person behind the mask was sneering at her.

"It's simple," Candy said softly. "Your mother told her."

The skeleton froze. The eyes behind the mask widened. "What did you say?"

"You heard me." Candy's voice took on a sharper edge, an almost accusatory tone. "It happened when they were both in that mental institution down in Portland, didn't it? Sapphire was there because her husband, a young man barely in his twenties, had died tragically in a car accident. She was pregnant at the time of his death, and after the baby was born, she wound up giving it to a foster family. In the months that followed, the loss of her husband and then her child literally drove her crazy. It's one of the reasons she wound up in that institution. And while she was there, she met another patient—a woman named Emma."

Candy thought she heard the skeleton repeat the name in a muffled breath of air. The pistol faltered for a moment, then steadied. "How did you find that out?"

"Both Sebastian and Sapphire had files on Emma. It wasn't hard to make the connection. The two of them—Sapphire and Emma—must have had an instant connection in that institution," Candy said, starting to talk faster now, "because Emma also had a child, didn't she? I saw a photo of her with an infant in her arms. That was Emma's child, wasn't it? So what happened to it?" Candy paused, letting the question linger briefly before she continued. "I can guess. She was forced to give up the baby, which made her own behavior more erratic. I'm not sure exactly what happened back then, or who she contacted, but it was enough to prompt *someone* to put her away in that place, probably to hide her or maybe just to get rid of her. And so, when she met Sapphire, the two women had an immediate common bond—they'd both experienced the trauma of having their children taken away. I imagine they talked quite a bit about that, perhaps even told each other their life stories. Emma probably explained how she'd been raised in an orphanage, and later moved to an isolated house out on Wren Island, where she was made a virtual prisoner. And how, one day when she was still a teenager, she had a strange little party, and Abigail Pruitt showed up on a boat and made her sign some sort of legal document. Emma must have wondered what became of that document, and she might have even searched for it herself, until one day, either while she was still on the island or perhaps after she left, someone gave her a clue. Someone told her about a certain key that opened a certain drawer: *To find the key, search that which binds.*"

Candy paused. "But you already knew about that, didn't you? You didn't need to read that note Emma placed in the volume of Pruitt history. You already knew. Sebastian did too. That's what you were both searching for. As far as I can figure, Emma must have mentioned something about it to Sapphire when they were in the institution together. And Sapphire must have told Sebastian—and he told you, right?"

"Something like that," the skeleton agreed, its voice so low and rough Candy could barely hear it.

She pressed on. "Sapphire knew what the key opened, and she also must have known what's still locked up inside that drawer—the document Emma signed on the island that day Abigail Pruitt came out to visit her. Emma probably told Sapphire about that too. And after Sapphire left the institution and took on her new personality, she figured that if she could get her hands on that document, she could use it in some way—possibly to blackmail the Pruitts, or at least that's my guess. So she stole the diary, recovered the key, and put it on the key ring with all the other house keys—essentially hiding it in plain sight. But before she could use it to do any harm, she was murdered. And after she died, her house—and all the keys that went with it—passed on to her sole heir, Cameron Zimmerman, and his family."

"The key ring," the skeleton said, nodding, as if finally understanding.

"The key ring," Candy echoed, her gaze narrowing. "That's what Sebastian was after, wasn't it?" Suddenly it dawned on her, and her eyes widened as one of the final pieces of the puzzle fell into place. "But you didn't know that until just now, did you? That's why you killed him, isn't it?"

The sudden clarity drove her thoughts now. "Because *he* knew where the key was at—but *you* didn't. That's it, isn't it? He *knew* the key he wanted was on this key ring." She held it up in front of her, as if it were an exhibit at a trial. "*That's* why he told Maggie he wanted to get his hands on the keys to the house as quickly as possible. And *that's* why he was holding the keys like that in his fist when we found his dead body buried under the pumpkins. He was trying to tell us something in the last few seconds of his life, after you'd shot him, and started piling pumpkins on his body—something that Sapphire must have told him before she died.

That the key was on the key ring in a drawer at Sapphire's house. But you didn't know! You thought the key was still hidden in the diary's binding—you showed me that when you searched for it just now. *You didn't know.*"

Candy paused again, this most recent revelation almost taking her breath away as her gaze shifted back and forth before returning to the frightful skeleton mask. "Once Sebastian rented Sapphire's old place, you thought you were going to spend several days with him searching the house. You thought you were going to find the key together, and Sebastian was going to share whatever was locked inside Abigail's box with you, right? You two had an agreement— a scheme. But in the end, he had no intention of sharing anything with you. He just wanted to get his hands on this key, so he could get that document, and then he was probably headed straight back out of town, cutting you out of any deal he was planning. And that's why you killed him, isn't it?"

The skeleton seemed to stiffen. It brandished the pistol. "I knew I could never trust him," the voice growled in a burst of anger. "He played me from the beginning. He said it took him a year to find me, and when he finally contacted me, he said he could make me rich. He told me he knew a secret no one else knew, and that if we worked together, he'd ask for only a small share of the fortune. So, yes, I helped him put the whole thing together. We even came up once or twice to check out Sapphire's old place, and just for fun, we scared a few of the renters. We were waiting until the place was empty—and then he had other issues he had to deal with for a while. But finally we figured out the perfect time to rent the house—and to sneak into Pruitt Manor once we found the key." There was a pause, and the skeleton's voice darkened. "But he had inside information. Something Sapphire Vine had told him. Something he didn't tell me."

"So you shot him," Candy pressed.

"Yes, I shot him. He betrayed me."

"But what's that document?" Candy asked, her eyes going to the locked drawer. "What makes it so important? Why kill for it?"

The skeleton laughed. "You still haven't figured it out, have you?"

"Tell me," Candy said, "and then turn yourself in. You can't get away with this."

"Do you suppose I'm stupid enough to tell you?" the skeleton said coldly. "You've done your job. You found the diary—and the key. That's part of the reason I shot him in that pumpkin patch—and buried him there. I *knew* you'd find him, and I knew *you'd* get involved. He told me we had to watch out for you—that you're too smart for your own good. He wanted to take you out—do you realize that? Early on, he suggested that we should just kill you to get you out of the way. But I had a better idea. I knew you had access to certain information I didn't have."

"So you used me?" Candy asked, incredulous.

"Don't be so stupid," the skeleton spat out. "Of course I used you. And now I have one more task for you. I want you to take that key you found, and I want you to walk over to Abigail's desk and unlock the drawer. And then I want you to hand me what's inside."

Candy hesitated. "And if I don't?"

She heard a click, as if someone had flicked off the safety on a pistol.

"Then you'll die—just like Sebastian did."

FIFTY-ONE

Again, Candy knew, she had no choice—and one way or the other, she decided she had to see this through to the end.

So cautiously, as if treading on thin ice, she edged forward, a step at a time, around the end of Abigail's canopied bed and past the small marble fireplace, then angling toward the writing desk. As she did so, the skeleton backed deeper into the shadows in the corner, keeping the pistol trained on her the entire time, ready to fire at the slightest provocation.

Candy approached the front of the desk, where she hesitated for a few moments, glancing out of the corners of her eyes at the discreet door to her right, next to the bed, that led into Cornelius Pruitt's bedroom.

I can make a quick dash for it, she thought. *Get away while I still can.*

But if it was locked, she thought, she'd still be stuck here, in this bedroom—with a gun pointed directly at her.

As if reading her thoughts, the skeleton spoke up. "Go

ahead, open it," the smug voice chided. "You're just as curious as I am to see what's inside it."

It's true, Candy had to admit. She was indeed curious.

She lifted the key ring, holding it in her open palm as
she studied it.

After discovering Abigail's diary hidden away in a side
pocket of the red purse, Candy and Maggie had searched
the diary's binding—and come up empty, just as the skeleton had a few minutes earlier. They'd been confused at
first, wondering if they'd misread the clues. But then Candy
remembered the keys clutched in Sebastian's cold fist, and
on in impulse, they'd started checking all the keys and key
rings associated with the house.

The ring of duplicate keys they'd found in the junk
drawer had held a number of possibilities, including a
smaller, flat metal key that looked like it might open a small
locked box or drawer. Maggie had known that most of the
keys on the ring fit specific locks and keyholes throughout
Sapphire's house, but this one had remained a mystery.

It was, as Maggie had called it, an orphan—a key without an associated lock.

There had been no way to actually test their theory—that
the orphan key on the ring opened the drawer in Abigail
Pruitt's writing desk—until now.

Candy took the small key between two fingers and lifted
the entire key ring off her palm. As she leaned forward,
toward the drawer, she repositioned the key, the flat end
aiming downward, the jagged edge pointed up. She held her
hand as steady as possible as she moved it toward the keyhole, though she noticed she was shaking just a little. If she'd
guessed wrong, she knew she was as good as dead.

She gently slipped the key inside, and turned.

The lock was old and didn't give way easily. She had to
coax the key around, turning it one way and then the other,
loosening the path, until something inside clicked.

She reached out with her other hand and pulled open the drawer.

Inside was a single yellowed letter-sized envelope, with the word *Emma* printed on the front. Candy recognized Abigail's handwriting from the diaries.

"Take it out," the skeleton ordered. It had come up a few steps behind her. "Tell me what's inside."

Candy did as she was told. She lifted out the envelope, opened the flap, which had been neatly tucked inside, and withdrew several sheets of folded documents on thick paper.

"Read them," the skeleton ordered.

Candy turned and shot a questioning look at the skull mask, and the eyes behind it. "Are you sure you want me to do that? You can just . . ."

"Read them," the voice said, more emphatic this time.

Candy took several quick breaths and realized her heart was beating faster. She unfolded the pages and scanned the top sheet.

"The first one's a birth certificate," she said, "for Emma Rose Pruitt."

"I'll take that." The skeleton hand darted forward, faster than Candy expected, and snatched the sheet from her fingers, then backed away again. "Next."

Surprised, it took Candy a few moments to refocus. But when she did, scanning down the next sheet in her hands, she knew instantly what it was. "This is it—the document Emma signed."

"And what does it say?" the skeleton asked. It sounded as if it was grinning.

Candy took a few moments to scan the text before her and look back through the other sheets, which were all clipped together. "It's a legal document, just like I thought," Candy replied, and then she looked up at the skeleton. "It says, basically, that Abigail would continue to provide a home for Emma at the house on Wren Island, as long as Emma agreed to disavow any legal claim to the Pruitt fortune." Candy paused. "It also says that none of her heirs can lay claim to the fortune as well."

There was silence in the room for a few moments as those words sunk in. Finally, Candy said breathlessly, "You're her, aren't you? Your Emma's daughter?"

It took the longest time, as the seconds seemed to stretch to minutes, but finally the skeleton reached up with one hand and slid up the skull mask.

Underneath was the face of Olivia March.

FIFTY-TWO

"So it was you all along," Candy said.

"It was me all along." Olivia's face looked pale in the dim light, and there were dark circles under her eyes. She looked on the verge of a breakdown, though she forced a smile, trying to make a strong appearance. "But you must have suspected at some point. You had most of this figured out."

Candy nodded, and there was a sadness to the gesture. "I did—though I was hoping I was wrong. But I had to make sure. If Olivia—if *you*—really had been kidnapped by someone else, and your life really was in danger, I knew I was the only one who could help you, because I had the diary and the key. So I couldn't take any chances."

Olivia was silent again, her mouth a tight line. After a few moments, she said in an almost mocking tone, "Well, I'm genuinely touched you were so concerned about my well-being. Unfortunately, I can't say I feel the same way about you." She reached out a hand, making a beckoning movement with her fingers. "I'll take those."

Candy glanced down in the documents she still held, then looked back up at Olivia. "What are you going to do with them?"

Olivia's brow fell and her face hardened. "Destroy them, of course."

"So that's it then? That was your scheme? Destroy the documents that would prevent you from laying claim to the Pruitt fortune? And then what?"

Olivia's eyes turned suddenly dark. "I am the grand-daughter of Cornelius Pruitt and Daisy Porter-Sykes!" she said, her words coming with some force, though she kept her voice low. "I have a legal claim to both those fortunes. And I plan to take full advantage of that claim!" Her face twisted. "There's a conspiracy here that goes back decades— more than sixty years. My mother . . ." Her voice trailed off as she looked down at the folded birth certificate she held in her hands. "I never even knew the exact day she was born. Did you know there are no records of her—except for this? Someone had all her other birth records destroyed. How, I don't know—but none exist. There's nothing that proves my mother was even alive. I know. I looked. That's why I needed your help."

"*My* help?" Candy asked.

"You had information I didn't," Olivia said, her voice taking on a haunting edge. "You knew Sapphire Vine. Your friend manages her property. You're at the center of every-thing that's going on in this town. So I shot Sebastian in the pumpkin patch, made up a few stories about a pumpkin patch killer to stir things up, and let you do the rest. And you delivered, like I knew you would. You found Emma's grave for me, and the diary, and the key. And you found this." She waved the birth certificate in front of her. "This *proves* it, once and for all. Now I can legally show proof of who I am, and I'm going to get what's rightfully mine."

Candy looked back down at the sheets she still held. Slowly she folded them up and placed them back into the envelope. "As long as these papers your mother signed don't stand in your way." Again, for a fleeting moment, she thought of making a quick escape, out through the side door to Cornelius Pruitt's bedroom.

But Olivia was quicker. She darted forward, grabbing the envelope from Candy's hands. She slid it inside her costume as she backed away, around the bed toward the hallway door.

"You've done your job," she sneered, "and you've been very helpful. But you know too much. I'm sorry it has to end this way."

She slid the skull mask back down over her face and stepped into the center of the room, where she'd have a clear shot at Candy, who still stood by Abigail's writing desk.

But at that moment, the door behind Candy burst open and Officer Molly Prospect rushed through, arms stretched out in front of her, holding the butt of a pistol in the palm of her left hand, her right index finger hovering near the trigger, both hands steadily aiming the weapon directly at Olivia. "Drop it!" she ordered.

For a moment, no one moved. The air tensed as Candy held her breath, and Olivia and Officer Prospect stared each other down.

Then the door to the hallway swung open and Tristan poked his head through, his tricorn hat tilted jauntily to one side. "Candy, are you in here? Everyone downstairs is looking for you. We have a . . ."

But he never had a chance to finish, for there was a shout. The next thing he knew, a skeleton was rushing toward him, seeking freedom through the open door.

"Stop her!" Candy and Officer Prospect yelled almost in unison.

And Tristan did. The skeleton brought up its hands, intending to push him out of the way—or perhaps just to shoot him—but at the last moment, he stepped elegantly aside, reaching out to grab the wrist of the hand that held the weapon. He gave it a jerk and a yank, and the skeleton spun around, growling in pain as it dropped to one knee. The pistol fell from its grip and clattered away across the floor.

"Hold her!" Officer Prospect sprang across the room, kicking the gun farther away, under the bed. After making sure she was all clear, she lowered her weapon as she reached behind her and pulled out her handcuffs.

It was over in seconds. Olivia March, with the skull mask still over her face, lay in a crumpled heap on the floor, handcuffed and defeated.

"What the hell's going on here?" Tristan asked, looking around the room with a shocked expression on his face. Then he saw Candy, who stood with one hand clutching the edge of Abigail's writing desk. She looked unharmed as far as he could tell. He crossed quickly to her. "Candy, are you all right?"

She felt a wave of relief engulf her as she watched Officer Prospect, who obviously had control of the situation, radio for backup. She also noticed her whole body was shaking. She took several deep breaths to calm herself. "Yes, I just . . . I need a few moments."

"Very well," Tristan said, his own face showing his relief. He stepped closer to her and placed a comforting hand on her shoulder, steadying her. "But don't be too long. Otherwise, you'll be late for your own surprise party."

FIFTY-THREE

She pretended to be surprised—and she did a very good job of it. She even had tears in her eyes. Real tears.

Maggie gave her a kiss and a hug. "Happy fortieth birthday, honey! And happy Halloween!" She'd been dressed as a witch. Candy hadn't recognized her until they'd all removed their masks and cried out happily, "Surprise!"

Everyone had been there, all in disguise for the masquerade ball—Doc and the boys, Cameron and Amanda, old Mr. Gumm, Ray Hutchins, Melody Barnes and her husband, Jesse Kidder and other coworkers from the newspaper, the Reverend James P. Daisy and his wife, Gabriella, town council chairman Mason Flint, Lyra Graveton and her husband, Llewellyn, local shop owners Ralph Henry and Malcolm Stevens Randolph, the Daggerstones and the Coffins and the Chapmans. They all hugged her, shook her hand, clapped her on the back, kissed her, brought her glasses of champagne, fussed over her costume, and generally wished her well.

Even Wanda Boyle had showed up, dressed like an Egyptian princess, accompanied by her husband, Brad, who had chosen the role of a Roman emperor.

She also saw Judicious F. P. Bosworth, who was presently visible, and surprisingly well engaged with the crowd. She gave him a restrained hug.

"I'm so glad you could make it," she told him, "though in the past you've helped me solve the murders in town. This time you were noticeably absent."

He smiled warmly at her. "This time you didn't need my help," he said simply, "but I'll always be there when you need me."

Doc and the boys told her the same thing. "We're always there for you, pumpkin, you know that," her father said as they embraced.

"And I'm always there for you, too, Dad," she told him. She lifted her wrist, showing off the blueberry bracelet. "And thank you for this."

"Anytime, pumpkin," he said with a grin. "Now let's party! After all, this is your pumpkin bash!"

Herr Georg Wolfsburger appeared with a flourish from a side room, wheeling a cart that held a tall birthday cake, which he'd personally made for her. *"Mein leibchen!"* he cried to her happily when he saw her. "You are beautiful! Like a fairy princess!"

She stood with Tristan and Maggie, Cameron and Amanda and Doc as they once again sang to her, and they clapped and snapped photos as she turned and blew out the candles on her cake—all forty of them.

A short time earlier, when she'd come down the stairs with Tristan, she'd been surprised that no one here on the first floor knew what had happened upstairs. "And we'd like to keep it that way for the moment," Tristan had told her. Before they'd left Abigail's bedroom they'd retrieved the documents from Olivia March, and Tristan had had a quiet talk with Officer Molly Prospect, who had relayed his requests to Chief Durr. "The police are going to announce shortly that they've made an arrest in the Sebastian J. Quinn murder case," he'd told her as they'd come down the stairs, "but they're going to keep some of the details under wraps for now, until we can sort everything out. Anyway, we'd like to keep the family name out of this as much as possible."

Candy doubted they'd be able to do that for long, but for the moment, she decided to let other people handle it. She'd done her part. Now it was time to let the experts do theirs.

As the evening wore on, and the ten o'clock hour approached, Candy started looking around the room. Someone was missing. Someone who'd promised he'd be here for her birthday.

Ben Clayton finally showed up at ten thirty.

She saw him standing under the arch that led out into the first-floor hallway, silhouetted by a light behind him, searching for her. She'd recognize his profile anywhere. He looked a little disheveled—he'd just come across the country, after all, flying first into Boston, then hopping on another plane to Bangor before driving down to Cape Willington. It was a long trip, and he'd been away for what seemed like forever, though it had been less than a week.

She crossed the room toward him, and when he saw her, he met her halfway.

He gave her a hug and whispered "happy birthday" in her ear. But there was something in the tone of his voice that instantly alerted her. When she looked into his eyes, she knew something was up. "What is it?" she asked, sounding worried.

"Candy, I have to tell you something. I know this isn't the best time but . . . things have been happening so fast and I . . . I've received an offer."

Her brows knitted together. "An offer for what?"

"For a job. In San Francisco. As managing editor for the *Chronicle*."

She looked into his eyes, somewhat confused. "But . . . that's wonderful news but . . . what does it mean?"

He smiled hopefully. "Candy, I've accepted the job. I'm leaving town. I'm headed to San Francisco. And I want you to go with me."

FIFTY-FOUR

The following Wednesday afternoon, she drove out to Pruitt
Manor.

A week had passed since her birthday party, the arrest
of Olivia March—and the bombshell dropped by Ben. And
today, Candy had a little unfinished business to tend to.

The Pruitts had left town the previous weekend. Mrs.
Pruitt had returned to her primary home on Beacon Hill in
Boston, and Tristan had flown off on Sunday to New York,
and eventually to Europe on business.

Ben was gone as well. The previous Friday had been his
last day in the office. They'd thrown a small party for him,
but it had been a subdued affair. Other than that, he left with
little fanfare. He'd flown out Saturday to the West Coast. He
had plans to return to Cape Willington at some point to pack
up his things, but he didn't know exactly when that would be.

He'd obviously been disappointed when Candy had told
him, after thinking it over, that she couldn't go with him—
her home was here in Cape Willington. But they both knew

it was the right decision. Neither of them had been completely sure about the direction of their relationship. In the end, it had been an amicable split.

So here she was, a single woman again—at least for the moment.

As she drove south along the Coastal Loop with the sea on her right, she could see the peaks of Pruitt Manor just above the trees, most of which had lost their leaves. The color of autumn was gone. The pumpkins were gone, too, and the harvest was behind them. Even Halloween was gone. But they had Thanksgiving and the holidays to look forward to . . . and another winter.

Candy had surreptitiously kept tabs on the comings and goings at Pruitt Manor, and she had timed her visit carefully.

The last she'd heard, Olivia March had been transferred to the Maine Correctional Center in Windham, northwest of Portland, which had facilities for female prisoners. Given the fact that she'd been a reporter for the *Boston Herald*, there'd been quite a bit of media hype in the city over her arrest, and out-of-town reporters had invaded town for a few days. But most of them were gone now, moving on to the next story, and Candy—and the Pruitts—had largely managed to avoid the spotlight.

Candy had also spent a number of hours on two separate occasions at the Cape Willington Police Department, explaining everything she knew about the case—although she'd left out a few parts, since she hadn't known them herself.

That was why she was driving out to Pruitt Manor today.

The courtyard in front of the manor was mostly deserted. But several of the garage doors in the adjacent building were opened. The Bentley sat in one of the bays. And as Candy had hoped, a certain butler was puttering around it, wearing an apron and gloves.

He stopped what he was doing and stared at her as she pulled the Jeep to a stop just outside the bay. She shut off the engine and climbed out.

"Afternoon, Hobbins," she said, and she squinted as she looked up at the sky. It was a beautiful late-fall afternoon. The sky was bright blue, and the ocean beyond Pruitt Manor, visible through the trees along the side of the building, looked almost as vivid.

"It sure is," he said, looking up with her. After a few moments he looked back down. "By the way, I don't think I ever wished you a happy birthday. So happy birthday, Ms. Holliday. You had quite an eventful evening, from what I've heard."

"You got that right." She wandered casually into the garage bay, admiring the Bentley. "That's quite a car," she said, staring in the passenger-side window at the interior.

Hobbins smiled. "You've always been an admirer of this car, haven't you? We talked about it before, a few years ago, if I remember correctly."

"You do," Candy said, straightening. "And you're right. We did talk about this car a few years ago. It was the first time I visited Pruitt Manor."

He nodded amiably. "Yes, that sounds about right, miss. You've been out here a few times since then, haven't you?"

"I sure have," Candy said. "I'm getting to be a regular visitor. Tell me, how long have the Pruitts owned this Bentley?"

"This one?" Hobbins scrunched up his face. "Well, if you remember correctly, miss, it's a 1993 Brooklands Saloon."

"That's right," Candy said. "A '93." She walked around the tail end of the car, admiring its lines and detail. "I assume you bought it new," she said. "I can't imagine the Pruitts would buy a used Bentley."

"Yes, that's true," Hobbins said, walking to his workbench and removing his gloves, which he laid down carefully. "Is there something I could help you with, miss? I do have to finish up my work. I'm driving back to Boston later this afternoon. I just had to wrap up a few things here."

"Actually," Candy said, "I do have one or two questions to ask you. Nothing on the record, of course. Just trying to tie up a few loose ends."

"Questions?" Hobbins gave her a wary look.

"There's two things I haven't quite been about to figure out," Candy said, "concerning Emma Pruitt. You've heard about her, right?"

The expression on Hobbins's face changed abruptly. "I'm afraid I can't talk about that, miss. I'm sworn to secrecy."

"I'm sure you are," Candy said, "and I admire the loyalty you and your father have shown to the Pruitt family. So since you can't really say anything, I wonder if I could tell you a quick story? You just have to listen. It'll take only a few minutes of your time."

Hobbins looked skeptical, and glanced at his watch. Finally he nodded. "All right, miss. I suppose I can give you a few minutes. So what's this story about?"

"Well," Candy said, leaning back against the Bentley and crossing her arms in front of her, "it's about the wife of a very wealthy man. Now, this wife is a fairly serious woman, and she doesn't put up with much nonsense. But she also knows the ways of the world, and she knows the value of being discreet. So when she finds out that her husband has fathered an illegitimate child with a young socialite from Boston, who'd been his mistress for a year or two, the wife knows she has to do something about it to protect the family's reputation and fortune." Candy paused and glanced over at Hobbins. "Are you with me so far?"

He nodded, expressionless. "I'm with you, miss."

"Okay, so, this wealthy man's wife tries to find out what happened to her husband's illegitimate child. But she keeps running into dead ends. So one day she decides to hire a detective, and he finally tracks down the child—who is a teenager now—in an orphanage in Lewiston. She has all records of the child destroyed, and then takes her out to an old estate on an isolated island, where the girl is made a virtual prisoner. She waits until the child's eighteenth birthday, when she is of legal age, and has her sign a document, disclaiming any rights to the Pruitt family fortune."

Hobbins gave her a tight look. "I can neither confirm nor deny such a thing happened, miss. In fact, for all I know, it's complete fantasy."

Candy tapped a finger on her chin. "Yes, you know, you're right—except for two things."

Suspicion returned to cloud Hobbins's eyes. "And what might those be, miss?"

"Well, for one, a Bentley"—Candy reached out and tapped the side of the freshly waxed car—"this Bentley, I believe, was spotted in the vicinity of the pumpkin patch, with its lights out, on the night Emma Pruitt died there, twenty years ago."

It took him a long time to speak. "And the second one?"

"Who took Emma's body out to Wren Island—on a boat—and made sure she was buried there?"

Again, Hobbins took a long time to reply. "Unfortunately, I don't know the answer to either of those questions, miss."

"I'm sure you don't," Candy said, "and for the record, neither would I if I were in your place." She paused, and her tone turned more serious. "But I do have a question I'd like an actual answer to, if you don't mind—what really happened to Emma Pruitt that night?"

In response, Hobbins grabbed a clean chamois cloth and walked over to the Bentley, looking for spots that needed buffing. He sighed. "All I can tell you is that she died of natural causes," he said finally in a low, confidential tone. "There was nothing sinister going on. The elder Mrs. Pruitt—the mother, Abigail—had been giving money to that young woman for years, especially after she had her baby, but Emma kept wanting more, even after Abigail's death. It became . . . unmanageable. I was asked to make a final payment to her—to drop off the money. For some reason she wanted to meet at a field out of town. I wasn't familiar with it and went looking for it, but I was never able to find her. I think she got the whole thing mixed up in her head. She went to the wrong place. There was no way to contact her. . . ."

"And she waited for you to arrive but you never showed up? Is that it?" Candy asked.

Hobbins nodded. "Something like that, miss. It was no one's fault. She was in a bad spot."

"And after Emma's death, you made sure she was buried on Wren Island, right?"

Again, it took him a long time to respond, but he finally nodded. "It was one of Abigail's last wishes. She'd even specified the inscriptions for Emma's tombstone. I did as she asked. I took the body out in the family boat myself."

"And you covered up the whole thing. As far as everyone knew, the body just disappeared."

Hobbins gave her a pained look. "As far as anyone knew, she never existed, miss. I tried to give her a decent burial and a good resting place, out there where she spent so much time."

Candy had suspected as much. It explained the last few pieces of the puzzle, and she decided not to press any further. She thanked Hobbins for his honesty, and was on her way back to the Jeep when she stopped and turned around. "Hobbins, another question," she said. When he grimaced, she added, "Last one, I promise."

"And what would that be, miss?"

"Well, I'm wondering, who told Emma about the missing key—and how to find it? You know, that little phrase she wrote down on a slip of paper and slid between the pages of a book on Pruitt history?"

At that Hobbins visibly lightened, and he gave her a quick wink and a sly smile. "Well, miss, that's an easy one to answer. I had to give her a fighting chance, didn't I? After all, she *was* a Pruitt."

"Indeed she was," Candy said, and she nodded to herself as she turned back to the Jeep. "Indeed she was."

EPILOGUE

As was their custom, he arrived at the house in Marblehead on Sunday afternoon precisely at four P.M. for tea.

Daisy Porter-Sykes was proper that way. She insisted on punctuality. She insisted on proper dress. And she insisted on good manners. So when he found her sitting in her dark living room, he was on his best behavior. "Good afternoon, Grandmother. You're looking lovely today as usual."

The ninety-one-year-old woman scowled as she turned up a cheek to her grandson, accepting his grazing kiss. "Don't get smart with me, young man."

He laughed softly. "You really must learn how to accept a compliment." He unbuttoned his sport coat and settled himself in the chair opposite her. "So, have you been well?"

"I wish I were better," Daisy said with a coolness in her tone, "but I suppose I'm as well as anyone can be at my age."

"Look at it this way. As least you're still alive."

"Don't remind me," Daisy said sourly as she leaned forward and poured out cups of tea for the both of them. "My quest for revenge keeps me alive."

"More precisely, your hatred of the Pruitts," her grandson said matter-of-factly.

At that, Daisy's thin lips curled up in a crinkled smile. "You know me all too well, don't you? Sugar?"

Porter Sykes waved a dismissive hand. "You know I can't stand that stuff. I'll take a strong cup of coffee if you have it. Or a brandy."

The old woman scowled at her grandson again. "You'll have tea with me!" she said sharply. "That's the whole point of our visits."

"Hmm, I thought the point was that you wanted me to give you a report," he said. "And since you insist, I'll take one sugar."

His grandmother complied, dropping a sugar cube into the cup and passing it to him. "And, yes, I do want you to *report*, as you call it. So tell me: What have you found out?"

He let out a breath as he leaned forward to accept the teacup, then settled back again in his chair, crossing his legs and arranging his coat around him. "Well, you were right, of course. The documents were in Abigail Pruitt's room, locked in a drawer in her desk. Apparently no one had been able to open it since her death. Why they didn't just take an ax to it is anyone's guess. As it turns out, they didn't know where the key was until Candy Holliday found it in Sapphire Vine's house. And, oh, yes, the authorities have arrested Emma's daughter—your granddaughter, I might point out."

"Don't call her that," Daisy sniped at him. "Her mother may have grown inside my womb, but she was a Pruitt. She was always a Pruitt—and so's the daughter. I did what I thought best at the time to protect our family, and I've never regretted my decisions. I had the situation well contained. I made sure there were no traces of her birth and stuck her in that orphanage. Neither Cornelius Pruitt nor your grandfather knew anything about it. But then Abigail Pruitt had to start snooping around. She was the most stubborn, damnable woman!"

Coolly, Porter responded, "Well, it was bound to all come out sooner or later, wasn't it? This way everything's on the table. We've scared all the rats out of their nests and into the open. It's a start. But surely you must have some regret that your granddaughter has to spend the rest of her life in prison?"

Daisy took a sip of tea, trying to swallow down her bitterness. "She's the grandchild of Cornelius—and that's all she is. That's all she'll ever be. The offspring of the man who destroyed me, and forced my husband—your grandfather—to take his own life at that wretched mansion up in Maine. Cornelius Pruitt launched a vendetta against this family and tried to destroy us all—and he almost succeeded a couple of times. But he's long gone, and now it's my turn to take revenge on his family."

Porter was silent. He'd heard all this before. His grandmother had lived with her simmering hatred of the Pruitts for more than sixty years, constantly plotting ways to strike back. Now she'd pulled him and his siblings into her web, and for some reason he'd let her do it.

But, no, that wasn't entirely true. His brother and sister were the ones who had initially bought into their grandmother's schemes. He'd only been persuaded later—and now one part of him regretted that he'd ever let it get this far.

But another part was intrigued by the possibilities that still lay ahead.

"We're getting closer," Daisy said, as if reading his mind. "I can feel it. Once we find those old land deeds that belonged to Silas Sykes, we'll be in a position to destroy the Pruitts once and for all."

"Ah, yes, the famous land deeds," Porter said skeptically, longing for something stronger to drink. "Roger thought he had those in hand, didn't he? Or at least a clue to their whereabouts, supposedly written down in Old Man Sedley's journal. But it was another dead end, wasn't it? At this point, I'm not even sure they exist."

His grandmother looked as if she wanted to slap him. "Don't talk like that!" she admonished him. "Of course they exist. I know it. We'll find them. We have to."

They both sat in silence for a long time, mulling their individual thoughts, until Porter shrugged and said, in a facetious tone, "I suppose we could just hire Candy Holliday to find the deeds for us. She's had quite a bit of success at that sort of thing lately."

His grandmother snorted at the suggestion. "You're taken with her, aren't you?"

Porter arched an eyebrow. "I'll admit I like her, yes. She's spunky."

"Is that why you arranged to have her boyfriend shipped off to the West Coast?"

At that, Porter frowned. "Ben Clayton? I had to get him out of the way. I knew if I made him the right offer, he'd never be able to refuse it. He was getting too close to the truth, anyway. I just had to make sure he didn't know who was behind the offer."

"So what now?" Daisy Porter-Sykes asked, her eyes hooded, her expression vengeful. "What's next for Cape Willington, Maine?"

Porter Sykes mulled over his grandmother's question for a long, long time, sipping his tea as the room darkened with the setting sun.

He had poked the hornet's nest several times now, getting interesting reactions. His latest effort, unknown to his grandmother, had been a discreet offer, made through back channels, for the Pruitt's private library collection. He'd heard rumors about what the collection might contain, and had taken a chance. It was possible, he thought, that there might be valuable information hidden away in some of those old volumes. He hadn't been surprised when the Pruitts refused the offer, or by the events that had followed. But he still hadn't quite figured out how to leverage it all to his—and his family's—advantage.

Finally, softly, he said, "I'm still working on that. But I can promise you we're not done with those people. We've only just begun. But we must bide our time, Grandmother, and wait for the right opportunity to come our way."

"Well, as long as it doesn't take too long," Daisy Porter-Sykes said bitterly. "I want to walk the halls of Pruitt Manor before I die."

"And you will, Grandmother, you will. I have a feeling that before this is over, you'll not only own Pruitt Manor, but half of Cape Willington—and Blueberry Acres as well."

AUTHOR'S NOTE

While the Cranberry Isles are real, Wren Island is fictional. You won't find it on any map. However, the Cranberry Isles ferries do exist, along with a great number of working ferries and mail boats providing seasonal and daily service to the islands along the Maine coast. Thanks once again to Todd Merrill of Merrill Blueberry Farms in Ellsworth, Maine, for providing details about fall mowing and burning procedures. Thanks also to the many fans, family, and friends who continue to support the series. For more information on the Candy Holliday Mysteries and Holliday's Blueberry Acres, visit www.hollidaysblueberryacres.com.

RECILPES

Holly Holliday's Pumpkin Chocolate Chip Bread

1 ½ cups flour
½ cup sugar
½ cup brown sugar
1 teaspoon baking soda
1 cup pumpkin, fresh or canned
½ cup vegetable oil
2 eggs
¼ cup water or milk
¼ teaspoon nutmeg
½ teaspoon cinnamon
1 cup chocolate chips
½ cup walnuts, chopped (optional)

Preheat the oven to 350 degrees.

Mix together the flour, sugars, and baking soda.

In a second bowl, mix the pumpkin, oil, eggs, water, and spices together.

Combine the pumpkin mixture with the dry flour mixture.

Add the chocolate chips and nuts.

Pour into a well-buttered loaf pan.

Bake for 50 to 60 minutes until a toothpick poked in the center comes out clean.

Take out of the pan and cool on a rack or board.

Holly Holliday made this bread for Candy's birthday every year. Happy 40th birthday, Candy!

Wild Rice and Pumpkin Pilaf

2 tablespoons butter
1 large onion or 2 shallots, chopped
2 cups wild rice or wild rice blend (usually with brown rice)
4 cups vegetable broth
2 tablespoons olive oil
1 cup cubed fresh pumpkin or squash
½ cup chopped mushrooms

In a large saucepan over medium heat, melt 2 tablespoons of the butter.

Add the onion and sauté until soft, about 5 minutes.

Add the dry rice and mix with the onions.

Add the vegetable broth, making sure the rice/broth ratio is correct.

Cook the rice 50 minutes (or according to package directions).

While the rice is cooking, cube the pumpkin or squash.

Heat the olive oil in a large skillet over medium heat.

Add the mushrooms and pumpkin cubes.

Cook, stirring until browned.

When the rice is cooked, stir in the pumpkin and mushrooms.

This recipe is a favorite of Doc's. Enjoy!

Melody Barnes's Pumpkin Soup

2 onions, chopped
3 tablespoons butter
¼ cup flour
4 cups vegetable broth
3 cups pumpkin, mashed or pureed
½ cup light cream
¼ teaspoon nutmeg
¼ teaspoon ginger

In a large saucepan, sauté the onion in the butter.

Add the flour and stir, cooking for 2 minutes.

Add the vegetable broth slowly, stirring while adding it.

Add the pumpkin mash.

Cook for 15 to 20 minutes on low heat.

Stir in the cream, nutmeg, and ginger.

Cook 5 minutes more on low heat.

This is a delicious soup to serve on a cold Maine day.
It's served at Melody's Café daily in October!

Candy Holliday's
Pumpkin Cheesecake Swirl

8 ounces of cream cheese, room temperature
8 tablespoons sour cream
¾ cup sugar
2 eggs
1 cup of pumpkin, canned or mashed fresh
½ teaspoon cinnamon
¼ teaspoon ginger
1 graham cracker crust

In a large bowl, mix the cream cheese and sour cream until smooth.

Add the sugar and mix.

Add the eggs one at a time and mix.

Take out ⅓ cup of the cream cheese mixture and put it in a smaller bowl.

Add the pumpkin and spices to the mixture in the large bowl and mix.

Spread the pumpkin mixture from the large bowl into a graham cracker crust.

From the leftover mixture in the small bowl, take table-spoonfuls and drop them over the top of the pie.

Use a fork or sharp knife and swirl the drops into the pie mixture.

Bake at 375 degrees for 30 minutes, or until the filling is firm in the center when touched.

Cool on a rack or board.

Store in the refrigerator.

This pie is great anytime, but especially on Candy's birthday!

Watch out for
B. B. Haywood's
next Candy Holliday Mystery!
Coming soon from Berkley Prime Crime!

In the quaint seaside village of Cape Willington, Maine, Candy Holliday has a mostly idyllic life, tending to the Blueberry Acres farm she runs with her father— and occasionally stepping in to solve a murder or two . . .

FROM NATIONAL BESTSELLING AUTHOR

B. B. HAYWOOD

TOWN IN A

Wild Moose Chase

A Candy Holliday Murder Mystery

It's winter in Cape Willington—and trouble is about to walk right into Candy's life. First, town hermit Solomon Hatch stirs things up by claiming to have seen a dead body in the woods with a hatchet in its back. Then a mysterious white moose starts appearing around town in the strangest of places.

Meanwhile, the town's annual Winter Moose Fest has drawn plenty of out-of-towners who've come to enjoy the Sleigh and Sled Parade, the ice-sculpting exhibition, and the Moose Fest Ball. As Candy runs around town covering events for the local newspaper, she begins to suspect a link between the body in the woods, the white moose, and several of the town's weekend visitors. But as she hunts for the killer, she's the one who's prey . . .

INCLUDES DELICIOUS RECIPES!

facebook.com/HollidaysBlueberryAcres
facebook.com/TheCrimeSceneBooks
penguin.com

M1181T0912

P.O. 000378831 20191202